FIX THE ROADS

A NOVEL

LEONARD BORMAN

CALUMET
EDITIONS

Minneapolis

CALUMET
EDITIONS

Minneapolis

SECOND EDITION December 2022
FIX THE ROADS Copyright © 2016 by Leonard Borman.
All rights reserved.

10 9 8 7 6 5 4 3 2

ISBN: 978-1-959770-99-2

About the Author

Leonard Borman is a native of Detroit, Michigan, where he resides as an accountant, husband, father of seven, and grandfather of eighteen. He received his bachelor's degree in accounting from Wayne State University and master's degree in history and literature from the University of Michigan.

Acknowledgements

I would like to thank my writing coach, Ian Graham Leask, who pushed me hard to produce a quality product, and Rick Polad for his copyediting. Thanks, guys.

FIX THE ROADS

A NOVEL

LEONARD BORMAN

Other books by the author

Our Jewish robot Future

Prologue

The visitors' lounge of William Beaumont Hospital provided Flossy Lovesong with the perfect view to observe the comings and goings of staff and visitors on the cardiac care floor. Her attention was poised, focused on watching for Margarita Haralson to enter an elevator and go downstairs for lunch. Once Flossy could confirm that Margarita was gone, she would compose herself, stride down the corridor, and enter *his* room. She would sit in the vacated chair by *his* bed, filled with joy. Flossy felt his affections were not Margarita's alone. Alexander Haralson was her lover.

The elevators stood in full view. Flossy had once asked Alexander to show her a picture of Margarita. As with all mistresses throughout human history, how a wife looks holds a certain mystique. Alexander had reluctantly showed her. Flossy was fascinated by Margarita's looks. She was tall, had an olive complexion, wore bronze highlight makeup, and dressed in conservative, but fashionable, sportswear. She looked expensive and would be easy to spot.

Flossy watched as three cardiac care nurses, holding patient charts, chatted behind the information desk. They could see Flossy, but connecting celebrity status to Flossy was unlikely. She had dressed casually, so as not to call attention to herself. By wearing flats, plain jeans, a light black sweater covering a white blouse, and no makeup, she could have been anybody. Alexander had commented many times on her natural beauty. "If dirt covered your face, you'd look breathtaking."

Sneaking into Alex's room wasn't a spy story. She would walk in right after Margarita left. If confronted by hospital staff or security, 'I'm Mr. Haralson's niece' was her prepared response. She watched as attendants pushed food carts from the service elevators to deliver lunch to patients. She expected Margarita to appear at any minute.

Flossy knew Alexander was a picky eater and would knock the lunch tray over onto the floor. He'd told her he viewed eating food as one of life's necessities, on a par with peeing. His menu was short. He would say, "I eat Italian dishes at home and Italian food at five star restaurants."

Alexander had first been admitted to the DMC Harper Hospital building, located about a mile north of downtown Detroit, with severe chest pains. Alexander's son, Dr. Roman Haralson, was a staff resident at the nearby Karmanos Cancer Center, but had insisted his father be evaluated and operated on, if need be, at the DMC. After being admitted, Alexander reminded his son, "I did tell you I was born in Harper Hospital—this ancient, decrepit mausoleum? When I was seven years old, I had a tonsillectomy in one of those germ-infested operating rooms on the second floor. I imagine sixty years later the same germs are now senior citizens roaming about, pushing walkers. Most importantly, Roman, your grandmother told me the nurses promised me a dish of ice cream afterward… any flavor I wanted. I'm still waiting. Get me out of this place. I love *you*, not Harper Hospital." Alexander had then added in a huffy tone, "I don't give a good goddamn if you work here. All I see roaming around the place are aliens."

Roman said, "Dad, watch what you say. Someone could be offended. And don't give me any sass. By the way, I've learned members of the Detroit Symphony often come here to perform. You'd miss a great show if I checked you out."

"That's okay. Expect me to perform a comedy routine every day for the nurses."

The next day, Roman arranged for Alexander's transfer to William Beaumont Hospital, where Alexander's heart condition would be evaluated. The official explanation was because of Beaumont's close proximity to home.

Flossy saw Margarita approach the elevator doors and push the call button. There she was, the same person she remembered from the photograph—tall, with that Italian complexion, bronze makeup, drop earrings, and an expensive dark blue outfit. Margarita's stride conveyed poise. She held her head high. Flossy raised a magazine and kept it high until Margarita was out of sight.

She then walked into Alexander's room and closed the door halfway. She found Alexander asleep, emitting a quiet snore. She bent over, kissed his forehead gently, and put her lips to his ear. She whispered, "Alex. Alex, baby, I'm here and so excited to see you." Flossy waited for Alex to wake up. He kept snoring away. "I've got so much to tell you."

Even though Alexander slept, Flossy kept talking to him. She hoped her Indiana drawl might wake him up. The visitor's chair stood beside Alexander's bed. "You look great. Good color, and you're clean-shaved. Who shaved you? Did you do that because I was coming to visit?" Flossy rubbed her cheek against Alexander's. She reached her hand under the covers and rubbed his thighs and his privates. "Right now, I want to pull the covers down and jump you. I'll bet my medicine is better than what they're giving you."

Alexander groaned and opened his eyes. She whispered, "I know any excitement will warn the nurses to rush in. Right now I'm feeling hard candy, mmmm. You were so brave to have a heart operation. You deserve some excitement."

Alexander turned his head and remained quiet. Flossy stood, pulled the covers down halfway, and tucked a napkin inside the collar of his hospital gown. "They brought you lunch, and I'm going to feed you." Instead, she began kissing him. "When you get better, I'm going to care of you. Tell Margarita to move back to Italy. Then we'll be alone." Flossy put her tongue in his ear. Alexander smiled. She grabbed his hand and started to kiss it.

Flossy began to cry and dried her teary eyes on the hospital sheets next to Alexander's head. "Alex, I love you so much. Think of my tears as me lying next to you when I'm not here. Rub the sheets near your head and you'll dream of me. I don't want you to be alone." Flossy put the fork filled with some vegetables up to Alexander's mouth. He shook his head.

"It's okay, baby. You'll eat when you're ready."

Flossy covered Alexander. "You make me so happy. You stood by me and arranged regular comedy club bookings for me, and I've become a big star, making lots of money. My only regret is that *you* haven't succeeded too. You're funny, Alex. Oh my, I've told you that a hundred times. And you never get sick of me repeating it. I love your jokes, and I wanted you to be a success like I am. You're so kind. You gave up your space for me to step into." Flossy's eyes watered. "I mean, you had the material and gave it to me. I can't thank you enough. I'll never forget the joke you told me after we met, when I wanted to take you to my house and screw you on our first date. You were surprised, saying, 'I'm not that kind of guy. I don't have sex with any woman on the first date.' We laughed. Then we went to bed. Where was it? Oh, yeah, the Hot Rod Motel."

Flossy giggled. "Baby, you are one hunk of a man."

She sat down and combed her fingers through his hair. "Do you remember when I told you I was going to jail? My sentence begins next week… I think for two years. Keep making up new jokes for me. My career's on hold, not over. I'm sad 'cause I have to say goodbye. I'll miss you and will think about you."

"I'll visit you," Alexander muttered.

"When you get better and I get out, we'll have a special time."

Flossy straightened up when she saw a nurse open the door and enter the room.

The floor nurse said, "Hello, I'm nurse Reynolds. How's Mr. Haralson feeling?"

"He's doing fine. I tried to feed him. He didn't want to eat."

Flossy and the nurse glanced at each other, which made Flossy uneasy. She stood, took Alexander's hand, bent over him, and kissed him on the cheek. "My time's up, *Uncle* Alex. I have to leave. Promise me you'll feel better the next time I visit you?"

Alexander replied, "I promise. I'll look like my old self."

Flossy stepped back a few paces, turned, and exited the room.

Nurse Reynolds approached the bed. She bent over and gave Alexander a significant glance. In a low voice she said, "Your niece seems quite enamored with you." She checked the sheet by his head. "It's damp, but, there's no need to change the sheets." The nurse paused and stood. "Your niece thinks you're a hunk of a man."

Alexander gave a sly smile. "She's very affectionate."

"Oh, and her accent. Do you have family in the south?"

"In south Detroit."

"Mr. Haralson, *please*."

"You're right. I must be mistaken." Alexander winked at the nurse. "I should have asked if she was in the right room." He looked at the nurse. "How could a young *zaftig belle mia* like her, speaking with a southern drawl, be interested in me? How could I be interested in her? I'm a married man. A retired accountant, respected and successful. My clients were pillars in the community. And, may I add, I'm the state budget director, appointed by Governor Robert Hatcher. I have an image to protect. How could I associate with a redneck girl like her who's going to jail? How could she be interested in an older man who's showing his age with a pudgy stomach? Yeah, I'm a *zslob* who can't shut his mouth."

After a slight pause, nurse Reynolds responded. "I agree. It's not possible she would be interested in you. If your wife asks about visitors, I'll tell her there were none. It's not the hospital's policy to meddle in family matters."

"You are a dear."

"There are many women who wish they were as lucky in love as she seems to feel with you."

Alexander replied, "I guess I'm a lucky dog." Then with a tired voice, Alexander muttered, "Woof," and drifted back into sleep. He began snoring again.

Nurse Reynolds found Alexander's medical chart, wrote some notes for the doctor, and exited the room.

BOOK ONE

Chapter One

HALLELUJAH, THE WORLD IS COLLAPSING

Alexander Haralson awoke drowsy from a nap. He rolled his head to his right and saw the head nurse wrapping a blood pressure cuff around his arm, while an assistant nurse on his left side inserted a thermometer into the corner of his mouth. He moaned, "What time is it? Where am I?"

The assistant nurse kept working, while the head nurse leaned forward and spoke in an undertone. "Mr. Haralson. Are you feeling any pain?"

Alexander shook his head. He pulled the thermometer out with his free hand, handed it to the nurse, and said in a groggy voice, "Taking my vitals can wait." He tried to reach for her nametag.

The nurse stood back, took his hand, and gently tucked it under the covers. "My name's Jennifer Reynolds, Mr. Haralson. Please, avoid touching any private areas."

"I wanted to find out if your private area was a magnet that attached your name tag to your uniform."

"Oh, my. You need to have your hands tied to the railings."

"Is my wife here?"

"No, Mr. Haralson. I haven't seen her."

"Good. Then we can talk privately. Were you here when my niece visited?"

She answered in a significant tone, "Yes."

"Did I tell you my niece is a stand-up comedian *par excellence*?"

"No. This is the first day I've attended you, Mr. Haralson."

"You introduced yourself as nurse Reynolds. I promise I'll remember your name... Jennifer. I have an exceptional memory for names. Yours has been stored inside my head, inside brain cells that recall names in a flash. But Jennifer, I need to know something. Have you heard any news about Detroit filing for bankruptcy?"

"Yes, Mr. Haralson. The local Channel 4 TV news reported this morning that Detroit's petition was accepted by the bankruptcy court. The city's officially bankrupt."

In a state of ecstasy, Alexander puffed, "Woof. I wish I hadn't been asleep when they reported it. I must write a comedy routine. It's almost poetic. Thanks for the information." Alexander strained to read her nametag. She laughed and brought it closer. "Thanks, Jennifer Reynolds, R.N. Love your nametag. Do you have any extras? I know someone who's dying to wear one... me. It radiates power. And let me compliment you and your staff. You've been an excellent nurse and news reporter. And tell your staff they've done excellent work emptying my bed pan."

"You are a very funny person, Mr. Haralson."

"I'd love for you to be in the audience when I perform my post-op stand-up comedy show. But first, I need to recover. And please, call me Alex."

"I thought you said your niece was a stand-up comedian?"

"She is. But, she's going to jail next week. I'm her replacement while she vacations."

Saying nothing, the two nurses looked at each other, resumed taking his vitals, and left the room when they'd finished their work.

* * *

After a short hospitalization at the DMC, Alexander Haralson was transported to Beaumont Hospital. The cardiovascular surgery team there completed tests and examinations, concluding his chest pains had resulted from a heart attack. They found severe arterial blockage and recommended a quadruple bypass operation as soon as the next day.

The doctors held a pre-op meeting with Alexander and Margarita, telling them about the planned surgery and offering a short narrative about the long and difficult road to recovery.

"Mr. Haralson, controlling stress and weight and doing cardiovascular exercises will become your long-term activity."

Margarita asked, "Doctor, are you serious? Who's going to watch him and tie him down when he's running around crazy? Not me."

The doctor looked at Alexander and said, "Mr. Haralson, the most important and immediate long-term therapy will require you to take daily walks. Mrs. Haralson, while your husband is in the hospital, the nursing staff will lift him out of bed three times a day, and you can walk with him for a half hour. Physical therapy will continue once the hospital discharges him. Alexander, you need to curtail strenuous activities and take this therapy seriously. I think retirement from work should be a major consideration. Our staff will visit again, once you're ready to be discharged."

Alexander became agitated on hearing about the cardiovascular therapy. "Don't be an obstacle. Listen, Doc, I've got work to do. My fans are waiting for my return to the stage. Forget about shutting down my career. I set my retirement date at age ninety-five. I plan to reach it, with or without you."

"Mr. Haralson, besides your genetic makeup, your high stress level caused your heart condition. If you keep up your present attitude and don't bring your stress levels down, you'll be a regular patient at the hospital. We won't be waiting at the entrance to help every time you're transported here."

The surgeon wrote a prescription and handed it to Margarita. "The medication he'll receive in the hospital will cause hypertension. We'll need to calm him down when he's home."

"Thank you, doctor." Margarita smiled at Alexander devilishly, as if failing to give him medication might prove to be a better option.

* * *

Alexander's bypass operation was successful. Within a few days, he was able to roll out of bed by himself to go to the bathroom and walk the corridors. Thus began his rehab phase to rebuild and return to his old self. Alexander had no intention of vegetating every day until he died. He wanted to reunite with the spunky self he'd known in the past. Margarita accompanied Alexander on walks. They strolled through the corridor, locked arm-in-arm. Nurses commented on how well they walked in sync, leaving out the end tag, "for their age." Nurses didn't need to read Alexander's chart to know his age. Alexander's main traits were gray hair and rounded stomach, while Margarita's portrait would be an ideal advertisement for women considering a face-lift.

* * *

Royal Oak, Michigan consisted of a lower-to-middle-class population. Its downtown design was an electric train model, with real trains choo-chooing through the center of downtown. Alexander often wondered why Royal Oak remained a free-standing suburb, when you considered its bordering powerhouse neighbors. Two miles north was downtown Birmingham, Michigan, a financially solvent city with a huge nest egg guarded by tightwads. Vaults of money filled Birmingham banks that could buy Royal Oak ten times over and have plenty of cash to spare. Birmingham was well protected. Roaming the downtown district was permitted, as long as your legs kept moving. Shoppers or gangs stopping to congregate met Birmingham's finest who encouraged dispersal. The message resonated. The word 'bruisers' best described the police force, which included women.

To the south, Eight Mile Road marked the City of Detroit's northern border. All of Detroit's departments ran functionally awry. Lack of concern and responsibility was evident, especially in the city's financial management. Council members enjoyed two hundred dollar salaries, lavish perks, twenty-four-hour limo service, comps at restaurants, and bodyguards. Was anyone surprised to conclude that Detroit represented a major bankruptcy waiting to happen? Detroit had no money in the bank but could enlist enough marauders to attack and loot Royal Oak in short order.

Birmingham's city council members were citizens, many of them in business, who attended council meetings, did committee work, and guarded the treasures. They made sure the founding principles that built and ran the city avoided debt, shunned overspending, kept crime rates low, and structured great school environments for students. On the finance front, they helped business owners prosper, encouraged commercial property development, and performed city services to help residents maintain their homestead properties. The city council also served as ambassadors of diversity who welcomed anyone who had made it in life. It was clear that you earned your way to live in Birmingham. Public-assistance housing projects mandated by the federal government were met with menacing fists and fighting words like, "I'll bet nothing would make you DC bastards happier than turning us into another blighted City of Detroit."

Birmingham's fiscal conservatism was complemented by Oakland County's Commissioner L. Brooks Patterson's monetary mandate: "Don't mess with my triple-A bond rating." Using the same theme, over and over, the words resonated with voters, who had elected him commissioner for three decades. Forget his distasteful political statements or the large number of publicized DUI arrests. Oakland County residents loved him. A *New Yorker* magazine reporter had once baited him to reel off a rant spouting distasteful diatribes about Detroit: "Commissioner Patterson, tell us how you feel about Detroit." Brooks replied to the reporter without phrasing any words deferentially: "Detroit is an Indian reservation." His feelings articulated that an aid package of blankets and corn could reduce poverty more effectively than money. Every Democrat reading Patterson's comments flung every negative piece of shit on the ceiling to see which would stick. None did. Newspapers and TV news tried hard to plant a racist label on him. They sent reporters to Michigan, seeking negative public reaction to the *New Yorker* article. Oakland County residents responded in lovable soundbites for TV news: "That Brooksy. He's such a little devil." Brooks eventually apologized with an "Oh, shucks, folks. I didn't mean to compare Native Americans with Detroiters. Indian casinos have a spotless reputation for honesty and are run with financial acumen."

Alexander had bellied up to the bar with Commissioner Patterson many times at political fund-raisers. Star Paving Company, a Robert Hatcher enterprise, was one of Oakland County's main contractors. Although Patterson and Hatcher conducted business, Patterson knew Alexander was Hatcher's pipeline, telling him which paving jobs he wanted completed ASAP: "I don't want to be running for office with a million potholes." When Commissioner Patterson heard that Alexander had retired, Patterson asked him what his retirement plans were. "I'm thinking seriously about becoming a comedian. My *shtick* will be about Detroit's long history of failure. Brooks, when I'm done telling my jokes about Mayor Kwame Black, you'll be declared a hero and put in the County Commissioner's Hall of Fame."

In contrast to Oakland County's surplus budgets, the City of Detroit managed its budget deficits by increasing taxes, issuing general revenue bonds, and overcharging city services for anyone forced to use them. Kwame's spirit of citizen concern could be described on a par with Marie Antoinette's "Let them eat cake." The con was to fool the suburban whites—have them believe Detroit was improving. With tax dollars sent from the state and adjoining counties, all remained the same. Needy blacks were sheltered in alleys, against garbage cans that served as refrigerators, and whites could delight in donated succor. The money landed in the politicians' pockets. Behind the scenes, Kwame considered repaying a loan from Wall Street as immoral: "The city don't owe anybody any money, and I'll murder any MF who says so." Hearing a threat from a huge, muscular person was a game changer. Alexander surmised that any banker owed money must be wondering why they agreed to lend him money.

Another method employed to increase cash streams was cash received from shakedowns and kickbacks. A one-party system in

control of Detroit meant money could be spent lavishly, without accountability. With Kwame in your face, a fallback position was to
avoid a challenge of how the money was spent. Kwame's mantra
was, "The money I spent on myself and my friends was meant to
better serve the city." Despite laws against stealing money for personal gain, judges sided with the mayor. Defining 'stealing money for personal gain' became a judicial gray area for judges in the
brotherhood. Anybody who dared disagree and publicly air displea-
sure would soon recant, persuaded by arm twisting or jail time on
specious charges. Others who complained loudly were found in the
trunk of a car.

The timeline of Detroit's financial decline spanned about fifty years. Along the way, newer revenue methods to prop up Detroit's finances emerged. Washington DC politicians and Michigan's
lineage of governors exchanged state funds for votes. When that
stream proved to be insufficient, surrounding counties became the
target. Kwame claimed that the suburban residents used many Detroit facilities, such as the art museum or Cobo Hall convention facilities. He rationalized that Detroit was entitled to receive money
for upkeep. L. Brooks Patterson stuck his chest out and attacked:
"Poor management by Detroit officials ran the museum and convention center into the ground. They never performed any maintenance." And he included the City of Detroit's Water Department.
"The underground water pipes are worse off than the blight above
ground." He won even greater voter approval by pointing out, "Why
should we give money when we have no say in running any of the
operations?"

'Making it' in Detroit meant you become the mayor, a city council member, the water commissioner, a water commission member,
or a city property inspector. The positions required no accountability. Each position served as a license to steal rather than a job to help
the citizens who elected you. The criminal system inside the City
of Detroit worked to perfection, with all cylinders in sync. Everyone became specialists in putting hands in tills or accepting bribes.
The bell on the ladder of thievery's top rung rang 'Hallelujah' every

day. Detroit residents were a conduit of free money by virtue of low educational standards. Elected officials exploited them by directing voters to memorize the mantra: "Keep yourselves unemployed because the city needs people in a state of perpetual dire straits. High poverty statistics bring in federal and state cash." Officials feigned helplessness. They were trained musicians strumming on heartstrings, which any sensible person knew was a complete con job. Detroit's principles of unbalanced budgets, borrowed money, failed garbage collection, failed police and fire protection, no street lights, and schools preparing students to be unemployed for life established the road to success.

Tourism was limited to a ride on the Detroit monorail system, which comprised a two-mile ride around downtown. Detroit gave it the euphemistic name *People Mover*, a Disneyland ride in a war zone. Other exciting activities included high-speed emergency vehicles blasting ear-piercing sirens.

* * *

In his hospital bed, Alexander found the TV remote control and began flicking through the channels for breaking news. On CNN, Wolf Blitzer spoke with a somber face and monotone voice—like he was reading an obituary—and said that the City of Detroit had filed papers in federal court seeking Section 9 bankruptcy protection.

Alexander howled with joy. Switching to Fox News, Sean Hannity, in a blistering 'I told you so' voice, ripped the city's Democrat administration as a bunch of thieves. Alexander later tried to quote a Hannity statement to friends. It was close, but not exact. "Those wolves pay themselves a superstar athlete's salary and spend all day lining up another con game to steal from the city treasury." Alexander switched back to CNN and watched Blitzer claim the cause was sixty years of questionable choices. "Let me call in our panel to discuss today's announcement." Alexander tried to shout, "You mean your gullible panel of political allies." He felt hot in the face; his blood pressure was rising.

Several nurses quickly entered the room, led by Jennifer Reynolds, R.N. She had an impatient look. "Calm down, Mr. Haralson. You're recovering from bypass surgery." She ordered an aide to take his blood pressure while she turned off the TV. Everyone waited. The aide read, "160 over 90."

"Stress is not good, Mr. Haralson."

"Come over here, honey. Let me rub your sweet *shiksa* behind. I'm sure my blood pressure will drop."

At that moment, Margarita Haralson walked into the room laughing and said, "Alexander, you're always trying to rub some babe's ass." Turning to the nurse, she said, "Honey, don't worry. He's harmless." Jennifer's eyes rolled. Margarita asked, "When will the doctor be here? I must ask him if rubbing an older wife's fat ass will lower your blood pressure."

Alexander smiled, "I'll take Norvasc."

"I'll bet your friend Hatcher doesn't use blood pressure medication."

Alexander kept quiet. She was right.

Margarita sat down in the visitor's chair, looked up at the TV, and immediately *kvetched* to the nurse, "The TV is off and covered with dust."

Alexander barged in. "You can't see any dust. The TV is turned off."

Margarita stood, walked over to face Alexander, and said, "I didn't come here to hear you jab at me." She took a towel, wiped the TV screen, turned it on, and returned to her chair.

On the TV appeared Kevin Paddle, the emergency manager whom Governor Robert Hatcher had appointed to deal with Detroit's bankruptcy. It was an earlier news segment, showing a press conference when he'd announced, in front of fifty microphones with continuous cameras flashing, the legal action taken by the State of Michigan.

As the state's budget director, Alexander had advised Hatcher months earlier, before the bankruptcy filing. He'd suggested Hatcher think of the money inside the treasury vaults as something precious, like his wife's privates, that should be locked up securely with a chastity belt.

Alexander asked Margarita for his cell phone. "I've got to speak with Hatcher."

"He's doing fine without you."

"I'm his high-powered advisor, his 'go-to' guy. He can't function by himself. And don't challenge me, either. I respect him because smart managers hire smarter people to help them run their businesses. Dumb managers, like our president, hire dummies—weak people shepherded by Huey Long types."

Margarita ignored him and flicked open a magazine. Impatient, Alexander calmly promised her he wouldn't make any outgoing calls. He emphasized, "But I need my cell phone by my bed, in case Hatcher calls."

"Alex, can you accept that your heart condition has rendered you a has-been?" Margarita placed his cell phone on the side table.

Alexander reached out and touched the phone. In a calm voice he said, "Thanks, dear."

"Alexander, can't you trust that I put the phone within reach?"

"When I'm dead."

* * *

Alexander's cardiologist, Dr. Arnold Lieberson, had discovered Alexander had suffered a heart attack. A stress test and catheterization confirmed blocked arteries, and a quadruple bypass would be needed. Dr. Lieberson was about ten years Alexander's junior. They knew each other outside the office, having met at several charity functions. At a Beaumont Hospital annual golf outing, they were paired with their wives. It was a one-time pairing. The Liebersons reported to the golf outing commissioner that Alexander had been obnoxious, making foul-mouthed remarks.

Alexander had challenged Arnold at the pre-op physical, saying: "I'm breathing, not huffing or puffing when I walk. I don't smoke. I don't have shortness of breath or chest pains. And I need an operation?"

"Let me be blunt," the doctor had said. "Your blood pressure is sky-high. Your stress level is high. I'm guessing it was caused by being married to a crazy Italian wife and having an out-of-control, five-year-old brat for a daughter."

Alexander bit his lip. He knew Lieberson's wife must have heard about the family dynamics from Margarita and passed the details on to her husband.

Lieberson had continued. "The heart catheterization we performed on you showed four blockages. The good news is your regular EKG was normal. The bad news is your exercise stress test results were a disaster."

"I'm a little chubby. I admit it. But I play golf for exercise. Arnie, I think you're overboard about the operation."

"You had a heart attack that went undetected. And I forgot to mention the stress caused by your benefactor, Hatcher, your ham-fisted employer. Does he know how to do anything without acting like Attila the Hun?"

"You're out of bounds, Arnie."

Pointing his finger at Alexander, the doctor sternly responded, "I'm your doctor. You're scheduled for a bypass operation, Tuesday, at eight a.m. Dr. Mohamadon will be in shortly to discuss the operation."

"Who is this guy? Is he a U of M grad?"

"No, he attended medical school in Karachi."

"Oh, goodie. And the name of the school?"

Annoyed, Dr. Lieberson replied, "I don't know."

"Great, Arnie. Would seeing his medical credentials be too much to ask?"

"Alex, do you hate everyone?"

"Only heart doctors who graduated from the Karachi School of Goat Butchery."

"You're so funny you put me to sleep."

"Excellent. Lenny Bruce and George Carlin succeeded because they ranted against the establishment. To me that means they liked the anti-establishment. I'm different. I hate the establishment, *and* I hate the anti-establishment."

"That's a non sequitur."

"Oh my, a law degree that complements your butcher's license."

"Jesus Christ, you're crazy. No wonder you're stressed."

"You didn't let me finish. You think I'm a nut job. What do you suggest? Should I call your thieving political buddies in the medical profession my role models? Arnie, never did I veer out of control during my accounting career. Clients marveled at my self-control. Everything I accomplished approached near perfection. I'm leaving the revisions to you doctors to second-guess my condition. You support my political enemies. But you're a stooge. Leave out medical school and you'd have flunked beginner's checkbook balancing. I love Detroit. What fries my ass is the kids' school money your buddies stole for vacations, cars, sporting events, clothes, and hookers. When I get better, I'm going to let everybody know that they allowed the *ganefs* to do what *ganefs* do best."

"And your son, the surgeon at the Detroit Medical Center. What does he think about your ranting?"

"Roman? My son, the doctor? He's too busy to get involved. He's busy stitching up knife and gunshot wounds inside Detroit's shooting gallery. The *k'nocker* signs more death certificates than I sign checks."

"You're on the operating table, Tuesday, eight a.m." Dr. Lieberson left the room, hands to his temples, shaking his head.

* * *

Alexander smiled at the memory of Lieberson's torment. His cell phone rang. Checking caller ID, he saw it was Robert Hatcher and, making eye-contact with Margarita, answered.

"Hello, Roberto, as distinguished from my daughter, Roberta."

"Alex, you should sound weak. I like hearing a strong voice. Your doctor says you're recovering nicely."

"The way I sometimes feel, if I get any better, I'll be in good enough shape to die."

"Always on stage. Relax, will you?"

"*Oy*, Robert, I saw you beside Paddle at the news conference. Your appearance reminded me of a man who meant business."

"Alex, you've got to get better ASAP. The jerks who plan to sue the city and state because of the bankruptcy are coming out of the walls. They're bigger babies than your daughter. They resent that I, Governor Robert Hatcher, want to take their candy money away. Look, everybody in government steals money. And yet these elected bums protest. They have the nerve to go after me, another chump to sue personally. What did I do wrong?"

"Bob, you didn't do anything wrong. You have deep pockets. They think that because they contributed chump change into the system, they've been short-changed and are entitled to a king-size return on investment. You've heard me say ROI, haven't you? Right now you're viewed as a pig, a villain taking away the old status quo. I'm a pig too, only smaller."

"Look what I have to face. President Barack H. Obama undermined me. That bull-shitter told them—and by them I mean Detroit's governmental pickpockets—that everything seemed swell. Let me define BHO's 'swell.' Brooksy balances Oakland County's budgets and earns a triple-A credit rating. The Democrats yell that his accounting is all smoke and mirrors. BHO overspends his budget, borrows obscene amounts of money, and yells that the government's S&P credit rating is low. Detroit's cash levels are at knee-level, and sinking. The truth is pension and health benefits are in a rocket trajectory passing Saturn, in tandem with BHO's bullshit."

"I loved Paddle telling the bondholders to expect five cents on the dollar. They thought they would be paid before welfare recipients. Uh, huh. I'll find out the names of the firms who floated that phony paper. Robert, you can be assured from the bottom of my new arteries that I will never invest a dime of your money where those jerks work. They thought all was good. Peddle the bonds to investors and collect fees, with no repercussions. Hey, that's not bad work. I think I'll go to work for them.

"BHO knows the city is in a shambles. He saw several buildings tilted at a forty-five-degree angle. His spin was, 'The City of Detroit is so fortunate to have a tourist attraction replicating the Leaning

Tower of Pisa. I congratulate the city for its ingenuity—such a marvelous work of art.'

"Robert, let's face it. I've been trained to steal money from large corporations. They call it shrinkage and can afford it. But these bastards steal from kids, stealing large sums and leaving scraps to run the schools."

"What do you suggest?"

"Follow their pattern. Chuck your values. Right now, they don't give a shit about the kids. When we're stealing it, I'll give them the Italian salute."

"Good, Alexander, good."

"Let's lie and tell everyone how good we were at managing their money. The taxes they paid into the system were a pittance compared to paid benefits. I was the genius who set it up for you. Don't we deserve hefty fees? Let's innovate another scam, become bigger crooks and put ourselves next in line to the cashier's cage."

"Alexander, what a wonderful idea."

"Woof." Alexander put down the phone.

Margarita walked over to the bed. "Alex, what are you doing? Hatcher's business is putting too much pressure on you. He'll kill you." A thought brought a smile. Margarita held it for a moment, then continued, "But if you want to die, who am I to stop you?"

"Thanks for the encouragement."

"Where are the insurance policies?"

"Bring me a gun. I want you to predecease me. I can collect on your nursing home insurance policy, you know."

"Darling, you can't continue this madness. Besides aiding and abetting Hatcher, your crazy, late-life desire to be a comedian was supposed to be a relaxing hobby, not a self-inflicted beating. You're so bad at it that you only got gigs in sex clubs—which may of course be your secret motivation. Your Sadie Mussolini routine goes down well with the boys from Temple, but *goyem* think you're an asshole."

"I like that. Next time, try to remember to add a sadomasochistic beating."

A nurse came into the room to take vitals and inform the Haralsons that lunch would be brought in shortly. An orderly walked in
carrying a tray, placed it on the side table, and said, "I've brought
you a delicious lunch." Alexander looked at the food and tried to
catch the orderly to remove the tray before he left. He was too late.
"M, just leave it. Fill out a suggestion card for me. Tell them I am
not a taste tester for pig slop."

"Alex, you are back to your normal self."

"That means I'm getting better. M, why don't you go downstairs and eat something. Bring me back something edible. I'll be
out cold for a couple of hours."

Margarita kissed Alexander on the forehead and left the room.
"*Oy.*"

Chapter Two

CAN'T RETIREMENT BE STRESS FREE?

Alexander woke from his afternoon nap and saw nurse Reynolds taking his vitals.

"You've had a good nap, Mr. Haralson," she said. "I noted that your vitals have improved. Blood pressure is 140 over 78."

Alexander turned his head and saw Margarita.

On cue, she said, "I saw your lunch tray. You picked at it. I'm sure you dream about my cooking."

"I do. Your *bucatini alla diavola* is sensational, to die for. But you always serve me enough food for three people. M, you're not surprised I have clogged arteries, are you? One day, I expect the doctor to tell me to avoid your cooking. What do I do then? Eat bird seed?"

"Relax, Alex. You're a long way from a stomach stapling."

Alexander looked at the ceiling. "I've seen enough news on TV about the bankruptcy." He fumbled about in his bed to find the TV remote and turned the TV off. Then he looked around and found a joke book. He wondered if he had enough arm strength to hold and read a book for an hour. It seemed impossible.

Besides his physical strength, Alexander worried about mental fatigue. Working in the field of comedy meant completing tasks that contributed to mental exhaustion: writing, rehearsing routines, setting up gigs, performing, and avoiding jokes that bombed halfway through the first weekend show. Even so, Alexander was passionate and committed to the work. He had put on a cast-iron disposition and charged into the breach, determined to become a known personality. There were plenty of obstructionists. The cast of characters included established comics, hecklers, and con artists who hung out to swindle a piece of your action.

Being a performer meant putting life's matters aside. Did that mean not caring about family needs and happiness? Alexander loved his family. Yes, there were plenty of friction and fights inside the Haralson family. But did it mean throwing Margarita, Roberta, or Caroline under a bus? Alexander would quit comedy before that happened.

Alexander never lost sight of the state and city finances. His mind wrapped around Detroit's lawyers or hired law firms. They irritated him. Simple solutions got out of control. Many of Detroit's court case failures resulted from poor legal advice or incompetence. The city's track record was pathetic. Nickel-and-dime lawsuits resulted in sizable judgments against them. It cratered budgets every month. Alexander wondered, *Don't those assholes know how to negotiate?* Employment lawsuits saw losses with significant settlements. Many times the lawsuit didn't need to be filed by a plaintiff. But because of poor management and not paying attention to knitting, lawsuits were filed against the city with open-and-shut results.

In view of the fact that the city debts were humongous, Alexander had suggested to Hatcher that the US Government negotiate with China and trade Detroit for the debt owed them. Hatcher claimed the feds would never do it. If the debt were repaid, the feds would turn around and borrow money from China again. Alexander's comedic thought process suggested pictures of Chinese politicians lining the wall as mayor, treasurer, etc. They transformed and acted like capitalists, while Hatcher and Alexander became the communists. What's so funny? They would own the place.

At one time, it was true that Alexander had been Hatcher's main financial man. Did that mean this would be his future for life? Margarita might have been right. Why hadn't he broken off his client relationship when he announced his retirement? Alexander had other options. Job offers in finance arrived from all directions; headhunters called him with job offers; confidential letters arrived with offers, as did offers to buy his accounting practice. Some offers Alexander received paid attractive salaries and bonuses. The offer he'd received for his accounting practice added an open-ended expense account. His job description consisted of keeping the client base happy, playing golf at posh country clubs to secure potential new clients, and eating dinner at expensive restaurants. Becoming a playboy accountant smelled enticing. So was the salary. "We'll send you and Margarita to vacation resorts to secure the client base and tell jokes to your heart's content." With offers sounding better with each phone call, Alexander had decided the best strategy was to hold off returning calls from recruiters.

Hatcher placed obstructions in his way and made the breakaway to retirement difficult-to-impossible. "I'm your oldest and most loyal client. I stuck with you. I could have found another accountant long ago. Your practice grew because of me. Now you want to retire and hang me out to dry?"

Alexander's love for Detroit fortified Hatcher's guilt trip. He wanted to help people by making an inroad into stopping corruption. The road he planned would help the state stay solvent and in turn help bankrupt school districts. Stifling regulations for industrial companies, one-sided politics, and non-existent ideas for growth were the accomplishments Detroit officials kept lionizing. TV reports spotlighted the lies. "Are we doing a great job, or what?" In a real world, population growth and financial success went hand-in-hand. Companies complained to Detroit officials that their politics made competing with companies in other states or countries difficult. News reporting repeated the same announcements made by companies. "We might have to close." Detroit officials called the bluff. "There's no foundation in the belief that our policies have caused financial and population decline." Opinions stayed the same.

And what about Flossy Lovesong, his love? Alexander could feel his head sink deeper into the pillow's softness. Alexander couldn't deny he loved having sex with her. He believed the more sex with Flossy, the more energy it generated in him to put in a greater effort to help her career. He was madly in love with her. She treated Alexander with kindness and thought him a god. His heart began to thump thinking about her. The freckled-face, redheaded Daisy Mae had caught Alexander's interest while they were both attending a school for comedy. She'd commented to him in a giggly voice, "My, you sure carry a hunk of manhood." Alexander replied, "You remind me of Red Riding Hood when she told the wolf, 'My, you sure are well-hung.'" Flossy had broken into hysterics. "Believe me when I say there're no socks stuffed in my undies," he added. Flossy fell forward in laughter and wrapped her arms around his neck. Alexander felt mellow touching the outline of her breasts and hips. He smiled, thinking he'd started school off on the right foot. "Have we formally met?" he asked. Flossy responded, "You're sweating. You okay, honey?" He was sure the odds of a hot romance were one hundred percent.

Flossy was a piece of work. Her mouth was formed in the shape of a crescent moon, and she had dirty-red hair, making her overall appearance look dim-witted. Alexander learned that she lived with her third husband. Very noticeable were her large breasts supported by a halter-top made of steel mesh. Why hadn't she gone to school to become a nurse? Forget rubbing Jennifer's body. He needed to rub Flossy's large body parts. Who could deny they had a high level of medicinal potency?

Alexander thought her comedic style fit the dumb blond mold, except with red hair. During one practice session, he saw an arm movement across her chest thwarted by her breasts. "My breasts are so big, I don't know what to do with them." Alexander, the clack, commented that if her husband didn't, he did. Flossy said Alexander might have to show her. Alexander responded he was prepared to demonstrate how a vacuum cleaner's on-off button worked. Remembering, he broke into a hearty outburst.

Margarita asked, "Alex, is everything all right?"

"I'm telling myself some jokes."

* * *

Alexander realized after the training session at the Zug Island Comedy Club that his career, just started, was in trouble. He had impersonated Joe Stalin and his reception was continual boos. Myths circulated from countries west of Russia that the real Joe Stalin was a dull person, lacking in humor. The only country that thought him a funny man was Russia, especially when he joked about starving populations. And Alexander came off as sounding even duller. The scoreboard on successful gigs read zero for fifteen. But Stalin had statistics in his favor. One hundred percent of the persons he ordered in front of firing squads were guilty of not laughing at his jokes. This assured no member of the Federal Assembly ever failed to laugh when Stalin told a joke. None of them wanted to be singled out by Stalin pointing an accusing finger in their direction. Another rumor circulated that, once, the entire Parliament had rebelled against laughing at Stalin's jokes. Stalin asked the back row to accompany the military personnel out of the Great Hall, and they were never heard from again. After that, all returned to normal, and Stalin was crowned comedian of the year. Alexander had once tried to duplicate Stalin. He threatened an audience with, "If you fail to laugh, I will lock you in a room and tell stale jokes until you do." Swearing and bottles thrown at him had proved an effective polling of Alexander's ability. He thought about changing to a stand-up philosopher style, but Mel Brooks' originality beat him. In his movie *History of the World*, such orators were referred to as "bullshitters."

But Alexander never quit. Performing comedy stood at the top of his agenda. Calls that he turn himself in to the police for committing the crime of comedic con artist sounded redeeming. Instead, letters from attorneys threatened lawsuits if no amends were received at places where he performed gigs. They demanded their money back, along with an apology. The letters stipulated they should be paid for listening to him.

* * *

He received calls from Governor Hatcher. They talked regularly, with Alexander telling his friend to lynch crooked politicians at every opportunity. "Take away their goodies. The roads and schools need to be fixed, and the city's sixty percent of vacant land needs a higher and better use." Alexander soon learned how difficult Hatcher's job had become. "None of these guys who run the city have a third grade education, and they're lecturing me on how to fix the roads. I tell them I'm a paving contractor. I should know."

His mind drifted back to Flossy. Her routines were hilarious. She told her audience that when she was a waitress, she used her large breasts as a cover to keep the soup warm until she served it to a customer. Alexander plotted how, sometime in the future, Flossy could be his perfect sidekick—a Sancho, a stooge. She was funny just being Flossy. There was no need to separate the everyday person from the comedian. She was perfect.

But alas, she was going to jail. Alexander knew her unemployed husband had gotten drunk and knocked her around one too many times. When it came to domestic violence, police protection on her side of town amounted to a two hour wait to respond. Instead, Flossy ran for the gun hidden in the bedroom and let a few shots ring out. The police arrived in less than a minute, cuffing and stuffing her into a police cruiser in less than five minutes. She was all about self-preservation. She wasn't a material person. She never asked for a handout. Alexander wanted to help her, but she'd refused. By comparison, he thought Margarita's qualities embraced self-interest and that she represented America's self-centered attitude, which Alexander bitterly resented. Margarita had asked him, after he announced his retirement, "Will you earn as much money in retirement as you did when you worked?"

Alexander was not going broke anytime soon, but he wanted some time and space to enjoy life. He wasn't planning on abandoning his family. He had family values and loyalty. They had three children. Two had become adults, and one was a five-year-old monster. Roman sided with Alexander's politics. As to the girls, Alexander was not sure how he felt about them. His older daughter was opinionated, demanded money, and wished her mother could divorce her father. Sometimes, Alexander wanted to shoot his five-year-old daughter out of a cannon.

Was the family unhappiness because of him? Alexander asked himself that question often. He wanted a laudable relationship. Perfect, no. But on a scale of one to ten, he felt their current relationship rated a three. Alexander thought that even if he acquiesced to the female side of the family on all issues, the relationship might only move up to a four. A seven rating would have pleased him.

A nurse came in and gave Alexander his afternoon medication. Alexander then drifted off to sleep.

Chapter Three

THE ZUG ISLAND COMEDY CLUB

Neither snow nor rain nor heat nor gloom of night shall stay these couriers from their appointed rounds. Alexander loved the postal workers' slogan, which he borrowed to apply to his own walk of life. The motto revolved in his head on his drive to work and when he marched through the firm's hallway to reach his office. He was happy to arrive at work and went out of his way to say "hello" to any employee who beat him to work, especially on snowy days.

Alexander had earned his reputation as a highly respected accounting practitioner. He demonstrated his love for accounting, serving on panels to strengthen the profession's rules and regulations. He was held in high esteem by clients, peers, co-workers, and secretarial staff. Skillful work made him renowned and earned him many professional awards. Alexander's status also included being a notable personal advisor. Anyone who approached him with a question or problem to solve found his office door open, with time to listen and dispense advice. The thought of retirement had crossed his mind many times, and he'd concluded that ninety-five would be about right. At sixty-four, he still had thirty-one more years. Alexander's strategy settled on a plan to groom a close friend and associate, Perry 'Pizza' Bufferino, twenty years his junior, to run the operation. Alexander would take a back seat, showing up to work each day for an hour or two, mainly to drink a cup of coffee.

Alexander was a great teacher, and Pizza was ready to take the reins. Alexander pondered when the transition would take place. Until then, he remained totally dedicated to his work.

Alexander was a realist. He knew he couldn't continue to work forever. What his firm lacked was a mandatory retirement age. Alexander wanted to make that decision on his own terms. As his firm's managing partner, he dreaded the thought that he'd begin to notice his brain losing sharpness. The possibility would force him to cut down on his workday hours or face the reality of retirement. The recollection of Sewell Avery, chairman of Montgomery Ward, illuminated his memory. The board of directors had asked the federal government to help implement a court order to escort him from his office. Mr. Avery was a stubborn man who had refused to leave on his own, so the feds carried him out the front door while he sat on his desk chair, defiant, with his arms crossed. This memory served as a cue for Alexander. You want to leave on your own accord. Don't go overboard by thinking a mushy mind can make the right decisions.

During his lengthy career, Alexander had faced many deaths of friends and family along the way. In his younger years, wakes and funerals had amounted to necessary days off from work to attend the memorials. As time passed, more deaths brought the retirement question out into the open. One day, Alexander was completely shaken from his apathy when he learned Pizza had been severely injured in an auto accident. His schedule shifted, which required Alexander to shuttle between running the office and running to the hospital to visit Pizza. Playing his normal golf games during the week was placed on hold.

Pizza died a month later. Alexander was upset and confused. Whom would he choose as managing partner? Whomever it was, Alexander would need to train the new candidate. Or would selling the firm and becoming a comedian be his calling? He was a high-energy guy, and doing comedy work would make him happy. What was he supposed to do—run around a track all day, wondering when a fatal heart attack would happen? Or window shop? Slowing down, finding a qualified associate to run the office, and teaching him the ropes could give any executive a heart condition.

Alexander would blame himself for any unhappiness he felt in an inactive retirement. Retirement was his last hurrah, and he'd dreamed of stardom since childhood. He didn't consider performing comedy gigs as a step down from his important work as an accountant. The low-life profession that comedy represented was not a pasture to roam about in all day and stop occasionally to eat. To work in comedy—and do well—required effort. He'd come to realize long ago that continuing either as his normal self or as a vegetating pre-corpse in retirement, he'd still become an unknown. That was a horrifying thought. The decision was made just by saying goodbye accounting, hello comedy.

The challenge stood in front of him. The change to comedian would put a face to his intimate feeling of hating everyone and everything. One of the perks he yearned for was the world being able to see the fun-loving guy he felt he really was. The thought of school and contacting clubs for gigs pumped his blood. The glitch came when Robert Hatcher told him not to leave accounting and to be his financial side-kick after he was elected governor. "I'll need you to sift through the bullshit," were Hatcher's exact words. Alexander thought they sounded more like an order. The timing was lamentable. The newspapers were skeptical about Hatcher being an able governor. Alexander wondered why he had to run for governor in the first place. The state of Michigan had plenty of crooks to choose from.

Alexander wanted to do stand-up comedy full-time in the worst way, and for good reason. Payback time awaited all the despicable people he hated—clients he'd ass-kissed, or government regulators who decided issues on whims or bribes. Then the monkey wrench thrown by Robert Hatcher landed in his gearbox. Did Hatcher have any idea that he was one of the many targets Alexander planned to scorch? Couldn't Hatcher fix the state's finances by himself? He owned a paving construction business that Alexander had whipped into shape. Wasn't that enough? "Why me?" Alexander babbled. "I have a chance to dive off the deep end into a free fall, and Robert

Hatcher offers a job requiring me to keep my sensibilities. How dare he." Comedy would have to fight to claim its rights to Alexander.

At a family barbecue, Alexander told everyone about Robert Hatcher running for governor and about the accounting work Hatcher wanted him to do. Every member of the family had an opinion that ranged from take the job to forget it. They said, "Hatcher's a crook," or "You could wind up in jail," or "Stay away from him." Alexander relished having a say-so over the state's purse strings. Like Santa, he'd tell Hatcher who was naughty or nice. "Robert, make sure they clap their flippers before you throw them a mackerel."

In Alexander's head, the comedy demons took him back. "Not so fast, Alexander. Hatcher doesn't have exclusive rights. In fact, you belong to us."

* * *

Alexander had never worked as a comedian, so he decided first to start at the bottom by attending classes and learning the craft at the HA-HA School of Comedy. No epiphany arose to enlighten his senses and lead him. The mindset to change occurred inside a calm individual—a planned, natural transition from accountant to comedian. Bob Newhart had done it, so why not a level-headed individual named Alexander Haralson? For years, his vision, his perception of life, had played out as melodrama—follies worthy of biting criticism. His favorite reenactment was the elderly lady on the floor, garnering enough strength to elevate her arm toward the camera and calling to her home alert system, "I've fallen, and I can't get up." His inner circle of friends howled at his antics. They encouraged him. "Go to school and train to be a comedian. Perform at comedy clubs. Join Riff Markowitz at the Follies in Palm Springs. The old *kockers* will love you." Alexander held a high opinion of himself and couldn't disagree. It's what he'd always wanted to do. Each day his friends' advice grew louder. The message filled his head.

Alexander planned to base his comedic persona on Lenny Bruce. He immersed himself, reading every morsel about the comic's life. He discovered police rap sheets galore. Lenny's life history had been that of a con artist who made good. What he learned about the content of on-stage performances could be summarized in the maxim that every decadent aspect of life should be considered meritorious. Drinking, drug usage, and adultery, to name a few indiscretions, didn't need rules of conduct. Using "fuck" in every sentence as a noun, verb, adjective, or interjection made his inner voice understandable. In reality, swearing during performances was considered a misdemeanor. But Lenny didn't care. When the police had finally moved in to arrest him, he said, "You guys aren't going to arrest me before I finish this set, are you?"

Lenny loved skin. He'd married a stripper, a hot *shicksa* named Honey Harlow. Lenny saw nothing wrong in being married to a woman who exposed the private areas of her body to the public most of the day. Lenny's act with a tramp for a wife earned him credibility. To Alexander's way of thinking, there was no drawback to a wife exposing her skin in support of advancing her husband's career. What about Margarita? Could Alexander's career advance while he was married to a woman whose life centered on family? Divorce Margarita, marry Flossy. Her name rolled off his lips, in a whisper. Projecting Margarita's idea of fun dances – the fox-trot, the hora, or the zoppetto—into a strip club would cause a riot. Honey's breasts were water wings that had inflated Lenny's career. For Alexander, the image of Margarita gyrating her hips, removing her bra, and flinging it into a crowd carried the weight of an anchor.

Alexander planned a comedic style that spared no one from embarrassment. His opening would warn the audience that he took no prisoners. "I live a quiet family life. Inside here, what comes out of my mouth will be a barrage to humiliate you. Take a Xanax if you suffer emotional distress or call my attorney."

Trying out options for a *nom de plume* that would conceal his identity and gain audience attention testified to his seriousness. Being recognized while calling people he knew derogatory names or describing unseemly behavior meant flies would be the only attendees at his funeral. Alexander compiled a list of possible stage names:

Stalin, Boris Tomashevsky—Russian names that resonated obnoxious, nose-picking individuals.

Alexander's wardrobe needed some thought. A disguise con-
sisting of a dirty T-shirt, jeans with holes, and worn tennis shoes
contained all the earmarks of someone who needed to return to a
previous life as a hobo. Clothing with holes needed to be worn, off-
the-rack Salvation Army stuff. A wig, black shoe polish, sunglasses covering half his face, a baseball cap with an English D, and
a T-shirt with a picture of Joe Stalin bearing the bold inscription
"Greetings from Uncle Joe" would be enough to confuse anyone
trying to link him to his real identity. The final touch to the disguise
included stuffing cotton in his Levi's genital area, with the hope of
keeping women's eyes gazing at his groin.

* * *

Alexander Haralson recalled his first appearance as a stand-up comedian at Dino's Comedy Club in Royal Oak. When he called them
out of the blue, the club was glad to give him a start, adding his
name to a performance roster. The booking agent told Alexander the
time and date of appearances had not yet been set, but that his open
mic appearance would be a five-minute segment. Alexander hung up
the phone and began to practice a routine.

About a month went by. Then the comedy club left a phone
message, instructing Alexander when and where to appear. After
hearing the message, Alexander froze. Would the routine help or
hurt him? He'd put in a lot of effort, and if the audience booed him
off the stage, he had no intention of leaving the stage or quitting
comedy. But afterward, he'd had to start over, seeking jobs below
improv comedy club standards.

He showed up at the club and was escorted into a ten-by-fif-
teen-foot waiting room. Inside, five performers waited on bench
seats with legs crossed, puffing on cigarettes or making cell
phone calls. The wall was painted battleship gray, with mirrors
for grooming oneself or practicing lines. The room resembled a
sports locker.

Alexander decided to come to the club with no routine. He was never short of things to say. And the last thing he wanted to do was act giddy, like a college freshman or a phony. He sat and let his mind wander. How should he begin? What jokes should he use? The stage manager woke Alexander from his trance and told him he was next on stage. During the wait, his mind hadn't generated any jokes. Alexander concentrated on telling himself to remain calm. Life would continue after he'd appeared, no matter what.

He heard his name broadcast over the loud speaker and walked onto the stage toward the microphone. He shaded his eyes and scanned the audience. Then he began.

"I have nothing to say." A silence filled the room. "This is my first performance as a comedian. I'm an accountant, and members in my profession are considered introverts. But I'm an exception. In matters of accounting, I'm considered an extrovert. Can you picture me working? Now that I'm retired, I've turned completely around into a comedic introvert. I would be a perfect host for Saturday Night Live. They hire introverts, famous actors who do a dull monologue. They don't get any laughs, but that's part of the fun. On stage, Freddy Kruger, with long fingernails that claw victims to death, is not funny. I can't imagine him ever being funny. But he's backed up by the show's regulars. By the time the show ends, he's considered an up-and-coming comic.

"Accountants think their accounting jokes are hilarious. As a rule, they stink. But there are exceptions. The funniest thing I've heard in all my years of work was a story about a junior accountant who wanted desperately to discover an accounting fraud. Frauds are discovered, but the results aren't a cause for high fives or celebrations. Someone's going to jail. A junior accountant I knew thought he'd discovered a company employee who kited some checks. Kiting is cashing checks and waiting for future payments to cover the shortfall. Let me say that kiting is a crime, but the operative expression *here* is *thought he discovered.* This accountant went crazy, jumped on a desk and yelled, 'I've found a fraud' about four or five times. Then he jumped down from the desk and ran like a crazy man through the office, shouting and repeating the same mantra—'I've found a fraud.' The accounting firm's manager took charge and told his employee to show him his findings. In a closed-door session, it was discovered that a five in the thousands column looked like an eight which had caused a footing imbalance, meaning there was no error. Within a day, the employee was discharged and the senior partner visited the client and begged forgiveness. 'Jared, believe me this kind of incident will never happen again.'"

A dead silence ensued. "I should have warned you this skit would have been more lively with a backup group of quacking ducks. May I offer a eulogy to conclude my time? Dear Lord, my lunacy is not your fault. Please forgive me for making an ass of myself. Ladies and gentlemen, as punishment for my inept performance, I will now go home and have sex with my wife."

* * *

Alexander's debut as a stand-up comedian had not been an unmitigated success. So being the methodical accountant he was, always walking in straight lines and taking deliberate steps, he eventually found the HA-HA School of Comedy in the phone directory. The Yellow Pages were filled with broadcasting schools. Under "comedy schools," there were precisely three. The others were named Jokers and Laugh City. The HA-HA School was located in Flat Rock, a community about twenty miles downriver from Detroit, a stone's throw from Detroit Metropolitan Airport. Flat Rock and Detroit were kissing cousins. Both were eroding from no-growth rot. When flying into Detroit and looking down, Flat Rock resembled a town constructed by children, made of model airplane wood and glue, awaiting someone's brilliant idea to torch the buildings and toast marshmallows.

Alexander enrolled and paid his tuition by check, which earned him a twenty-five percent discount. Margarita would be unaware of Alexander's comedy exploits until canceled checks were returned by the bank. It was the preferred method. She'd ask him about a check made out to a comedy school. And then Alexander would drop the bomb about his lifelong quest. He'd inform her that refunds were not given, and therefore his new endeavor must proceed.

On the first day of class, he noticed that his facial features, strongly suggesting a particular variety of eastern European heritage, went unexamined by his fellow freshmen. They appeared to be mostly imbeciles, resembling cartoon characters who couldn't spot a refined Jewish man if they tried. Later, Alexander would reference them as originating from the "Tribe of Bumpkins," while he descended from the "Tribe of Israelites" who had come out of Egypt. God had led these hillbillies out from the Tennessee caves and marched them up mountains to become moonshiners.

Seeing a real-life Howdy Doody, Daisy Mae, or Elmer Fudd in action was funny, and easily launched Alexander into hysterics. One classmate, Pimples, scared everyone. Her face resembled a volcano landscape. Alexander classified her as a dermatologist's retirement annuity. She approached Alexander once during a break, and he ran like hell to hide in the men's room. The school's head instructor, Bernie Schwartz, suggested Pimples find another line of work. As a student, she was dumped. In time, the student dropout rate increased. The main reasons were late tuition payments or realizing everyone laughed at *them*, not their jokes. Alexander survived, realizing the school kept him enrolled for the money. Bernie was no fool. Alexander was a landsman, and Bernie sensed Alexander had bucks in his wallet.

Alexander found class workshops a pain in the ass. Instructor and student class critiques infuriated him. He looked down his nose at them. "You dumb asses are telling me how to do a routine? Nobody bosses me around."

"Mr. Haralson," protested one instructor, "this is only the first day of class!"

The owner of the HA-HA School of Comedy, an Italian named Frank Amenero, approached Alexander asking him, "How about buying me out?" Alexander replied he'd married an Italian, had Italian clients and Italian friends and relatives. "From left field you're asking me to do business with another Italian? Don't take it personally, but after a lifetime living and dealing with dagos, I've had enough."

Frank roared with laughter. "Alexander, you're funny."

"You knew I had money? What gave it away—my designer clothes, my Allen Edmonds shoes, my expensive glasses, or my BMW parked outside?"

"Stop, Alex. My guts are splitting."

* * *

The Zug Island Comedy Club accommodated exhibition performances for students of the HA-HA Comedy School. Zug Island and the comedy club were separated by the River Rouge Canal, which flowed into the Detroit River. The club sat on the mainland, and the island was a world unto itself. The comedy club building had for seventy-five years been a bar where steelworkers who worked on Zug Island congregated after work. There was a small stage where bands played for late night crowds. The owner, Freddy Kaye, later added a comedy club format on nights when the band had a night off. As a result, there was no necessity to renovate the inside. One stage served both.

Zug Island, besides being utilized as a steel mill, had been used as a chemical waste site. Its decomposing wildlife included the remains of rats, squirrels, and opossum. And let us not forget dead birds. Law enforcement was controlled by deadly gases. The spewing poison polluted the overcast sky every minute. If you resided on the island, you never saw the sun or the moon. The inside of the comedy club replicated the chemical overcast. A dungeon is usually described as being in a basement, but the comedy club was the only place in the world where it was located on the first floor, above ground. The basement rooms were, by comparison, less contaminated. A sea of dim lights struggled to illuminate through the dust glued to the dinginess. Every square inch of everything was permeated with chemical waste: the floor, the ceiling, the chairs, the tables, the silverware, the beer mugs. Alexander looked around and concluded that the conditions allowed a pulmonary specialist to print money.

The school arranged for Alexander, Flossy Lovesong, and a funny looking guy, Pork Chop (real name Howdy Longjohn), to perform at the comedy club. It was frequented mostly by low-income wage earners who stopped by for a drink after work. It also served as a venue for Freddy K to have students perform before a crowd of drunks. Freddy didn't care about the jokes. He earned extra cash coming from fees paid by the school's owner and from additional patrons who got drunk. Directions to the comedy club were passed out by the comedy school's owner a day before the show. There were no posters announcing a Hollywood special. The club was centrally located in a swamp of human disgrace—everyone knew where. Zug Island had a reputation to protect.

The school's gong-show format would be in effect. Freddy K would send back a report on every performance. The idea was to catch a rising star. That never happened. Failure at generating meaningful laughs meant trying your luck at other employment opportunities, such as enrolling in stenography school, or applying for a job as a school crossing guard. Alexander wasn't worried. He knew they dared not expel the best cash customer they'd ever had. Even so, Alexander planned to give a peak effort compared to the Royal Oak open mic flop. He was excited and had rehearsed hard, anticipating a spectacular performance.

Alexander was familiar with the area and the comedy club's building. His client, Robert Hatcher, had his factory nearby. The place had always been a bar, older than Methuselah.

Alexander drove to the comedy club in his new BMW 750i. That this was a mistake dawned on Alexander as he entered the uneven and weed-infested parking lot. History had dubbed Detroit the car capital of the world. He'd heard that slogan a thousand times. Might his brain cells have been disconnected because of dementia? Alexander, *dumbkoff*. What were you thinking? Detroit builds American automobiles. Germany builds BMWs. His brain softened, realizing jobs in Michigan depended on local retail support. Alexander wondered how soon lookouts—workers on the line—would spot his car and castrate it. He began to bang his head on the steering wheel, realizing the car was toast. He'd worked his ass off to buy it, and the *goyem* would demolish it like a *piñata*. Alexander looked outside for the Angel of Death.

It's terminal, he thought. I'll have to call a funeral home for cars to make final arrangements. I loved this car. *Oy*, if they find out I'm Jewish, I'm dead too. I'll ask the hooligans to kill me and leave the car alone. Just look at me. I don't even have to say one Yiddish expression. If they sense I'm Shylock from my demeanor, I'm dead. What am I thinking? These assholes don't read books. And they sure as hell don't read Shakespeare. I feel better already. Just to be on the safe side, I'll say a prayer and make my way inside.

Alexander assessed the other cars in the parking lot as most likely belonging at a cardiac care facility for wrecks. Windows of cellophane were held in place by duct tape, colored in a pastel battleship gray. Differently shaped fenders with one side painted rose and the other side painted purple served as replacement parts. The BMW would soon provide the newer replacement parts. Alexander started to cry—goodbye my lovely.

Howdy pulled into the lot in a pickup, Flossy in a dull-green Ford Contour. She parked nearby and rolled down her window.

"Oooh, baby. You're sporting a real nice car."

"Thanks, honey."

"The locals are going to love marring the finish."

Alexander replied, "That's what I'm afraid of. What I need is a local denizen with holes in his pants and a mouth half-filled with teeth, looking for work, to guard my car."

"I'll drive you home, if your car's missin' tires."

"I'm sure my wife will appreciate your help."

"I can't wait to meet her."

Alexander began to perspire.

"My husband doesn't mind if I bring someone home late." Flossy smiled and gave Alexander a wink.

He laughed.

They got out of their cars, ready to walk inside. A big black-panel truck with oversized wheels pulled into the slot where Alexander and

Flossy stood. The tinted window lowered, presenting a mean-look-ing dude with stone features. A toothpick hung from his mouth as he eyed the BMW. Alexander started to breathe hard. Flossy took a step sideways and stood quietly.

The toothpick wiggled as he spoke. "You the comedian to-night?"

Alexander nodded.

"You don't look funny."

Alexander turned and put his arm around Flossy and led her to the entrance. "Does that offer to drive me home still stand?" Flossy turned her head and smiled. "Sure does, honey."

They entered and walked up to the bar.

Chapter Four

INSIDE THE COMEDY CLUB

Inside the club, the bartender instructed the students from the comedy school to find Freddy K at the end of the bar. Freddy was easy to find, wearing a silk shirt with pastel pants, resting an arm on the bar and smoking a cigar. Alexander, observing Freddy's facial features, labeled him a fellow yid. Freddy's introductions were quick. "Go backstage. The show starts in ten minutes."

Alexander inquired, "Did you just return from a trip in the Caribbean, or did Zug Island turn into a tropical paradise?"

Freddy returned a look of disdain.

Alexander quipped, "Better watch out, Freddy. I do a mean gig when I talk like Reichsführer Himmler."

Freddy glared.

"Katz, or is it Kaplan? Did I ever do any accounting work for you? I have a nearby client, Star Paving. Are you acquainted with its führer, Robert Hatcher?"

Freddy stared at him, and said, "Are you some kind of smart ass? Fuck off, and go in back." Freddy turned away and puffed on his cigar.

Alexander met up with Flossy and Howdy. Before they could say anything, the loud speaker blared for everyone to take their seats as the show was about to begin. They huddled and told each other to "break a leg." Flossy went onstage first. Her routine began by telling the audience she was a minister's daughter. Her dad had bought a repentance mobile. Now you didn't have to wait to go to church on Sunday. She joked that business was good. The sins male parishioners confessed in the privacy of the mobile home's bedroom were arousing. Her best gag was:

Parishioner: "I came here to confess that I've committed adultery."

Minister: "Damn it, man. Didn't I cure you of lust the last time you were here?"

Parishioner: "You did. But my wife got so mad at me one day, she told me to stick it somewhere else."

The audience started a slow laugh in unison.

Flossy came off the stage into the back room. Alexander gave her a good-job hug and said, "Don't take the poor laughs as personal."

It was Howdy's turn. His routine was a redneck speaking to a redneck. His jokes were old, but hillbilly made everyone laugh.

Next came Alexander. He walked at a fast pace, jumped on the stage, grabbed the microphone stand, and pressed his lips against the microphone.

"Thank you, ladies and gentlemen." He shaded his eyes and said, "Do I see any beer drinkers?"

A weak voice responded, "Yeah, baby."

Alexander pictured a laugh meter reading zero. "I see everyone's dressed for the occasion—jeans, work boots, and wrinkled T-shirts. I'll assume you're not a group that shops at Brooks Brothers regularly?" Dead silence.

"They sell fancy T-shirts and underpants. You can say what you want, but the high-priced stuff has better value. They don't shrink after the first washing. And they don't wrinkle. The Dollar Store stuff you guys buy might be wrinkle-proof. But wearing the same underpants for ten days, you can sure smell gamey." The only sound was beer being slurped.

"By a show of hands, how many of you finished elementary school?" To Alexander's surprise, about a third raised their hand. "I was told I wouldn't be performing before an audience of doctors, so I'll take it down a notch. How many of you are able to balance your checkbooks?" Alexander's view of the audience changed to open mouths with missing teeth. "I see dental checkups aren't big around here either. You do know that toothbrushes were invented a while back?"

"Why don't you shut up, asshole."

"Hallelujah, someone in the audience just woke up. The rest of you can stay asleep. You, with the splendid vocabulary—would it surprise you to know that I'm a checkbook-balancing kind of guy, with a mouthful of my original teeth? I put on a clean pair of underwear daily. I'm also a member in good standing of the NAACP." The crowd woke up. A chorus of talking began. One patron shouted, "Who the fuck let this guy in!"

Alex quickly replied, "Oopsy. I got mixed up. That's for a Detroit comedy gig. I really meant the John Birch Society." The silence continued. "I'll take your silence as a vote of confidence." The crowd began to murmur. "I remember now. Yeah, you guys are the NRA bunch. Am I right?" The crowd quieted.

"I'm going to shift into third gear to resuscitate you. I go to a university, where I'm majoring in comedy." Alexander reached in his pocket and pulled out a piece of paper. "The scripted routine I hold in my hand came from the school's treasure vault. This stuff is gold."

Alexander opened the paper. "Anyone want to buy a newly built Zug Island home?" Alexander scanned the audience with his free arm. "It'll be cheap. The builder, I've heard, will guarantee it melts to nothing in five short years."

The audience stared at Alexander in cold silence. Other heads turned to neighbors with questioning faces, as if to say, *was that supposed to be funny?*

"How's your city's finances? When auto plants closed, I was able to correlate mortgages for houses in critical condition. Just like your city hall. Besides needing a paint job, the shingles on the roof look like old shoes. Let me guess, your Melvandale is flat broke.

You'd better get your gears working. Detroit spends millions they don't have on marbled municipal buildings. They're eating Clams Casino for appetizers, while you peasants are warming up a can of pork and beans for your entree." Angry stares faced him in unison.

Alexander quickly realized his routine was playing to the wrong crowd. Heart palpitations started to unhinge him. Another dead joke, and he imagined his BMW would be on its way to a junkyard.

Alexander sucked in his stomach and tried again. "A couple of older, single persons at a nursing home mixer meet and have a conversation. The man asks the lady, 'How old are you?' She replies with a swish of her arm, 'I'm very sorry, but that number is unlisted.'"

Dead-pan described the audience's reaction. Alexander remembered this was a Jewish joke. Still he continued, "What are you waiting for, a drum roll?"

Alexander looked over at Howdy and Flossy sitting at the end of the bar. Howdy stared with an open mouth. Alexander felt his head throb. Flossy was laughing. She blew Alexander a kiss. He felt some buoyancy. He decided to continue with the planned routine and then get the hell out of Dodge.

"I'm an environmentalist. Did you realize the comedy club where we're located is one hundred feet across an inlet from a major toxic chemical dump, known as Zug Island? And that Zug Island was not, repeat not, a resort island? And that the only way on and off the island is by rail over a bridge? Prisons are built on moated islands. Alcatraz Island prisoners travel by boat to get there. Now that's sexy. Think about what you have here. The only other way to cross over would be by swimming across the Rouge River Canal. Escaping from Alcatraz means encountering sharks. That's safer than swimming across the Rouge River. The chemicals in this river will peal your skin off in seconds."

At that moment, calling McDonald's to ask if any hamburger flipping jobs were available seemed a smart alternative. At least he wouldn't have to endure any more agony.

But Alexander would not let go. He sucked it in and started again. "I hope you know everything in the immediate area of Zug

Island is toxic. You're safe inside this building, though the tables look like they were coated with poison substituted for varnish." Alexander looked at the audience for a laugh. The locals' appearance personified decay: rotting teeth, thinning hair, gaunt faces, clothes soaked in chemicals, and skin (if exposed) a dullish rust and gray. Alexander shifted into his Russian accent. "Did you forget how to laugh? If you're hating my guts at this time, good. My expensive automobile is parked outside the front door. I dare you to harm it. My name is Harry Alexanderofsky. And if anything happens to my puppy, my Russian comrades will skewer you and roast you like a pig over a barbecue pit."

The audience laughed, some shouting, "You're full of shit."

But Alexander wasn't done. While play acting a coughing spell, he choked out, "Does anyone have any cough medicine?"

Freddy K walked over. "Finish up, already."

"Piss off, Freddy. It'll take a pack of your goons to get me to stop." Freddy left in a huff.

"Let me lighten up. A salesman is on a trip to London. The flight attendant gives the passengers the usual information regarding seat belts, etcetera. She announces, 'Now sit back and enjoy your trip while your captain, Sheila Miller and her crew take you safely to your destination.' When the flight attendant arrives with the drinks trolley, the salesman asks her, 'Did I understand you correctly? Is this plane really being flown by a woman?' 'Yes, sir,' replies the attendant, 'In fact, the plane's entire crew is female.' 'Oh my God,' says the salesman, 'I'd better have two gin and tonics. I don't know what to think of being on a plane with only women controlling it. Do you think you can arrange for me to go up to the cockpit to see for myself?'

"'Yes, of course sir,' says the attendant, 'But that's another thing you might like to know—we no longer call it the cockpit.'"

Alexander swung the microphone in a wide circle when no laughs emerged. "I see my laugh meter just plunged to zero. From the looks on your faces, if I swung two microphones, I suppose you'd relate to a stripper swinging tassels attached to her nipples."

Alexander felt impotent, limp. "What's the matter? Haven't you ever seen a comedian die doing his act in this dive? Where I live, just saying, 'Zug Island' gets a boatload of laughs."

Booing and yells broke out. "Go home, moron." Audience participation unleashed as Alexander sidestepped beer cans. He blurted, "No cleanup will be necessary. The building's architect also designed a duo purpose for this place, namely a pig sty."

Alexander had said something that finally caused the audience to laugh in earnest. "Ouch!" He slipped on the beer-soaked floor, lost his balance, and hit the deck. The audience roared. Encouraged, the audience launched a cannonade of beer cans. Alexander protected his head with his arms. Common sense suggested he should stand up and escape. With every direct hit, howls and high fives emerged.

Flossy approached to help but was forced to stay back, fighting off the incoming beer cans. Howdy had already run out of the building toward his pickup when the commotion first began.

Then the name-calling started. "Alexander, you're an asshole" won first place. Alexander's mind drifted into automatic. From his prone position he mumbled, "My car. *Oy*, why did I drive my brand-new baby to this chemical dump?" Alexander remembered that earlier he couldn't find a watchman for his car. "These *meshuga* ghouls will chop off the fenders and give the remainder a sledge hammer makeover." He shouted, "Flossy, call the police, call my wife, call anybody. Run for your life." Flossy told Alexander to escape and meet her at her pickup truck. She picked up some cans and flung them back, getting closer to the door.

Alexander, still in harm's way, shouted, "Freddy, you mother fucker. You egged these morons on." Alexander believed the crowd would get tired and leave. Imagining his car destroyed, he prayed that Flossy was nearby and hadn't driven away. Call and tell Margarita that Mexican banditos had destroyed his car? He imagined Margarita saying, "Not to worry. I'll drive alone through a high crime area to pick you up. I'll be there in twenty minutes." Alexander knew he was on his own. When he got home—if he ever got home alive—he dreaded the thought of feeding M more BS about how precisely he decided to become a stand-up comedian. It would prove tricky, but not impossible. He tripped on an electrical cord and fell on his tush. His face was covered with lacerations and bruises. As he ran outside, the rednecked goyem were in the process of converting his BMW into scrap. Tire irons and hammers whaled away. After the windows were shattered, hammer claws ripped the interior. A gunshot boomed. Someone was practicing shooting, using the car as a target.

Alexander ran into the industrial waste night, looking for Flossy.

Chapter Five

THE SAFETY NET

Alexander sprinted through the industrial network of Melvandale in fear of the rioters who had by now trashed the inside of the Zug Island Comedy Club. By following a zigzag route through the streets, he hoped to escape detection and arrive at his client's industrial building safely. The twilight helped him avoid the obstacles of parked trucks, garbage cans, and scrap metal that lined the streets. The neighborhood was a dump, and dumps had landmarks. He recognized every caved-in, tatty building he passed.

A horn blew in the distance and grew louder. Alexander was short of breath and wanted to stop or slow down. He imagined goons in a truck were closing in ready to grab him. He heard the yell of his name and the sound of a blowing horn. He stopped and looked around. A panel truck pulled alongside. "Hi, honey. I didn't forget about you." It was Flossy. "You lookin' for a lift?"

A drenched but happy Alexander stood in his tracks and didn't move. "I'm exhausted."

Flossy looked Alexander up and down. "You, sir, resemble a ghost looking for a grave. Hop in, and take a load off."

Alexander opened the passenger door, got into the seat tush first, leaned back, and collapsed. "I ran. I was afraid a truckload of thugs would spot me, jump out, and dispense justice for my lousy jokes and insults."

"When you're riding with me, you're safe." Flossy pulled a .45 from her jacket and patted it. "Did you ever shoot a gun?"

Alexander said, "Couple of times. Right now, it wouldn't have made any difference." Alexander glanced at Flossy's gun. "I'm too dogged tired to pull the trigger. From now on, I plan to bring a body-guard along to any future gigs."

Flossy laughed.

Alexander said, "Who would believe a happy hour gig could turn into a riot? I thought the patrons were supposed to be drunk when we performed. Whatever the club served, it turned them into beer-can-throwing professionals."

Flossy turned to Alexander. "Next time, baby, I've got your back. Where're we headed?"

"To my client's paving plant, in the Chowder Street industrial area, a couple blocks ahead."

Alexander remembered the feds, several years back, digging up the roads everywhere to look for Jimmy Hoffa's remains. Alexander had heard stories his killers first buried him in Macomb County under a road paving project. When the Feds went digging in Macomb County, Alexander was sure Hoffa was replanted below Chowder Street's pavement. Who would look in a dilapidated area? He murmured, "Jimmy, so sorry we're running over your face."

Alexander wiped sweat from his eyes with his sleeve. His head throbbed from running. "Flossy, around the next corner there'll be a sign that reads Star Paving. It's probably locked up for the day, but I'll get out and attract attention. I'm sure a security guard is still around and will let us in."

As Flossy rounded the corner, a drab and unlit Star Paving Company sign emerged. Seeing it, Alexander chirped, "It's beautiful."

A chain link fence surrounded the property, topped with spiraled razor wire. Alexander saw a guard shack, climbed out of the truck, and ran toward it. The guard shack was open, but he found no one inside. He reached in his back pants pocket for his cell phone. It was gone. "Damn."

Alexander could see the main road leading to the complex's main building inside a fenced gate. He walked over and tried to unlatch it. Surprisingly, the gate opened, and when Alexander went inside, it closed automatically. He took a few strides, but suddenly stopped. Something felt scary. Alexander was now locked in, and three guard dogs, more specifically dobermans, were racing toward him. Alexander jumped on the fence and tried to climb up and crawl over. A look upward reminded him that concertina wire was atop the fence. "That wire'll slice me in half." He looked toward the dogs. "Christ, they'll rip me apart." He started to scream. "Flossy. Help! Save me!" He looked down, and the dogs readied to leap up. "Down boys. Stay down." Alexander thought he should recite a couple of prayers, but "Oh, Shit" was the only one that came to mind.

Flossy saw what was happening with Alexander. She yelled, "Hang on, baby. I'm coming to get you."

Even so, Alexander tried to save his skin by hanging still and pulling his legs up to straddle the top of the fence. Two dogs snapped and jumped at him, an action that shook the fence like an apple tree. He screamed, "Flossy!" One dog stood ready for Alexander the prey to fall and be ripped apart into Alexander the disintegrated. The dogs kept barking and snarling, never taking their eyes off him. Flossy jumped out of the truck and fired a gunshot into the air. "That'll wake them up."

A voice from the building cried out, "Who out dere?"

Alexander recognized the voice and responded, "Henry! Is that you?"

Stillness suddenly filled the industrial swamp. Distant sirens could be heard. Alexander waited for Henry's reply.

"Henry, answer me. It's Alexander Haralson, Mr. Hatcher's accountant. You remember me, don't you?"

In a sing-song, the reply said, "Mr. Alex! Oh, my Lord. Hallelujah. I heard a gunshot. You okay?"

A shadow emerged from the main building. Alexander recognized the figure. The caretaker, and Robert Hatcher's bodyguard—

the larger-than-life, ex-football player—walked toward the gate. He yelled at the dogs, "Perry, Patton, Hun, get yo asses back where dey belong."

The dogs looked at Alexander and back at Henry. "Get," said Henry with a sweep of his arm, pointing to the main building. The dogs gave one last look at Alexander and beat a retreat.

Alexander climbed down. He and Henry hugged and then stepped apart. "You look de same," observed Henry. "I thought you'd gain weight when you quit work, doin' nothin'."

"Nah, I kept busy, but you look more rounded. That'll happen when you're not playing football."

Henry chuckled. "Yah, dat'z true. Gosh, it's great to see you."

Henry looked at Flossy. "I don't remember. Is dat the misses?"

Alexander laughed and said, "No, but a very good friend. She fired the gun to get someone's attention." Henry's smile faded to a serious look. "What you be doin' here?"

"I was at the Zug Island Comedy Club. A fight broke out, and I ran for my life. My car was destroyed."

"What was you doin in dat dive? Sounden' like you and the misses habbing some marital problems?" He looked toward Flossy. "But you seems to be doin' okay."

Alexander didn't want to read Henry the *magilla* about his comedy career and his relationship with Flossy. He fumbled for something to say but decided to say nothing.

"Henry, Flossy will drive me home. Is there anyone who could escort us to I-75?"

"Sure. You probably thirsty. Wait here. The dogs are gone. You'll be safe. I'll get you some water before you leave. And Mr. Robert, he here and be glad to see you too. Wow, that car business heavy duty. I'll get a driver from the dispatcher to take you. Dat Freddy K, the owner of dat club, always causing trouble. The city need to close it down."

Alexander fumed inside. Freddy K, a Jew, *owned* that cancer-transmitting citadel? He'd let a room full of drunken *goyem* work over a landsman? Alexander hadn't forgotten he was in the process of a makeover, a new Lenny Bruce. "Henry, if I ruled the world, I'd hang Freddy K by his feet, dowse him with barbecue sauce, and let those dogs feast."

"I bet you would."

"Flossy, you're in charge."

"Anything you say, hon."

Alexander spoke, inspired by a vision that had jumped into his head from the pages of Orwell's *1984*. "You'll be the ruling dictator. Flossy, you can write any law you want and call it the law of the land. You can lie, cheat, commit violent acts, spy on citizens, deny free speech, and so on. For everyone else, it's a crime if they're caught. I'll have you know the conviction rate in societies using this system is always one hundred percent."

"I'd never understand the laws," pondered Flossy. "In school, I got a C plus in reading."

"Henry, I'd help you arrest anyone daring to pursue happiness or believe in honesty. Sentence Freddy K to thirty years in a gulag. Feed him *yushka*... that's sewer water soup. He'll have the runs for the rest of his life. You'll get his brain cells to think straight. That SOB Freddy took advantage of me. I'd like to go back and burn the place down."

"OOOeeee. Now you talkin'. Yes, sir. I have some friends with big muscles who throw der fist with speed. I seez scrapes on your face. Dat owner, he hurt you. He made a mistake. Mr. Hatcher mad at him too. Mr. K telling the police Mr. Robert using inferior material to make the streets. Bull shit! Mr. Robert only use de best. That owner needs a whoopin'.

"Let's walk to the main building and find Mr. Robert. He be lookin' for an excuse to give some payback to dat man. Anyway, I know'd Mr. Hatcher be happy to see you and the misses. Nobody goin' to bother you." They turned and walked to the building's entrance. Henry said, "Wait here." He turned and went inside the building.

Alexander laughed when he left. "Henry thinks we're married, and nothing will convince him otherwise."

Alexander could attest to Freddy K's claim of using inferior material. He knew Robert Hatcher pocketed money from over-billing. He could also attest to Hatcher laundering money and to the possibility that Jimmy Hoffa's remains were buried in a sub-base material mix under a concrete pavement job. And he believed there were other unidentified burials, courtesy of Star Paving. But Alexander kept quiet.

Flossy noticed Alexander's face. She hugged him and said, "I see that getting into scrapes isn't your everyday happening."

"No, it isn't. Thanks, babe, for saving my ass."

The guard reemerged and gave Alexander and Flossy each a bottle of water. Alexander acknowledged thanks by raising the bottle. Twenty minutes passed. Alexander thought that Hatcher must be discussing strategy with the 'boys.' Suddenly, the building's overhead doors rolled up. Two Lincolns pulled out and parked near Alexander. The driver's window opened. A bald, muscular head belonging to a muscular body rasped to Alexander, "Someone's coming out to see you."

Alexander turned toward the building. Out of the building's interior strolled Robert Hatcher, with open arms, saying, "How's my friend, Alexander Haralson, C.P.A., accountant extraordinaire?"

"I'm doing great."

They greeted each other with a hug.

"Can't you stay out of trouble?"

"I thought you said I *should* get into trouble, so you'd have the enjoyment of saving a friend?"

"I remember that. So how's Margarita?"

"Getting crankier with age, along with fretting about sprouting wrinkles."

"Your young daughter. What's her name?"

"Roberta, the brat, who learned the word pedicure before the word happiness."

"Oh, my."

"Robert, you look great. Your hair is still dark. I don't see any gut hanging over. Business must be good. With that smile on your face, you must be divorced. Did I miss anything?"

"Very funny, Alex. Yes, I'm still married to the same woman, and yes, business is good, but that's only part of the reason. I've got to look good on TV. It's obvious you haven't heard any rumors, outside of me being an SOB. So let me throw you for a loop. I plan to run for governor."

"What? Wow. Will you be called Governor SOB?"

"Good comeback, mister." Robert eyed Flossy, checking her out head to toe.

"You dog. Good for you. I like the looks of your friend." Hatcher kept a steady gaze on Flossy.

"Robert, meet Flossy Lovesong. Flossy, meet the next governor of the state of Michigan. Robert, a run for the governorship is good. It'll shake the trees, and the state could use a good housecleaning. You've got my complete backing. Let me know how I can help."

"Thanks. And I won't ask what the hell you were doing at the Zug Island Comedy Club. Follow me."

A third car, a limo, pulled out of the building. The front doors swung open for Hatcher and the back ones for Alexander and Flossy. Inside were a couple of Star Paving's disciplinary guards. The two men were tall and muscular, which Alexander knew to mean 'show them your highest respect.' Salute, if necessary. Each man, in this instance, had four bad sides. Hatcher made the introductions. "Alexander, meet Gino, and the driver's Frenchy."

Alexander replied in a calm voice, "Nice to meet you... gentlemen."

Robert leaned toward Flossy. "You'll come back to my building for your truck. Sit back and relax." He looked at Alexander. "For you, Mr. Troublemaker, I set up an appointment between Freddy and me where you come out to be the winner." Alexander whistled as he inhaled and fell back on the seat's backrest. He admitted to himself that sitting among a human arsenal felt good. This adventure was about to turn out differently. Robert Hatcher was going to bat for him. Freddy K was about to learn a lesson.

As the limos drove toward the comedy club, Hatcher told Alexander that Freddy was a bit too cozy with the local police department. When they arrived, police cars with lights flashing manned the parking lot, and a crowd hung around outside, behind the crime scene tape. A hoist held up Alexander's car, vertically. An officer lifted the tape and allowed Hatcher's entourage into the parking lot. Robert surveyed the parking lot and focused on the hanging car. He turned to Alexander and asked, "Is that yours?" Alexander nodded. The police had been waiting for the right person to consult, to determine what should be done next. That person had arrived—Robert Hatcher.

A police officer came over to the car. "Hi, Mr. Hatcher."

Robert leaned toward the window and said in a firm voice, "We'll take over from here."

The officer said, "Sure, Mr. Hatcher. The owner is still in the building." The officer backed away, went to his squad car, and drove off. The other officers followed suit. Alexander observed the vindication of one of his core beliefs—the entire world moved with money as its fuel. In full view, Alexander watched tax dollars and police bribes in action. Back at the warehouse, the court ruled in favor of Robert Hatcher. Freddy K was left to the executioners to dispense justice.

Alexander watched as Hatcher's lead cars emptied. Alexander mumbled to himself, "Jesus Christ. I've only seen roughnecks in movies. What's going to happen?" The door where Alexander sat opened. Gino exited first. Then Robert exited and leaned back into the car. "Stay in the car with Frenchy."

Alexander slunk down. Peering over the front seat, Alexander saw Star Paving's finest lead the way to the one-on-one meeting between Robert Hatcher and Freddy K.

The driver turned on the radio's local twenty-four-hour news. A news flash announced that a large disturbance was in progress near Zug Island. Alexander leaned back against the headrest. "Whoa, baby. Get me home!"

Frenchy looked in the rear-view mirror and said, "The TV stations will be trying to get some pictures."

Alexander retorted, "Is the operative word, *trying*?"

Frenchy broke out in laughter. "You're a funny man."

Alexander blurted, "*Oy*."

Frenchy asked, "Did you say something?"

"No. You heard the gears grinding in my brain." Alexander's thoughts turned to Robert Hatcher's plan to run for governor. "*Oy*."

Frenchy again asked if he had heard Alexander say something.

"The gears in my right and left brain were working at the same time."

Frenchy laughed. "Wait till I tell de boys what you said."

The next *Oy* rolled inside Alexander's head. So Robert Hatcher planned to run for governor. Where the hell did that idea get traction? Alexander knew Hatcher's methodology for success. He would employ the Chicago style of government. All government contracts signed by the elected governmental head would pay one-third to government executives, one-third to union heads or alderman, and one-third to the contractor. Hatcher fit the contractor slot. He did quality paving jobs, in a timely manner, at the lowest bid. Having good networking relations with various state transportation departments placed his company in the loop, with money flowing from a spigot into his pocket. Robert Hatcher was a rich man and would be a very rich man when he left public service. Alexander wondered how he could get inside some of this action.

He looked up and caught sight of Hatcher returning. Hatcher got inside the car and told Frenchy to head back. "Alex, say hello to Margarita for me."

Alexander acknowledged Robert's wishes with a nod. He sighed. "I'll be heading home, then." However, another order of business caught his attention. He sniffed several times, then turned to Robert.

"Do I smell smoke?"

Chapter Six

DINING WITH DANGER

"We're late," boomed Margarita, as Alexander dragged himself through the doorway. Her remark wasn't only said as a reminder of a social engagement but as an excuse to ambush her unsuspecting husband. For several months now, Alexander's commitment to the Ha-Ha School of Comedy had kept him away from home, sometimes all day, and sometimes several days a week. Margarita was clueless where he went or how he spent his time. She'd asked him several times to tell her his whereabouts, but his answer was, "I'm busy launching a new career."

She'd had enough. Alexander walked into the house, knocked out from the day's events. Margarita, playing a stereotypical Italian wife, felt she had a God-given right to bury her husband under a verbal avalanche. She launched into a tirade, slamming him with every derogatory remark or expletive ever said or written in human history. Not satisfied, she included remarks she believed a female T rex might yell at her husband—"I'm going to squash you and drive my spiked teeth through your heart!" When finished, Margarita felt proud of her effort, silently declaring herself the husband-beating champion of the year.

Alexander stood still and sucked it in. He was exhausted and had not been looking for an argument when he returned home. He'd expected a light dinner, a hot shower, and to collapse into a bed to rest from the day's tumult. Instead, Margarita had ambushed him without a chance to breathe or think. Earlier, he'd defended himself against a beer-can-throwing barrage, with a two mile run to safety. Wasn't that enough? Looking up at Margarita, he answered his own question. Her pose, with one arm resting on the banister and one leg standing on the first step, said it all. Missing was a rawhide whip. Alexander imagined Margarita delighting in his suffering as would a warden welcoming back a prisoner from an afternoon of forced labor.

He replied, "So I'm late."

Margarita elaborated, "I said, *we're* late. We have a dinner date with the Tashins." Alexander realized that she was wearing dressy sportswear.

"Oh." A silence ensued. Margarita signaled her disdain, staring at Alexander with piercing eyes. A hallucination appeared to Alexander—Margarita's mouth wide open, rivaling a saber-toothed tiger's jaw with drooling jowls, ready to bite his arm off. To show off his wounds and tattered clothing to her, he edged a shoulder and arm toward her. Margarita remained silent. Alexander started up the stairs. He said, "I love your show of concern. Admit you're relieved I arrived home in one piece."

"Get cleaned up and dressed, *veloce*. I'll call the Tashins and tell them we'll pick them up in fifteen minutes."

Alexander was halfway up the stairs when he stopped and said, "It'll take me an hour to get ready."

"Run. Don't give me excuses. Change your shirt and pants, comb your hair, and bandage your scrapes. Roberta has some designer bandages in her bathroom drawer. Your choices are Snow White or Dora the Explorer."

"You could be more civil."

"Get real."

"So I played a spirited game of touch football with friends and ran late. That isn't a crime."

Margarita snickered. "You played football? Really."

Alexander continued upstairs. He had been beaten and humiliated enough. He cautioned himself to finish the day without any further trouble to incur her wrath. Like a good soldier, he followed Margarita's orders, went into the bathroom, and in the mirror viewed a beaten face with blood still oozing. *Not horrible*, he thought. *But not pretty.* Earlier, Flossy had given him a rag to wipe the blood off his face. His clothes were stained and ripped. In the medicine cabinet he found plain bandages. Alexander looked upward. Thank you, God, for saving me from humiliation. I knew you were the only one who would answer my prayer. Alexander's face was sore, and he washed his wounds using a washcloth, dabbing them with care.

After getting groomed and dressed, he bounded down the staircase and joined Margarita. As they walked into the garage, Alexander told her they would have to drive her car. "I had a car accident earlier and got a lift home."

Margarita moved close to Alexander's face and looked under a bandage. "Oh, is that why you needed bandages? So where's the car?"

"It had to be towed."

"Where?"

"To a scrap yard. It was totaled."

Margarita fumbled for something to say. Her eventual reaction was a prayer entreating understanding, aimed heavenward. She blurted out, "I married an idiot." Lowering her gaze to ground level, she said, "Tonight, honey, you're going to be on your own. I plan to embarrass the hell out of you. I'll lead the Tashins to ask you what happened to your face and why you're wearing bandages. I can't wait to hear your explanation."

"I'll tell them the earlier story about why we're late. They'll be sympathetic."

Margarita chuckled and said, "Go for it, big boy."

The Haralsons got into her car and they drove in silence. This continued all the way, even as they pulled up the driveway and waited for Anita and Cyrus. Everyone was all smiles as they got inside the car.

Anita started the conversation. "We haven't seen each other in a while," she said and asked how everyone was feeling. Margarita and Alexander commented that they felt fine.

Anita asked, "Alex, are those bandages?"

"I had a small accident. I'm fine."

Margarita told the Tashins she'd called Jimmy's restaurant to tell them they had a reservation and would arrive late.

Alexander said, "I don't know why Margarita called. Jimmy Kilikas, the owner, knows me and wouldn't give up the table." He then looked at Margarita. "Everything will turn out okay." She kept her cool by looking forward and saying nothing. Her face betrayed the real story—inside, *en fuego*.

Anita turned the conversation to families as Alexander drove toward the restaurant and asked about Roberta. "You mentioned before that she was a handful. Has anything improved?"

Margarita sighed and said, "Roberta is exhausting," and left it at that. Alexander pulled into the restaurant's lot, which was full. The only parking space available was one especially reserved for Alexander. He drove into it and turned off the motor. Unbuckling his seat belt, he said, "My very own VIP parking place. I must be important."

They went inside Jimmy's Grille, a Birmingham 'must go to be seen' place, a hangout for rich attorneys, rich doctors, and rich businessmen. Middle class acquaintances were labeled the neighborhood illegal immigrants and encouraged to dine elsewhere, helped by the maître d ignoring them. If they asked when a table would be available, he shooed them away by telling them there was a two-hour wait.

The restaurant was located at the corner of Maple and Telegraph. Although the restaurant owner's name was Jimmy, the restaurant's name had been chosen to commemorate the late James Riddle Hoffa, the ex-president of the International Brotherhood of Teamsters Union, an ex-con released after serving four years in prison for extortion. The parking lot of the restaurant was the scene where, on July 30, 1975, Jimmy Hoffa was seen getting into the back seat of a car. Police reported the next day that he'd had a meeting with two local Mafia leaders, whom police suspected had kidnapped him. He was not found in the trunk of a car. In fact, his remains were never found. He was reported missing by his wife when he did not return home for supper. Subsequent police investigations turned up no trace of his whereabouts or any evidence.

Alexander's parking space was where they'd found Hoffa's car. Alexander had coveted the spot. He took the trouble to learn where the exact parking space was and laid claim to it.

Jimmy K did everything first-class. The building's redwood and chrome siding was eye-catching. Inside, the decor was expensive—marble floors, hardwood tables, and plush leather chairs. Contemporary paintings hung on the wall, lit with recessed ambient lighting. The restaurant attracted the preferred clientele—spenders. The wait staff was tops, and so was the food. Jimmy's was rated a five star restaurant by food critics. The group walked into the restaurant where a duo played quiet music, allowing conversations to be heard. A hostess greeted them.

"Good evening, Mr. Haralson. I have a table ready for you and your guests. Please follow me." With menus in hand, she led them past a crowd waiting to be seated. Alexander kept his eyes straight ahead. To him, eye contact meant, *"You mean there were people ahead of us? Tough luck, suckers."*

Once they were seated in Alexander's favorite booth toward the back, the manager, Roger Hornbeck, approached the table. "Good evening, everyone."

Alexander ordered a bottle of white wine and said, "I love this place. You've done a fabulous job."

Roger thanked Alexander and said a waiter would be by shortly to describe the specials and take their orders.

With Roger running the operation, the restaurant's popularity had soared. Alexander never said a word to anyone, but he knew the restaurant did well because he was in charge of the books. Alexander hadn't revealed the owner's name to Margarita. But she guessed Alexander was the accountant, with all the special attention he received.

Alexander had sat in on many meetings when the restaurant changed hands after Jimmy's death. At one particular meeting with the wait staff, Jimmy K had commented, "Make sure not to refer to the steaks as 'dead meat,' or use the expression 'swimming with the fishes.'"

Knowing that Margarita was in a mood to make trouble, Alexander jumped in to direct the conversation. "I'm going to say something about my daughter. Managing a brat is work, and Margarita has done a great job."

The Tashins looked at Alexander, startled.

Without realizing it, Alexander launched into a comedy club routine.

"Let me enlighten you. Roberta Haralson is a five-year-old child, completely ungrateful by anyone's standard. Watching TV once with a bored expression, she huffed to my wife, 'I want a new toy.' The brat's mother replied, 'Darling, you have toys in unopened boxes.' Roberta looked at Margarita incredulously. Her mother reminded her about the new clothes she was wearing. The little darling stomped her foot. She wanted the Salvation Army to stop by next week to pick up any 'old' clothes and toys dated more than two months. Roberta then dictated a new order. The word 'new' must be in front of every noun associated with personal items—shoes, American Girl dolls, dresses, and toys. Thank goodness she has a way to go before she reaches the word 'car.' I ask you, is this a description of a well-balanced child in the early stages of life, on her way to developing into a well-adjusted, mature adult? Don't answer that question."

The Tashins broke into laughter while Margarita sat nonplussed.

Margarita hissed, "How far do you plan to take this?"

"Very far."

Margarita looked at the Tashins and said, "Plan on a funeral in the near future."

Alexander was in his element—he had an audience. With an air of confidence, he continued. "We're required to put up with brats. We're expected to love them while we hide in closets. How amazing. At a high point of mischief and at the highest point of arrogance, they demand and challenge the world to say 'no.' We run for safety.

Once we're inside our hiding places, we open the curtain and concede defeat. 'Anything you want.' Our cowardice guarantees survival for the brats. Just think, our natural response is to run from disasters, brawls, and now brats. In astrological terminology, they're called death stars."

The Tashins howled. Cyrus told Alexander he should try the brat routine at a comedy club. Margarita fell back in her seat, exasperated. "I'm hearing that comment for the fiftieth time."

Alexander smiled, feeling rejuvenated. He couldn't wait to return to the comedy club school and practice his lines for his next gig. He looked at Margarita.

She responded, "Get that silly-ass smile off your face."

"I can't. I'm on a roll."

Margarita shook her head and put on a brave look in the face of defeat.

Anita commented, "Together you two are real comedians."

"Anita, I'm not a comedian," responded Margarita. "I'm a vampire. Alex is a wannabe comedian. I'll go home and do what I do best—dress in a black gown and watch it flow in a breeze while I stir a boiling cauldron."

Laughter erupted.

"Margarita, you say the funniest things when you're on edge. By the way, I've been meaning to ask why haven't you and Alex moved to Florida? The weather's warmer. There are cultural events. You could split your time between Florida and Michigan."

Alexander continued where Anita left off. "And save on inheritance taxes. Anita, you make a good case. I have retirement plans that would keep me here. And let's not forget our precious Roberta. If we could board her at an obedience school, the thought of moving to Florida would take on traction."

Cyrus cautioned Alexander. "Be nice." He nodded toward Margarita. "She might fool you and become a rival comedian."

Alexander mumbled, "Oh, help."

Cyrus continued. "I'm curious… why the bandages? Did Margarita bop you on the head?"

"No. No domestic violence. I had a car accident. Lost control and hit a utility pole. No broken bones, just lacerations."

"You're lucky... no stitches."

"Yeah. You could call me that."

The wine arrived and was poured. Toasts to good health and friendship were proposed.

Cyrus picked up the conversation. "While we were waiting for you, I saw a strange news story on TV. Some bar, a comedy club in Melvandale, caught on fire. They suspect arson. The picture at the scene showed a car in the parking lot sitting upside down. Ouch. It looked expensive. How do you flip a car over in a parking lot? And who would drive a car worth over five hundred dollars into that area?"

Margarita looked at Alexander. "Did they show a close-up of the car? Did it look like a BMW 650i, Michigan license number EL6 H27?"

"It was hard to tell. Anyway, the reporter at the scene said a suspect ran from the building. He was described as an older man wearing jeans and a T-shirt. They said they would check the car's license number. The report said the police suspected the older person who ran from the scene was the arsonist."

Margarita leaned close to Alexander. "Go ahead. You can tell me if that was your car."

Alexander replied *sotto voce*, "You're thinking because Robert Hatcher's business is located in Melvandale, and I was his accountant for many years, and Robert Hatcher has Sicilian partners, he started the fire. Am I right?"

"Uh, huh."

"Is 'no' a believable answer?"

"Your mother should have named you Pinocchio. You've been a bull-shitter from day one." Margarita turned to the Tashins. "Alexander has some news concerning that Melvandale fire."

Alexander grinned and picked up where she left off. "The gossip about Melvandale is about one of the city's favorite sons, Robert Hatcher, my friend and former client. He will be declaring his candidacy for governor."

The Tashins responded 'wow' in tandem.

Alexander continued, "Ol' blue eyes will try to hit it out of the park."

Margarita sat with a blank stare. "What just happened? That rotten *chevalyek*. He's running for governor?"

"Yes, my dear."

The Tashins looked at Alexander and Margarita with a puzzled look and then at each other. They sat back, nonplussed.

"Let me help, M. You wanted to use the word duplicity to describe Hatcher but couldn't spit it out." Alexander looked toward the Tashins. "Margarita's vocabulary is limited. She meant to say Robert Hatcher is a scoundrel, which he is. I think as governor he'll make sure the state will get whatever is needed to start back on the road to recovery. Might I also mention he'll be using the phrase 'kick-ass' more than 'compassion'?"

Margarita asked Alexander if he planned to help Hatcher's campaign.

"I already did. When Hatcher told me his plans, I said, 'congratulations.' In my mind, that statement cost me five thousand dollars."

Margarita huffed.

Alexander continued. "Listen, without going into details, he's helped a lot of people out of scrapes."

"Like hiding the name of the BMW's owner."

"I was referring to Robert providing jobs to underprivileged and uneducated people."

"You're referencing his workers. When they're not breaking up roads looking for Hoffa, they're breaking skulls."

"Thanks, Margarita, for that clarification. Look, he'll make sure everything goes in a straight line, like going through a car wash."

The waiter approached the table and described the specials. Dinner orders were given.

After ordering, Cyrus commented that he thought Alexander was right about being under an obligation to support Hatcher. "M, it's only a check," he pointed out.

Margarita, fuming inside, managed to give Cyrus a pleased look over the top of her glasses for flushing out an important detail.

Alexander said he supported Hatcher one hundred percent. "He was a good client." Hatcher had profited from Hoffa's disappearance in a big way. "After it became clear no suspect would be charged with murder, the investigation changed to finding his remains. 'Family closure' was the PC term used by TV reporters. Hatcher and I laughed at their stupidity. Anybody with half a brain could have concluded that ninety percent of Detroiters, deep down, didn't give a shit where he was buried. Only ten percent did. They were the paving contractors who were assigned to dig up the streets and let crime investigators sift through the gravel base in hopes of finding human remains. Hatcher's workers then repaired the street, deposited large checks in offshore accounts, and went home. A week ago, Hatcher finished his seventh dig-up and street repave job. The jobs come about when business becomes slow."

Cyrus said, "Alexander, get into comedy. Find a foil. Margarita, you'd be perfect. Be part of a comedy team, like Martin and Lewis."

"Cyrus, think about what you've said. Martin, an Italian, was a foil for Lewis, the Jew. I, Margarita, an Italian Jew, would not be a foil for my husband, the Jew."

Cyrus replied he meant no offense.

Alexander admitted he'd had thoughts of doing comedy work after retiring from accounting, but he hadn't pursued them. Margarita looked at Alexander with a wary eye.

"I could train and try to work on my mechanics of delivery. I'm never short of jokes. As to material, I observe minute detail in my surroundings. Nothing ever passes me by. Call me a bloodhound. I notice what people wear, what they look like, and how they converse.

"I could put together a routine, tearing them apart. Take no prisoners. Everyone and everything is fair game. You're right, Cyrus. I've wiped enough asses. Now, it's payback time.

"I see stardom, and not just from being bathed in limelight. My star in the sky a hundred light years away may have died out, but the photons it emitted still live and are streaming down in formation to illuminate my glory."

The Tashins sat in a funk.

Margarita groaned. "Like going in line through a car wash."

The evening quieted down as dinner arrived and was eaten in silence. After everyone danced and ate a dessert, they were exhausted. Anita said, "Let's go home."

Alexander paid the check. He said his goodbyes to friends, some wait staff, and Hornbeck. The group left the restaurant. The drive home was silent.

After dropping the Tashins off at home, Margarita told Alexander she planned to go to court to have him committed, first thing Monday morning.

Alexander smiled. "Go for it girl."

Chapter Seven

ALEXANDER GETS A BIG SURPRISE

After a morning nap in his room at the William Beaumont Hospital, Alexander rolled out from his hospital bed, slid his feet into his slippers, and walked down the corridor. Gradual improvements in his health were evident. He walked without scraping the floor, suffered less fatigue, and felt physically stronger with fewer aches and pains. Even though he felt better, Alexander kept an eye on his pace, making sure not to overtax himself.

The operation was a blessing of sorts. Being confined, he had more free time to walk around and think about matters, which he had so desperately missed. Before he entered the hospital, business matters had demanded his attention and interfered with his time to think. Now he could relax and sort out pressing personal matters, such as the benefits of working for Robert Hatcher, managing his comedy career, keeping his marriage intact, and dreaming about his intimate relations with Flossy. He also had time to reminisce. There were good memories he had put aside or ignored because of his hectic work schedule.

His mind drifted to a couple of years earlier, when he and Governor Hatcher had attended a Lions-Packers game on Thanksgiving Day. Alexander remembered it was right after Hatcher won the election for governor. The newly elected governor called and said, "Let's get together on Thanksgiving. We can go to the Lion's game.

I've got great seats." Alexander thought the call from the governor-elect a bit strange. Feeling overworked, however, he welcomed
the thought of some time away from the office. "Robert, I love your
idea, but it's right after the election. Don't you have more important
matters?"

"Spending an afternoon relaxing with an old friend is what matters," the governor had said.

"Thanks, Robert. Rubbing elbows in public with the new governor will strengthen my resolve to support you in your effort to
squeeze every welfare sponge dry."

"You're always over the top, Alex. I'm counting on making a
statement by appearing in front of a large crowd with the sharpest
man in finance at my side. Call it a symbol of hope, a resurrection
of Detroit."

"Cut the crap, Robert. Call the Ford family and tell them their
stinky football team's record mirrors the collapse of Detroit. I know
deadbeats when I see them. I think half the college teams could whip
our sissies."

"Alex, you'd better not spout off at the game. We're in their
stadium."

"I'm not scared of being thrown out. If they do, call Margarita
and tell her I'll be eating Thanksgiving dinner at Mother Wattles
Soup Kitchen. When she's through, you'll think the Fourth of July
came six months early."

* * *

Hatcher picked Alexander up at home and they drove to the stadium,
located in downtown Detroit. The limo passed burned-out buildings, vacant land, and industrial sites where only steel girders of
collapsed factories remained. Hatcher and Alexander looked about
and said nothing. It was painful to see Detroit's devastation, block
after block. Alexander leaned toward the driver and said facetiously,
"When you see a new structure that has all its bricks intact, that's
Ford Field."

Hatcher smiled. "That started the day off well."

Governor-elect Hatcher and Alexander got the VIP treatment when the limo arrived. They were escorted by police to Hatcher's private viewing box at Ford Field. Alexander knew Margarita was preparing Thanksgiving dinner. He anticipated a day spent in an air of relaxation, a change from taking baby Roberta and Roman's children to the Thanksgiving Day parade. Roman, his *go to* son, had agreed to substitute as grandfather. Alexander's Thanksgiving Day plans were now happily split into time spent with a good friend and then family.

The game started at noon. With the Lions, the doormats of the NFL, opportunities to cheer a good play would be few and far between. That left plenty of time for conversation. Alexander had noticed Robert Hatcher was a more confident man these days, a more assertive person than he'd known in the past. Alexander hoped to duplicate Hatcher's success. Once he was rambling comfortably along his new walk of life, the comedian would blossom and became a sought-after performer.

Hatcher's campaign had mopped up his challenger, Henry Ouster, a protégé of the outgoing governor, Jennifer Granholm. On the campaign trail, Hatcher accused Ouster of being her lapdog. "She's incompetent, and if he's elected, he'll be your next incompetent governor." Hatcher reminded voters of Granholm's swashbuckling spending habits, calling her a Robin Hood in drag. She robbed money from her political enemies and gave it to her friends. Granholm tried to help, campaigning for her would-be successor. She made a big mistake, telling the unemployed to eat less if they were hungry. Her insensitive remark sent voters to the polls in droves. In one day, what had polled as an even race turned into a landslide by election day. Hatcher's campaign had stressed responsible spending. After Granholm's remark, he kept his mouth shut. The final tally was seventy-five percent in favor of inaugurating Robert Hatcher as governor of Michigan on January first.

Alexander thought he'd been invited by Hatcher to relax, drink whiskey, and talk gibberish. A chance to take their minds off politics was well deserved. Hatcher told him how glad he was the campaign had ended. "Kissing babies and kissing voter's asses was tiring," he had said. Hatcher also told Alexander how much he appreciated his work as personal tax accountant and finance man for his multi-million dollar road construction business. Alexander gave himself a pat on the back, hoping his career as a comedian enjoyed equal success. Besides challenging the IRS about their questionable tax deduction inquiries, Alexander's eyes were sharp to recognize where Hatcher's company should invest new money. New equipment and new paving techniques were needed for roads to survive cold winters. Costs would be higher. Alexander had recommended buying out competitors. It was a successful tactic. He'd made Robert Hatcher one rich guy. Hatcher told Alexander he knew he sat on a pile of money, but that he missed the daily snowstorms of additional dollars falling from the sky into his pocket. They toasted each other during the game with single malt scotch, joked, and smoked cigars. With Hatcher firmly entrenched, each could let loose.

By halftime, the Packers were ahead thirty-eight to ten. It appeared the Lions' season record would remain unblemished with no wins. Hatcher's box was spilling over with campaign contributors, politicians, and state officials. He shook hands and hugged everyone. Hatcher remarked to a contributor he would make sure an important building contract was awarded to him. "You showed me your loyalty. I don't forget friends."

Shouts of "Remember me, governor?" could be heard from the opposite side of the room. Everybody wanted to shake his hand. He was the man to meet. Hatcher shouted back, "I'll shake everyone's hand." Hatcher had indicated earlier to Alexander that he loved to match a face with the amount on a check. Hatcher made all decisions. The box with a state-regulated, sixty-person room capacity was filled with twice that number. Etiquette changed to trashy, as sober revelers got drunk. Drinks spilled, and food fell on clothes or the floor. Alexander avoided the rowdies, engaging in conversation instead with anyone who appeared sober. The obnoxious jokes for his stand-up routines stayed in the closet. He would launch them at the right opportunity.

At halftime, Hatcher descended to the football field's fifty yard line. A standing ovation of cheers and applause greeted his introduction to the crowd. He remarked that his goal as governor would be to build new industries in Michigan and bring back old industries that had moved away. "I want Michigan and Detroit to return to the national limelight they once enjoyed." When he finished his speech, he returned to the club box to watch the rest of the game. Alexander liked what Hatcher had said. The part about returning to the limelight fit the goal that Alexander envisioned for himself.

The game progressed just as disastrously for the Lions in the second half. Many of Hatcher's guests left. They showed their faces in the box and then it was time to go home. Once the crowd thinned, Alex enjoyed himself, eating and drinking for two people. He sat back on a couch, stuffed. He was going to have to fake eating Margarita's lavishly prepared Thanksgiving feast. It was in a quiet moment, with both men sitting together, that out of nowhere Hatcher said, "Alex, I want you to be my budget director. I know it's been years since you were my tax consultant, but you still show that old zip, even in your senior years."

Alex smiled, taken aback by the invitation. He looked at Robert and thought, *is he serious?*

"I need a change, someone capable I can trust. I had Josh Hillman in mind. He's a good finance man, but he's not you."

Alexander nodded.

"With him, I'd feel like I was carrying a hundred extra pounds."

"Bob, I don't know what to say. Are you sure? You know I'm not that well versed in government finance. My hair is gray, and it'll be a lot grayer if I say yes."

Hatcher retorted, "Alex, relax. You're a finance genius. You're a fast learner. Government work will be a breeze in short order. There'll be plenty of time to get up to speed. You point the direction, and I'll implement the decisions. Knowing you, you'll have the *chanukahs* to help me."

Alex laughed. "Robert, you're drunk. They're *cahunahs*."

Hatcher burst out laughing and said, "What did you expect from a dumb *shagetz*?"

"Alex, I've had you in mind for the job since making my victory speech on election night."

Alex tried to humor Hatcher, saying, "I'll talk with my family tonight. I want everyone to hear it first from me. If I accept, there will be other friends I'd want to tell before the news becomes public. I'll call you with a definite answer next week."

Bob smiled. "It's a deal."

Conversation and laughter reverberated in the half-empty suite. Friends came over to shake hands and say goodbye. Hatcher was busy. It gave Alex time alone to ponder some pros and cons of Bob's job offer. Aspects of Alexander's business relationship with Robert Hatcher resurfaced in his mind. Parts of Bob's road construction business appeared seemly. Italians ran the Hatcher Concrete Road Building Company's operation. Being a capable administrator, a capable finance man, and a capable public relations person made Robert Hatcher the perfect front man.

What stood out in Alexander's memory, however, was an old contract to repair the City of Melvandale's main roads. They were the ones he passed every time he drove to Hatcher's industrial complex. How could he forget to repair the roller-coaster roads and the ones with deep potholes? Alexander remembered he never got a definitive answer about whether that contract had been completed. Hatcher had brushed him aside, saying everything was fine. Alexander, very busy at the time, had visited and inspected other finished jobs, but never got around to inspecting the Melvandale road job. It remained a perennial work in progress. He thought it was a microcosm of Robert Hatcher's character. Alexander's thoughts were mixed and he did not lean toward either accepting or rejecting the offer.

Alexander knew Robert Hatcher ran his end of the business with perfection. It showed. As a campaigner, he had appeared on TV dressed impeccably, speaking in a golden voice as either a spokesman for the company or to answer a reporter's question. His Italian partners performed their side of the business with equal perfection. The paving jobs filled their schedules, and jobs were completed on time. Star Paving's reputation was enviable.

The football game was in the middle of the fourth quarter when Hatcher told Alexander he wanted to leave. They got up from their seats and walked briskly toward the limo, with no stops to shake hands with well-wishers. Alexander got inside Hatcher's limo and waited for the governor-elect to finish talking with a few state officials. Any reason to be impatient and shout "Hatcher, let's get going" belonged to another day. Alexander sucked in all the pomp associated with a head of state. He loved every minute. Where else, other than on TV, could he see unending adulations for his good friend?

Standing near Hatcher was a tall, broad-shouldered bodyguard whom Alexander had never met. He surveyed the crowd with his arms crossed, ready to rip off the head of anyone he thought might cause the governor harm. This bald brute, Alexander imagined, was just waiting for someone to try so he could spring into action. What better way than busting a few skulls to keep in top form? Hatcher, too, could prove tough in a tight situation. A tall, muscular person, he'd played basketball for MSU. Opponents learned to fear his elbows, earning him the nickname 'Meat Cleaver.' High school and college classmates kidded him by asking if TV's Theodore 'Beaver' Cleaver was his brother.

When Hatcher finished with the crowd, he entered the limo and plopped himself on the back seat, next to Alexander. The bodyguard opened the front door and sat in the passenger seat. Hatcher elbowed Alexander and observed, "It was a lousy game for football fans but a great game for the governor-elect. Everyone's attention was focused on me, and I'm delighted." Hatcher sported a toothy smile and swayed his head side to side. "I must tell the Lions' coach to keep up the losing streak."

Alexander commented, "My, my. You sure love to sport that smug, tough-guy smile. Flexing your fists complements it."

Hatcher laughed. "And aren't we in a happy mood. How is it possible we stayed friends all these years?"

"Because you don't wear a brown shirt and never will. I've learned drinking large quantities of liquor loosens and raises the dark inner voices from the bottom of a person's soul. That's when *hidden* prejudicial thoughts expose themselves as *spoken* prejudicial remarks. They're all about the same thing. "I'd like nothing better than relocating all Jews to the bottom of the Atlantic Ocean. I've seen you drunk on many occasions, and you've never made a disparaging remark. The reason is, we hate the same type of person—über liberals."

"You're bad, Alex. You bring out the worst in people. I like that. Anyway, the others you allude to compare me to a dictator, like Kwame Black."

"Kwame's a *gonef*, unlike you. Besides, he doesn't know your inner kindness like I do—unless you've got a plan I don't know about, such as sending Afro-Americans back to Liberia."

"That's where I'd like to send Kwame Black. He's ruined Detroit and those... what do you Jews call black people?"

"Schvartzes."

"Yeah. Those *schvartzes* keep electing him, and he keeps stealing money for himself. Some day his stealing and harming people will come to an end. I'll enjoy escorting him into a prison cell."

"I believe you would. Your methods can sometimes be sinister. I wouldn't want to hear about justice being dispensed illegally."

Hatcher smiled and began to make a call on his cell phone as the motorcade pulled away. The crowd waved. Hatcher waved back with one hand. The other held the phone. Alexander looked out the window, smiled, and drifted into thought. Thrilled at being invited to the Thanksgiving Day game, Alexander thought Hatcher might ask him for more campaign money. He'd already contributed, and he knew Hatcher could have financed the entire campaign himself. His campaign fund bulged at the seams. Politicians always overindulged when going after money. But Alexander also knew Hatcher measured the degree of friendship by individual cash inflows. Everyone knew special favors were to be disbursed after January first in direct proportion to cash contributed. Alexander, as a friend, expected no favors. The amount he'd contributed was generous. Hatcher had called to personally thank Alexander. Was the special treatment, being taken to the Lions' game, some kind of payback? Maybe Hatcher wanted to share his success and happiness with an old friend, and nothing else.

Hatcher ended his call. "Alexander, what are you doing with your time, besides working on my account?"

Alexander thought, *what is this?* Hatcher campaigned for governor, Hatcher was elected governor, and Hatcher knew Alexander discretely and competently handled personal assignments such as finding investments for clients' money. Was he about to ask for a favor?

"I'm trying comedy. Retirement was not a stop sign. But you knew that."

"I thought you'd play more golf."

"I still play, just not as much. Reading is a new preoccupation. I have the time to catch up with books I've neglected. Poe rattles my brain. Call it my preoccupation with mortality."

"Wow, I'm in intellectual company."

The motorcade exited the Ford Field parking lot. The driver veered the limo to skirt around the traffic, inadvertently hitting a deep pothole with a loud thump. Alexander and Robert were sent skyward as the bodyguard grabbed for the steering wheel. Hatcher scooted close to the driver's ear and screamed, "You shithead! What the hell are you doing? Are you drunk?"

The driver apologized and asked if anyone was hurt. But Hatcher wasn't satisfied, and screamed again, "Shut up, you moron!"

The driver remarked, "Potholes are everywhere you drive. The state needs to fix the roads."

"Did I not say to shut up?" Hatcher didn't need a reminder that Michigan roads were in bad shape. He sat back and turned to Alexander. "Why couldn't that problem wait until after I'm inaugurated? This campaign has taken a toll. Right now, my marriage has hit a huge pothole of its own and needs attention."

Alexander's eyes narrowed. He'd heard rumors Hatcher had marital problems bubbling up from the gubernatorial campaign. Women openly fawned over him, which upset Harriett. And Alexander was aware that Hatcher was a skirt-chaser. Robert made no effort to push back his admirers. Other office holders indulged, so why not him? Hatcher's blue-blood wife, Harriet, thought campaign wifely duties consisted of shaking hands and having the back of her hand kissed by aristocrats. On the campaign trail, dingy male voters with missing teeth had a habit of reaching in to steal a kiss from her. But when she looked to Robert for relief, he only responded with a smile and a wink. Robert was a good looking man. He was swamped with female voters hugging him and trying to plant their puckered lips on any available skin.

Alexander knew Harriet fumed at Robert's campaign style, which eschewed whistle stops. Her preference was to show her bubbly personality in small groups. In contrast, schmoozing in a large room was his forte. If they drank a glass of beer, he followed suit. The Lions' game had proved a great venue—schmooze, eat, laugh, and drink. His actions had made direct contact with eighty thousand fans. Alexander observed Hatcher's maneuvering and upbeat behavior at the Lions' game—it was mission accomplished.

Looking out the window at the urban debris that confronted them as they drove away from the stadium, Alexander diverted his thoughts to a more positive image and reminded Hatcher of the motorcycle poker run his friend had organized to Lake Huron. "Christ, seeing Harriet riding on the back of your bike as your 'bitch'—I estimate that garnered about fifty thousand votes. The newspapers didn't know what to do with the story. Great campaign maneuver."

"In contrast, that ass-kissing liberal media thought my opponent Henry Ouster conducted a 'proper' campaign. What a joke. He goes to a union hall, gives a rousing speech, drinks lemonade, and leaves for the next union hall. Net new votes—zero. His wife Portia dresses like a cleaning lady. At one debate, I told Ouster to apply for benefits at the unemployment office after the election. I'll make sure his application gets speedy approval."

Settling into the back seat, Alexander determinedly maintained his effort to reinforce Hatcher's ego. "That poker run was a stroke of genius. You rode a tangerine-colored bike, spit-polished chrome, wearing expensive leather duds, with Harriet's arms wrapped around your waist. Call it poetry in motion. The cherry on top was your 'do-rag' and Harriet's bandanna. The rednecks rode with a hip politician and loved it. When I saw those grubby characters' expressions, the election was over."

They both roared with laughter.

"Listen, Robert, I understand why Harriet's pissed. She thinks life is meant to be lived traveling a straight road. But the governorship is pothole city. You're driving a life detour for the next four years. You're in for more rough times than just marital problems."

In the background, Alexander's own marriage preyed on his mind. His semi-retirement was straining family relations. Stand-up comedy, he hoped, would fill a need and return harmony back into the household. The logic was, the more time away from home working, the greater the harmony. Did that sound like a detour? Alexander avoided analyzing his situation too closely and silently stared ahead as they continued to pass more examples of Detroit's devastated urban landscape.

Hatcher awoke him from his somber reverie with a slap on his knee. "Alex, I can't express how desperately I need you as my budget director."

Alexander carefully changed his expression to neutral. Struggling with his demons, inner fireworks erupted, strongly suggesting he grab onto something for dear life. *He wasn't kidding*, Alexander thought. Looking skyward at the hovering clouds, he expressed a silent plea: *God, you are my copilot, right?* And he felt the Almighty answer: *Alexander, nice to hear from you. Being omnipotent, I can read your mind. You want to inflict pain on people as a stand-up co-median? Accept the budget director job offer. It's my way of inflicting pain on you.* Alexander turned to Hatcher and told him stand-up comedy gigs might have to wait.

Hatcher yelled, "That's the funniest acceptance I've ever heard in my life!"

"Wait until you hear this. I thought you invited me today to ask for more campaign money."

Hatcher again broke out in laughter. "Jesus Christ, you are funny."

Alexander kept a straight face. "I wasn't kidding about becoming a stand-up comedian. It's been a lifelong dream. That's how I planned to spend my twilight years."

Hatcher turned serious. "Are you nuts? You're telling *moi*, a good friend, you were considering saying 'no' to my job offer? I ought to stop the limo and have Adolph throw your ass out."

"Was that his birth name, or did he wait until he became a bruiser to change it?"

Hatcher scowled. Alexander looked back out of the window. Thugs mulled at street corners, angry faces staring sullenly as they passed. Observing the ominous reality of this local scenery, Alexander said, "Bob, let's put the idea of saying 'no' on hold."

"Wait, Alex. I'm prepared to give you loads of latitude. You know which budget concerns are my priority. Twist balls. I don't care. I need you to squeeze expenses. And don't let any legislative girlies get in the way. Tell them you're not going to be persuaded by any sweet talk or newspapers to open the spending floodgates. I want the budget under control."

"Thank God Betty Friedan died. I'd worry what she'd do to you if she heard what you just said."

"Alexander, you know me. On occasions I can be manipulated on small matters. But the state's finances are off limits. Don't you dare dangle your temporary hold decision on me. Keep your brain working, buddy. I'm confident your dumb idea of stand-up comedy will fade." Hatcher moved to within inches of Alexander's face, his tone suddenly containing an edge of menace. "Right, buddy?"

Alexander did not back down. "Do you know what I'm giving up to take the position? I planned to shake a rebellious fist at the world, an opportunity to rant on multiple levels. I was in an existentialist prison ready to saw the bars loose and escape. I asked myself, 'Alexander, are you ready to throw your life away?' If the answer is no, your dream of pursuing stand-up comedy is *kaput*. But my brain kept yelling, *Say, yes. Tell yourself, yes. Have the world fear you. It worked for Stalin*."

"I'm calling 911."

"Listen, you Nazi. I have a chance to call anyone I want an asshole without remorse or pity. I've imagined the response—'Who called me an asshole? Alexander Haralson? I thought he was a quiet, stick-to-your-knitting type of guy. What's gotten into him?'"

Hatcher shifted away to the far side of the car, observing Alexander with a slight frown. "You're scaring me."

"Do you have any idea how far I've traveled on this crazy idea? Stand-up comedy was a plan to reinvent my life. Dress like a *schlump*. Wear the degenerate dress code. Grow long hair and keep it uncombed. Wear a stingy brim hat to cover the bald spot. Wear cracked, imitation black leather kickers with pointed toes. Wear a sport shirt and jeans that appear to never have been washed. Lose weight. Not advertise the flab. Change my name to something funny, like Boris Thomashevsky. How's that sound, Robert, huh?"

"Who?"

"You're a *sheygetz*, a *goy*. Tell me that name's not perfect. Imagine the announcer at the comedy club, blasting out, 'Get your hands together. Let's welcome Boris Thomashevsky.' Nobody needs to know Thomashevsky was an early twentieth century high-brow, melodramatic singer and actor. I need to hold onto his passionate character persona. Forget the eastern European clothes the real Thomashevsky wore. The audience will think they're in a synagogue."

"Alex. You're nuts. You're beyond nuts!"

"I compare my switch into comedy to meeting a young hot woman by chance, rolling around with her in a sweaty bed, and, in a state of heated passion, agreeing to her proposition, 'Dump your wife and marry me.'"

Alexander moved closer to Hatcher and continued with a sweeping gesture. "As a comedian, I need to fit a role. Jerry Sienfeld, Rodney Dangerfield, Billy Crystal, and Jewish-cultured but non-Jewish Robin Williams are possibilities. Larry the Plumber showed up in overalls, told redneck jokes, and cashed large checks for his performances. Nah. I considered his style too *goyish*, impossible to pull off. Then I thought, what about Lenny Bruce? Perfect. I'd take over from where Lenny Bruce left off—a modern day Lenny Bruce. The similarities were no different from his day until now. Lenny played a lowlife, rolled in feces, got close to the slimy feel and smell. He came across as crass. No mother would claim him as her son. I realized I was so un-Lenny because I grew up with stability in my life. My starting point was with parents who worked hard and forged a strong, conservative family unit. I lived and loved that environment. Now I needed to throw it all away, get it out of my mind. How could I possibly bring this conservative upbringing into the act?

"No scientist was born yet who could link an accounting career to stand-up comedy. I found that out at Freddy K's Zug Island Comedy Club. The public views accountants as antiseptic, believing they're highly moral. In contrast, the comedians who work in stand-up comedy are an infestation of rats. I doubt any performer follows even one of the Ten Commandments. I'm not sure they'd know what they are. They'd slit their mother's throat just for a shot in the footlights."

There was a long pause as Hatcher took in the seismic implications of Alexander's rant. "As a friend," he finally responded, "I should tell you to see a doctor Monday morning. But I have a better idea. Be a stand-up comedian. Do it from a building in Lansing. Make every government beneficiary's life miserable. They have full stomachs, but not the stomach to do productive work. And productive work isn't about collecting signatures for an idiotic ballot initiative. These spongers are the target. I don't see a problem in linking a comedy career with the role of state budget director. Raise hell in Lansing. I'll give you carte blanche."

Mischievous thoughts danced in Alexander's head. He'd heard enough crap from children dumping elderly parents onto the state for care. "Robert, it sounds insidious and mischievous. 'Somebody's got to take care of granny,' the children will say. '*We* can't take care of her.' Then I'll respond with faultless logic. 'We're out of money.' I plan to cap costs in every department. You go to the taxpayers and ask them to pony up. See what they say.

"Robert, we'll disengage freeloaders, no matter what their age. I'll suggest lowering taxes and returning the savings to taxpayers. Oh, the happiness they'll feel. A crowd will parade, blanketing the state capitol building with signs saying, 'We love Alexander Haralson' or 'Michigan Equals Moochers & Garbage.'

"But wait. The stand-up comedian is now filling the budget director's head. Robert, you've freed me!" Alexander's mind finally focused with searing, inspired clarity. "I don't need to decide which one. I don't need to choose by saying she loves me, she loves me not. I have a clear head. I don't need a wall to bang my head against a wall. I don't need to be a human sacrifice and set myself ablaze. I don't need to take a header off the Penobscot Building!"

The limo reached Alexander's house. Adolph jumped from the front seat to open the door for him. "Robert, make the announcement on Wednesday. I'll meet you wherever. You can show my face and tell Michigan to meet their new budget director... er, how about Joe Stalin?"

Half-groaning and half-laughing, Hatcher exited the limo with Alexander. They stood in the middle of the road, shook hands in united agreement to forge ahead with their financial crusade, and said goodbye.

Chapter Eight

MARGARITA HEARS THE NEWS

After his walk, Alexander returned to his room at the William Beaumont Hospital and sat in the visitor's chair next to the window. Outside, against a picturesque background, Detroit's downtown skyline reflected the sun's rays. Inside, the smell of cleanliness pervaded his hospital room. His mind improved as he sensed how Margarita had received the news of Governor Hatcher's job offer. He didn't need to rack his brains to recall.

Alexander had stood in the road when Hatcher dropped him off after the game, not paying attention to traffic. He'd never imagined the day would change so dramatically. A car had approached and honked. Startled, Alexander opened his eyes and shuffled quickly to the curb. He looked up and saw his house. He looked for Hatcher's limo, seeing only a trail of leaves and dust still swirling. The serious tone of the conversation on the ride home with Hatcher continued to consume him. The next task would be marching into the house and telling Margarita about the job offer. Telling the news to anyone outside the family would be at his own discretion. At that moment, however, he was too *farmisht* to think or talk straight. The children would be next to know. He'll tell them while sitting at the Thanksgiving table.

The idea of playing games with his grandchildren before Thanksgiving supper danced in his head. A pleasant and relaxed atmosphere should pervade the festive day. Alexander couldn't contain his excitement about the future. He'd face Margarita and tell her how his day had gone with Hatcher. Be assertive and don't fall flat and develop chicken legs. He wandered up the driveway to the rear entrance.

Alexander opened the screen door, walked straight into the kitchen, and hugged Margarita from behind while she was placing a dish of stuffing in the oven. Propping his chin on her shoulder he whispered, "Hatcher offered me the job as state budget director."

Margarita turned and stared at him with a menacing look.

Alexander said, "I see we're in for an argument. I'd much prefer a fight over who eats what part of the turkey's carcass."

Margarita put her lips to Alexander's ear. "Are we moving to Lansing?"

"Well, yes and no. It'll be a temporary home. Let's say I'll need to stay over some nights after working late. You'll be here to take care of Roberta."

"*Mio marito*, we are not a band of gypsies." With puckered lips, Margarita continued. "My darling, you do such a good job making funny jokes when we are with friends."

"I'm pleased you liked my routine."

"Didn't you say you wanted to become a stand-up comedian?"

"I did," replied Alexander, spiritedly. "Hatcher offered me the job, allowing me the opportunity to unleash and rant against anyone collecting state funds. I'm thrilled."

"I've got another job for you to consider. How about being a full-time father to Roberta? Take her to Lansing. You remember her, don't you? Your daughter, the brat?"

Alexander peevishly walked to the breakfast table. The situation with Margarita was no detour. He could feel her eyes follow his every step.

Margarita waited until Alexander sat, then barked, "What's gotten into you lately? You're obsessed with stand-up comedy, and now you're into politics?"

"I'm trying to fulfill a wish. Hatcher has invited me to be part of his team, a call to action to fix the state's ills—potholes and the like.

He told me to lower state expenses, cut out unnecessary programs, and cut lazy bastards off welfare."

"It's hard for me to believe you allowed Hatcher, that blue eyed *shaygetz*, to hook you with Nazi claws and drag you into his insidious web. I never liked him as your client. I still don't."

"Did you vote for him?"

Avoiding the question, Margarita responded, "And his wife is a name-dropping nosey, waiting for the world to kiss her ass."

"You didn't answer my question."

"Yes," Margarita finally admitted. "Are you happy now?"

"So what do we do with Roberta?"

"*You'd* like to drop her off at an orphanage."

"Let's not talk drastic measures. Chalk up her conception as an accident. I'm the insurance company required to pay damages.

"But right now I'm happy, apprehensive, dizzy, and delirious— all in one! The job offer was a God-send. So, okay, I'll watch over Roberta in Lansing."

"I've never seen you so off the walls. You will?"

"She's a family pothole. The big picture rules. Hatcher gave me carte blanche to rant against stupidity and injustice. I hope to fulfill God's wishes. *Tikkun olam*, repair the world. In my case, that means fix the roads. I've heard a calling telling me not to allow fairy tales to rule as law in God's stead. I believe in Hatcher's plans as governor. And I plan to uphold honest principles and help him."

"You're still off the wall. Anyway, *tikkun olam* belongs to Caroline. It's a liberal thing."

"I'm stealing it away from her."

"You plan to tell everyone? When?"

"At supper. Soon is best. Hatcher plans to broadcast my appointment to his department heads next week."

"You've got it all figured out."

"I'm at the starting line, ready to lunge forward. The more I think about the job, the better I feel. Relax. We'll find a house in Lansing. Roberta will find another group of spoiled brats as playmates."

Alexander stood.

Margarita ordered him to sit down. "You're not walking out of here so fast."

Alexander returned to the breakfast table.

"I suppose you think at the end of the line, when Hatcher's term runs out, a rainbow will appear with the banner 'And they lived happily ever after'?"

Alexander answered with a strong voice, "Absolutely."

"You and Hatcher are full of it."

"You could be surprised." Alexander stood up again. "The food looks delicious." He left the breakfast room.

Chapter Nine

GETTING OUT OF BED CAN BE DETRIMENTAL

Awake, with his nose resting on top of the hospital blanket, Alexander looked straight ahead at the clock on the wall. It read clear as day 8:12 a.m. He wanted to be asleep, but his brain wouldn't let him. Reaching out his arm, he fished for his glasses on the nightstand, instead knocking over the water pitcher. Hearing the thump made him realize he'd worn his glasses to bed. In his imagination, the eyeglasses transformed from a medical aid into a metaphorical tool, providing insightful focus on the insane reality of his comedy career. It was little wonder he lay awake. With all the tubes and monitors attached to his body, Alexander couldn't easily roll onto his side or get out of bed to walk around. He was stuck there with his brain waves aflutter. On one occasion, Alexander had reached for his glasses and almost fallen out of bed. Fortunately, the nurses had been alert and prevented the fall. Since then, the guardrails attached to the bed had been raised permanently. Imprisoned physically and mentally, Alexander had plenty of time to think.

The Zug Island Comedy Club was added to Alexander's list of disasters. The reality of becoming a comedian in retirement was now compared, in his mind, to that of a pilot who nose-dived his plane into the ground, where it exploded. Alexander couldn't pinpoint what was amiss. Have someone manage his career? No chance. We're talking about the egotistical Alexander Haralson. Seeing that audiences found him boring, a shift in attitude to curb his ego was in order. A deflated ego hurt. Maybe recording a YouTube video on how to scratch mosquito bites would prove more worthwhile, or how to swat a mosquito that landed on your testicles. He'd picked up a ton of jokes from the Internet, but that his delivery stank was one of his major faults. Good comedians looked funny, Alexander rationalized. They didn't have to say a word. When you saw them, you just laughed. When you saw Alexander, you snored.

Since entering the hospital, his sleep patterns had become sporadic. They'd changed to four hours at night and two hours in the afternoon. A positive was that no glasses of water would be knocked over or pills scattered onto the floor. A call button for the night nurse solved that problem. Trips to the bathroom proved a blessing. Besides emptying his bladder, they showed that his lower body was slowly gaining strength. Alexander dreamed of the day when his life would return to normal, running on schedule.

Sometimes Margarita slept overnight on a recliner in his hospital room. Listening to her rhythmic and trumpet-blaring snores now, Alexander mentally compared them to a rooster's morning call. He was in a wide-awake, if slightly disoriented state. Scooting his tush to the edge of the hospital bed, he looked to see if he'd brought earmuffs to the hospital. He longed to shower, find clothes to wear, and head over to Starbucks to meet his buddies. It was at this point that Alexander realized wearing glasses didn't help much after all—he still couldn't keep track of the time clearly. The wall clock read three a.m., not eight a.m. Christ, what's wrong with me? The sun won't be up for another five hours.

Besides her snoring, Margarita was an annoyance in other ways. She'd turned off his cell phone and left it out of reach. She'd also quarantined his laptop computer. Alexander had pleaded with her to be allowed to use his electronic equipment. "I can't do any work, I can't read or send emails, and I can't retrieve Internet jokes. What do you expect me to do all day?"

"Pay attention to me," Margarita had replied.

"All day?"

She nodded with a big smile.

"Then, tonight, don't fall asleep. I plan to smother you with a pillow. This place makes it very convenient to dispose of you and complete the vow 'until death do us part.' The elevators are nearby. All I have to do is push the B button. The morgues are in the basement."

"Your mind's rambling."

Drowsily, he reached for the remote that Margarita had forgotten to quarantine along with the other electronic gadgets and turned on the TV. Drowsiness started to overcome him as a Charlie Chan movie filled the screen. He'd seen every one five times and was in no mood to hear a repeat of corny aphorisms delivered by a non-Chinese actor. And, oh my, the Chinese racism—it never quit. How many times did Charlie investigate a murder at the Lee-Kee shipbuilding yard? Hmmm. Let me count. And his Americanized name Charlie… was that a change the scriptwriters made from Chu-Gum?

Alexander shifted uncomfortably about in his bed. He checked the clock again—still only 3:35 a.m. He fluffed the pillows and propped his back against the headboard. He thought about turning on the lamp to review budget reports or read a novel and remembered he couldn't. Margarita had also confiscated all reading material. He couldn't even call Roman in the middle of the night and tell him about his mother's cruel treatment.

When Roman came to visit him the following day, Alexander told him, "I'm going nuts. I'm a candidate for a nervous breakdown."

"Dad, back down until you get home. If you end up in the psych ward, you'll be tied to a bed and talking to yourself all day."

"What's the difference? I'm tied down here and talking to myself."

"Dad, you'll be home for Thanksgiving. You'll be home to carve the turkey."

"Can I go home today and practice?"

"Relax. Thanksgiving is still a month away."

Alexander continued to reminisce about disastrous gigs he'd played. The problem, he soon realized, was not all routines played to the right audiences. After his disastrous performance at Zug Island's Comedy Club, he had a one-off gig at an American Legion Hall. Alexander had thought the audience of forty-to-fifty-year-olds would laugh themselves silly at his mother-in-law jokes. So what if half the audience were mothers-in-law? The men would howl. The women would laugh, too, if only at themselves. He'd expected a big ovation at the finish.

His comedic tirade had opened with promise. "Boy, how mother-in-law jokes have changed," he'd announced. "If I said I'd read about some cranky old bat who was shot by the son-in-law, the laughs would pour in. Those jokes always start the same way. The old girl shows up to the house unannounced. You're in bed, putting on a show with your old lady, and the phone rings at ten o'clock. *Coitus interruptus*! Your wife answers and learns her mother is coming the next day to visit for a week. Staying at a hotel isn't even a consideration. She'll be staying with you in the next bedroom. Clear logic says a squeaking bed in the nighttime ain't the sound she wants to hear from her daughter's bedroom. She brings a stethoscope to amplify her suspicions. How many of you have been in that situation? Do you think she'd just say to herself, 'Don't mind me, you lovebirds. Pretend I'm not here.' No way. She's actually thinking *Oh my God, my daughter's having sex!* So would it surprise you to hear the son-in-law isn't happy? He decides a swift remedy is needed. He grabs a gun. Bam. DOA. Mother-in-law is tomorrow morning's headlines.

"But that story's stale. The audience expects the comedian to be innovative. The world wants spice—tabloid-headlines-type material made to sound funny. In addition, the son-in-law perp wants his story printed in all the major city papers across the country, wants to play it to the biggest audience. A shotgun doesn't cut it anymore. The son-in-law decides to whack her using some ingenuity. "Now, what I'm about to tell you is what actually happened.

"So, this man drove his mother-in-law's car into his garage. He stuffed her in the front and handcuffed her to the steering wheel. She was screaming when he left her in the closed garage with the engine running. When she stopped screaming, he left with his buddy to play a round of golf. When he came home four hours later, his mother-in-law was lying on a gurney, attended by an EMS team. But she was alive, and he'd counted on attending her funeral and seizing her money.

"The police approached him and said, 'We need to have a word with you, right now. Your mother-in-law told us what happened. Listen, when you go to kill your mother-in-law, make sure you finish the job… no pulse, no heartbeat, no breathing. If you do that, you're in clover. When the police arrive, she ain't going to give any testimony. They'll look to you to tell them what happened. You say you don't know nothin'. Sweet. You're off scot-free. The police will ask who tied her to the steering wheel. You tell them you don't know. In fact, you give that answer to every question, because if she lives and tells the police what happened, you're headed to the station for further questions. Your next move will then be to look for an attorney.'"

Alex had thought the planned routine was great. The audience didn't agree. For one thing, the wives saw themselves as victims. *Murdering my mother is supposed to be funny?* Alexander imagined them warning their husbands, *You laugh at his mother-in-law routine, and it's no sex for a month!* The husbands morph into wimps and meekly reply, *Yes, dear*.

The audience's silence had been like a knife plunged into Alexander's guts. Evidently, nobody could laugh at themselves. And nobody laughed at him. He remembered the hall's manager approaching him afterward, asking if he thought sick jokes was such a good idea. Alexander had responded, "I guess next time the jokes will need to be sicker."

When it came to comedy, Alexander ignored the possibility of failure. After this depressing experience, he'd trudged ahead and interviewed for other gigs, knowing there was a one-hundred-percent chance of slamming his head into a brick wall. He answered an ad asking for headliners at a late-night club in Detroit. This caught Alexander's eye, but his cranium took the day off and didn't read carefully between the lines. When he showed up, the club owner dubbed Alexander 'Sir Stupid.' The ad was seeking bar maids geared for nude dancing. Still, he'd tried to persuade the club owner, Clarence Jones, to let him audition. He got an earful. "Man, what chew thinkin'? Doin' a routine on Detroit roads and the IRS? Alex, boy, nobody in dis area owns a car. And nobody care about potholes. In springtime, dey become sandboxes for the kids. And as to dealing with the IRS, nobody around here pays no taxes. Incomes in this neighborhood are three feet below the bottom of your balls. We're the welfare folk. Or did dat not dawn on you?"

"Clarence, have pity. Let me do an audition."

Clarence took a deep breath. "Shit man, go ahead."

Alexander went on stage, stood in front of the microphone, and cleared his throat.

"We live in Detroit, aka the Dirty D. I've scanned a dictionary and found no word starting with a D to be happy. Happy, that starts with an H. Let me give you a list of D words. You tell me which sounds happy—disgrace, degenerate, delinquent, dead, detox, dominatrix, dentist, dandelion, DDT, decay..."

Clarence came over. "Best you hall ass out of here. You got nothin' to show." He turned to a waiting group of nude girls. "Girls, over here so I can take a look. Start dancin' and bouncin' those titties."

Alexander reflected, *was there a successful gig in his future?* Then he remembered the one good thing that had come out of his Zug Island Comedy Club gig. He had found Flossy and bonded with her. The bad thing was, it was the first of many failed performances. He looked up and pleaded, "Dear God. I'm an Aristotelian-type thinker. I make sense of the world by explaining it in my jokes. So explain to me why no one laughs at them?"

Failure hadn't been an option. A lifetime of beliefs and experiences molded into jokes awaited an audience. Comedy would be the avenue to say what he wanted. It was supposed to fulfill a dream he so badly desired. But it didn't. Audiences screamed, "We don't want to hear stupid jokes berating people."

In his mind, Alexander retorted, I want to even some scores. I can't do that to my family, even though I'm treated like a slave.

All Margarita and Roberta need are whips. And Caroline, my social work daughter? She knows everything, on every subject, every minute. It's a perpetual chorus of *Do this or that*, or *You don't know anything*. Alexander thought maybe talking fulltime to himself wasn't all that bad.

Chapter Ten

THE CAREER PATH

Back at home, recuperating from his operation, Alexander gulped down his breakfast of a banana buried in a bowl of yogurt and a side of toast overloaded with marmalade. His acid reflux erupted, forcing him to double over and grab his stomach. My *kishkas* are killing me. He eschewed any thought of using an OTC preparation or prescription to relieve the upset. He felt the world was plotting his discomfort for daring to become a Lenny Bruce-type comedian. The rumblings in his head, also plotting against him, sounded a more threatening message—we'll fight you. We'll pound your soul into submission. We don't need any more loud-mouth assholes spewing stupidity. Quit, or we'll retire you into a permanent quiet.

Who were these enemies? And how were they going to fight him? Alexander knew the answer to the second question—not laugh at his jokes. That made the answer to the first question self-explanatory—the entire world. Alexander's ego argued he was the chosen, a token Jew roaming from comedy club to comedy club with the express purpose of changing the world. Fix the roads was his message. The City of Detroit was imploding from inside forces. Elitists had set up a totally corrupt government, from the mayor on down the administrative pyramid. Every taxpayer investment account was located. Every purse and wallet was searched. Every taxpayer was lined up against the wall, arms up and legs spread. Every pant pocket was patted. All money was seized, even loose change. In Alexander's imagination, any wretched soul pleading for some loose money to buy food found all pockets a virtual desert. Authorities laughed. "It's our moral obligation to take all your money." That obligation included stealing board of education money that was supposed to run the public schools.

Alexander had decided Detroit comedy clubs would be the perfect venue for his activism. That's where the thrust of his attack would be most effective, blasting the bastards in their own backyard. He wouldn't need a microphone. He'd speak loudly enough to make sure everyone heard. Alexander whispered to himself, "Attack. I'm coming after you bastards."

What Alexander didn't realize was that his cognitive judgments were becoming unhinged. This was evidenced by his eating habits, which had changed from chewing small bites of food with deliberateness to gouging the food at a high rate. Alexander's changed dining habits made pigs at the trough look genteel. They grunted, chewing each delectable bite slowly, turning a head to friends and family, letting everyone know they were enjoying the slop's flavor. Alexander, using civilized utensils, shoveled food like coal into a furnace.

There were other changes of habit he was equally unaware of. No longer was there a right or wrong side of the bed to roll out from. Since starting comedy school, sleep had become erratic. And since the Zug Island fiasco, Alexander hadn't shared a bed with Margarita, trying instead to fall asleep sitting in his home office, on a chair with his feet on the desk. Since this had proved futile, he stayed awake and stewed, feverishly, over the recent unpleasant incidents—Freddy K not controlling the crowd at his comedy club, allowing the rednecks to throw beer cans and possibly injure him, allowing the drunks to demolish his pride and joy, the BMW 650i. And there was Margarita's lack of concern for his injuries, while trashing Robert Hatcher's candidacy for governor. Alexander's subconscious thoughts judged the world as stupid, spurring his inner Lenny.

The episodes preyed on Alexander's mind, laying the blame on Margarita for her unsympathetic attitude toward his retirement plans. Margarita was unaware he harbored thoughts of clutching a sharp, twelve-inch kitchen knife and stabbing her as she slept.

Doubts festered as he sat in his office chair. He reasoned that the odds favored him achieving success doing gigs in front of a comedy club audience versus a prison audience.

On a monitor, Alexander's brain waves would have scared the hell out of anyone. "Look at that brain pattern," viewers would scream. "Run for your lives!"

At that moment, the only person in the whole world he loved was Robert Hatcher, the savior of his ass. Damn, he was the governor! How about that. And he told me I was his man. Asked me to help with the financial minefields. Alexander had decided he would.

After cleaning up the breakfast room table, Alexander went upstairs, without a kitchen knife, to check on Margarita. She was asleep. He dressed and prepared to leave home to attend a comedy school class. Frank Amenero, the school's owner, had probably already heard Alexander's four a.m. voicemail, in which a sampling of expletives described Alexander's feelings. He wasn't finished. As he walked out the front door, he shouted to Margarita, "You do remember what you said you would do the first thing Monday morning? It's show time, honey—monday in the a.m., the time you planned to file papers at the Oakland County courthouse to initiate a hearing having me declared insane. Need directions? In case you forgot, take northbound Telegraph Road for about ten miles. Look for Mack's Retail Entertainment Store at the corner of Dixie Highway. Once you're inside the building, they'll fit you in a dominatrix costume you'll love, along with a whip that you'll find useful."

Alexander slammed the door shut and walked to his Hertz four-door sedan rental with automatic transmission and air conditioning as extras. He sat in the driver's seat and gagged from the smell—a vanilla-scented air freshener that he couldn't find to throw away. He engaged the engine, which started with a sound similar to scratching a blackboard for fifteen seconds. Why wasn't this car the one he'd driven to Melvandale? Alexander scheduled a meeting with his insurance adjuster, a meeting with a new car dealer, a meeting with the car rental agency to find the lost and annoying air freshener, and a meeting with Frank Amenero.

He stopped at Starbucks to chat with a few cronies before heading to the comedy school. The coffee shop reserved a special table for the older men who shared the same problem as Alexander—their wives didn't wake up to fix breakfast. Alexander waved hello as he strolled to the order line. He picked up his grande chai latte and walked to the table. He sat on the open seat next to Itsy Bergman. Itsy and Alexander had attended the same high school and were still buddies fifty years later. "Itsy, what's with the long face? Having a problem taking a leak?"

"Shut up, you *putz*. Every day Brenda keeps yapping orders—where we should eat, and where we should shop. I'm going broke, but her fancy jewelry stores thrive. She accuses me of being a lousy husband when I don't pay attention. I tell her I'm losing my hearing. With a low sensitivity level, she starts yelling. What a pain in the ass. Some days I'd like to kill her."

Alexander leaned in and in a voice only loud enough for Itsy to hear said, "I can arrange that."

The other half a dozen guys at the table paid no attention. Itsy looked at Alexander, aghast.

"I'll have her cuddled up next to Hoffa."

"You're not funny."

"You want to hear something funny? Close your garage door and start the car."

"Alexander, go home."

Alexander put his face up close to Itsy's. "Do you think paradise awaits me at home?" He had scolded Margarita for ignoring her homemaking chores. "The responsibility of washing a sink filled with dishes falls on my shoulders. And with a new week beginning, mealtimes follow the same pattern. I have to make my own breakfast. You couldn't even set the timer to turn on the coffee maker in the morning." Margarita was not off the hook. He'd have more to say to her later. Alexander relished the drama. In assuming the life of a comedian, he'd find the small faults in others and exploit them to a larger-than-life image.

I shall return, he vowed.

Chapter Eleven

ALEXANDER LOOKS FOR WORK

A *mature car* for a *mature man* was how the used car salesman, Freddy Botchett, described the ancient Cadillac sedan he felt Alexander should consider buying. Alexander drove Margarita's prized Lexus GS 350 to Detroit's mecca of used car lots, located on Livernois Ave. There were hundreds of cars on display, but he agreed with Freddy. The Cadillac sedan interested him most, despite—or perhaps because of—its rusted, dented panels and wobbly tires. Alexander thought its problems were limitless. He smiled at the sick thought of the car being destroyed by hooligans. He so wanted to do a comedy routine right there on the inner city car lot. An inner voice rang out—*I dare anyone to make me angry by trashing this car. I welcome anyone hijacking this car.*

Alexander was determined not to quit because of recent failures. There would always be jobs—he just had to create them. Self-instruction number one: canvas neighborhoods. He'd drive around in seedy areas and survey the local denizens. Locate homeless shelters. They would be an obvious place to perform. The problem was, no building sign would show him where. So he decided he'd track the homeless to gathering places under bridges. Their clothes would not be a recent Brooks Brothers purchase. This would lead him to a hive of homeless activity. He'd park the car and introduce himself to the head honcho. In his head, Alexander appointed himself the only suburbanite to take pride in buying a heap of junk and driving it through ritzy neighborhoods, waving to neighbors. Maybe he should take a test drive around the block. No worry whether or not the streets were in good condition. Alexander's interest centered on the denizens who roamed them. If an axle broke in half after hitting a pothole, the car would be left where it failed. A call to police headquarters would bring a squad car. Special privileges would be accorded him. He kept his yearly City of Detroit 1000 Club police membership dues up to date. A flash of his membership card to the officer, and he'd get a lift home.

Alexander wondered if he needed a head check. He didn't need to test drive the Cadillac to evaluate its condition. The interior benches with exposed springs were enough to confirm it was a piece of junk. He started the car and found the noise level ear-splitting. On questioning the salesman, Alexander learned the muffler had rusted to zero effectiveness and that the clanking engine needed a tune-up. Another overlooked fault was the tailpipe spewing oil. Alexander's neighborhood would issue a smog alert the minute he opened the garage door and started the engine. What the sickly car needed was a rosary recited for it.

After this careful consideration, Alexander found the $750 junker to his liking. It was more than suitable for cruising inner-city neighborhoods. Alexander knew the streets from his childhood. His roots were in Detroit. He owed the city some payback. *Hey everyone, a home-grown comedian who grew up in this neighborhood has returned to entertain you.*

Alexander recalled taking Margarita to the Elmwood Casino, across the river in Windsor, where Milton Berle was a yearly headliner. Berle had put on a great show. The jokes he told stayed the same from year to year, but his style was infectious. You laughed from the front door of your house to the club and then back home again. The fun crashed when Berle decided to retire. Alexander was disheartened. Berle retired. Haralson bombed.

Detroit was the city where tourists came to see the destruction caused by the liberal politicians. Alexander expected that children would shout with excitement, "Daddy, look at all the burned-out buildings and the people sleeping on the sidewalk." This was the place where financial death reeked. This was the location for him to spew hostility. He would speak for himself, but in his heart he spoke for all the citizens unable to control the disaster but were forced to pay taxes to prop up the duplicity.

In his mind, Alexander became a spy, a James Bond on the lookout for homeless persons to exploit. He remembered an overlooked matter. If Boris Tomashevsky was his stage name, he needed to look the part, develop a persona. A pair of khakis and a sport shirt looked weak. He needed to look Russian. He started to mentally dress himself with an expensive pair of slacks, matched with a silk sport shirt and alligator shoes. Alexander didn't stop with a snazzy wardrobe. A pillow would create a portly waistline. Cotton inside the shirt and mouth would add to the bulge. Didn't pictures of Russians portray obnoxiously fat porkers? What better image could there be to seek gigs?

The massacre at the Zug Island Comedy Club continually preyed on his mind. If the car were hijacked or beaten to a pulp, no tears or sobbing would result because of a $750 loss. The car would serve a more useful purpose in a beaten state. Alexander was the only human on earth who wondered if there was anything as funny as someone driving a decrepit automobile. Someone pulled up to him at a stoplight in a comparable junker. They looked at each other. The man was black and gave Alexander a curious look. Alexander waved and said, "Hi neighbor."

Alexander planned a routine about parking expensive cars in less than pristine parking lots. He wondered if he should plan to insult the homeless members of his audience as rusted out ghouls to get them fired up. This thought caused his brain to silently roar with laughter. How could they be insulted? I'm delivering them reality. Isn't that what comedy was all about? Reality checks. Nobody is immune to an overblown ego, stupid remarks, or allowing society's failures to ferment.

The thought of mingling with the down-and-out excited Alexander. They'd enjoy a live show, sitting and watching Alexander trying to be funny. It would be a change of pace. They deserved it. Their lives followed the same monotonous pattern—go to the state office, stand in line, collect the welfare check. Alexander thought if he was in the same position and did what they did, he'd develop a case of carpal tunnel in his hips. That back and forth to the state offices will do that to you. A new line of work would be to hire an attorney to collect workman's comp. Either way, at the end of the day you'd be sitting on your ass with nothing to hope for.

If they didn't like the routine, what would they throw? Dirty laundry? Oh my. Alexander suddenly realized the suit he really needed was a twenty-year-old Armani.

The *schmutz* on clothes and tables of the venues he had in mind scared Alexander. This wasn't your polite, antiseptic, suburban dirt that sat still on the rug until you used your five hundred dollar vacuum cleaner. The slums had dirt with imbedded neuropathological vermin. No one cleaned the rooms, so the dirt provided fleas and ticks with a warm bed.

Alexander started to entertain second thoughts about pitching his act to the homeless and down-and-out. Thinking of the men's room sanitation condition in the shelters horrified him. Did anyone wash their hands after taking a leak or a dump? Did anyone have anything other than a sleeve to wipe a snotty nose? Oh my. Inside the mind of Alexander, a routine blossomed—a demeaning exposé of homeless people. Alexander gave them names: Stinky, Schmutzick, and Toothless. Heckle me. I dare you. I'm Boris Tomashevsky. Are jokes about the downtrodden out of bounds? Alexander probed himself further. I've heard others tell jokes about my ilk. I can take it. Take a caliper and measure the thickness of my skin. So laugh at yourselves. And laugh at people like me. Ripping on successful people and lowering them to cockroach height will warm your hearts. Be happy. Aren't you satisfied, you despicable peasants?

Alexander finished his drive around the block. He saw Margarita's car sitting where he'd left it. It was still in one piece. How long would that last? The neighborhood was filled with walkers, gradually gathering to examine the shiny Lexus GS 350. He sighed.

Alexander completed the deal with the used car salesman, signing the paperwork and paying the $750 in cash. Freddy counted the money and handed over the keys in a dainty way that suggested the car was stored in a showroom and sported a new car smell.

After Alexander got into the car and started it, he noticed the cigarette lighter was missing. He stuck his head out the window and yelled, "Hey Freddy, where's the lighter?"

Freddy walked over to the car. "There wasn't any."

"Bullshit. Do I look stupid? You snatched it. What else did you steal while I wasn't looking?"

"Piss off, Haralson." He did an about face and walked toward the sales office.

Alexander got out of the car and opened the gas tank cover. The cap, too, was missing.

Shaking a fist, Alexander yelled, "I'll never recommend you to anyone as a used car salesman."

Freddy ignored Alexander and kept on walking, counting the money. Alexander got back into the car, calmed himself, put it in gear, and peeled off. He drove through the neighborhood looking for a homeless shelter. He noticed a down-and-out man in baggy jogging pants and a hoodie pulled low over his head and followed him. The man walked up the steps of a local church and entered. Alexander parked the car and followed him in.

Once inside, Alexander looked around for someone in charge. That proved to be difficult because the interior was dim. Alexander wondered if the light bill was paid or if the church kept the lights off to simulate the afterlife.

A hand touching his shoulder caused Alexander to jump almost to the ceiling and scream, "Jesus Christ," pronouncing the Savior's name with distinct emphasis on each syllable. When Alexander landed, he saw a kind, angelic face. "This is the right place. He lives here."

Alexander was disarmed, more by seeing the priest when he'd expected to see a janitor. He calmed down, respectfully acknowledging he stood inside a Catholic church. He fumbled for something to say. "I need help."

"You've come to the right place. I'm Father Bernard."

"Don't let my clothing fool you," Alexander joked, as he mentally regained his balance. "What I'm wearing for underwear doubles as my stand-up comedian wardrobe. Boris Tomashevsky is my name."

The priest continued to look calmly at Alexander. "I can help," he said again.

"Hey, Father. I see you're having difficulty discerning my inner message. I'm like a road—a slick surface to gloss over but an inner foundation of rock-solid comedy that will, I'm quite sure, bring to the surface the difficult nature residing within. Call it an exorcism by way of comedy."

The priest continued to watch Alexander, saying nothing, as if waiting for something.

"Would it be possible to see the unfortunate flock? Seeing that I bring no harm or malice, I could entertain them and maybe bring a smile to some desolate faces for a few seconds. I promise, no off-color jokes."

"I don't see why not. We hold AA meetings here. There's a meeting going on right now. I can ask the leader if he would welcome you."

The priest looked at Alexander, smiled again, and walked toward an assembly room. Alexander waited.

As Alexander's mind continued in overdrive, a thunderbolt hit. "Ashburn!" He lives in this neighborhood. Alexander took out his cell phone, found his name in the directory, and called his number. "Won't he be surprised to hear from me."

A weak sounding "hello" answered.

"Ashburn?"

"No. You called a hotel."

"Is this the Cass Avenue Cat House?"

A suddenly alert voice responded, "Hey, buddy."

"This is Doctor Boris Tomashevsky calling. I'm a doctor of internal orifice inspections. I just gave you a hearing and comprehension test. By the answer you gave me, you're in good health. Now answer me this question, does a resident by the name of Ashburn Haralson live there?"

"Hold on. I'll see."

After about a ten minute wait, a sleepy voice answered, "Hello?"

Alexander jumped in, "Is this Ashburn?"

"Yes."

"It's your favorite cousin, Alexander Haralson."

"Who?"

"Cuz Alexander, the annoying cousin. You do remember me?"

The phone was silent.

"Let me help you recall some pleasant memories. I remember your father, my uncle, being a religious man. He prayed hard when his horse was in last place at the top of the stretch."

"Why did you call, Alex?"

"I wanted to invite you to our house for Thanksgiving dinner."

"It just turned May first last week."

"You're family. I wanted to make sure your social calendar was open for Thanksgiving. By the way, I'm at an AA meeting in a church in your neighborhood, where a comedy gig for a roomful of classy Cass corridor subpar citizens is about to begin. Can you come by?"

"Who's the comedian?"

"Oh Ashburn, I do love your level of perception and discrimination. I'm sure only the top comedians are allowed to perform here, and to perform *gratis* for the *feces de-la feces*. Ashburn, I want to do my part to entertain the financially-challenged citizens."

"Will there be any nude dancers?"

"Ashburn, I feel confident speaking for the Catholic Church—no. Wake up and get out of bed. You're not a member of the idle rich. It's past eleven. You missed breakfast."

"Can we end this phone call?"

"Yes, of course. But you'll miss out on a present I have for you. Parked in the street is a Cadillac sedan. Come by the church and drive me to the lot where I parked my Lexus. Drop me off, and it's yours. You'll be able to drive to our house for Thanksgiving. I'll tell Margarita to expect you. You'll have plenty of time to shower and rid your twisted, uncombed hair of fleas."

Ashburn hung up.

Father Bernard walked back. "We're almost ready. Wait here. You can begin in a few minutes."

"Thank you."

Alexander walked into the assembly room and was handed a microphone. All was quiet. Eyes were busy focusing.

"I'd like to thank Father Bernard," Alexander began. "I'm new to performing comedy. I'm here to put a smile on your face. However, I must warn you. Don't take any remarks I might say as personal. My mouth sometimes runs off, and I'm embarrassed at what I may say. For example, the ads for medication that appear on TV. They're downright nasty and criminal. Some guy says take NyQuil to help you fall asleep when you have a cold. That sounds simple enough. Then, the announcer reads the side effects. 'It may cause dizziness having a forty-percent alcohol content.' The label warns that liver disease is possible. Then you hear some other ingredient causes rashes and a one-percent chance of cancer.

"Okay. Let's get back to what happens if you don't take the medicine… insomnia. You're awake, coughing, sneezing, and wiping your nose. Your chest hurts. It's decision time. What's the lesser of the two evils?"

At this point, Ashburn entered the room. Alexander smiled. "There is another option. Call 911, or call my dearest cousin who lives in the neighborhood." Alexander acknowledged Ashburn. "He'll drive you to a nearby clinic in his newly acquired Cadillac. He's an Uber driver—reliable, dedicated, and coherent between the hours of one and two in the afternoon.

"I'm so happy to have been of service. Your worries are over. I now leave you in Father Bernard's capable hands. Thank you." As his impromptu audience looked on with a slightly stunned expression on some faces, Alexander grabbed the somewhat disheveled-looking Ashburn by the arm and walked out. Ashburn drove him to the used car lot without saying a word. Fortunately, Margarita's car was still in one piece.

* * *

Back at home, Alexander went right to work scanning want-ads for adult entertainers. Phone calls offering to perform volunteer gigs sparked some interest but no takers. After an hour calling various clubs and retirement villages, a rural nursing home was delighted that a comedian had finally answered its ad, and Alexander was hired. The job would be weekly, during a mid-afternoon quiet session. Alexander had thought quiet sessions at nursing homes lasted from morning to night. The home's director, Harry, had said he wanted light jokes. Alexander cringed, but agreed to take the position. Containing his Lenny Bruce style would be difficult. A quiet Lenny Bruce had never existed.

* * *

Alexander polished up a Lenny Bruce routine, lowering the heat to Bob Newhart style for the senior citizen crowd. He pulled up to the Almost In Heaven Nursing Home, which was located somewhere in Michigan. The intersection was two dirt roads with no street name signs. Alexander felt like the first visitor in the last two years as he walked through the lobby to the reception desk. Dressed in wrinkled polyester pants, an underarm, perspiration-stained T-shirt and twenty-year-old gym shoes, Alexander could have sat in the audience and fit in. Laser, a golden retriever house dog, walked over to where he stood and looked up. Alexander, not fond of pets, looked down and tried to shoo him away. Laser didn't back away; he licked Alexander's hand and sat down at his feet. The receptionist said, "I see your straight man showed up," and grinned.

The receptionist directed Alexander to where the show would be held, and Laser followed right behind. Inside the dining room, an elderly lady said, "I see you have a friend." Alexander looked behind and saw Laser still following him. He muttered, "Jesus Christ, will somebody please call the Humane Society?" Harry, the director, walked up to greet Alexander and patted the dog's head saying, "Good boy. Now run away." Laser stood still and wagged his tail.

It was Alexander's first gig in a nursing home setting. And it would take nerve—even guts—to try out his passion in the more restrained, Bob Newhart style. Janice Corkland, the facilities director, walked over with a bright smile and Harry introduced them. "I'll leave Janice to explain how things work," he told Alexander. Harry turned away to talk to one of the attendant caregivers. Surveying Alexander's clothes, Janice's facial expression shifted from welcoming to disapproval.

"I didn't expect you'd wear inappropriate clothes."

"Janice, the routine is what matters."

Janice walked away ahead of Alex, evidently unconvinced, as she led him over to a small area that had been cleared for him in the common room. Facing him, the residents were either settled in comfy chairs or propped up by their walkers. Janice picked up the microphone and announced that Alexander Haralson had come to entertain them. As she handed him the microphone, Alexander scanned the audience and estimated nearly all of them were widows. He wondered, besides Janice and himself, how many people in the room were actually alive.

"Before I start, will you please turn off your cell phones and turn up your hearing aids?"

Deadpan city. "Is this a funeral home? Let me say, your nursing staff had better check state regulations. If the state inspectors spotted the violations I've seen since arriving, they'd close this place down in a hurry. So far, I've been in a head-on collision with a walker, run over by a wheelchair, and banged my knee on an oxygen tank."

With still no response, Alexander said, "Let's try this. By a show of hands, who's alive?"

Just then, a man who was evidently a widower, a *shill*, shuffled in front of the stage. "I'm lost." The timing was impeccable. Alexander broke into a hysterical laugh and knew exactly which routine to play. "Ah, the resident stud. Mister, what are you looking for?"

"The men's room."

"If I show you where to go, do you remember the drill of standing at the urinal, zipping down your pants, and taking out your weenie?"

A moment of silence gave Alexander more ammunition. "May I ask your name?" The man was evidently putting a lot of effort into processing an answer. Alexander said, "Might it be George, or Wilbur, or Chief Pontiac? By the looks of your pants, you're not using a napkin at feeding time. Or might it be you've raced to the men's room all day but always came up ten feet short?"

The man's face suddenly brightened as he finally announced, "Orville."

"Everyone, give Orville a hand. It took him about five minutes to remember his name—let's congratulate him!" Alexander laughed. No one else did. "So, Orville, I'm glad you finally remembered your name. Orville, how many men live here?"

This second question took a little less time to process. "I think I'm the only man."

"Look at all the women here. You must *schtupp* the pick of the litter every day."

The expression on Janice's face stiffened from disapproval to horror. She walked over to Alex and hissed, "Can you tone down your act?" Then, turning to the elderly man, she quietly offered her assistance. "Mr. Wilson, let me walk you to the men's room." As Orville gratefully took her proffered arm, she turned her head and scowled at Alexander. "Don't you dare say a word until I get back."

"Janice, have Orville stop by when he's done. I need to ask him a few more questions."

The facilities director returned a glaring look and left with Orville.

Turning back to face his audience once again, Alexander continued. "I'm an accountant, and I can safely say I disagree with those people who say Michigan is in a recession. Look on the bright side. You buy tons of health aids—diapers, prune juice, and raised toilet seats. Prescriptions are paid by Medicaid. Can I tell you something? You folks should be ashamed of yourselves. Think of all the hardworking taxpayers whose tax dollars are used to pay for government subsidies to keep you alive. You're probably taking fifteen pills, three times a day. The most potent is probably Bayer aspirin. I guarantee the nursing home wants you to stay alive. They collect your social security payments in lieu of a monthly check, which might bounce.

"In case you forgot, your children cleaned out your bank accounts and sold your home furnishings, specifically the couch and chairs with stains and odors. Here, they don't have the headache of day-to-day care, like wiping your shit off the floor. It's win-win for everyone."

Janice Corkland re-entered the room and stormed over to Alexander. "Get out. Now!"

"Where's Orville? I need to say goodbye to him."

Janice looked toward the main entrance. A muscular security guard came over to Alex and said, "I think it best if you left, now."

Alexander retorted, "I love doing gigs *pro bono*." He turned to the audience. "My next performance will be at a funeral home. I'll expect to see many of you there."

Laser growled at him as he exited the building. Not understanding why his irreverent tactics had produced such an unappreciative response, Alexander took this failure personally. Should he have started his first geriatric gig with some bad jokes from fifty years ago? Was there any place in the world where he *could* have a successful gig?

BOOK TWO

Chapter One

ALEXANDER CELEBRATES THANKSGIVING AT HOME

Encouraged by his continual improvement, the Beaumont hospital's cardiac surgical staff held a conference with Alexander and Margarita. They explained their decision to discharge Alexander, allowing him to leave the hospital the next morning. They reached this conclusion in part due to observations noted in Alexander's medical records by Jennifer Reynolds, R.N. She stated Alexander walked without any breathing difficulty and that his blood pressure and heart monitor readings fell within normal ranges. The doctors still issued warnings. "Once home, Alexander, continue walking and breathing exercises twice a day."

"And work at lowering your stress level," Dr. Mohamadon, the lead surgeon, ordered. "It's my most important recommendation."

Alexander smirked and thought, *they want me to stay calm?* He knew he could. But taking orders was against his nature, even if coming from someone looking out for his best interests. Only one doctor's order received Alexander's wholehearted agreement—no heavy lifting. He looked at Margarita and smiled. "My days of moving furniture are over. How wonderful." Margarita scoffed. Alexander thought of the orders Flossy gave him. These he viewed with more seriousness, especially the ones indicating she wanted to sleep with him. He knew an 'I'm too tired' excuse would rankle her.

A cardiovascular resident entered Alexander's room later in the afternoon to perform the final step before his release from the hospital. This required removing two sternal wires hanging from Alexander's mid-section. The doctor slowly pulled out one wire, and then the other. Alexander cringed as he watched the doctor win the tug-o-war. He thought his chest was a dam and blood would immediately gush out. Nothing of the sort happened. He mentioned to the doctor that the procedure scared the shit out of him and asked why the wires hadn't been removed earlier. The doctor explained they facilitated in administering stimulation in case of a heart attack. Up to this point in his life, Alexander's attitude toward caring for his health had been as light-hearted as anticipating a summer romance. Now, hearing the doctors, everything turned serious. Did he dare adventure down the demanding path of a career in comedy at the risk of another heart attack?

That night, as he lay in bed, Alexander thought about how he would face the world. Getting back to driving a car would be a blessing. He needed his life back. Being ill failed his 'I'll do what I want to do, when I want to' test. His morning routine would have to change. A morning cup of coffee dropped a few notches on the priority list. He'd leave home wearing sweat pants, a T-shirt under a sweatshirt, and running shoes. Then he'd head out to physical therapy. Alexander knew the operation had worn him down and caused much of his fatigue. But so did the medication. He needed a strong voice for comedy. For now, and most importantly, he felt happy that he'd be spending Thanksgiving at home.

The day his release was signed, Roman visited his father to help him pack and drive him home. Margarita threw Alexander's hospital garments in the laundry hamper and everything else in the garbage. Roman handed his mother the discharge instructions regarding prescriptions that needed to be filled. "Dad, Mills Pharmacy would be best. It would be a nice walk. And—I've said it umpteen times— you're going to have to take it easy from now on. You have a serious medical condition that requires your attention and patience. You can't start running around on the first day out. I'll keep repeating this until I see you taking care of yourself."

"Will going around and kissing the nurses goodbye be detrimental to my heart?"

Margarita piped in, "You could give me a kiss."

"Of course, dear." Alexander walked over and gave her a hug and a kiss. "Thank you, dear. You've been a wonderful caregiver. I must be careful not to squeeze you too hard. My ribs already hurt." Alexander then asked Margarita if she wanted to say goodbye to the nurses.

"I'm sure you can handle that job," she responded, wryly.

Alexander turned and headed straight to the nurses' station.

As he approached, Jennifer said, "Hi, Mr. Haralson. I see you've been discharged. We'll all miss you." Another nurse asked Alexander to tell a joke before he left. "Sure," he answered. "It's an oldie and still a goodie. A woman suspects her husband is cheating. She visits her sister and calls home. The maid answers. 'Is my husband home?' 'Yes ma'am.' 'Can I speak to him?' 'No, ma'am, he's in the bedroom with a woman.' The wife says, 'Don't disturb him, but listen closely to my instructions. Go into the library. You'll find a gun in the desk's second drawer. Take it out, go upstairs, shoot my husband and the woman, go downstairs and toss the gun anyplace in the backyard. I'll find it later and dispose of it. I'll wait on the line.' After twenty minutes, the maid picks up the phone. 'I did what you told me. I shot your husband and the woman.' 'And the gun?' 'I went outside and threw it in the swimming pool.' 'The swimming pool?' 'Yes, ma'am, the swimming pool.' There was a silence. 'But we don't have a pool... Is this 514-734-8536?'"

The nurses broke into hysterics. Alexander looked around and saw Margarita staring at him with an expressionless face as she registered that the tag line had been their home phone number. "Are you finished? I've got a nail appointment this afternoon."

Alexander approached her. "I love you. Your laugh is so infectious."

He then turned and approached Jennifer. "Jenn, you've been a dear." He gave her a hug and kiss. "I hope I didn't break a rib just now."

"Mr. Haralson, you're fine. My vote is that you've been a special patient. It will be dull around here without you."

"Thanks again. I hope you can come visit me when I appear at a comedy club."

The wheelchair arrived. Roman helped Alexander stand and then reseat himself in the wheelchair. With Margarita alongside, he pushed his father into the elevator and through the lobby to the front entrance. Caroline had brought Margarita's car around earlier to the main entrance and was sitting in it waiting for her father. Alexander, proud of everyone's efficiency, got out of the wheelchair and climbed into the passenger seat by himself.

Roman stuck his head in the car. "Dad, promise me you'll remember not to lift anything heavy. Carrying a book is your limit."

Alexander ruffled Roman's hair. "Thanks. I feel great having you as my son and doctor." Suddenly, he opened the door again and reached up to hug Roman, awkwardly, beginning to tear up. Both father and son were surprised by this unexpected gush of emotion, revealing the cracks in Alexander's professed irreverence toward the world.

* * *

On Thanksgiving afternoon, Alexander was able to walk downstairs, descending slowly, using extreme care, and holding on tightly to the handrail. Thanksgiving was a favorite holiday for the Haralson family. The energy Alexander exerted walking down a double flight of stairs was worth the effort. To him, Thanksgiving could be considered the most sacred day of the year.

This yearly ritual required Alexander to carve the first slice of Margarita's turkey, with all family members present. Besides the family, the Haralsons' home was large enough to accommodate a host of friends, cousins, and clients. But being incapacitated didn't allow Alexander to betray a Haralson family tradition and push this responsibility aside. It was 'Carve the turkey, or else,' patterned after Patrick Henry's "Give me liberty, or give me death." If Alexander had still been confined to a bed in a cardio-surgical ICU, he'd have insisted the turkey be brought in and carved bedside, with an over-crowded hospital room of friends and family in attendance. Every Haralson family member feared a family breakup if this patriarchal ceremony wasn't performed.

The Haralson tradition began on Thanksgiving Day, 1957. From his pulpit, Abe Haralson, Alexander's father, sermonized to the family that God Almighty had decreed an immutable law: Woe to anyone transgressing the unpardonable sin of snacking by eating a hot dog at the Lions' game or starting to eat dinner before the elder Haralson carves the turkey. There was one more personal warning Abe Haralson passed along: And woe to anyone who dares to believe I've had too much to drink to perform this duty. He'd assured everyone that no feuding, shouting, or throwing of punches would ever divide the family, as long as the Thanksgiving family tradition was kept alive. Abe had then reminded everyone to help themselves to his famous punch, the Haymaker, which traditionally accompanied this festive event. It carried a dreaded wallop.

Every year, the topic of old Abe's curse was raised, with questions tossed at Alexander. The most notable was, "When did God speak to Abe?" Like the nativity ritual, Alexander was forced to repeat the story. "I sat next to my father at a Lions-Packers' football game. He signaled to the hot dog vendor he wanted a hotdog with mustard. When the vendor handed him the hotdog, I saw that my father had a strange look on his face. I asked if he was feeling sick. He told me he'd just seen an apparition. I played along because I was young and didn't know what an apparition was. Dad said he'd gone into a kind of trance, which he later told me was God speaking in soft tones, saying, 'Abe, I see you're eating early. Can't you wait until dinner is served at home?' My father said, 'What's the big deal? I'm hungry. And besides, we'll be eating turkey leftovers for a week.' My father told me the vendor was God, who'd said, 'You are evil and drunk. A curse will reveal itself after the football season, and it will be severe.' I asked my father if he was a comedian telling a joke. He shook his head. I said, 'I think your story was funny.'

"By the next Thanksgiving dinner, Bobby Layne, the Lions' star quarterback, was traded to the Pittsburgh Steelers. My dad said, 'God added an addendum to the curse. The Detroit Lions wouldn't win another football championship for fifty years,' which came to pass. My father cried as he related to the family that no future quarterback could duplicate Layne's throwing arm to work the magic that won games in the last minute of play. My Uncle Sam laughed and told everyone at the table that Layne drank a magic potion during halftime called Johnny Walker. The family never did split up, and no family member ever dared miss the annual turkey carving ceremony."

* * *

A joyous group was assembled in the dining room, waiting for Alexander to put in his appearance. The heart bypass operation one month earlier had kept his sails lowered. His doctors had ordered him confined to bed rest. The doctors had also ordered him to take a regimen of pills that made him tired and, at times, light-headed. But being with family and friends on Thanksgiving was important, even if he ate nothing.

Alexander despised the doctor's recommended diet of mainly fruits and vegetables. "You mean I'll have to eat those barfy salads for life?" was his comment to the hospital's discharge nurse.

The nurse, no stooge, replied, "Let me see. Instead of the hospital's main telephone numbers, I'll get you a complete list of local funeral homes."

At the foot of the stairs in the Haralson home was a wall separating the dining room from the hallway. Alexander now walked the length of the hallway and entered the dining room. Margarita, Roman, Caroline, extended family members, and other well-wishers were there to greet him. For the occasion, even Roberta had been transformed into an angel in her elder sister's arms, wearing a little white dress and halo-style hairband. An upbeat Alexander said, "Hi everyone." Family and friends turned and cheered. They gushed with effusive appreciation that their friend and father was well enough to join the group and celebrate.

"Margarita, where's that turkey-shaped fruit sculpture you threatened to concoct for me?"

A delighted Margarita replied with a smirk, "I have it in the refrigerator ready for you, my darling."

Alexander groaned. "Keep it away from me. I can hear it groan like a faked orgasm. Tonight is special. I want to eat real food."

Margarita gave Alexander a warning stare. "Right now, I'd like to drop the fruit sculpture on your head."

"Pay attention, everyone. Italian blood is boiling." General laughter ensued.

However, Alexander's jovial runway entrance into the dining room to greet everyone belied his ingrained conceit. He launched into the comedy routine he hadn't been able to resist preparing for this familial come-back.

"Don't I look grand?" His getup of silk pajama bottoms, warm-up jacket with scarf, and velvet slippers broadcast a comedic wardrobe. The slippers he wore had inscribed insteps in needlepoint reading, "It's good to be the king."

"I was able to dress and groom myself in appropriate fashion, instead of the natty hospital garments stained with pungent bodily fluids and uncombed hair," Alexander boasted.

Margarita interrupted him, determined to ward off the pending verbal onslaught. "You might have checked your ego at the door."

"Be nice, M. It's my coming-out party, and I'm feeling great. I'm pushing the bypass operation's importance to the back of the bus. The doctors may have released me from the hospital, but I'm eager to be released from household confinement."

A cheer and applause erupted in agreement.

The momentary tension between husband and wife evaporated as everyone approached Alexander and gave him a hug and kiss. No one was left out. Small children were lifted to give grandpa a chance to show affection. The scene resembled a reception line at a wedding where everyone waited their turn to congratulate the bride and groom, enthusiastically participating in the parade of affection. Even Ashburn Haralson—whom Alexander detested—embraced his cousin.

After Alexander was released from his cousin's clasp, he pointedly brushed off his clothes. Ashburn lived in a skid-row hotel with roaches and mites. Alexander reasoned they might have hitched a ride in his cousin's long, shaggy hair and now try to jump ship onto his own clean clothes. Alexander started to fantasize about perpetually ridiculing Ashburn in comedy sketches about fleas nesting in hair. His mind shifted to focus on another celebrant, his daughter Caroline, who had come to Michigan to join in the celebration. She now lived in New York, and it bothered Alexander that she was still single. Alexander planned to tell her to move out of New York to a colony of single men, or recommend that she tattoo an engagement ring in an intimate place. *It might encourage suitors to shop for a diamond ring in a jewelry store*, he'd tell her.

Dr. Roman Haralson saw his father was becoming tired and escorted him to the table's place of honor at the head of the table... his usual seat. From there, Alexander stood up and waved, saying, "I'm sorry I didn't greet everyone personally. I see my morning coffee group from Starbucks is here. Herman, Itzy, Jake, Ralph, thanks for joining us. I'm glad you came." Alexander sat down again, shifted to a relaxed position, and looked around.

On a platter in front of him was the turkey, but Alexander wasn't quite ready to perform the Haralson tradition. He waited for everyone else to sit. Then he shouted, "I have the scissors. The ribbon-cutting ceremony will begin when I say so." He observed hungry eyes staring at the resplendent turkey, the centerpiece of a loaded side-table, accompanied by dishes of roasted vegetables, mashed potato, and other traditional fare. However, no one dared to tell him to hurry up. "Relax, will you," Alexander teased them. "And keep the conversation light or else I'll stand and do another comedy routine. Important conversations will come later."

Eyes rolled, and chatter inevitably shifted to the topic of Governor Hatcher's incompetence. This prompted Alexander to stand up again. "I'll have you know, my blood pressure has not gone up one notch in response to your unsubstantiated drivel about Hatcher. Anyway, we are at a religious happening. I feel elevated. The turkey's head has been cut off. Call it a sacrifice. Both the turkey and Governor Hatcher are staying put!"

Alexander placed his hands over the turkey and addressed it. "Sorry, old chap. The lions are anxious for me to begin slicing your carcass."

Itzy suggested that someone call Alexander's doctor to cut back his medication.

Alexander responded, "I make one apologetic statement, and you guys start biting my ass. This isn't a comedy club."

"Will someone call an attorney and have Alexander declared insane?" shouted Ralph. "He might slit his wrists carving the meat!"

"Ralph, shut up," responded Alexander.

Swashbuckling the knife a couple of times, he finally cut into the turkey and then looked back at his friend. With the knife in full view he said, "Ralph, you'd better watch that this knife doesn't land in your back." He placed the first slice on his own plate. Everyone applauded. "Ladies, I'm turning the responsibility over to you to carry the platter to the kitchen and carve up the remainder of this corpse."

The meat on his plate and some cranberry sauce would be Alexander's food intake limit, for now. He stood and tapped his water glass with a spoon. The room quieted and everyone's attention focused again in his direction.

"Surgery killed my appetite. I've lost twenty-five pounds, which I welcome." Showing his stomach to the table, he commented, "Now I'm trim and sexy, a stud." Everyone applauded in agreement.

Picking up a glass of water, Alexander then said, "I'd like to toast everyone. Without your help, right now I'd be in a box." A cheer erupted. "I'd like not to toast the crooks who for the last fifty years have run Detroit's finances into the ground, creating city grounds that rival the look and smell of a garbage dump."

No one said boo. All were in agreement.

"I'll take your silence as a vote of confidence."

Alexander sat down, and the family and guest toasts began while the gathering awaited the sliced turkey to be brought back in. Some toasted good health and the turkey, others Alexander's life-sustaining medication and Roman, the doctor who watched over his father. And even Alexander's liberal-anarchist daughter, Caroline, participated in the cheering and toasted God for all His gifts.

Sitting in his chair, Alexander said, "Haven't we forgotten something?" Everyone looked puzzled. "We forgot to toast the New Year! In my book, Thanksgiving has taken over first place, as the new, New Year. Happy new, New Year!"

Roman leaned over and asked, "Dad, are you okay?"

"Of course I am. My world's been thrown for a loop because of the operation. For me, the Jewish high holidays and January have moved to second and third place, respectively."

"Alexander, what are you saying?" asked Margarita. "You love Rosh Hashanah. You stuff yourself with brisket and gefilte fish. The way you talk, it's as if the government plans to ban the holiday because of high calories."

"You're onto something, Margarita. Everything important begins with food. The high holidays should be renamed the heart-attack holiday. Everything important centers on food, with the express purpose of clogging your arteries, getting you on a gurney, and shipping you in an ambulance to a cardiovascular surgeon to cut you open. On the Sunday Sabbath we eat a cream cheese, onion, and lox bagel sandwich. The current New Year's Day is an eat and drink free-for-all, especially the deli meats. Here we get to eat the lean meat. Isn't that a smart way to spend the holiday?"

Everyone nodded in agreement, and Margarita was about to say, 'Dinner is served' when Ashburn Haralson, Alexander's cousin, whom Alexander frequently referred to as the offspring of his uncle's one night stand with a stripper from the Gaiety Burlesque, turned to him and said, "I want to hear if the cardiologist found out you had a heart condition because it was a cold heart?"

The room went silent. Alexander looked at Ashburn with a smile. "Oh my. Ash, I forgot you were here. And seated next to my friend, ah..." Alexander searched for a name, waving his hand. "Herman!"

Herman laughed.

Ashburn continued, "Did your doctor diagnose dementia because of the heart condition or old age?"

"Margarita, I've found a *shill* for my comedy shows. Ash, you've got nerve. You came wearing your one and only suit, an off-the-rack Salvation Army label, and you feel superior enough to pepper me with your political trash. I wish I had a flamethrower to fry your nuts off. I drove into your neighborhood to perform a gig for the unfortunate, and what thanks do you show? I feel attacked and rebuffed.

"But let's put our differences aside today. I mean, what an honor to have you among us. I didn't mean to demean you, especially after a long pilgrimage to our house in your new Cadillac sedan. We're glad to invite the underprivileged like you every year, because otherwise you'd have to eat the leftovers from last year's Thanksgiving dinner at your favorite soup kitchen. You must tell me the name of your homeless shelter. I plan to make a contribution to pay for the winter season's air conditioning."

"Whoa," was heard from many in the room, instead of laughter.

"Dementia, Asburn? No, I haven't experienced any dementia or memory loss. I still remember where to stick it in."

Margarita raised her voice in warning. "The children! Alex, watch what you're saying."

"Yes, dear." He turned back to Ashburn and said, "And please, Ashburn, change yourself into an irrelevant guest. To help out, we can reseat you in the garage or in your car." He turned back to Margarita. "See, no harsh words for the *doofus* this time."

Margarita firmly declared once again that dinner was served and glared at Alexander as she invited everyone to start helping themselves to the food on the side table. Once the family and guests got up to serve themselves, the tension relaxed. Dinner conversation shifted when they all came back with their plates. Alexander deliberately kept quiet, wanting the table conversation to flow before he said anything more.

Everyone had heard about the operation, but curiosity peaked to rehear the story of which symptoms had prompted it. Alexander's version, since the hospitalization, had changed several times. In this version of his condition, heart problems had been waiting to happen. An overworked anybody would have been done in.

"Heart problems force you to retire. You take naps. You go to doctors' appointments. You go to synagogue to understand mortality. You live life in slow motion until it's over.

"The retirement gods played a cruel hoax on me. My plan was different. I was looking for a new profession. I planned to work harder and do more with the family. I didn't retire because of health reasons. My tanks were full of energy. I didn't contemplate a couch potato life, eating and growing fat."

"A bummer."

"Thank you, Herman. You can every so often make an intelligent remark. Yes, I retired from accounting. Yes, I planned to play more golf and hang out more with friends. I also wanted to become a stand-up comedian, a comedic luminary, a celebrity. That would be how I envisioned spending a big part of my time. Since then, I've had time to think and reorganize my future, even while keeping all the important stuff floating in the air."

"I want to know when you're coming up for air," said Herman.

"Margarita, I might have to ask Herman to leave. He's causing me stress. Herman, annoy Ashburn."

Rocky, Alexander's grandson, broke in and asked if Alexander liked the hospital food.

"My boy, the fruit flies will have a ball procreating in my intestines." Alexander the warrior charged on. "Don't be surprised when I return to the hospital with a case of unstoppable diarrhea. I hope their toilets will be large enough to handle the expected overflow."

Rocky laughed. Roman leaned in and said warningly, "Dad, cut it out."

"Oh, and all the balls I had to juggle—coffee with friends, pastries optional, nine a.m. tee time, one p.m. lunch with business cronies, two p.m. phone call from Margarita complaining about everything, four p.m. call from Robert Hatcher asking about the state of his finances, arrive home at six p.m. to discover Margarita has made dinner plans I didn't like. The smattering of miscellaneous calls were equally annoying—my social-worker daughter calling to tell me how rotten her conservative father is, calls from the same daughter asking for rent money which she lacked due to the numerous causes she contributed to, phone calls from Margarita to tell me Roberta is spoiled, or for me to come home because she lost her cell phone, miscellaneous calls from charities soliciting money and asking if I would join their board, more calls from Margarita that the toilet was stopped up or that the cleaning lady or plumber didn't show. I have gray hair to show for my efforts."

"Alex, it's me, Herman the stress pusher. Tell everyone how you got started in comedy."

"Herman, my new-found straight man, thank you. I'm glad you asked. Margarita and I were in Italy, visiting her family. We were attending a performance of *Norma* at La Scala. After the completion of a passionate aria by the lead soprano, an older woman near where we sat, shabbily dressed, stood up and pleaded heavenward in a shrieking voice, 'I have heard your angel's voice. I am ready to die. Take me.' The audience ignored the woman and kept applauding. I, however, took note of the lady, somewhat impressed and sympathetic, thinking idyllically that this was not a bad time to die, surrounded by musical beauty. The audience quieted, but the elderly lady fell to her knees, raising her hands in prayer. Her voice pierced the quiet with, 'Please take me.' The audience turned to watch the shrieking lady.

"'I'd had enough,' I said. 'Jesus Christ, lady, die already.' The lady approached me and blurted an Italian expletive. I replied, 'Lady, Norma dies in the last act. Why don't you join her?'"

Margarita broke in. "I remember that incident. I said then you were disgusting. You still are."

Alexander said, "Quiet, M. Otherwise, everyone will think you're part of the act."

He continued. "Margarita huffed and went over to the poor lady, apologizing for her brute husband's remark. I thought, this is perfect. The opera house may hate me, but they've *heard* me! This was a formula—insult them into laughter. Insult them if they're down-and-out, like Ashburn. In fact, insult them if they're breathing."

Herman asked, "Is it working?"

"No."

A roomful of guests broke into laughter.

Ashburn said, "I didn't laugh. I want to know about the operation. What were your symptoms? Heartlessness? Disgust?"

Alexander responded, "Sorry, Ashburn. There were no symptoms. I was referred to a cardiologist after a regular physical where I flunked the stress test. From then on, it was all business."

Rocky asked, "What did you do in the hospital all day?"

"Collected jokes on the Internet that I thought were funny. There were a lot of jokes from a lot of comedians. What was I supposed to do… confined to my bed? Were Margarita and I supposed to talk all day about revising my will? My computer made for good company. I skyped with friends and family, especially those curious to gaze at my chest incision. Other times, I was able to Google information about comedians. I was astonished by the amount of information available about their comedic styles. I started to feel better. Laughter is better than heart medication."

"What became of your clients?"

"Oh, Ashburn, I knew it was your continual cranky voice insistently interrupting from afar. Sitting so far away, and through mental telepathy, I recognized that your bullet-point, liberal manifesto complaints were about to be unleashed. I know you're referencing my star client, Robert Hatcher, now the governor of Michigan. Sorry to inform you, Ash, but you voted for the loser. I've told you before—get over it. Hatcher's my client, my friend, and, in political social jargon, my main man. If you'd followed your elementary school friend, Stinky Horowitz, into business, you'd be rolling in dough today. We might have been able to celebrate Thanksgiving with your family in a ritzy neighborhood, cutting the first slice of turkey. But no. Not you. You spend your life calling Hatcher a crook. Let me tell you something. Hatcher thinks your ilk are a bunch of lazy welfare crooks. Looking at you, I can't say he's wrong. You won't have to pick through a garbage can when you get home. M, pack my cousin Ashburn a care package from the garbage can in the kitchen."

Alexander saw Herman ready to speak and pointed a finger. "One remark from you, and I'll come over and whack you with a drumstick."

"Alex, relax. I'm your Sancho at Starbucks, remember?"

"You are my jester with a limited life from six a.m. until I finish my second cup of coffee."

"Are there any more cobwebs inside any heads that need cleaning?"

Caroline said, "Your remarks are violent and bullying. I'm offended."

"I've warned you enough times to plug your ears. I do my best to improve the world, and from what I see, no one's doing a better job than me. When I get back into comedy work, I pity anyone who gets in my way. Did you see the turkey? It was sacrificed, honorably. I plan to rip the world open with punishments no one knew existed. Woe to anyone being crucified. The fourth nail will be pounded through your nuts."

A commotion erupted in response from all sides of the table: 'Alexander, you need help.' 'Dad, take it easy.' 'Give him some Xanax.' 'Take him outside for some air.'"

Margarita fell back in her chair and wiped sweat from her brow.

Alexander smiled, "I'm glad to see everyone's so thankful for something. Be unthankful to the powers that ran Detroit into the ground, and especially unthankful for the good work of the board of education. I hope you're all enjoying the evening. I must return to bed. I'm tired."

Alexander stood and walked to the stairs, slowly. He began to whistle "Hava Nagila."

Chapter Two

ALEXANDER LOVED FLOSSY'S PERFORMANCE

Alexander sat in his favorite chair, with the recliner tilted back about halfway and his feet stretched out resting on the ottoman. The home office he'd built over the garage ten years earlier served as an inner sanctum that guarded his privacy. It was Agatha Christie who best described it: "...a room where a man *lived*, where he both worked and took his ease." Before leaving for the hospital, he had warned Margarita: "The tiniest details of the messes I left, how I arranged them, are etched in my head. Woe to anyone who enters, touches, or moves anything." When he came home from the hospital, he checked the office, looking for anything suspicious that might suggest someone, even Margarita, had intruded into his space. The first thing he noticed was that no layer of dust covered the office. Well done, was his silent acclaim. The room's contents were in the same place, fixed as before when he had left for the hospital. Books and business papers lay around on his desk and chair. Pens, legal pads, and letters were scattered about. So were pictures of friends and family and golf mementos.

Margarita came in and handed him the mail. "Here's your precious mail, dear. And hurry up sorting it. I want the Valu-Pak coupons." She looked around. "See, Alexander, I called the cleaning service. This place matched the look and smell of a pigsty. Ah, here's the papa pig." Margarita pinched Alexander's cheek and kissed his forehead. "Oink."

Alexander was glad to get back into his element. The office over the garage was his home away from home, built in anticipation of his retirement. He could make private phone calls, work on government budgets, watch TV or a movie in privacy, and most importantly practice comedy routines, which he captured on video camera. About the only time he was interrupted was when Margarita called him for supper.

Things were changing for Alexander. Managing time was a throwback from his accounting career, when punctuality was a religion. In retirement, time faded to a *maybe* or an *on or about*. The only place where he saw the exact time was on his very expensive Rolex watch. But other important matters needed attention, most notably worrying about Flossy in jail and obtaining her release. And the worst thought that crossed his mind each day was feeling his stand-up comedy career slipping away into collapse.

Years earlier, Alexander had quit smoking on orders from his internist. He now thought smoking a cigar would add to his comedy act. The only time he'd cheated was while playing golf. He asked Margarita, "Dear, did the doctor say I could smoke a cigar while playing golf?"

"Alex, what does *no smoking* mean in your world?"

"What about letting me get my jollies off, sniffing or chomping on an unlit Corona? I mean, that can't be harmful."

"Alex, smell all the garbage trucks, waste disposal systems, or exterminator's daily rat collections you want. What I don't want is you within one hundred feet of a cigar. Your golf clothes, which you always made me wash, smelled of cigar smoke. Sucking in tobacco juice or spitting tobacco particles from the unlit cigar are both disgusting. Forget it."

The comedy clubs had banned smoking. Even so, Alexander remembered George Burns and Groucho Marx smoking cigars while they worked. It was part of the act. They were illusionists. Their grip and twirling a cigar while inhaling and exhaling convinced the audience a funny joke was gelling in their heads. Blowing a puff of smoke meant a joke would be released any moment.

Cigars weren't mind-altering. A sedate George Burns or talk-ative Groucho Marx was a story teller. Lenny Bruce fit into the smoker's club too. But Lenny didn't dare toke on a joint while performing. The part of his brain that began the act would be fried by the end.

* * *

Back in Alexander's office, his phone buzzed. Governor Robert Hatcher's ID came up on the screen. "Alex, will you and Margarita be able to make the inauguration?"

"Unless I collapse with heart attack number two, we plan to attend. Robert, we want to see you sworn in, and sometime during the day you'll need to swear in members of your cabinet, namely me. The inauguration ball, however, may present a problem. Sitting on your ass, eating and drinking for hours can be exhausting."

"There'll be a lot of walking."

"Ah, an added bonus. A PT session."

"Alex, take your time finding and settling into local housing. Call Sandra. She's the hot realtor in town. By the way, how's that hot chick you worked with at the Zug Island Club?"

"She's fine, Robert."

"Jullian told me about a comedy club act he saw. His description sure sounded like your woman."

"It was."

"Jullian said they took a survey of the men attending the show. The ratio of erections was one hundred percent."

"Robert, did they pay attention to her material? Her jokes were my creation."

"Ha ha, Alex. She got the audience in an uproar when she said she got mad at her husband, took out her Glock 9mm, and fired the gun at her husband. Great joke, Alex."

"Robert, it sounded funny. But that was no joke. She's serving time in prison for attempted murder."

"You sound serious. You wouldn't be thinking of asking me for a pardon?"

"Well, yes and no. Robert, I forged your signature on a temporary release to get her out of prison. I need your signature on a full pardon ASAP to keep the paperwork kosher, for my sake, and—by the way—for you. She's the one taking umbrage against your opponents. She's doing a great job turning every minor offense against you into Mt. Everest."

"Thinking about unseating me as governor?"

"No. Every day my most important priority is staying alive. I don't want another heart attack."

"How long was her sentence?"

"Two to five."

"We can't have a precious hottie looking at the world through bars, can we?"

"No. Robert, it wasn't fair. Her husband slapped her around plenty. One day she took her gun and shot at him. She missed. The judge found her guilty of defending herself. If I'd been the judge, I would've found her guilty of failing to kill him."

"Where's her husband?"

"He left town on my recommendation. I had the owner of the comedy school tell Flossy's ex-old man to take up residence near the north pole. I felt Santa could teach him the difference between naughty and nice. Look, Robert, I admit I pulled some strings without checking with you first."

"Alex, you, of all people, took some levity with my authority? You're forgiven. Besides, my call was to ask for some help from you. I need you to check out an Odetta Flanken for me. She's about to be appointed to a high position, president of the teacher's union. I can envision her climbing a ladder to become governor. She's got an organization behind her, and she plans to be vocal. Every move I make will be watched and reported to her first. I smell a recall bubbling in the wings."

"I know a Flanken family. I've met Gregory Flanken at some charity events. As I remember, his wife, Odetta, is a black woman. Have I got the right person?"

"Yes, you do. You amaze me. You have a phone directory in your head. By the way, what kind of a name is Flanken?"

"Robert, it's pronounced *Flanken*, spoken with a short 'a.' It's a Yiddish word that means a strip of meat from the front end of the short ribs of beef. Let me get to work. I'll check her out for you."

"And I'll follow up on your hot comedian girlfriend. I'll find her case number and sign the papers to make her permanent release legal."

"Thanks, Robert. But seriously, Flossy's an important ticket to your future. She's a big supporter and will rip on your opponents from a comedy club pulpit. I'll write the script, giving her all the lines. You need her."

After hanging up the phone, Alexander was relieved. He congratulated himself for getting away with overstepping his authority and foisting some heavy-handed maneuvers onto Flossy's loser husband, Almont. He didn't like bullies and remembered when Frank Amenero from the comedy club called to give him a message from Freddy K. "Freddy K said to say he's sorry for the rough treatment you got at the club. He said the patrons were, let me pronounce it as best as I can, *shick-kers*. He said you'd understand. Seems your friends have a convincing way about them."

Alexander had smiled and asked where Bernie was.

"He's in the hospital. His leg's in a cast, and he has a sore rib cage. Bernie said when the fire broke out, his official story was he tripped over something exiting the building."

Alexander's face brightened at the news.

He flicked the TV on and pushed the DVD into the playback recorder, pushing the "play" button. Flossy had mailed Alexander a disk of her latest gig while Alexander was in the hospital.

Speakers blasted, "Let's hear it for our star. The woman they call the Indiana Interloper, Dental Flossy Lovesong."

The waiting audience greeted her entrance with enthusiastic applause. Alexander watched as Flossy strutted out from a stage wing to the center stage microphone.

The show was at Vince's Comedy Club in downtown Lansing. Alexander recognized the club's decor, having held one-on-one meetings at the bar. He knew the club owner, Fred Babcock, who set up Flossy's gig. He scanned the screen, looking for people in the audience who worked for the state. Seated at a table was State Treasurer Jullian Hebrow, along with members of his staff.

Earlier in the week, Jullian and Alexander had talked by phone to discuss state finances. The treasurer acknowledged that a light at the end of the tunnel had started to appear. "Alexander, your cash analysis shows improvement in cash management."

"I expect tax revenues to improve in the next six months and into next year," Alexander had responded. "Businesses are spending money on improvements and maintenance to keep existing sales. Expansion will strengthen next year. We've worked to show where costs could be cut. We're taking the load off everyone's back."

"Hatcher is pleased. Is anything still a major problem?"

"The roads. They're in terrible shape. Like something imported from a third world country."

"Hatcher is trying to secure funding for road projects from Washington. But it's not working. Those bastards are playing with people's lives."

"Jullian, Washington DC is in a deep state of dysfunction. In general, seniors don't see, don't hear, and don't eat much. They're happy to be alive. Washington knows many families are working two jobs to make ends meet. DC is mainly concerned with elderly parents. They vote. Senior citizens should be considered liabilities because of their drain on the state. But Washington has to pour money into the areas where the seniors are likely to vote in the next election. Even if they die, seniors still show up to vote."

"What do you suggest?"

"Fix the roads. Find the money elsewhere. If they aren't fixed, lawsuits from defective roads will be in themselves a major budget item."

"We need a spokesman to sell the idea."

"I've got an idea. Go to Vince's Comedy Club. There's a performer I want you to see. She'll put everything into perspective. I know she has the talent to sell government programs."

Alexander set Jullian up with show tickets. He had no inkling Alexander was Flossy's secret promoter or about their relationship.

He simply told Jullian that Flossy was a natural-born comedian.
"I've seen her perform before. Her routines carry comedic political baggage, clearly aimed at drilling holes in assholes." The state
treasurer countered, "I've seen her promotional pictures. She's one
hot-looking number."

* * *

Back in his office, Alexander continued to watch Flossy on the tape.
She walked on stage wearing a three-quarter-arm-length brown blouse
with white polka dots, an ivory shell, a pair of black pants with a flat
front, side zipper, and narrow legs. She wore open-toed wedge shoes.
Flossy loved to tease Alexander's foot fetish with dark red toenail
polish. The clothes accentuated her figure and turned Alexander into a
howling wolf. Margarita called upstairs, "Alex, are you okay?"

"I sure am." The pants fit her well, but not skin tight. Just
enough provocative suggestion. A beautiful coral beaded necklace
hung to just above her large, voluptuously shaped breasts. If she
wore earrings, nobody noticed.

Her demeanor seemed relaxed. Her toothy smile was infectious.
In addition, Alexander had helped promote Flossy by giving tickets
away to the transportation department. He spotted a table of staff
members and looked to see who else had attended. He marked down
some names on a legal pad for future reference. The crowd was pretty much all male. Smiles in every audience camera shot abounded.
It was tough to determine if the eyes he saw were focusing only on
her body. He reasoned, how could they not?

Flossy shaded her eyes and scanned the audience. "Hey, look at
my face. I don't do nude gigs anymore."

Laughter and howls erupted.

"Kathy Griffin gets the face looks. If she tried to do a strip tease,
the audience would trample each other by the time they reached the
exit. By scientific standards, her body was an evolutionary experiment gone bad. God felt bad for her and intervened. He attached
a couple of lemon halves for tits. God punished her vanity. They
drooped."

The audience whistled and roared.

"Half the money you paid to see the show will prove to be well spent. One job for me is to vacuum the business of politics from your brains. You get a two-fer—hear some jokes, while enjoying eye candy." Flossy rubbed her breasts. Cheers erupted. "Or would you rather go home and look at your wife's lifeless body? I guarantee she can't tell jokes."

The loud audience reaction ran on.

"I can see you animals out there. By a show of hands, how many out there want a quick jump in the sack with me?"

Yells of "me" erupted, with most every man raising his hand.

"I can't help you. My case worker at the department of social services told me sleeping around town didn't qualify as a day job eligible for supplementary benefits.

"For the gentlemen who didn't raise your hands, I'll assume your wife is sitting next to you. She's daring you to raise your hand.

"For those women who raised their hands, your eyesight needs a checkup. Does this crowd look like a women's club?" The howls were deafening. "Sourpuss City, better known as 'The View,' is on TV, weekdays at eleven a.m. Their idea of an all-star guest is a transsexual turned from he to she walking around with a permanent five-o'clock shadow."

The noise rattled the glasses on tables. "Morality is important to me. I'm still a virgin when it comes to cosmetic surgery." There was enough light for Alexander to see men blowing kisses and reaching for her.

"My case worker questioned me about the ethnic group I belonged to. On the application, I checked the 'other' box and wrote, 'Between red neck and trailer trash.'"

Laughter erupted again.

"I decided since I've become such a comic sensation, I make my dermatologist sit in a waiting room for forty-five minutes before examining me. At my gynecologist's office, I'm a priority patient. When he finishes my exam, I tell him I don't take Medicare." Laughter kept coming.

"How about our governor, Robert Hatcher? He's a stud. Broad shoulders, slim waist. It's about time the voters in Michigan elected a sex symbol. Hatcher's looks will get him on the cover of GQ.

"Jennifer Granholm was touted as the beauty queen who'd save Michigan from financial ruin. 'Jobs will abound,' she bellowed. 'I'll convince companies to relocate to Michigan.' How? With higher taxes? Or doing gigs on her back?

"I believed her campaign *spiel*. I voted for her, twice, and just like she promised, I got a job. My employer said I was talented and was the perfect choice for the combined job of entertainer and cleaning lady. I vacuumed tips off the floor and chairs with my beaver—notice I didn't use the term 'snatch'—to pick up tips. I didn't want to confuse you with a word that's a noun *and* a verb."

As a mark of the festivity's evident success, a patron fell off his chair at that point. Flossy improvised. "Someone check that guy out. He might call the occupational and safety board, and I might get a citation for causing injuries telling jokes.

"I'm a product of the strip clubs I've worked. Detroit has two growth industries—casinos and gentlemen's clubs. Why they call it a gentleman's club escapes me. Furniture stores sell furniture. Gentlemen's clubs have no gentlemen patronizing the premises. It's really a zoo. The trainer throws red meat into the lion's cage and runs for his life. In the clubs, I was the red meat. I worked at a club called The Pubic Hair. No pretenses there. Men came in and had me do a private show in the Champagne Room. They claimed they worked for a women's shelter organization… tried to rescue me and take me home."

The noise level shook the ceiling.

"Uh, huh. I told those clowns I wasn't some lost dog trained to do tricks, sitting upright on legs, with my arms begging for food. Everyone was after me. One guy showed up with his face covered, wearing an oxygen mask. I said, may I presume you do not want your wife to find out you're in this type of establishment? The audience volume increased. Wait. Tell me you didn't tell your wife you're leaving the house to take the car for a wash, did you? Is she dumb enough to believe you'll be home in a couple of hours?

"Last month, my husband and I were on the verge of a divorce. I decided it was better to stay married, until death do us part. So I loaded my Glock and said I was headed to the pistol range. I served time for using my old man for target practice."

Flossy ranted on. "Who's in charge of the priorities in this state? Last week I hit a pothole and lost control of my car. Luckily, I was able to stop on the shoulder. And thank God, no bruises. I got out of the car and inspected the front end for damage. The tires were bent like something you'd see in the funny papers. The minute I bent over to look, all I heard were screeching tires. Three truck drivers pulled over to help. They inspected my rear end and saw no damage. I was disappointed. With my beautiful ass on display, I expected limos to pull over. Instead, I got three toothless critters.

"'Madam, can we help?' they said.

"They said 'Madam.' Imagine that. I'm earning good money now and can buy nice clothes. Just one year ago, when I walked around wearing *schmattas*, I was called a slut. They came, they saw, they tried to conquer. A degree from Yale doesn't make you better in bed than those jeans-wearing truck drivers. All *yous* have your brains in the same place. Did I tell you I tried to shoot my husband?"

Alexander was no linguist, but he loved to hear her Indiana drawl. Flossy's voice carried strength through a sound that flowed with silky texture. He couldn't help but laugh and giggle, hearing her tell the audience what *he* wanted to say to them: "I love you."

Chapter Three

A COMPETITOR JUMPS INTO THE FRAY

Alexander stretched out on his couch, relaxing his head atop an armrest. He was tired and knew he would soon drift off to sleep. The ceiling was white, not like sleeping under the rich, dark night with its brilliant, twinkling stars. His mind began to reminisce back to a time before the heart attack. He, Mr. Smart Guy, had put that oxygen mask story in Flossy's routine. He was the guy who wanted to help straighten out Flossy's life. He'd gone to find her, which involved a trip to the strip club where he'd heard she was working. He dared not go inside the club dressed as Alexander Haralson, the state budget director. That would've been a death sentence for his marriage and his job, if he'd been found out.

Alexander remembered that he first looked for camouflage in an old pile of clothes stored in his basement at home. He surveyed jeans, dingy shirts, and sneakers stacked in the corner and tried on a sampling of each to find that none of them fit snugly. Then he had an inspired idea: go inside the club dressed like a *schlump* wearing a mask and carrying an oxygen tank.

He found his mother's oxygen equipment in the guest room closet. It was in the exact spot where he'd stored it twenty-five years earlier. No one could possibly guess his identity. Pleased, Alexander thought *Mom, you've saved my ass*. The tank and mask were covered with dust and spider webs. Alexander took the equipment and wiped it clean. He was ready to hunt for Flossy.

Alexander parked in The Pubic Hair's parking lot. He opened his car door and exited. He was now careful not to drive an expensive foreign automobile. Alexander dared not have a repeat of the Zug Island Comedy Club fiasco, where his BMW had been destroyed. He instead drove a rental car, a four-door Chevy. The car blended in with the other parked cars. To his surprise, in the club's lot were a Mercedes, three BMWs, and several four-door Lincolns, Cadillacs, and pickup trucks. Alexander thought *better safe than sorry*. So far, so good.

Dressed in Levis and a sport shirt, he hobbled toward the club's entrance, wheeling the oxygen tank, his face covered by the mask. Alexander pretended he had emphysema. He reached the front door and began his act gasping to exhale in earnest.

It was a bright day, which caused Alexander to enter and stay by the door. Alexander waited until his eyes adjusted to the dim light inside the club. When they did finally adjust, he observed that skin city abounded. He saw a blond hostess staring at him. Two bouncers wearing sunglasses and earphones stood at attention next to her.

"Come on in, honey. I have a table ready for you." Alexander feigned gasping and looked up. Without speaking, he pointed where he wanted to sit, and the hostess escorted him to a table.

The club's setup was a three-ring circus with a long bar rail. About seventy-five customers packed the bar. Alexander looked around the club, hoping he could spot Flossy without asking anyone. Nearby "Ooos" and "Oh baby, give me some lovin" were the only chants he heard, even though the foundation vibrated from the loud music. On the way to his table, Alexander spotted the Macomb County road commissioner. He'd worked with him on some road jobs built by Robert Hatcher's construction company. Determined to remain incognito, Alexander held his face mask tightly in place. Groebeck Highway had been newly repaved in order to accommodate the club. Hatcher was the contractor. Alexander realized he was in the right place to find Flossy. Looking around, he estimated there were at least twenty-five strippers entertaining customers.

After sitting down, a pair of hands started to rub his shoulders. Breasts encircled his neck. A sexy voice purred, "I love your gray hair." Before leaving home, Alexander had added a bit more cover-up by dousing his hair with talcum powder. "Baby, I see you're missing some drinks for us."

Alexander turned to look up behind him. She was a long-haired, dark brunette, her hair held back with pins to expose her ears. Alexander gave her the head-to-toe inspection. The outfit she wore consisted only of high-heeled shoes. "My, my, my," he responded. "Looks like you have goosebumps. Honey, you need a mink coat to keep you warm. I'm short on funds, otherwise I'd buy it for you. Would you like me to buy you a pair of earmuffs?"

The dancer remained silent.

"I'll assume you're the entertainment."

"I am. I'd love to do a special dance for you."

"You're so nice, I'd love to nibble on your ears. But I'm into older women. You know, a thirty-ish woman would thrill me."

Alexander took out a fifty dollar bill. He motioned for the waitress to bend over and listen. "I'm looking for a redhead. I know her by the name of Flossy." Alexander noticed the dancer's eyes look at the money while he spoke. "Know her?"

She reached for the money saying, "I'll look around."

Alexander pulled the money back. "I'm not the police or trouble. Just an old friend who's concerned about her. We worked some comedy clubs together."

He handed the dancer the money, and she left. She disappeared into an unlit section. Alexander sat quietly. About ten minutes passed, and then he noticed a dancer leaning against the bar, looking in his direction. The lighting was dim where she stood. She wore a mask, and Alexander couldn't be sure she was Flossy. He gestured encouragingly for her to walk toward him. Flossy, he remembered, was simple-looking. She started toward him with bouncers on either side.

She looked as if she had more years on her body than the other dancers, but Alexander was still unsure if it was Flossy. She wore four-inch, high-heel pumps. Her outfit was styled dominatrix leather, with the crotch and buttocks cut out for display. Her breasts were exposed in full, protruding through an opening. Flossy was eye candy. As she neared him, Alexander lowered his mask a bit and asked, "Are you the Lone Ranger?"

Flossy sized up Alexander and took off her mask. "It's you, Alexander. Honey, you were the guy who chased my husband out of town. I love you. You threw the fear of God in him. He packed up and ran like hell." Flossy put her hand on his oxygen mask. "Jeez, what happened? You have a heart attack?"

"No. My heart is good. I came here to find you. Let me buy some drinks."

Flossy waved the body guards away. "I'll move you to a seat in a private champagne room and bring the drinks to your table. We'll be able to sit and talk privately. Just keep the money flowing."

"No problem. It's state money." Alexander commented, "You look hot. I'd love to see you dance." Flossy escorted Alexander into the private room. She smiled and walked toward the bartender.

Alexander waited for Flossy. He looked about for familiar faces and mentally filed the City of Warren in the back of his mind. They needed an investigation. Paying a sizable tribute to Robert Hatcher for allowing naked dancers to roam around seemed appropriate. Alexander guessed the owners of the club paid off the city fathers. Where was the state's share?

Flossy returned with some drinks. Alexander had already put his mask back on before she came. "What's with the mask?"

"I can't be seen in public. I mean, inside a strip club."

Alexander explained he'd been appointed as the budget director for Governor Hatcher. "You're about to do a pole dance for a celebrity."

Flossy smiled. Then, showing stronger feelings, she said, "You came to visit me in jail. But I didn't hear from you afterward. I missed you."

Alexander explained. "You disappeared, and I tried to get in touch with you. I found out you'd been released from jail, and I didn't know where to call or find you."

"I'm only out of jail temporarily. The club owner here, Amarando, has an arrangement with the local police. We get a week's leave from jail and must dance here. Next week I'm back in jail."

"I got you pardoned on the gun charge."

"That's the arrangement for the job. Technically, I'm serving time for solicitation."

"Are you paid anything?"

"We can only keep twenty percent of the tips."

Alexander's mind churned. "Life's kicked you pretty hard. Let me see what I can do."

Flossy led the way through a door that led off from the main bar area into a dimly lit room, with a single, plush red couch positioned in front of a small pole-dance area. The room was clearly staged for both performance and a more intimate server-client association.

Once she'd closed the door, Flossy raised her glass. "Let's drink a toast. We found each other."

"We did." Alexander told her he'd come to meet her about a legit business proposal she'd love. "Good money. I need to meet you someplace outside the club's fanfare."

Flossy stood, kissed, and licked Alexander as he talked to her. She told him she wanted to hear him out but needed to continue playing the part, just in case the manager, Amarando, came to check on them. Flossy sat on his lap facing him and placed his hands on her ass, inviting him to rub her buns. The arousal for both was immediate. "Stop talking," Flossy said as she leaned forward, shoving her breasts in his face. "I'll never forget what you did for me. Alex, baby, you saved my life. Almont was ready to kill me." She nibbled his ear. "I've got the hots for you. I'd love to screw you right here."

Alexander replied, "I'm glad I brought my oxygen tank."

They giggled.

Flossy said, "We can't be exchanging cell phone numbers here."

"Is there a place we can meet and talk nearby?"

"Norm's Coney Island. It's on Gratiot, a couple of miles south of Metro Parkway. You can't miss it."

"Don't they keep an eye on you?"

"If I don't show up at the club on time, they'll hunt me down and kill me. Norm's tomorrow morning, around eight thirty."

Alexander smiled. "I'll be there. If you're late, don't worry. I'll wait all day. Let me give you some money. Dance for me. No one will suspect anything."

Flossy came around to Alexander's back. He leaned back and said, "Show me those jumbo balloons in action."

"Sure, honey. Right now, I'm so hot, I'd fuck you anywhere."

"Whoa, baby."

Flossy moved to center stage and danced, holding and swinging around a pole. In a short time, Alex was hyperventilating. She sat on Alexander's lap and stuck her tongue in his ear.

"Holy Christ. You'd better slow down. I could have a coronary."

"Please don't. I need you."

Alex took out his wallet and handed Flossy a wad of twenties, without counting them. "Tomorrow."

Flossy helped Alexander stand and walked him to the door. They exchanged loving goodbyes and kissed. Alex walked out into the open air with his oxygen tank and mask, still playing the part of a heart patient, loving every moment that he was alive. Reconnecting with Flossy had spawned delirious, wild fantasies. He opened the car door and got in. He sat staring at the car parked in front, waiting until his mind came safely back to earth, before he finally drove away.

* * *

Emerging from his erotic memory, Alexander stayed put on the couch, still on a high from Flossy's tape and reconnecting at the strip club. He recalled another memory of Flossy, when she had first confided in him. She'd been waiting to speak to Frank Amenero, the comedy school's owner. He and Frank had just finished a conversation and shaken hands. Frank had turned away to announce in a loud voice, "Class will start in about an hour. Start writing some routines."

Flossy walked over to Alexander.

"Woman, you look like hell."

"Can we talk privately? Frank said it would be okay if we used his office."

A surprised Alexander escorted Flossy in and closed the door. On closer inspection, Flossy's face had a small bruise, and her skin was coated with perspiration.

Flossy put her arms around Alexander's neck. "My husband and I had a fight. He bad-mouthed me, called me a bitch, and slapped me. I'd had enough and ran for my gun. Just as I pulled the trigger, he pushed the gun aside, swung his fist, and hit me." She pointed to the facial bruise. "The bullet hit the ceiling, alerting neighbors, and then cops came and charged me with mayhem." She started to tear up. Alexander held back asking whether mayhem included assault with a deadly weapon to produce gross bodily injury. "I'm out on bail. My lawyer told me I'd probably do two years in jail." She put her face next to Alexander, holding him close. "You've got to help me. You're my only hope. I need my husband killed. Otherwise, he'll kill me. I saw what your friends did at the Zug Island Club." Flossy turned Alexander's head and stuck her tongue in his ear. "Shoot that bastard."

Alexander's mind was elsewhere. Wow, thought Alexander. No question she was a hot number. As usual, Flossy's jeans fit loosely. But any man looking at her would see the sexy body beneath them. The loose fitting jeans were an enticing accessory. Her red hair about shoulder length completed the package.

Alexander held her at arm's length. "Did you ask Frank for help?"

"Yeah. He and Bernie promised to protect me. They know all about my domestic problems. I asked them to beat up my husband."

"Why didn't you run away? Divorce your husband and start a new life far away from Michigan. Maybe you have family in another state? Go far away."

"That's what I planned. I have family in Indiana. But if I moved there, Almont, my husband, would find me. I don't know what to do." Flossy rested her head on Alexander's shoulder. "I'm alone. I'm stuck here." She cried and looked up. "Freddy and Frank are useless. I saw them start trouble for you. Now Freddy's banged up, and Frank's your lap dog. Honey, you're tough. I can see you get things done. I like that in a man. I'm your lap dog. Let's lay down on the couch and get it on."

Alexander was mindful she wasn't *schtupping* to get ahead in life. She was scared and doing what she had to do to stay alive. Alexander told Flossy he didn't know what to say.

"Flossy, I'll talk *mano-a-mano* with Frank. He and Freddy will deliver a message to Almont to stay away from you or else. For now, cop a plea on the assault charges. You'll probably do time, but I'll come visit you. Things need to cool off."

Alexander hugged her. "You're a sweet gal. You've got spunk. With a gun in your hand, I'd be afraid of you. By the way, I thought your routine at the Zug Island Club was great. You'd make a great stand-up comedian. You're funny. Keep working at it, even while you're in the tank."

Flossy kissed Alexander.

"I'll keep my promise and get Almont out of the picture."

"Thank you, so much."

Flossy slipped off her jeans and began to unbutton Alexander's shirt. Flossy whispered in Alexander's ear, "Baby, let me give you a down payment."

Alexander and Flossy began. The noise level inside the school increased by fifty decibels as their mutual arousal found expression in loud moaning and shrieks of pleasure. Alexander imagined everyone in the building had stopped what they were doing, run toward the commotion, and was listening. After fifteen minutes, Alexander and Flossy shrieked louder, a reverberating sound signaling they were in the throes of reaching simultaneous orgasms. Their sexual fervor resulted in overturned tables that matched the sound of kettle drums and flying desktop articles sounded a complementary cacophony as they hit the floor. A bookcase crashed downward, reminding Alexander of the climactic cymbals ending the opera *Pagliacci.*

The door to Frank's office swung open. Stunned, the student comedians and college staff observed the mess. Alexander buckled his belt and ran his fingers through his hair. Flossy adjusted her bra and buttoned her jeans and blouse. She grabbed loose strands of hair and lined them up evenly behind her ears. She then opened her shoulder purse, took out her compact, and looked in the mirror. She wore no lipstick. Grabbing Alexander's arm, she started to giggle. "That was some quickie." Alexander joined in the laughter.

Nobody moved. Flossy chimed, "Franky, you'd better get a good cleaning crew. I thought I sneezed from a chill. But I realized there was dust everywhere."

Alexander laughed.

The office help, teaching staff, and students stretched their necks to peek farther inside the office.

Alexander and Flossy continued laughing. Flossy animated a theatrical routine, looking at the office help. "Sorry, girls. You'll have to clean up the office."

Alexander suggested to Flossy they go out for a drink. Flossy replied, "Sure, honey."

"Wait here." Alexander walked to Frank and escorted him to a quiet corner. "The fun days with Flossy are over. She's told me about the two-year anger management vacation she might have to take. Let me give you my anger management orders. You and Freddy had better tell Almont that, in the best interest of his health, he should relocate to the north pole—visit Santa's workshop. Almont won't be happy with the move, but no one back home will give a shit. He'll get acquainted and adjust to life with seals and polar bears as close neighbors. I don't want anyone laying a hand on her ever again. I'm holding you and Freddy accountable. She'll need gigs to support herself. Did I hear you say you'll arrange them? And her tuition, if she came back for classes, would be free?"

"Oh, yeah. Okay."

"Good."

"I'll come by tomorrow to check on the gigs you've arranged for her. Any questions?"

"No, no. I guess I'll see you tomorrow."

Alexander nodded approval, smiled, turned, and escorted Flossy out of the building.

* * *

Flossy and Alexander met at Norm's Coney Island the next morning for a late breakfast. Flossy could leave afterward and head straight to work. Alexander arrived early at the restaurant in the same medical disguise he sported at The Pubic Hair. He settled into a booth. That way, as soon as Flossy walked in, she could slide in next to him without talking to anyone. The other way around, every guy in the joint would try to hit on her.

Flossy entered wearing jeans and a plain white blouse. She carried a large shoulder handbag and wore brown loafers. Dressed casually, Flossy looked the way Alexander remembered her. She walked over to the table, lifted Alexander's mask, and gave him a kiss on his lips, saying, "Hi, good looking." She sat down next to him, and ordered coffee and an omelet. Curious looks indicated the other patrons' interest. Alexander commented, "You look magnificent."

After relaxing from staring at each other, Alexander resumed the conversation. He told her all about his problems—his wife, his kids, his loneliness, and his failure in stand-up comedy. "But I want you to go back into comedy. I want you to be a success. You'll be my surrogate. You'll tell jokes that I wish I could tell to an audience."

After hearing about his family problems and his proposal, Flossy posed a central question. "Why would you want me to go back into stand-up comedy? Why continue as budget director? You've got enough money to divorce your past life. We could spend all the time we want in bed or on a beach. I'd soothe your hurt."

Alexander realized Flossy had a point. Being a Lenny Bruce-type stand-up comedian didn't sound so exciting compared to forgetting everything and getting it on with Flossy. The start of an old-age crisis seeped out of its hiding place. Alexander needed to address it.

"I've got a message to tell the world. They'll listen to you."

Flossy said, "I don't know if it will work. I hurt too." Her police officer of a husband had turned out to be an auto mechanic who worked in a garage, doing oil changes. At home, after work, or on weekends, drinking and watching sports on TV with friends, was his idea of fun. Flossy sometimes told jokes to try them out on this wild bunch. But her main job was collecting empties and handing out another round of beers. She fought off his friends' hands and lips when they tried to take liberties with her. One time Almont, her husband, told her he owed money to some loan shark. She didn't wait for the request she imagined he'd make. She found his Glock and fired a few shots at him. The divorce decree stipulated he'd receive the gun in the settlement.

Flossy told Alexander she'd started to work at The Pubic Hair Club to pay the basic bills. The only drawback was she had to pay some booty tribute to the club's owner. The hostess was ordered to steer men toward Flossy to sell drinks and dance. A fortyish nude dancer wasn't the pick of the litter.

Alexander reassured Flossy he would work hard to make her career in comedy soar. He explained she might have strong feelings for him right now because he'd agreed to help her advance her career. But maybe there'd be a day when she'd want to run away from it all. Maybe she'd meet some man with plenty of money, looking for a decent woman who'd been kicked about in life, sweet, born and raised in Indiana. "If nothing else, I'll make sure next time you don't marry a grease monkey."

Alexander remembered that Flossy had given him a big kiss. "I accept the proposal," she'd whispered.

Chapter Four

A POST-OP VISIT TO THE CARDIOLOGIST

Margarita drove Alexander to Beaumont Hospital's cardiovascular rehab center. He was eager to bypass the registration process, jump onto the treadmill, and begin his first workout. His entire body felt sore from the operation. Yet Alexander was prepared to do any exercise regimen, however difficult, to get back into shape. He counted on physical therapy as his channel to return to a life of seriousness, to further his comedy career. And getting into shape meant a healthy diet and plenty of rest. Allow himself to turn into a flabby old man? Never.

Today, Alexander wore an old sweat suit Margarita found in the basement. He moaned that he'd been made to look like a homeless person. Margarita replied, "So what. Rehab is not a blacktie event." Alexander countered, "I've told you this before. I will not allow myself to be seen anywhere looking like a *schlep*. The Salvation Army should thank me. My old Armani suits are the premium duds that fill their clothes racks."

"I wish you'd find space for your corny jokes. They remind me of your age."

The rehab center's welcoming receptionist sent Alexander to an intake office to fill out information and medical forms. Alexander presented Dr. Lieberson's written rehab orders, required to complete the registration and begin sessions. Margarita drank coffee and read a magazine in the lobby while Alexander grumbled about the wasted time filling out forms and answering questions. He was escorted around the facility by a rehab docent. He saw the gym filled with treadmills, stationary bicycles, and weights. A gray-haired population exercised on the machines and gossiped with the person on the adjoining piece of exercise equipment. He asked the docent about the attrition rate, being a stickler for statistics. "How many persons peel off the machines from a heart attack?" Alexander gave the facility a forensic accounting in his head as he waited for an answer. He never got an answer. Seeing the docent mark down something on a piece of paper, Alexander assumed he would be reported as a troublemaker.

Alexander was introduced to the rehab staff and told them, "Never in all the years of working did I experience shortness of breath, except during the cardiologist's silly treadmill test. I came to gain back my strength. I'm ready." Alexander confided to the nurses he'd changed careers and had become a stand-up comedian. "I'm working to build upper body strength to be more talkative." The staff indulged him with wows. "When I start back to work, I'll send tickets to everyone to attend a show. Can I start now?"

"Sure, Mr. Haralson. Let me take your blood pressure and issue you a heart monitor."

"Stand by. I'll do a comedy routine when I'm done."

With an acceptable blood pressure reading, and a heart monitor attached, an eager Alexander jumped on the treadmill, set the MPH speed dial, and turned the conveyor belt to "On." He walked for twenty minutes, quitting when he felt exhausted.

Alexander went to the nurses' station, removed his heart monitor, and couldn't resist beginning a routine. "My wife is an Italian, and Italians have no sense of humor. Let me explain why." Some of the nurses gathered around him. "An elderly Jewish man is granted three wishes from a genie. The genie tells the man whatever he wishes for his wife will be rewarded ten times more. 'I want to be young and handsome,' says the man. The genie says he'll grant the wish, but issues a reminder about his wife's good fortune. 'I don't care.' 'And for your second wish?' 'I want to be a billionaire.' Again the genie tells the man his wish will be granted and warns his wife will be even more wealthy. 'No problem,' says the man. The genie asks for his third wish. 'I want a mild heart attack.'" The nurses roared. Alexander was careful to never tell Margarita that joke.

Alexander emerged from the gym and met up with her. He told her the routine resembled military training and proceeded to describe every movement in detail. Margarita jumped in. "Alex, make sure you don't repeat the same details to me every day. It's not a public service announcement."

* * *

The Beaumont Hospital cardiology recovery program, which would allow Alexander to regain his independence and be able to drive alone, served as an incentive to put a strong effort into PT. When he reached the milestone, Alexander could be his own person—to go where he wanted, whenever he wanted. As he started feeling stronger, he enjoyed physical therapy more.

Margarita was his driver for now. He constructed a makeshift countdown calendar, on which he could cross off the current day and study how many days remained. Each time Margarita drove Alexander he reminded her that he would soon be behind the wheel. Margarita humored him with a syrupy, "Yes, dear." It was evident to Alexander that she didn't really care. In her estimation he was a child, and she'd change his diaper, if needed. No one loves changing a diaper, but the dirty job has to be done for those you love.

* * *

Alexander visited his cardiologist about a week after starting cardio-rehab. Going forward, Dr. Lieberson became the lead post-op doctor in charge of his medical condition. The surgeon's responsibilities had ended. The blood pressure, heart rate, diet, and weight were important now. To Alexander, what counted was the number of weeks Dr. Lieberson would order before Alexander could drive alone.

Alexander sat with Margarita in the doctor's waiting room of the DMC Medical Center branch in West Bloomfield. The suburban Beaumont facility appeared to be well maintained compared to the DMC downtown Detroit facility. Alexander wondered why his son couldn't have been chosen to practice at Beaumont Hospital. It's about ten minutes from my house, he thought. It's clean, and it's five miles north of our third world city. And my medical records can stay in Royal Oak, not sent to downtown Detroit to be stored in the basement with rats. I take Margarita to Beaumont Hospital for her doctor's appointments, and I never have a problem. My son intervenes and says I need to have my surgery done in his resident hospital. So I travel to the sewer collection capital of the world, from where the golden medina Birmingham flushes its toilets and sends its effluent downstream. And my son thinks I should've had my surgery there. What's wrong with this picture? Alexander fumed.

"Mr. Haralson," came the booming voice of a short, stocky nurse. He turned toward Margarita. "Are your eardrums intact?" Alexander stood and walked toward the nurse. He scowled at her. "Are you a spokesperson for a hearing aid clinic?" From her name tag, Alexander identified the nurse as Julie Butler, and she explained that she'd perform the preliminary vital checks before leading him into the examination room. She asked what current medications he took. Alexander handed her the list he'd prepared for the appointment. She glanced at it and nodded. She noted Alexander had missed a question on the personal form.

"Are you retired?" she asked.

Alexander was taken aback by her question. "You should have asked, 'What is your occupation, Mr. Haralson?' You focused on my hair. Note, for your records, my hair is gray, not silver. The answer to the non-medical question of occupation is *comedian*."

Julie raised her head and gave Alexander an irritated look.

"Don't worry, Julie, telling you one of my jokes couldn't make you laugh. You'd fit in perfectly as a member of my audience. Welcome."

She did an about-face, and gave a quick and explicit instruction: "Strip down to your shorts." Then she exited the room and closed the door. Alexander did as she asked. As he removed his slacks, his underpants came next with Flossy still on his mind. Five minutes later, the door flung open as Julie pushed an EKG machine into the room. In total silence she hooked up the probes to Alexander. "I said strip to your shorts."

Alexander looked down and replied, "Oh. Just call me a showoff." He put his shorts back on.

Julie gave Alexander a glance and ran the test. When she finished, she gathered the equipment, saying in a gruff voice that Dr. Lieberson would be in shortly. Glaring at Alexander, she left in a huff.

Dr. Lieberson came into the exam room wearing a lab coat and a tie, suit pants below the white coat, and brogues. He stuck out his hand saying, "Alex, the last time we met was before your surgery. How have you been feeling since the operation?"

Alexander shook Arnie's hand. "Never felt better. Can you make this appointment short?"

In a firm voice, Dr. Lieberman said, "Sit down, Alex." He cuffed Alexander's arm to take his blood pressure. "One thirty-five over eighty-five. Not bad."

"My handshake and blood pressure should tell you I'm well. I really need to be home making phone calls to line up gigs."

Dr. Lieberson gave Alexander a quizzical look. "You need to lower your stress level and regain strength before you start up with any activities, especially *strenuous* activities. I'm not a Santa Claus who can grant you that wish of getting better in a short period of time. You're delusional if you think otherwise. I'd suggest a cruise. That's a good start. Find a lounge chair and lie flat on your back by the pool. Watch some movies. Enjoy your time with Margarita."

"As in reconnecting our marital sex life?"

"You're kidding yourself. Marital relations at your age are problematic. If it happens, feel lucky and go for it."

Alexander's mind focused on Flossy and he said, "Then that's exactly what I'll do."

Dr. Lieberson ignored Alexander's remark. "The blood tests you had done earlier in the week showed good results. The EKG you just took indicates your heart is functioning well. There's nothing else to say but take your medication and book a cruise. You're doing fine. My advice—relax. You're free to go. Set up an appointment in three months."

"Arnie, when can I start driving a car? What about going to a comedy club to watch a show? What about saying it's okay to go for an early morning coffee?"

"Alex, as I said... in moderation. Give it thirty days. Then drive your car for short trips. I suppose early morning coffee at Starbucks won't hurt. Don't you have an automatic coffee maker?"

"Arnie, are you married to a Jewish princess?"

"Yes."

"Does she wake up early to make you breakfast before you leave for work?"

"Okay, Alex, I hear you."

"In my case, I'd have to put the grinds in the coffee maker, set the timer, and push the 'On' switch. My Italian queenie wouldn't strain herself. So Starbucks, here I come. Besides, I have to see a friend and apologize. Before the operation, I punched him in the face and broke his nose."

"What? Alex, you've got some serious issues. Fighting is not recommended. And it must have caused some stress—maybe the heart attack."

"We got into an argument. I reminded him I hadn't forgotten when he snitched on me to a teacher in the second grade. I swung at him and landed a haymaker. I felt better afterward and told him we were even."

"Sixty years of pent up tension? Alex, no wonder your heart attack was a time bomb waiting to happen. I hope your next appointment isn't inside an ICU. A visit to a therapist would be good. You need to figure out what's troubling you. Call me over the weekend. I want to know how the next few days go."

"Would you like a report about my intimate relations with Margarita? If you want, I'll call you after the cruise with a full report."

"Christ, Alex, ease up."

* * *

On the drive home, Alexander told Margarita that Dr. Lieberson thought he was doing well. "Keep taking the prescribed medication and continue going to the rehab center, were his recommendations. He gave me permission to drive. Your designated driver job is cancelled."

"He said you can drive around place to place?"

"Yeah. To Starbucks and back home. And he recommended we take a cruise."

"Italy is so beautiful this time of year."

"You think Italy is beautiful any time of year. You'd love to move back there and leave me hanging at the immigration office. You'd make sure the authorities know I'm an undesirable alien and shouldn't let me enter. You'd let them know that the first time the authorities let me in turned into a disaster. We met at your father's pastry shop and married in Detroit. What a mistake. You whined, 'Where are the mountains? I planned to exchange vows atop a mountain overlooking a vista.' The only panorama you saw were burned out houses and factories. Move back to Italy. I should be so lucky.

"I'll arrange a Caribbean cruise on an Italian liner. There'll be plenty of fellow *Italiano* travelers. And there'll be plenty of Italian dishes for me to eat and land me back in the hospital. We'll both be happy."

Alexander didn't waste a minute, going into action right after returning home from the doctor. He called his favorite travel agent, Valerie von Meer, to make arrangements. Alexander thought Valerie was skilled in her work, which meant Alexander could count on her to arrange suitable accommodations. Alexander and Valerie *kibbitzed* before hanging up. He told her about his operation and Thanksgiving supper with the family.

Valerie told Alexander how happy she was about the good news. "I'll get back to you soon as I can with travel openings."

"Do you know what I love about you, Val? You're in an elite club of persons I cherish. Your work is performed in a professional manner and completed correctly the first time. No excuses about doing the job halfway. Can you imagine my heart surgeon saying, 'Oh my, I finished two arteries, and, oh my, I had you scheduled for a quadruple bypass. Sorry, but I'm scheduled to tee off in fifteen minutes.'"

Valerie laughed and said she'd report back to him. Alexander thanked her and hung up.

"Margarita, pack your bags. We'll be taking off to the Caribbean."

* * *

Alexander didn't follow Dr. Lieberson's exact prescribed directive concerning driving an automobile. One day he decided to visit Flossy at the women's correctional facility, instead of taking an afternoon nap. Alexander knew the idea was dumb. He suffered from fatigue and needed the rest. The second dumb thing was driving more than the allotted one hour per day. He knew becoming overtired or overstressed could lead to a serious accident.

Alexander decided to take the chance. It was the first time since returning home from the hospital that he'd felt better, and the time to visit Flossy was now. He decided to take some liberties and not let the opportunity pass him by. The waiting time for the doctor's order allowing him to drive without restrictions had been stressful. And maybe a visit could help him find some relief from his stress. Ah yes, relief. The only other option would have been a sick joke. Margarita would be his permanent designated driver. Alexander wanted to see Flossy before he left home to cruise the Caribbean.

Alexander and Flossy had talked by phone, but Alexander always shortened their conversations, fearful that Margarita, who roamed the house, might sneak up on him and eavesdrop on his conversation. Worse, Alexander thought he'd suffer a fatal heart attack if discovered.

On the phone, Flossy told Alexander that part of her day was spent attending behavioral modification classes. Flossy described the social work class. "Instructors suggest to inmates how to resolve conflicts without resorting to violence. What a crock." Flossy said if the same set of circumstances happened with Almont, she would do a repeat performance with an added dimension—ambush her husband and finish the job. "I'd have it all planned out. He'd think I was angry and be running for the gun. He'd come chasing after me trying to beat me to the dresser where the gun was stored. He'd stand like a target in front and block me from opening the drawer. But I would outsmart him. I plan to buy a snub nose and conceal it in my bra. I'd pull it out, point the gun, and say, 'Almont, let's begin our divorce proceedings.' I'd keep shooting until I was sure he was dead."

Alexander howled. He told Flossy that being around her he felt safe, that he could breathe air freely. "Christ, I'd like to hire you to whack Margarita. I'll recommend to Governor Hatcher that he hire you to whack all those Detroit criminals. They won't be hard to identify. They wear fancy clothes and have bulging pant pockets stuffed with money."

Alexander suggested, "Let me visit you. We'll have time together." Flossy loved the idea. "But Alex, baby. They don't have private rooms for us to be alone."

Alexander laughed. "Shucks."

* * *

One morning, Alexander told Margarita he was off to conquer the world. He went to cardio rehab, cut it short, and then went straight to the women's correctional facility. While driving, Alexander's mind switched to automatic pilot, which reminded him his life was floundering and running on fumes. One good thing was he missed Flossy, and that void could be filled, prompted by his strong desire to visit her. He hoped being in her company would recharge something, though at that moment only God knew what the something was.

Alexander walked from his car toward the building. He knew he was going in the right direction. The sign over the entrance read "Visitors." That's all you needed to know. "Women's correction facility" was superfluous. Once inside, the reception area contained visions of dinginess. The linoleum floor was coated with grime, complemented by sounds of heated swearing and odors from overstuffed trash bins. Chairs were anchored to the floor so they couldn't be picked up and used as weapons or stolen. The scene was a 'holy shit' experience. Then he noticed something else. His slacks and sport shirt stood out compared to most of the other visitors. The general dress code appeared to be sleeveless T-shirts revealing bulging biceps, necks covered with tattoos, and do-rags wrapped around the forehead. The 'wife beater' code. In addition, all of the approximate twenty visitors wore Levis sporting impressive belt buckles that could be used as weapons.

Alexander sweated, waiting in line to announce to the desk clerk the name of the prisoner he wanted to visit. This individual gave him the once-over from head to foot. Alexander handed him the completed form identifying who he was and whom he wanted to visit. He received no special courtesies. "Cubicle four," was the clerk's directive as he issued Alexander his visitor's pass.

Once sitting down inside the viewing room, Alexander told Flossy, "Christ, there're some mean-looking guys out there."

"You haven't met the women they're visiting. I've talked with some, and they've all tried to kill their old man at one time or another. I'm in good company."

A guard stood nearby. Alexander nodded his head toward the guard. "Are they allowed to eavesdrop?"

"They're checking on whether we're talking about planning a robbery or murder."

"So, nothing's confidential. They can tell the supervisor what we talked about? Well, I've got a plan. When you get out, take me to a gun store and shooting range. I'll make sure you get a top-of-the-line gun, and I get some shooting lessons. No one's going to overhear our good times, especially when we're screwing."

"What about your wife?"

"You can shoot her. Claim she was an intruder."

Alexander and Flossy were separated by a bullet-proof partition. "I see guards on your side. Christ, you'd think a war was about to break out."

"Don't worry. Nothing's going to happen."

"When you get out, you can become my bodyguard. I'll feel so much safer."

"I'm glad you came. Maybe you'll be able to visit me more often."

"Ouch. I'm scheduled to go on a cruise with Margarita. Doctor's orders."

"What! Screw the doctors. I'm rotting in hell, and you're out cruising and having fun?"

"Relax, Flossy. Things will change. When I get back I'll have energy. I'll work with you to become successful. I'm frustrated and not making it. Instead, I want to spend my efforts on making you successful. I've patterned my style to match Lenny Bruce. He was funny. His material played to a liberal choir. Even if you didn't find his material funny, you listened to his rants and respected his philosophy. I'm conservative. My rants were met with hissing and hatred. My audiences consist of 'privileged peasants.' I'm insulting them. They think I'm one of those conspirators who plans to take away their government benefits and escort them to their new housing projects—park benches."

"No, Alex, you weren't funny. But now I'm taking over. And Margarita won't get in the way of my act. When I get out, you buy me that gun you promised. Your Italian hussy will be victim number one."

"One Italian wife in a lifetime is enough. But I'm keeping her until the end."

Flossy sighed. "You're disgusting. I'll bet you have a rant inside. Tell me one. Make me laugh. I dare you."

Alexander stared at Flossy for a moment. "Did you ever wonder why certain letters of the alphabet would allow themselves to be the first letter of words that denigrate themselves and become the doormat for words that insult? The word 'Detroit' comes to mind. Could someone take pity on themselves and change the first letter so it says 'Letroit?' Give someone else a bad name. L is so much better. L means love. L begins lively, luscious, or luminous. Is there a word starting with D that says happiness in some way? Let's try—dragon, demon, damage, damp, dandelion, danger, dark, DDT, death, debacle, debt, decadent, decay, destroy, defamation, delirium, delinquent, Delilah, demolish, Detroit, dentist, depressed, despot, detox, derriere, dysfunctional, douche, dumb, drought, danger, disbar. The only happy words I know are delicious and delight."

Flossy laughed through the list as Alexander sermonized. Without paying attention to time, visiting hours flew by and were suddenly over. They felt a little sad, the time spent too short. "I enjoyed visiting, even though we only looked at each other through a bullet-proof partition." They tried to touch through the glass. "I'll call you when I return home." They parted with faces streaming with tears.

Alexander exited the women's correctional facility. Despite his emotional response to seeing Flossy again, and having to leave her behind in that seedy hell hole, he felt much better. He found his Kia sedan with ease. It stood out compared to all the new trucks with shiny chrome bumpers. An embarrassment. Wife beating must be profitable. He slid in behind the sedan's wheel. He was suddenly befuddled and wondered how in such a short period of weeks he'd wound up romantically involved with Flossy and her working class ilk, loving this new-found energy. He sat staring out the window, daydreaming about Flossy's lovely face behind the bullet-proof glass. He came around when he heard other cars honking in the lot. About to start his car, he realized he'd left the driver's door open and pulled as hard as he could on the door handle. He heard some metal drop behind the inside door panel. The energy he exerted to close the door was an expression of sympathy and frustration at having seen Flossy behind bars, and his anger about where his life's career was headed. The door boomeranged open. "You fucking piece of shit," he shouted, which turned the heads of a variety of tough-looking types who'd been visiting their women. They glared at Alexander. He interpreted their looks as a sign they were ready to fight. Alexander wanted to pick a fight, too—with himself. He got out and opened the trunk. He saw the tire wrench and fantasized shaking it menacingly and clunking the main troublemaker—himself. Alexander was on edge, feeling sure everyone hated him. How would he be able to garner an audience he didn't alienate? With each setback, he crept closer to a meltdown. Then Alexander forgot about ripping on himself as he realized it was the audience who deserved the punishment.

Alexander mused. How come I don't see another Jewish *punem* around here? How come I'm always the token Jew? Where are my people, the *gonefs* who drive a Lexus hybrid? There were plenty of Alexander's 'landsmen' he felt belonged in jail. Some Jewish attorney friends came to mind. Bernie Madoff's wife belonged here. She was no innocent *chicksa*. She belonged in the cell that Leona Helmsley had vacated. Alexander started the car and exited the parking lot. He drove in a sedate manner. He would have preferred to burn rubber to get the hell out and away from the crazy *goyem*. It was a perfect analogy—he was blowing smoke out his ass.

Alexander wondered how he could be enchanted by a hillbilly. Or was she a redneck? He laughed at himself. "I sound so culturally insensitive." And at the same time, he knew he could easily hate his miserable wife and bratty five-year-old daughter. Is there such a thing as familial prejudice? Flossy and Alexander had spoken about happier days in childhood and in early marriage. Neither could explain what had happened to make everything so crazy. Alexander told Flossy he'd started out to change his life in his retirement years. He wondered whether stand-up comedy was a pretense for escaping the loneliness he felt.

"Everyone hates me," boomed Alexander to the empty car. "I had a fist fight with an old school chum. I make fun of crippled and homeless people. What's wrong with me? I'm trying to make people laugh. Maybe I should make a profession out of trying to make people cry." Gathering steam, he warmed to his self-castigation monologue. "And don't give me the 'I should see a therapist *shtick*.' My wife thinks there's nothing mentally wrong with me. I'm a normal person, she says. Yet she insists I schedule an appointment with a shrink—for her! I had dared not ask her to explain the logic. I think she's crazy, and I don't think an appointment would help. She won't change. It's a waste of time and money. She would still be the same miserable crank after the sessions."

Alexander encouraged Flossy to talk about her life and had learned her family were average jerks. But she loved them. They tried to steer her life in the right direction. Yet everything she did was mistake after mistake. She married a complete jerk and dropped out of school to become a waitress.

"The only thing that helped me gain control of my life was aiming a loaded gun at my husband," Flossy had said.

"Enrolling in a comedy school took guts," Alexander responded. "It was a big deal. But the effort had its obstacles. You've had a life of hard knocks, but you're still standing."

Alexander thought Margarita could learn some life lessons by bringing Flossy along on the cruise. He could tell Margarita, "Let Flossy lead by example." M would then understand what troubled their marriage. He'd crow, "Why can't you be like Flossy? Learn how to speak with sweetness?' Alexander could hear Margarita ringing his bell. "This pistol-packing *shiksa* picked up a gun and shot at her husband? This is a picture of sweetness? This tramp is in jail for attempted murder? She must have screwed the judge to get the two year cupcake sentence. To you, the know-it-all, this is a classy lady?!" Alexander would dare not remind Margarita that the Italians had plenty of sharpshooters in their ranks.

Margarita already knew that. "Let me tell you, Mr. Hotshot," she'd fire back, "Italian murder rates are high because everyone knows the laws of Italy. The church or the Mafia are backed by guns. Minor or major infractions aren't distinguished. You're just dead. In Detroit, the authorities water down murder to a minor infraction. That's why it's a mess. Excuses like poor upbringing mean you're free to go. If I ever get back to Italy, stay out. I'd make sure you'd be a marked man."

Chapter Five

ALEXANDER AND MARGARITA TAKE A VACATION

Alexander and Margarita were sipping coffee when Roberta walked into the breakfast room and said, "Where am I going to stay while you're gone?"

Alexander turned to his wife in disbelief. "Margarita, Roberta's not taken care of?"

Margarita was silent.

Alexander snarled, "If I growl, will you wake up?"

"Alex, wouldn't it be better if you could be civil and remember that Roberta is your daughter?"

"Forget civility. Our suitcases are loaded in the trunk, we're ready to leave for Florida, and you forgot Roberta?"

Alexander's blood pressure started to shoot up. "I gave you one checklist item to complete before we leave. One!" Alexander held up his index finger and wiggled it for emphasis. "Babysitting arrangements for Roberta... and you forgot about her? Since we're running short of time, I know what to do. How about stuffing her in a comfy cage at the dog pound?"

"Alex."

"Why not. She whimpers like the other mongrels. Her bark will mimic the ungrateful city of Detroit residents when I take away their goodies."

Margarita stood up suddenly and rushed to call her sister, Lunetta, who to Alexander's delight, didn't suspect what the consequences would be and answered Margarita's call. He hovered near his wife, waiting to overhear the conversation. Lunetta answered, and without any fanfare Margarita told her that Alexander had booked a weekend cruise on short notice. "We're leaving for the airport and need a sitter for Roberta. It's only for a few days." Margarita knew it was a lie. Alexander had booked a seven day Caribbean cruise. But she was desperate. "You and Roberta will have such fun." She pitched it as more of a courtesy call than asking for a favor.

They waited for Lunetta to reply. Margarita tried to resolve the delay by asking her sister if she wanted to speak to Alexander, who could explain the mix-up. While Margarita spoke, Alexander said in a firm voice intended to be overheard by his sister-in-law, that he would smite Lunetta with the biblical sixth plague if she said no."

The "No!" Lunetta shrieked could be heard by the entire population in the state of Michigan. The matter was clarified when Alexander asked Margarita if she'd said 'no' to babysitting Roberta or 'no' meaning God, please save me from Alexander's timorous plague.

Margarita told Alexander, "Why do you find it necessary to scare her? She already has ingrained fears because of you. For your information, Lunetta said 'yes' to watching Roberta."

Alexander grinned.

"Lunetta asked one favor. I'm to bring Roberta into the house with her suitcase and to tell my husband to stay in the car."

"My pleasure," was Alexander's cheery answer.

* * *

With time being a factor in dropping off Roberta in time for them to catch the plane, Alexander drove with recklessness to reach Lunetta's house. He knew the directions, but as he drove onto her street, the houses were a blur.

Margarita screamed, "You're going past her house!"

Alexander turned the steering wheel, slammed on the brakes, and jumped the curb, forcing everyone into their belts before coming to an abrupt stop. One wheel came to rest on the front lawn.

An unfazed Alexander said, "We're here. I'm glad it's your car. When we get back, Hatcher has arranged a new BMW for me on the state's dime. Geeze, another car for me to destroy."

Margarita screamed at him, "We're lucky to be alive!"

Roberta started to cry.

Alexander ignored the commotion. "I'm glad everyone wore their seat belts. Where's your sister?"

Lunetta ran outside toward the car. "Is everyone okay?"

"Yes," answered Alexander, in a casual manner, as if this driving escapade happened every day. "Hurry up. We have a plane to catch."

Margarita got out of the car and opened the rear door. Lunetta stood nearby. Roberta sat in her car seat, whimpering with folded arms. Margarita coaxed her. "Darling, we're here. Auntie Lunetta will take care of you while Mommy and Daddy are gone."

Roberta ignored her mother, petulantly turning her head away.

"Mommy will buy you a present while she's away."

"Let me handle her," piped Alexander.

Margarita opened up her vocal chords for the world to hear. "Alex, keep back!" Leaning toward Roberta, Margarita soothed, "Ignore Daddy. He tried to kill us and is now trying to annoy everyone else."

Lunetta addressed Alexander, "I suspect you were planning to take her on the cruise and leave her there."

Alexander snickered.

Lunetta went over to the car and said coaxingly, "Roberta, you should keep away from your father. I shall take care of you."

Alexander voiced, "You can have her for free."

Lunetta wagged her finger at him. "And you're going to pay for the damage to my lawn. Look at what you did. I'll send you the bill for my new landscaping."

Alexander gave her a deadpan look.

Lunetta opened the door for Roberta. Alexander opened the trunk and took out her suitcase. He flung it on the lawn. "Looney, she's all yours. Take care of the precious cargo."

Lunetta awaited Roberta with open arms as the child climbed out of the car, pointing a shocked expression at Alexander. In response, he offered a jovial goodbye, "*Hasta la vista*, baby."

Roberta bawled, standing next to her aunt. She turned back to her father. "I hate you."

Alexander replied in a babyish tone, "I hate you too. So there."

The situation was onerous, and Lunetta's cringing face showed it. Alexander imagined hearing Lunetta question herself about how she got suckered into taking care of Roberta.

Lunetta gave Alexander the 'once over,' clearly irritated. In a sarcastic tone, she said, "Life must be good, Alexander. You're wearing a tan leather jacket, a loud print sport shirt, dress slacks, and brown loafers. You almost look civilized."

Alexander looked at his slacks and shoes. "It's good to be rich in America." Alexander traveled in style with Margarita. On a trip with Flossy, he'd worn trashy clothes. Flossy's summer wardrobe consisted of flip-flops, a cheap T-shirt with a local hardware store logo, and thread-worn jeans imbedded with ketchup stains. Her get-up reminded him of Flossy's family as he'd seen them in photos.

Lunetta wasn't finished. "I don't like you calling me looney."

"Tough shit. Margarita, get in the car, *molto velacito*. She might change her mind."

Margarita hesitated, then said, "Goodbye, dears." She went over to Roberta and Lunetta and kissed them goodbye. "I'll send you pictures by e-mail," she said placatingly.

Margarita hesitated, waiting for a reaction, while Alexander cleared his throat, prodding her. Both her sister and daughter regarded her in silence. Sighing, she looked away and headed to the car, waving a last goodbye. Alexander couldn't resist turning back and saying to Lunetta, "Enjoy trailer trash's rendition of Honey Boo Boo." Turning to Margarita, he said, "Get in the car, already. Stop thinking and let's start rolling. You're giving your sister a chance to renege."

They jumped into the car, and Alexander peeled rubber as he backed off Lunetta's battered lawn. The car's wheel dropped back onto the pavement with a thump. "The car's fine," said Alexander.

He straightened the wheel and headed in the direction of the airport. The immediate concern was the flight reservation to Florida, and they were running late. Alexander put on his race-driver hat, clocking ninety miles per hour on the freeway.

"You were disrespectful to my sister."

"That's how I act to anyone I don't like."

"Does that include me?"

"Of course not. Since she came through in the pinch, my opinion of her improved by one percent, and don't ask me to explain." Alexander couldn't have cared less if Lunetta lacked the prescribed number of brain cells to care for a child. He delighted dropping a forty-pound sack of shit on her. He imagined Lunetta saying, as she watched the car shrink in the distance, "First, you drop the kid off, and then you drive off to soak up some sun. What's wrong with this picture?"

Margarita voiced her concern to Alexander. "I'm worried about my sister caring for Roberta. And I don't care what you said. The way you behaved was shameful."

"Your sister is capable of feeding Roberta, maybe not as well as in a dog pound, but she will be fed. Anyway, I'm more interested in the dynamics of the two. Who will kill whom first?" Alexander thought it a definite possibility Roberta could throw a fit and dismantle Lunetta.

Margarita adjusted her seat and leaned back on the headrest.

Alexander looked over. She seemed oblivious to his speeding. "My mind is fixated on boarding a cruise ship a thousand miles away, stuffing myself on rich foods, tanning by the swimming pool, and watching the warm glow of picturesque sunsets."

Margarita began to giggle. "Wait till I lead you to body parts you've been ignoring. I'm sure you'll find me entertaining."

Alexander returned a hearty laugh. Alexander was cocky. While on vacation, he imaged being the stud of studs, unleashing his passions, and taking full advantage of Margarita.

"While we're on the subject, my dear, I hope that while we're on the cruise you're planning to tune out Hatcher and stand-up comedy."

"I'm okay with that. I brought some books to read—a few Lee Child mysteries."

"Really. I was testing you. You're actually going to tune out Hatcher? Ha!"

"No. I don't have any plans to manipulate you or anyone. Lies may gel in my head, but none will be spoken. Pretend I'm a sober Lenny Bruce."

"What about the conniving Alexander Haralson, CPA? You can't trick me into believing you've never cheated your clients out of money."

"For sure I've always tried to cheat the IRS. I viewed it as one crook cheating another crook." Alexander chuckled. "My clients knew what I was doing on their behalf and overlooked the duplicity. I mitigated my dishonesty by wearing an expensive pin-striped suit, as successful professionals do. The clients loved me and in the end saved money, as evidenced in the form of a Treasury refund check.

"And what's happening now? We're driving on a Detroit free-way to the airport. All governmental entities are racing head-to-head for the title of biggest thief. Percentage-wise, Detroit won. The gov-ernment lackeys went bankrupt. They didn't have a printing press stored in some out-of-the-way warehouse, while diverting money into offshore banks. Talk about manipulation. The federal reserve did it by pumping money into the investment banking houses to bid up the stock market. A multitude of sins can be forgiven. They saw Detroit as a big loser and stopped sending money to cover the losses. Christ, I should forget about comedy and become a politician."

Margarita awoke to the remark, "Will there be any notable ce-lebrities on the cruise?"

"None that I'm aware of. And if there is one connected with the state of Michigan, I'll start an investigation into how the fare was paid."

"You're disgustingly good, and I wouldn't expect anything less. I know you check up on my spending. When I hear you say, 'M, was that dress you bought really necessary?' I know the Haralson version of the IRS has audited me."

"I'll be turning onto the airport exit soon."

Alexander and Margarita traveled light. A small suitcase filled with underwear, jogging suits, and swimsuits was all.

Margarita moved closer to Alexander and licked his ear. "This isn't a pleasure cruise for nudists, is it?"

"No, but good grief, the way you're talking, I might have to stop at the next motel."

"Control yourself. We'll be on board the ship soon enough."

"You're right. As much as I'd like to stop, the thought of parking your car in a cheap motel parking lot scares me. I don't want anything to happen to it. Can you imagine when we leave the room and find the car dismantled? This is not the place to call for help."

"Yeah, I remember now. Did something happen to your BMW?"

"A run-in with locals did her in."

"Hmm. If you say so, darling."

"Thanks for the forgiveness."

"By the way, turn your cell phone off until we get to Florida. I want your sister to get the voicemail greeting. We're sending a message. We're not turning back."

"What's Lunetta supposed to do with Roberta if she can't get her under control?"

"Tell her to drop the little darling off at the pound."

"You sure know how to win friends."

"Darling, I'm not naive. For now, it's hard to believe the bumpy roads we're on lead to paradise."

"I sense you're planning to go back into comedy."

"Maybe with you laughing at my jokes. As a clack, you'll split everyone's side. You could do it, honey."

Alexander called Delta Airlines on his cell phone. With one hand on the wheel and the other on the phone, he found out the plane was running about a half hour behind schedule. He let out a breath of relief. "For the first time in a long time I'm relieved the plane's running late."

"I know you're a stickler, but no need to bust a gut. I checked the information about the cruise line. We're booked on the *Costa Classica.*"

"I knew you wanted an Italian cruise ship."

"Thank you, dear. You'll be glad to know that Captain Schettino will not be the officer in charge."

"And Captain Schettino is who?"

"The officer who captained the *Costa Concordia* and capsized it onto rocks hugging the shoreline."

"Would you like me to call the captain and suggest he keep his full attention on navigating the seas versus navigating to the bar to pick up dames?"

"Alexander, you have such a way with words."

"And I'll tell him an Italian food critic is on board."

"Thank you, dear."

"I'm glad I brought along a food critic."

"Don't get smug… and wipe off that stupid grin."

"Wow, the world will never read about us in a detective novel. We aren't into discussing murder, robbery, or adultery."

Margarita glared for a split second at Alexander and said dramatically, "That's daytime TV talk show and soap opera stuff. At our age, it's past tense."

Margarita and Alexander had married for the best of reasons, besides being in love. Their partnership would function by each putting the concerns of the other above their own. Wasn't that what love was all about? Each knew the strengths and weaknesses of the marriage. The challenge was to keep it intact, come what might from the vicissitudes of life. At the moment, their daughter Roberta, without any formal training, showed how to effectively wrench a parent's gut. As a solution, Margarita and Alexander clubbed each other instead of adopting a common course in disciplining Roberta.

There were other obstacles. Did the marriage vow 'for better or worse' allow a path for Alexander to walk around and define his persona? Did the change allow leeway to tell audiences about his crazy wife when he acted the role of a nut and a cheating husband? Were Margarita's responsibilities limited to standing back and putting up with the reinvented Alexander? She told him, "Gays may come out of a closet. But houses have more than one type of closet. You, my dear, emerged from the one marked *Meshuggah*."

As they neared the airport, Margarita sensed Alexander's intentions. She told him, "I want a new life. You found comedy. I want to find myself. I'm throwing an olive branch. All past indiscretions are forgiven. I don't want to even hear about them." Alexander hadn't meant to stir the pot with his adultery remark. But he didn't regret saying 'adultery.' His brain was unharnessed, and he couldn't shut his mouth. Alexander should have known Margarita knew about his past indiscretions. She knew some of his clients' wives, whom she had referred to as 'tramps' after a client dinner. "I didn't like the way Felicia rubbed your shoulder," she had said.

"She backed away when you asked her where she had found out I had bursitis."

In Alexander's practice, the husband was always the breadwinner, but the spouse's signature on a tax form was critical. In some instances, due to a husband's work schedule taking him out of town, and at the wife's request, Alexander had pitched in as a substitute in the husband's marital duties department.

Margarita had no inkling about Flossy. She was his love, serving time in prison while he went on a cruise. Alexander could be devious. According to him, somebody had to go to prison and somebody had to live it up on a cruise. He imagined her release date would be the sixteenth of April. The prison doors would open. So would the door to a nearby motel room.

Alexander could kick himself for suggesting Margarita join the comedy group. Don't dance around, he told himself. Finagle Margarita into numbness. What a delicious word. The trip's purpose would be to regroup his comedy act.

At the moment, Alexander dreaded Margarita leaning toward him, muzzling him, and saying, "I've always been faithful to you." His inner demons danced in hysterics. Let's see you finagle out of this, they mocked. Alexander tried praying. *Christ, I really do need a shrink*, he thought. He dreaded the thought that Margarita slept around. Imagine me saying that about my wife. You mean you were a tramp like Lenny Bruce's wife?

Alexander couldn't make the faithful statement to Margarita. *What do I do? I hate lying, except to the Internal Revenue Service.* He wondered if the manly thing might be to jump off the ship.

On the plane, Alexander waited for Margarita to say something. The silence needed to be ended and the noise from the dropping anvil heard. Was the fat lady ready to sing?

Thank God for widows and divorcees, of whom many were clients. They were the honeybees roaming the pasture for the nectar of a rich new husband. To sign up for a matchmaking service was gutless. Follow Helen Gurley Brown's advice: "Let your body do the talking." Many widows and divorcees were sex-starved. Intentions were private, and a classified ad would be tacky. Overstated personal wealth, overstated career success, and overstated family functionality described every eligible male or female's personal data. Credentials were inflated by one hundred percent. Harvest time occurred every day. Forget the notion you had to wait until fall to be considered ripe to pick.

With Flossy, it was a perfect landing in bed. Her bells pealed. Her whistles shrieked at a pitch so high, only Alexander could hear. They were the control tower way of telling him he was on course.

Widows signaled interest by the tightness of the condolence hugs. Alexander had received many such squeezes that seemed lacking in sincerity for the husband. A gravelly voice saying "Please call me next week" certainly didn't tag the rest of the sentence… "so we can discuss inheritance tax matters." Christ, the old man's not even buried, and the widow's in heat. Alexander didn't see himself as the most handsome guy in the world. The metaphysical nectars emanating from his body were on automatic pilot. The inner devil smiled at Alexander's diabolical self. That hit the nail squarely.

Paradise came into view as the plane approached the landing strip. Outside the window, blue skies beamed, and palm tree fronds rustled. The ocean surf rolled with whitecaps, leading the charge into the beaches. Alexander showed his cell phone to Margarita, saying, "Dare I turn on the phone and check for messages?"

Margarita smiled. "Don't you dare."

A waiting cab hustled them through traffic to the pier where the cruise ship was berthed. Passing through security, the next stop was the cruise ship's desk to check in before boarding. Afterward, Alexander and Margarita wheeled the one suitcase they'd brought toward the gangplank. A photographer on the gangway officially commemorated the occasion, clicking away at a family with smiles and clinking champagne glasses. Ah, the good life. Adventures outside their everyday lives awaited.

On viewing the family with a keener look, Alexander's stress level began to rise again. His head bleeped an alarm. His thoughts turned existential. *Why?* he thought. God rested on the seventh day, but mysteriously kept the forces of mayhem constantly in motion. The Sabbath, his vacation, was planned to evolve into a slow news day. But nothing ever went along with God's grand scheme. Instead, things always happen at the oddest times. A universal law held that God is under no obligation to wait until you finish your round of golf before initiating a fatal heart attack.

Alexander whimpered to himself, *holy shit*. He recognized Odetta Flanken and Gregory, her husband, as the family being photographed. At the gangplank edge, he stood motionless lamenting God's cruelty. I thought I'd be taking a cruise without any interference. I'm ready to take my first step onto a floating pleasure palace, and I get hit with a left hook. God, couldn't you have booked the Flankens on another cruise line or a cruise leaving next week? You know, this is all your fault. Hatcher gave me the assignment to learn more about her. Couldn't it have waited? And you, dear God, know I have a heart condition. I need rest, and you throw a monkey wrench at me. I'll bet you're laughing, aren't you?

Alexander stared at the Flankens and thought, *Look at you. Mr. and Mrs. Parents of the Year. You darlings even brought your two children with you.*

Margarita came over to Alexander. "Is something wrong?"

"Right now, the happiest thing would be to learn that we are at the wrong pier."

Margarita looked up the gangplank and glanced at the Flankens ahead of them. "Alex, let's go aboard. I'll get you a drink. You need to calm down and explain why you're suddenly so upset."

Chapter Six

ALEXANDER LOOKS AND SOUNDS LIKE
HE'S GOING TO JUMP

Alexander and Margarita were walking up the gangplank to board the ship when, about halfway, a photographer greeted them. With his arms spread, he attempted to corral them toward a scenic spot for a picture.

"Easy, cowboy," asserted Alexander. "We put on clean clothes this morning," he added when he spotted the nametag "Rocco."

Rocco quickly withdrew.

"How often do you wash your hands? They're filthy."

"I can assure signore my hands are clean."

"Ah, a man pretending to be honest. Rocco, how many *happy* faces came aboard today?"

"Everyone, signore."

"Rocco, scratch one hundred percent. Look at me. This is what a miserable face looks like."

"I am sure signore will smile when I pose him with his arm around his dear signora."

"Are you a betting man?"

Rocco mumbled at first and decided to keep quiet.

"Rocky, when and where will all of today's pictures of the lovebirds be displayed?"

"In the hallway leading to the casino, early tomorrow morning."

"*Grazie.*" Alexander took Margarita's arm and led her toward the ship's entrance. She turned around and shrugged her shoulders at the photographer.

"I'm ready to cruise."

"As am I, darling."

Their suitcase was checked at the registration desk, and they were told it should be in their cabin within an hour. Once they were onboard, Margarita said, "Ah, the Blue Grotto Lounge. Let's go in for a drink and relax." They walked in, sat, and placed their orders with a waitress. "Alexander, will you tell me what is the matter? It took one minute after getting out of the cab for you to become unglued."

"I saw a couple I know, whom I'd prefer not to include as my fellow passengers. Her name is Odetta Flanken, and her crooked political fund-raising husband is Gregory. Hatcher mentioned last week that Mrs. Flanken has emerged from an underground crypt and hatched a lifelong ambition to run for governor in the next election. He assigned me the job of fact-finding all her political warts when we return home. Now, the operative expression 'when we return home' has been rendered *kaput*."

"So you saw her. That's no reason you have to stalk her while on vacation."

"Should I lie to Hatcher and say that we didn't meet anyone? I prayed we wouldn't meet anyone we knew. No such luck. I've met Gregory at charity events. He knows who I am, and we'll be acknowledging each other along the way. We may even engage in a duel. Word that we saw each other will get back to Hatcher. Right now, I feel violated and spied upon."

"Darling, I plan to do whatever I want. I suggest you do the same."

"I hope we're not seated with them at the same dining room table."

"Oh, I'd love that. Imagine, two hot-blooded women jousting for interest in the same man."

"Me?"

"Darling, you are a prize. I've seen some of your female clients show most unusual interest in you. They always lead with an overdone smile."

"My mistake. Poor Gregory. It seems he'll be doing the babysitting with Odetta spending her time making a play for me. Believe me, she doesn't need to search for campaign donors among the passengers to put money in a campaign war chest. She's drowning in money from her husband's net worth and her union's PAC funds."

The waitress arrived with their drinks. They toasted a happy voyage and that Alex's blood pressure would return to normal.

"Alex, let's finish our drinks and inspect our room. Then we'll come back on deck to say 'bon voyage.' And maybe see my competition waving goodbye with a toothy smile."

"M, I can't wait to see you in action."

* * *

Upon opening the door to their stateroom, they saw a queen-sized bed, a sitting area that included footrests with the chairs, and a bathroom with a shower and jacuzzi.

"Alex, this room is wonderful. You must let the travel agent know that the suite made me very happy."

"M, you're right. I thought the room would be the size of a closet, like in older cruise ships where you were forced to sleep in a fetal position. Not anymore. Everything has expanded, even prison cells." Alexander regretted this remark as soon as he'd uttered it. The medication or a medical condition to be diagnosed on his next doctor's visit served as his excuse to himself.

"Prison cells. How did you know that?" asked Margarita.

Flossy had told Alexander many facts about prisons that he'd never known. He suddenly realized the comparison with cruise ship cabins was perfect. "As budget director, you discover new avenues where money was spent or needs to be spent. Americans are concerned about the comfort of prisoners. Can't have the world thinking we're mean by putting criminal politicians inside cells, sleeping on wooden mattresses. Anyway, I saw the state's budget from last year.

Included was replacing the older, non-clogging toilets that flush human waste in a jiffy into the sewer system. Kohler's state-of-the-art
crapper, currently on sale for $625 each, features a quiet and more ef-
ficient flushing system. That means less water used because the waste
remains in suspension. It's a stinky smell until a plumber arrives to
clean out the sewer system. My salesman pitch would say, 'What the
toilet lacks in efficiency, it makes up in design. It's a piece of furniture
you could proudly show off to your family and friends. Install one in
your living room.' What we do for our crime denizens amazes me."

Margarita looked at the stateroom's toilet.

"Yes M. This ship's facilities are A-one. But the prison's toilets
are far better. They hold steady when a fat ass plops down. Let's take
a walk around the ship."

A nonplused Margarita commented, "I hope what you said was
a joke."

"No, it wasn't. I'll tell you when it's a joke."

Alexander and Margarita walked about the ship and found various attractions. They passed the casino, pool area, fitness center,
Topsider Bar and Grille, La Cuisina restaurant, Stardust Theater, and
the computer room. Alexander had brought a computer key fob. It
contained last year's state of Michigan budget files and the proposed
budget for the next fiscal year. Alexander did not need to spring a
lie on Margarita and carry a computer on board. She was under the
impression that Alexander would avoid working while on the cruise.
But Alexander had other plans. A quick peek at the financial numbers he'd seen suggested someone had increased the prison budget
for a payoff at the end. Discrepancies in every category of the state
prison budget were off the charts. The toilets ordered for the reno-
vation amounted to about twenty-five percent more toilets than the
amount needed for existing prison cells. Hatcher had ordered Alexander to lower the overall budget by ten percent, but the numbers
he'd reviewed before leaving home showed a budget increase of
seven to eight percent. Someone was pulling a fast one, and Alexander was not happy. He murmured, "I'll find the *gonef*. Overspending
isn't a murder mystery."

* * *

They found a convenient spot against the railings where they could see the ship's mooring lines loosened and secured inside the ship. There was no fanfare when the ship moved away from the dock and drifted into the channel leading to the ocean. The only observers were some nearby passengers.

"I miss the foghorns and well-wishers who lined the docks throwing streamers," commented Margarita.

"I remember the times when we left Italy for home. It was a big event when ships left port. A tugboat pulled you away from the dock and positioned the ship straight toward the channel. Everyone stayed, waving goodbye until the ship's berth was out of sight."

"What's everyone doing now?"

"Headed to the dining room to find their table number. What I'm doing is admiring the water. It's a paved road on which inclement weather resembles a thoroughfare full of potholes."

* * *

After the ship exited the channel, Margarita and Alexander went directly to the dining room to learn their seating arrangements for dining. They were assigned to table four, with seating for six, which would include the Haralsons from Birmingham, the Crowleys from Baltimore, and the Fajistus from Atlanta. Satisfied with the arrangements, Alexander asked the maître d' where the Flankens were seated. He checked his seating chart and said they were to be seated at table eleven. Alexander looked about and spied a card holder on a table that read "11." He was relieved at the distance between their tables. Margarita asked the maître d', since she was born Italian, as was the captain, and as the ship was an Italian liner, what night they could expect to be invited to sit at the captain's table?

He answered, "The way you look, my dear, I would expect the captain will be pleased any night."

Alexander looked at the maître d' saying, "M, I'm sure the captain will have sensual thoughts, asking if you might want something

harder than liquor." Alexander leaned toward the maître d', looking
for his name tag. "Am I right, Alfredo?" They stared at each other
for a minute before Alfredo lowered his gaze.

* * *

Alexander and Margarita walked to their stateroom to unpack, wash
up, and change clothes. They had plenty of sweat to wash off from
the effort spent to get Roberta to Lunetta's house, the effort spent
rushing to the airport to catch a plane, the effort spent from an anx-
iety attack because certain despised fellow passengers were aboard,
and the effort spent getting agitated because an oversexed Italian
captain was steering the ship. Sitting on the edge of the bed, Alexander had the additional task of thinking about who might be stealing
money from the state. The early on-board relaxation he'd imagined
was melting away at a rapid rate.

Alexander's thoughts of his failing comedy act added to his
self-pity. He imagined a wanted poster with his picture hung in
every Starbucks Coffee location, with a simple message: "WARN-
ING! If you see this man doing a comedy routine, do not laugh at
his jokes. Instead, call the police." Alexander was well aware he'd
heard hissing and booing at recent gigs. At first, Alexander attributed the negative reactions as an aberration. He reasoned the act had
kinks that needed to be massaged. When the reactions turned to
silence and yawning, he fully realized how badly he performed as
a comedian. His style had changed to insulting audiences and stir-
ring up the dormant hatred that smoldered in their guts. Audience
anger reached him with calls of "You bum," and "I want a refund."
No one was unaffected. The residents of the nursing home gig had
shaken their fists with the last gasp of reserved strength God had
saved for them before dying. Even the loving pet dog, Laser, hated him in the end. Word about his disastrous gigs had got around
town. Organizations and clubs one by one labeled him a *persona
non grata* and canceled appearances. Graphically, Alexander's career resembled the buggy whip sales chart in its last throes, nose
diving before impact.

Alexander kicked himself for opportunities he'd let pass him by. I should have bought a comedy club or a comedy school when my career began to flop. I should have bought The Zug Island Club or the HA-HA Comedy School. What was I thinking? Hatcher would have strong armed the owners into selling it to me. Or Alexander could have started a club from scratch. Alexander and Margarita had vacationed in Palm Springs, California, many times. There was a theater named the Follies, whose performers were required to be over eighty years old. The owner was Riff Markowitz, a comedian who headlined the variety show. He was hilarious. I could have duplicated his format in Detroit, thought Alexander morosely. A comedy club along Eight Mile Road would have fit in alongside all the nude bars running in both directions. His mind drifted and he fantasized about putting Flossy in charge of the entire operation. Was there still a chance to do that?

Even while suffering from the negative fallout, Alexander's long-term plan did not include the compromise of planting his ass in his recliner and operating a controller to change the TV channels. To Alexander, TV was a placebo. He thought himself a go-getter. Ideas of becoming a politician as his next venture danced in his head. His destiny, he told himself, was to change into a lying politician, which would bring him success. From the newspapers, he saw how politicians viewed and treated their constituents. They spoke down to them as mental illiterates. "My friends, if you want to read about recorded world history, you'll find it printed on the label of your favorite beer can."

Alexander's spirits sank. With all his knowledge and abilities, was there anything worthwhile he could accomplish? Why not agree to volunteer for charity work? Why not play more golf? Alexander loved the game. He shrugged in despair when he recalled how much more he'd loved the game when friends and family were alive and able to meet him at the first tee. His vista revolved in an era of decline. Others, with mended hips and knees, had retired from the game and taken up pushing a walker. Some had moved away to retirement destinations—cemeteries, hospital cardiac care units, nursing homes, or hospices. To Alexander's way of thinking, charity work was handing out brochures at a meeting or making phone calls to solicit money. He'd reduce his efforts to writing sizable checks, as long as he didn't have to solicit for an organization.

He recalled family members—parents, aunts, uncles, and cousins—who'd died in a steady stream, and whom he'd cherished. They were the ones in a crowd who saw Margarita, the children, and me off on our trans-Atlantic trips. Left with great memories of playing baseball with friends, hearing family stories at dinner, listening to life values being stressed as most important, or being taken to a Tigers' game had made Alexander into a man. What am I to do with myself? he wondered despondently. The vacant hole took the place of buoyed, cherished, and loved remembrances. It seemed his children, the educated older ones, didn't want to hear about the family anymore. They laughed, saying the older family members were insufferable, overbearing, and dysfunctional. His social worker daughter's quip, "They were bums," instantly summed up her view of the Haralson family's roots. Where did that leave Alexander? Who in the world could he tell about his happy earlier life? Alexander loved those bums. They were drinkers, something Alexander admired.

Alexander had lived the high life. His career in accounting accelerated after college graduation. He'd cultivated clients and grown his practice. His reputation earned high fees, some paid on the couch in his office. Some female clients even willingly paid extra for Alexander's spectacular tax services. The happy ending of his story line was satisfied clients.

Other business professionals abandoned careers at midlife. He knew one such person, Freed, who'd thrown his professional life in the trash to live a happier one eating pineapples and growing pot for a living. On one occasion, Alexander and Margarita visited him in a dense Hawaiian jungle. On observing him in all his natural glory, Alexander asked Freed, "When was the last time you took a shower?" The response from the dope smoker was, "Shit, I don't remember, maybe three years ago." Alexander believed him. The dirt caked to his skin looked permanent. Freed's crusted beard and caveman hairdo made him look like the Hawaiian mountain '*Schmuutzman*,' as Alexander referred to him, a Yiddish word translating as 'pig-pen' in English. Freed had felt insulted. "Alexander, use my correct name. It's now 'Hikaru.' In Japanese, that means radiance."

Alexander had looked at Margarita and said, "I think we should leave Hikaru to his air pollution." They immediately said their good-byes. Alexander always commented to friends that Freed had hit the skids, but secretly envied seeing the guy's new-found happiness.

Alexander stated a lamentation he carried in his head. It was addressed to Freed. "Dear Lord, you let this human being's soul fall through a crack into a mud pot. He landed in Oz and morphed into a pig's life of believing himself superior, while we're slopping about with fat bank accounts and justice on our side."

Alexander walked out on deck as his head churned with all the noxious events of life. Perhaps it was the rocking motion of the ship's slow trajectory on the choppy water that echoed the unsettled state of his own mind. As he stood by himself on the ship's deck, looking back at the shoreline, he felt it was a metaphor for his own increasing alienation from reality. The setbacks he'd experienced were proving to be impediments, metaphorical clogged arteries. If they'd represented his lifeblood, Alexander would be in a hospital coronary care unit, with doctors injecting him with medical fables.

Alexander wished he could replace the past. What fell through the cracks were aunts, uncles, siblings, and parents, all of whom were dearly missed. He couldn't deny what they'd meant to him. He ruminated that they'd paid attention to him. He was included when they played baseball or went to a Tigers' game. They took him on trips to visit relatives in other cities. They concerned themselves about his schooling, asking what he was studying. They'd encouraged him to succeed.

Then one day it was like they went away and never returned. It wasn't abandonment, just life's rotten realities. Growing up and death had combined to cement the separation. Now that they were all gone, where was he supposed to go? Establishing new relationships with a wife, children, grandchildren, and business associates filled the gap, which felt funny. Weren't the old timers relatives? Did he have to relearn how to be in a family? The old friends had gone the funeral home route. Where were the new friendships to be made and nurtured? How do you make friends with trust fund babies? If there was a common thread that brought old friends together, it was that they all went down the path of hard work and study. Alexander Haralson had started near the bottom, risen to a high level in life, and learned the tools of his trade, believing all this would ensure happiness and financial security for him, forever.

Flossy was the person who'd awoken Alexander, made him realize the path to happiness was to pioneer into an underground life of rednecks, drunks, country music, worn-out jeans, a customized dragster, and a trailer to call home. All he really needed was a woman who could shoot a gun, cook crispy fried chicken, and turn the bedroom into a playground. Blacks, Indians, and asians were rejected by Alexander. Collard greens, curry, and egg foo young were not favorite foods.

Chapter Seven

ALEXANDER AND MARGARITA
SIT DOWN FOR SUPPER

Margarita and Alexander entered the dining area and were greeted by Alfredo, the maître d'. The chandeliers above them shimmered in opulence as he welcomed them with a short bow and asked if the ship's accommodations met their satisfaction. "Yes," was the dual response from Alexander and Margarita. Alfredo thanked the Haralsons and ordered an assistant to escort them to their seats. Starched white table cloths and sparkling silverware were subtly complemented by a single white orchid at the centre of each table. The theme was expensive, tasteful elegance. On the walk over, Alexander had glanced toward table eleven. Only one couple was already seated, the Flankens not yet having arrived. Alexander and Margarita were the last to arrive at their own table. The process of introductions managed itself agreeably. It began and concluded with handshakes, smiles, and comments of "So glad to meet you." Alexander and Margarita were hungry after a difficult day of final arrangements and travel. In casual conversation, it seemed the other couples were in a similar mood.

The table learned that Gordon Crowley was a retired corporate attorney whose family included three children and five grandchildren. Gordon's face was a bit ruddy, but he looked overall in good health. The Fajistus were Japanese-Americans. Hideo, Alexander estimated, was in his mid-fifties. He worked for General Electric as a VP in charge of the electrical engineering department. Alexander sat in a bit of a quandary. What was he to say about himself? A recovering heart attack patient, the state of Michigan's budget director, or a comedian whose career was about to crash and burn? Or tell everyone, "Margarita and I have a dysfunctional family with two grown children and a five-year-old mistake for a younger daughter. We love her so much we decided to leave her with my wife's sister." Alexander played it safe. He said he'd retired from accounting but had been hired by the governor of Michigan to manage the state's finances.

A glance at table eleven saw Gregory, Odetta Flanken, and their children about to be seated. Margarita noticed Alexander looking across at them. He said in a low voice to Margarita, "I don't see a toothy smile."

It was Hideo who captured Alexander's attention.

"Detroit is in Michigan?"

Alexander nodded.

Hideo first laughed and then in a giggly voice commented that he'd read about the city of Detroit's precarious state of affairs. "I've read newspapers. The mayor sounded like a crook. Ha, ha, ha."

"You used the word precarious in referring to its finances. I agree with you. Everyone's a crook. I'm new to the job, an apprentice crook-in-training. Everyone claims that in a short time I'll advance to a journeyman-professional crook. In the short term I've been in my position, I can see that stealing money is easy. Controls are almost non-existent. What bothers me is that nobody cares. It's steal, steal, steal, then spend, spend, spend. Detroit's most endearing and descriptive motto best describes its essence—Murder Capital of the World. Being killed in a drive-by shooting is the equivalent of dying from natural causes."

Heido's expression changed from animated curiosity to seriousness.

Alexander continued. "Don't feel bad, my friend. The number of murders has declined. It directly correlates with the size of the city's population."

Gordon Crowley interrupted. "How can the city expect to make a comeback?"

"It doesn't. The plan is to retain the status quo by electing bubbling idiots who'll continue to wreck the city, unless an all-out civil war begins and wrecks it in a shorter period of time. My job is to recommend ways for the governor to improve the business climate. As director of the budget, I've made several suggestions such as to encourage compartmentalized businesses. Have someone start up a new minor league team and name it the Detroit Deadbolts. Or open a new cleaning business and name it the Detroit Money Laundering Company. Or open a tool shop named the Detroit Machine Gun Emporium."

"Are you serious?"

"Yes. Gordon, Americans have no idea how bad the conditions in Detroit are. There is no other city in North America that compares. Every street has abandoned homes or vacant lots—structures with stately designs that stand like gravestones in cemeteries. Burned out homes aren't safe. Homeless people, drug addicts, and prostitutes live inside this cancerous environment. Imagine a city gentrified by thugs using matches. Schools are training grounds for gangs. The only jobs available for teenaged children are drug dealers and pimps. The best thing for Detroit would be for the undertaker to close the lid on its coffin, take it to Woodmere Cemetery, and bury it. Detroit could join and revel in eternal bliss with all the crooks that have sapped its guts of strength."

Dampened by this passionate diatribe, the table's conversation quieted for a few minutes.

A voice interrupted the momentary silence. "Hello, Alexander."

Alexander looked up and saw Gregory Flanken. "Greg, what a surprise. Are you on this cruise?" Margarita turned to look in Greg's direction. "Margarita, I don't know if you've ever met Gregory Flanken."

"No." With her best smile, Margarita said, "I'm very happy to meet you."

Alexander scanned the dining room. "I see Odetta is seated with your children, and another couple is sitting at your table. Who are they? Some precious leftovers from a democratically controlled homeless shelter you brought along to stir meaningful table conversation?"

Gregory's face turned angry.

"Greg," responded Alexander, in full creative flow, "let's not slow down. Meet the Crowleys and Fajistus. We were just talking about Detroit."

Alexander stood and faced Hideo. "Meet the man who opened the door for World War Two Japanese retribution by allowing Toyotas and Hondas to be imported. Thanks to Greg's efforts, your low-cost manufacturers have been allowed to undercut our automobile and electronics industry, while American manufacturing is being choked by imposed regulations." Alexander faced Greg. "Oh, Greg, their TV sets are so lovable. Personally, I would have granted Japan retribution by allowing them to drop an atomic bomb on Detroit and call it even."

Obviously offended, Greg Flanken turned away and headed back to his table. Alexander faced his own table and announced he had a second job—moonlighting as a comedian. He sat down.

"It's no surprise that we are on politically opposite sides. Greg's political party ran Detroit for seventy-five years, with every job occupied by a member of his party who swore an oath to steal as much as possible from the city's treasury. I'm disgusted and angry with him. He made sure poor residents slept on park benches outside in the cold. The state gave Detroit money to help, but it was never spent or given to those in need. Greg was the bag man, seeing that his rich friends became richer. I'm going to see that Greg is put in jail."

Gordon Crowley said, "Wow. I read stories about how badly Detroit had deteriorated. Your description paints an awful picture."

"Visit Detroit. I'll give you a personal tour."

"Uh... thanks."

Alexander picked up on Gordon's apprehension. "Don't worry, I'll see that we're escorted by security."

* * *

The following morning Alexander looked out the window and saw it was sunny. He shook Margarita. "It's the same routine, as if we're home. You don't cook breakfast. How about going to the dining room?"

Margarita was notably silent as she got out of bed and dressed to sit by the pool. They covered their swimsuits with jogging outfits to wear inside the dining room. Margarita turned to confront him. "Alex, how many more people are you planning to insult today?"

"My dear, as many as will listen to me. By the way, I have no intention of making light of the passengers. What I'm seeing are older persons with walkers, canes, and oxygen tanks. By comparison with my heart condition, I'm in perfect health. Let's walk for about a half hour after breakfast."

"Good idea."

The Flankens were not at breakfast when Alexander and Margarita were seated. "I see your enemies are recovering from the aftershock of your bombing raid last night."

"Maybe they jumped off the ship."

Margarita shook her head in disbelief.

Hideo and his wife were at the table. The Haralsons and Fajistus talked casually without any bombs being thrown. They finished breakfast and went their separate ways.

Alexander and Margarita walked the ship's circuit for about a half hour. When finished, Alexander said he felt great. "I'm going to the computer room to check on e-mails. The casino is right down the hall."

"Alex, don't you want to see the picture gallery?"

"Yes. Let's see if we can find the Flankens."

They searched and found the picture.

Alexander spoke first. "The family looks happy. I'm sure they're practicing posing for campaign pictures. Looking good supersedes plans to bury the state."

"Hatcher must not like her."

"I don't think it's her. She seems pleasant for a liberal. It's her husband. He's a bastard."

"Is he Jewish?"

"If you mean is he a stereotyped money-grubbing individual the answer is yes. His Sunday Sabbath follows the ritual of eating a bagel with Philadelphia Cream Cheese and lox. He celebrates Passover, passing over any jewelry purchases. He's a *goy* in drag."

"You sound as if Scrooge took lessons from him."

"In the end, Scrooge changed. Greg Flanken will never change."

"Do you think Michigan will elect a black woman for governor?"

"Yes. And Hatcher knows that better than anyone. She speaks intelligently, with a little bit of a melodic voice. She's smart—a graduate from the U of M. She has a teaching degree. And yes, she's a bit plumpish but not oversized."

"I'll bet she can put you in your place."

"She's probably got a good haymaker she learned from Abe Haralson. Let's meet up in an hour by the pool. See you later."

Alexander left Margarita and entered the computer room. It had about twenty-fve computers, with seven or eight people already typing or reading. Alexander signed in, plugged in his thumb drive, and brought up the state's finance files on the screen.

As a good accountant, Alexander Haralson could put values to assets. He could also put income and expense numbers to any company's operations. He knew construction costs to build roads. And nobody understood costs better. Calling him a pawn broker, an appraiser, an estimator of manufacturing, defined him to a T.

Alexander had an inkling Hatcher wanted to run for public office at some point in his career. Alexander told Hatcher the company books had to be believable. If someone found out about cheating, his political career would immediately end.

What came out on the computer screen was a corrupt Robert Hatcher. Alexander hadn't worked on the state's account while he was ill. Whatever accounting mischief Hatcher and the previous governor had unleashed was now obvious to the bloodhound Alexander Haralson. He knew that Hatcher had appointed him because of Alexander's good name. What Alexander saw on the computer screen was the Chicago format of distributing project costs. A third went to the construction companies, a third to the government officials who voted to screw the taxpayer, and a third to the man who planned and executed the financing—Robert Hatcher.

Hatcher had ballooned the budget to get a better payday and collect the past money he'd missed receiving while Alexander had him on the straight and narrow. Alexander could feel the blood flowing faster through his neck arteries. He grumbled in a low voice, "That mother-fucker. He made all that money from paving, and now he's out to steal more. He's making Kwame look like a saint."

"Hello, Alexander, you don't look happy. Are you all right?"

Alexander looked up and saw Odetta Flanken. "Yes. I'm fine. I dread thinking about the workload that will have piled up while I was gone."

"Greg told me you are the new state budget director."

"That's true. If you want to talk about the education budget, there's no need. I'm planning to slash it in half."

Odetta gave Alexander a suspicious look.

"Don't worry. It won't be that bad. But I do plan to cut budgets in all departments. Detroit's finances are impacting cities and counties across the state. If Detroit could come out of bankruptcy and be run in a professional manner, all manner of good would emerge, especially for the school system."

"The school system is performing respectably."

"If by 'respectably' you mean overspending your budget and raising taxes to meet obligations, you're going to need to present a very persuasive outline. I have no intention of proposing to borrow money or raise taxes to make ends meet. There are many school districts outside of southeast Michigan that are doing well. They stay within their spending limits, and the children are adequately taught the basics to perform well on state exams. You've got competition. Charter schools are eating your lunch."

"You've got your defenses up."

"I'd say I'm ready to land a haymaker."

* * *

Margarita had wrangled a place at the captain's table with some elderly Americans, stuffy Europeans, and a lively South American couple. Alexander's head was spinning, sorting out all the different languages spoken. English was spoken with Spanish, British, and German accents. The captain showcased rotting teeth and flirted shamelessly with Margarita in Italian. The only native English speakers besides themselves were the Flankens. They were seated at the opposite end of the table, not that they preferred to be seated closer. It was torturous to converse, and the food in Alexander's view was pig slop. Yummy White Castle sliders danced in his head. The level of conversation sickened him. He could no longer sit amongst the drivel that fell from their mouths like geriatric gravy. He waited for a calm moment to excuse himself.

The waiter placed a fruity mass of dessert in front of him and, without being thanked, said, "Prego." *Why can't they wait till you thank them*, thought Alexander. Sons of bitches. Alexander imagined the cruise coming to an end, and he felt horrified by the prospect of returning to his life in Birmingham where more of this awaited him. Two more nights floating on a calm sea, a luminous expanse of beauty accented with warm temperatures, would soon change from unbounded fantasy back into snorting, humdrum reality. He already felt the stress building in the center of his chest and neck. When he returned home and picked up Roberta from Lunetta's kid-pound, did he expect his little daughter would hug him and say, 'Daddy, I missed you?' For damn sure Roberta wouldn't. He could expect no better from his son the doctor or his daughter the social worker. Informing them that mother and father had returned home safely and relaxed might bring an 'Oh.' But that was it. Did Alexander expect them to ask how the trip was, how the food was, if their parents had fun? God, no. Bring me a pair of cement shoes, he prayed plaintively.

Alex pushed away from the table, excused himself from the elaborate dessert that looked like psychedelic vomit, and sauntered out of the dining room onto the side deck where lovers stood under lifeboats. He strolled along past the swimming pool to the ship's stern. The warm night was brilliant with stars, and the wake of the ship spread to the misty night horizon, making him think of the life he'd lived before coming on board.

Here he was retired, but he still felt like a boy. The time had passed so rapidly that he wondered if God was cheating him in some way. God, of course, was an accountant like him, who could make numbers do anything. Numbers can part seas and wipe out a generation of firstborn. A life of accountancy, and how nothing but stress. Ach, it made you want to barf!

He wished Flossy was standing here with him right now. She would stand behind him and put her hands up to wipe his tears away. She'd say, "What's upsetting you now, my lovely old fart?" She liked to push her pelvic bone against his buttocks, the same way he would do to her when they stood in queues at the coffee shop. They arced off each other, and he longed for her. He could not stand to think of her sitting in that prison, so instead he thought of his idiotic old cronies in the coffee shop near his house—the one that had banned him after so many years of his patronage. *Prego, prego, prego.* They served crappy coffee anyway. Diarrhea was more interesting than their weak bilge water. In Alexander's imagination, they'd already put up a "Wanted" poster that the old men had taken on a smart phone—the face of a furious Alexander Haralson, photographed while being arrested.

They told me I stank as a comedian. They didn't understand the concept of apprenticeship. They will soon—sons of bitches, stinking geezers with urine-smelling boxers they forgot to change.

* * *

Part of the fun on a cruise meant letting your hair down in front of other passengers. Included was an impromptu performance by passengers arranged by the social director. Doing a short gig, acting completely crazy by playing an instrument, tap dancing, singing a song, or telling jokes—anything to ease the tension, let loose the gases stored inside. The event replaced the regular entertainers who'd earned a day off. Alexander was on a tear. Already crazy, he wanted everyone on board to know it. Maybe he would disembark a relaxed human being, ready to return to whatever challenge life demanded. But that seemed unlikely.

Margarita signed Alexander's name on the performer signup sheet. *Oh, boy, she's got me into a mess*, he thought. *I hope when there aren't any laughs I don't fall down on the floor with another heart attack. I must ask the social director if any former burlesque strippers signed up to perform.*

Doubts seeped into Alexander. What was he supposed to say? Insult members of the audience? Tell them the old Zug Island jokes? Tell them how miserable he felt about his life? Tell them he planned to become Buck, who in *Call of the Wild* transforms from a lazy domestic husky to an Alaskan wolf, howling on a mountainside? He'd found his roots all right. Buck changed from a lazy-assed dog eating canned dog food, into a wolf leaping at someone's jugular. Hey, everyone, I found my roots. I've turned from a lying, cheating family man, into an IRS cheating accountant, to a comedian who can't stand the looks of your overweight bodies and sagging face lifts. The reason I decided to become a comedian? I was inspired by Buck being regenerated from a meek, work-at-nothing pet, whose entire existence consisted of greeting his master and being rewarded with a pat on the head. Then the SOB threw a stick for the next fifteen minutes for him to chase. The other twenty-three hours and forty-five minutes Buck was on his own time to eat, sleep, and find a nearby tree to take a leak.

* * *

When Odetta was introduced, Alexander thought her gait as she walked to the microphone resembled a bowling ball with legs. Her muscular arms had evidently developed during her fist-shaking, union leader speeches. She was well groomed and portrayed a happy and sunny personality. Alexander imagined that in an arm wrestling contest he would be easily tamed. She sang "Summertime" in a coloratura that resonated pleasantly in his head. Alexander surmised her voice training came from years in a church choir. While she sang, he felt his blood pressure lower. When she finished, the audience erupted into applause. She was good. Hatcher would need lessons in everything to compete with her. Alexander would suggest to Hatcher that linking Greg and Odetta Flanken as crooks who stole millions of dollars for personal benefit as the best avenue of attack in the next election. They'd need to do something to undermine her appeal and credibility.

The announcer invited Alexander Haralson, as the next performer, to come to the stage. Alexander showed a confident if sardonic smile as he picked up the cordless mic from its stand. He shaded his eyes to look in the audience. "Is my wife here?"

A "*Si*" came from somewhere behind the bright lights trained on Alexander.

"We had dinner with *el capitan*," he began.

The same female voice shouted provocatively, "That's Spanish. It's *il capitino* in Italian."

"Thank you, dear. As you can see, ladies and gents, I can always rely on my Italian wife. It seems the captain is partial to Italian women. He's been trying to get my wife into a private parlor so he can take some measurements. He wears clothes that are two sizes bigger than his frame. He wants to give an appearance of losing weight, but I wasn't fooled. To cover his wine belly, he's wearing a parachute for clothes.

"Did you know my wife and I wore life preservers to bed last night? These Italian sailors are notorious for running ships aground. A combined women-and-Lambrusco potion make a perfect mixture for veering off course. When the ship tilts and lands sideways on the rocks, the captain acts surprised. His line is, 'I can't tell which way is up.'

"I never understood the waiter doing a war dance on a Caribbean cruise—you know, when the waiter serves food, says '*grazie,*' and bows. Cruising in Europe, wearing top-drawer clothes, the courtesy custom might add to the ambience on the Mediterranean, but this is the Caribbean. A dinner outfit of Bermuda shorts, a Tommy Bahama sport shirt, and athletic dock-siders don't command ritziness."

The audience laughed politely. "You are alive, right? I know the jokes are old. I'm not one of those talented Jewish jokesters who do a fabulous delivery. This is my coming out, a debut to people my own age." Some laughter lit up the room.

"I was in the lounge this afternoon. Let's call it the prune juice saloon. The fun was the people singing with the karaoke machine. That was what I call a show. Seriously deteriorating bodies with stomachs awaiting liposuction operations, trying to croon with the likes of Doris Day and Judy Garland. Men tried to sing along with Bing Crosby's 'White Christmas.' I loved every minute. I'll report to my ear doctor when I return home. There has to be a disease when the thought of your wife's nagging by comparison sounds sweet." Laughs picked up.

"I snuck by the body exercise facilities. No face in this crowd looks familiar. It appears your weight training room was the kitchen. I won't tell anyone. When you return home, tell your friends you lost three ounces." The audience roared.

"I can't thank my wife enough for pointing out this show to me. Everyone asks me where I get material for my shows. Probably no different than any other method star comedians use. They tell stories about experiences that fall outside a world that is normal for you and me but not for the people living in that outside world.

"I must tell you this story. How many people admire a plumber walking through your front door, with wrenches in hand, with clothes smelling of sewer water, his billing meter ticking away at a rate of $175 an hour? Hearing your silence, I'll assume I'm not at a plumber's convention. Let me start over. How many people admire a carpet cleaning jockey walking through your front door with a steam cleaning apparatus, wearing white coveralls? I can see your carpet cleaning consensus prefers a pig sty.

"Me, I prefer the outcome from the plumber's services. Sure, it's nice to have a carpet cleaner brighten the interior, but the plumber wins hands down. You can forgive the plumber's sloppy appearance because afterward your toilet flushes or your sink drains. Running every couple of hours to McDonald's to relieve yourself has to have an end. Did you get the pun 'runs'... an end? I guess not.

"Let me go this route. Don't you feel better knowing appearance plays no role in effectiveness? A short or tall plumber, or a short or tall carpet cleaner makes no difference. You probably haven't noticed you're being fooled by the commercial ads showing a medium-height, clean-cut person carrying the tools of the trade into your house.

"Let me be the first to tell you… the service persons in the pest control ads are not the ones who arrive at your front door. The worker sent to rid your house of pests is not a clean-shaven individual, unless it's a woman. Start with the fact that spraying for bugs does not require a college degree, nor a high school diploma. You could do the work. The tools of the trade are sold at hardware stores and have instructions included. The assumption is you can read. But if you're stuck not understanding the printed word, you call your mechanically inclined brother-in-law to give you a papal interpretation.

"Back to the uneducated, insect disposal service person. The spray they use kills whatever uninvited guests live in your house. You don't see the results of their work. In many ways, it's better not to see carpenter ants lying dead under your expensive inlaid wood floors.

"In my experience, the demeanor of the service person for eradicating insects was most important. In my case, her name was Marge. She was a clean-shaven pest control worker who looked more fitting alternating time between being a pro-football defensive tackler and an artillery gunner carrying seventy-five pound shells to load into a cannon. Marge meant business when she arrived. She carried herself with assurance that *she* was the right person for the job. The fact that she might be a lesbian played no part in my judgment of her. In fact, she brought happiness to our household. Roaches didn't stand a chance with Marge on the job.

"Marge played a Jekyll and Hyde role. The quarterly visits always started with her asking how things were. I told her, 'Nothing unusual. The usual aches and pains and visits to the doctors.' She looked at me with seriousness and asked about spiders, flies, etcetera. I felt stupid trying the same line to elicit a smile every time she arrived. 'Flies live in my office, roaches live in all the bathrooms, and ants are circling the refrigerator.' She flashed a blue light to inspect the house and began dispensing a spray I can only classify as deadly. I left her to quietly go about her work. When she left, she handed me a pen to sign a billing slip. The key to her successful visit was her parting statement, 'Call if you see anything crawling around.'

"There always was. Post Marge, going into the bathroom was a roach convention I needed to break up. I called the pest control company and told them Marge needed to make a repeat visit.

"The operator asked me the type of pest. I told her a roach was scouting around the bathtub for new digs. She needed more clarification, asking what type of insect. Being curious, I'd studied the roach genus on Google. I learned there are German and Oriental types. I told the operator, 'I couldn't tell. They all look the same to me.' I was asked the wing color. Apparently the operator did not connect with my pun, so I replied that the Oriental was yellow, and the German wore a brown shirt. I broke her ensuing silence by repeating my request. 'Honey, just send Marge, ASAP.'

"Well, that afternoon I spotted Marge's truck pulling up the driveway. She was dressed in full combat uniform, down to the combat boots. She carried her spray can assault weapon. I opened the door. She pushed me aside and walked past me with fire in her eyes. Did I mention Marge was less than refined? She roared, 'Let me at 'em' as she marched past.

"I called upstairs. 'M, are you in the bathroom?' A faint reply came back, 'I'm in the bathtub.' I ran upstairs into the bathroom. 'Get out of Dodge. Marge is here.'

"'Who's Marge?'

"'Marge the roach killer, that's who. You'd better move quickly. The roaches, in very short order, will be swimming and running for cover.'

"My wife got out of the tub in a hurry, dressed, and came downstairs to the kitchen, where we waited for Marge to return and tell us the results of her latest roach onslaught. I told my wife Marge's last visit had been overkill, but somehow some roaches still managed to survive. 'Marge does not want to receive another call to come back. The front office might demote her.'

"Marge came into the kitchen and stood in front of us. She declared, 'They're dead.'

"I was afraid to ask the next simple question. But M forged ahead fearlessly. 'Did you clean up after them? You know, the ones that were sprayed?'

"I didn't know if the next funeral was for the roaches or for my wife.

"I stepped in to protect my wife. 'Marge, my wife meant to say, did the roaches check into the roach motel?'

"Marge smiled. 'They sure did.' I saluted her as she exited."

Signaling his finale with a flourish, Alexander waved to his audience. "I've filled my time quota and my bladder. Goodnight folks." And he left the stage.

The applause erupted immediately. Alexander put the mic back in the carriage and made a dash for the men's room, a precipitous exit that did nothing to diminish the din. He beamed a smile of self-satisfaction. Inside the men's room, he walked up face-to-face with the mirror and gazed. He couldn't wipe the smile off his face. He thought *Gosh, Flossy would be proud.*

Alexander went back into the audience to find Margarita. On stage, a pudgy, well-dressed woman began to sing Vera Lynn's blockbuster "We'll Meet Again" to close the show. Alexander found Margarita and sat down.

She grabbed his hand, nuzzled next to him, and whispered, "So this is what you've been doing."

Alexander nodded.

"I'm glad the captain wasn't sitting next to me. I went to the ladies room during dinner and learned '*El Capitan*' has been entertaining other women, particularly American types, before this evening."

"Jesus, stay near a life preserver. That fat pig might actually steer this ship onto the rocks."

The social director went on stage after the last act and thanked all the participants. When the lights came on and everyone stood, many gravitated toward Alexander. The conversation was focused on questions about how long he'd been a comedian, where he'd learned to be one, and who wrote his jokes.

Alexander, not answering directly, shrugged his shoulders, giving everyone a here-and-there answer. He realized a crowd of people wanted to listen to the comedian, not the straight man.

"I can't tell you how much I appreciated your reaction to my jokes. I've played gigs at comedy clubs, but you folks laughed—a first for me. Hell, by this time, they've usually turned me into the garbage dump, with all the food thrown at me. Salad dressing was the only missing ingredient.

"But I'm not going home to pick up where I left off. I'm going home to become a politician."

Everyone began to laugh.

Alexander looked at Margarita. "I think I'm headed in the right direction. I can't wait to get home. Stay here, I'll be back in a minute. I need to say hello to someone."

Chapter Eight

BACK TO WORK

The comedy routine Alexander performed for the cruise passengers rewarded him well. His face would soon be seen in many foreign countries. Many passengers had their smart phones on and had recorded the rising star-comedian's performance. *They'll take it home to show all of their friends*, thought Alexander, triumphantly. An add-on was the selfie everyone wanted with him. He was shocked at having turned into a cruise ship sensation. Passengers could not have known about his disastrous record of comedy gigs at home. Alexander kept that news private. Margarita had been in the dark about his performing. On board a cruise ship, Alexander could pop out of the cake as a hidden talent and in fifteen minutes turn into a comedic star.

Alexander fought off the crowd, looking for Odetta. They spotted each other, walked closer, and greeted with new-found respect. "I came by to say, Odetta, you were great. Inspiring."

"Thank you. And where did you learn to do comedy? You were great also."

"It's a long story for another day. We'll see each other in Lansing." Both paused a moment to take stock of the other. Then Alexander returned to the ongoing congratulatory atmosphere.

Alexander was met with hugs, high fives, and kisses from many women passengers. They chimed, "Alexander, you were fantastic!" and "When are you coming to Arkansas?"

Alexander replied, "I'm going first to meet up with my wife, take her to the bar, and then do some serious drinking. Anyone want to join me?" Cheers erupted with shouts of "We'll join you." Alexander located Margarita, who was standing and waving. In an instant, he ran to her. She nuzzled his ear. "Your oversized ego is showing."

Alexander replied, "My prostate is excited too."

A Red Sea path cleared, and Alexander and Margarita exited the theater arm-in-arm, waving to the crowd. Alexander said to Margarita, "I think we should get plastered. And no drinking any of your sissy Italian wines." When they arrived at the karaoke bar, adoring fans cheered their entrance. Alexander whispered to Margarita, "Once more into the breach."

"Am I in the presence of Shakespeare?"

"Just because I signed off on-stage doesn't mean I can relax. I've got to stay in character and keep the jokes flowing. Pick me up when I collapse from exhaustion."

People, mostly couples with silver hair, kept arriving and showering him with praise. Suddenly, a reality check caused him to mentally pause. "What have I become, a comedic bard?" Alexander attributed his comedic success to a mysterious miracle of divine providence. What had changed? Alexander's obnoxious self had played out a carbon copy of the disastrous gigs performed back home. But this time, he knew the fat lady had finally sung by the applause that roared for him in response. Why search for a reason? Alexander took the ball and ran.

Within minutes, another wave of well-wishers entered and surrounded the Haralsons. Sweat rolled off the busy bartenders. In due time, everyone was drunk. Margarita mingled with men in white officer's suits. Alexander looked in her direction, and mused, "I see the captain sent his lieutenants to steer her to his cabin."

The Italian assemblage broke into laughter in response to something Margarita said. If the laughter continued, Alexander noted, he would have to go over and remind Margarita *he* was the comedian.

The evening rolled into a success. When Alexander took stock of the groupies standing next to him, he realized one had grabbed his legs and slid to the floor in intoxicated adoration. On his hands and knees, he inadvertently barfed on Alexander's pants and shoes. Another drunk grabbed Alexander and stood holding onto him and slobbered drool on his sport shirt. Inspecting his clothes, Alexander pondered that the chances of getting reimbursed for cleaning them was zero. But why care about the cleaning cost? For Alexander, all this was a small price for being adored.

Alexander kept an eye on Margarita's location. He wanted to remain in her field of vision. That way mischief would be in plain view. Alexander saw her emerge from a group, which parted to allow her to go in front and lead them. They were drawn by her sensuous smile toward the bar and dance floor. Alexander was amazed. He felt like he was seeing her again for the first time. But then, she was in her element—socializing with Italian countrymen. She saw Alexander and upped her smile's intensity. She gave no gesture for him to join her. Alexander stayed back, rubbing elbows with the American drunks and relishing in her satisfaction. Joining her group would put a damper on the evening.

A man slurred, "She is one hot babe."

Alexander nodded and said, "Yep. Where're you from?"

"Atlanta, Georgia. When you're booked into a comedy club in town, make sure the hot babe is with you."

"I sure will."

"By the way, I saw Cotton Watts perform in Atlanta. He was a hoot."

"Remember any jokes?"

"An old one, performed by a favorite woman comedian I know. She told the story about a nurse who once saw the initials SAS tattooed on a patient's penis. She asked him if he worked for Scandinavian Airlines. He answered, stick around honey. I'm from Saskatchewan."

The bar roared. The drunk man said, "Say friend, bring that comedian with you."

"I will. I'm sure my wife won't mind." Laughter erupted. Margarita stopped dancing and looked toward Alexander. Ever vigilant,

Alexander acknowledged her with a wink. She locked arms with her dance partner and walked to the bar.

"Alexander, you and your friends are having so much fun." She got close to his ear. "You're, um, upstaging me."

"Imagine that. And I did it without revealing my tits."

"Oh, you are naughty. Let me introduce you to Officer Fallalia. He's the chief mechanic of the ship's engine room."

Alexander acknowledged the officer with a short bow.

"I'm glad you made sure the ship was well stocked with shafts." Alexander bowed again.

"*Piacere*," the chief mechanic responded coldly, as he turned back toward the bar crowd.

Margarita came to Alexander's side. "It's a good thing he doesn't speak English. We'd be locked up in the dungeon. Why don't the Italian officers think you're funny?"

Alexander sighed, "Is that a surprise? They're looking for entertainment that doesn't include jokes."

"Let's stay together. We do know how to have a good time, don't we?"

Alexander and Margarita spent the night drinking and dancing. When the gaiety subsided, several hours later, they retired to their stateroom. Somewhere between standing and collapsing into bed, Alexander told Margarita he'd pushed the pause button and that the party could continue in the morning. Alexander planned to greet fans and accommodate the enthusiastic solicitations with an early appearance poolside.

* * *

Normally an early riser at home, Alexander sat up in bed, yawned, and stretched. He looked at his watch. It's seven a.m., he observed to himself. I'm on vacation, or did I forget? I give myself permission to go back to sleep. With that, he fell back on the pillow with open eyes. Turning his head, he looked over at Margarita snoring in a rhythmically harsh tone. He realized he was naked, and lifted the blanket. So was Margarita. He cupped his hands behind his head and thought *What time did things get frisky?* Then he sat up, perplexed. He remembered falling into bed, fully clothed. But here he was, naked. He peeked again to admire the seductive vision of his wife's firm, shapely body as her breasts rose and dropped rhythmically. *Alexander*, he admonished himself, *shut up, thank the gods, and go back to sleep.* He lowered himself onto his back and closed his eyes.

Then he sat up again with a start. "Christ, we need the lounge chairs next to the pool," he blurted out loud. Reaching for his glasses, he jumped up from bed and headed to the bathroom.

When he came back, he stood over Margarita with a return of the vigor that had resulted from his triumph last night. "Margarita, you need to get up. I'm due on stage in a half hour." Margarita did not stir. How am I going to awake her? he wondered. "Margarita, you've got to get up." Alexander's pleading evoked nothing. He stepped back and began a joke he knew would annoy her. "Did I tell you about the salesman who, on a trip to London, heard the flight attendant say, 'Now sit back and enjoy your trip while your captain, Sheila Miller, and her crew take you safely to your destination.'"

He then launched into his all-women, cockpit joke. As anticipated, this tactic secured her attention.

Margarita looked at Alexander with a pit bull stare. "Don't tell me you told that joke at a gig?"

"I did. Specifically, at the now fire-ravaged Zug Island Comedy Club, and it went over big."

"Bullshit."

"Don't make a big deal out of this. I just wanted to get your attention. We need the lounge chairs by the pool."

Margarita rolled out of bed and put on a sun outfit. "Am I to understand that my role in our comedy arrangement is the same as my wifely duties? You bark orders telling me do this, do that, and I follow orders?"

Alexander was nonplussed. "Well, yes..."

Margarita smiled quietly... their marriage was back on track. Together, they hurried outside to pick the most desirable lounge chairs next to the pool and claim territorial rights. Once they'd placed towels and beach bags filled with suntan lotion on the loungers, Margarita said, "Let's do breakfast."

"Aye, aye, *commandant*. By the way M, I'm expecting the captain to be on the bridge steering the ship, where he's supposed to be. I'll have a heart attack if I see him eating in the dining room."

They entered the dining room and walked to their table, where special treatment awaited them. The waiters pulled out the chairs for signora and signore, and handed them their napkins. Margarita, with an overdone smile, thanked the waiter. She turned to Alexander and asked, "Why the special attention?"

Alexander shook his head and shrugged his shoulders. "I wanted to ask, how did we wind up undressed last night?"

Margarita smiled and said, "You were sound asleep. I took care of everything."

"Everything?" Alexander smiled and reached for her hand.

"You were already aroused."

"I must call Dr. Lieberman with a report."

The waiter came, and Margarita said to bring a sumptuous breakfast. "Surprise us."

Alexander continued, "Today's the royal voyage climax. Oh, shit. Here comes some of last night's audience." The enthusiastic fans approached the table, and the royal couple greeted them. Eventually, Margarita asked to be left alone so they could eat. "My comedic husband and I will be at the pool after breakfast. Please stop by."

In relative peace, Alexander and Margarita savored the breakfast of eggs benedict with hollandaise sauce. The coffee, a dark roast, was the perfect blend to keep them awake for the day. In lockstep, they walked to the exit, Alexander making a point of tipping the waiters and maître d'.

Alexander and his princess walked toward the pool area. It was unclear to Alexander whether the sun or his ego filled the sky with light. And what could be grander than groupies surrounding an idol, with continuing acknowledgements from where they'd left off the previous night?

The success he'd found on the amateur stage in the ship's ballroom ignited a strong desire in Alexander to return to the comedy clubs in Detroit and secure a gig. He realized this might be difficult because his humor was meant for older people who went on cruises, not toothless assholes from God-knows-where who frequented the Detroit comedy club scene. Why did people go to comedy clubs, anyway? To laugh at poor saps who thought they might be funny? Nah, he would leave the comedy scene to Flossy. He was crap, and she was funny. Perhaps a different kind of comedy would do the trick—politics. Detroit needed another funny man running the show... sure, why not? He could see the headlines: Wisecracking Accountant Steals Election With Humor-Based Reality.

Alexander's mind churned. And the more it churned, the more everything made complete sense. Leave the comedy clubs to Flossy. She deserved the success. He'd buy her a club to run. Flossy was the person who'd woken him up. Alexander finally realized that success was a paved road to your own kind of people. Detroit and the surrounding suburbs didn't fit. A life of rednecks, drunks, country music, a customized dragster, and a house trailer wasn't his calling after all.

Alexander knew he was full of himself right now. That wouldn't stop him from telling old jokes. To an elderly couple by the pool, he quipped, "Your husband looks alive, but I'll speculate his schmuck died ten years ago." Tears of laughter launched. The general response swelled to a high pitch.

"Your husband is hilarious," choked a laughing admirer to Margarita, who also joined in the gaiety. "I'll expect to see your husband on the Ed Sullivan Show."

Alexander replied, "Lady, I'd love to. But the only thing left with Sullivan's name is a marquee on a Broadway theater, where David Letterman does his TV show." He spared her the usual insult. She'd laughed at his jokes.

It seemed as if everyone stopped by. The entire morning was spent greeting passengers, while the sun warmed and tanned them.

Alexander toweled Margarita and covered her in suntan lotion, enjoying the newly discovered sensuality of touching her smooth curves. "Too much sun, my dear? I'll arrange for lunch." Alexander and Margarita would enjoy the day as if it were the entire week. A dreadful thought then came to him. The ship would pull into port the next morning. What a bummer.

Chilled champagne arrived in the white-gloved hands of a wine steward, who poured the bubbly with elegance. Alexander toasted the success of the past evening with "Lenny Bruce would be proud."

Margarita downed the flute and said, "I plan to devour the champagne and guzzle the salmon salad you ordered for me."

Alexander looked at Margarita with a smirk. "I see you're planning to arrive somewhere between tipsy and dead drunk. When your nose tingles, I suggest you ease back."

The luncheon plate arrived, and Margarita squealed with delight. The Atlantic salmon sat atop a bed of mixed greens, with a touch of radicchio lettuce. The champagne glasses were topped off. A dessert of tropical fruits served with raspberry sauce caused Alexander to comment, "The chef must be religious. The food resembles Joseph's coat of many colors."

"First, a comedian, now a rabbi." Margarita saluted Alexander with the champagne flute and then drained the glass." She immediately called the wine steward for a refill.

"The way you're headed with that bottle of champagne, you'll be doing an impersonation of Joe E. Lewis. While swigging a high-ball, he used to quip, 'I don't drink any more than the man next to me, and the man next to me is Dean Martin.'"

"Alex, I love how you tell jokes." She leaned in. "Tell some dirty ones while we're screwing."

They giggled.

"By the way, when I got on top, you asked, 'When did you get released from prison?' Who were you talking to? Me? Where did you come up with that ridiculous idea?"

"I was asleep when I said it. I'm sure it was no one I knew." Alexander thanked God Margarita seemed more interested in cruising her champagne high than pursuing this vague memory. He wanted to hold onto their newfound intimacy, not rock the boat.

The crowd stayed at a distance, observing the cooing couple.

"Alex, Let's take a break and go for a walk. Even though I'm woozy, I don't understand something, and I'm curious."

Alexander jumped up from the lounge chair and commented to the admiring crowd that he and his wife needed airing out. After he'd helped Margarita to her feet, they walked toward the stern and viewed the ship's wake.

Margarita broke the silence. "If you were planning to become successful in comedy, why did you accept a position in public office?"

"My, my. You sobered up quickly. I've been a loose cannon. As of yet, no serious damage has happened to the hull from the battering, and no cannon balls have been discharged by accident. The ship, however, is rocking in heavy seas."

"I love your metaphors."

"They are good, aren't they? Anyway, I'm sick about what's happened to Detroit. Hiroshima, the day after the bomb dropped, looked better than Detroit has in the last twenty-five years. Its downfall happened because the Greg Flankens of this world, who gained power, thought taxpayers' money could be better spent funding the high life. They believed money stolen from the school system was replaceable by implementing higher taxes. As a result, the Detroit public school system, once the envy of the country, collapsed. It now stands in shambles. How could anyone say they cared when they saw failing students and crumbling school buildings? They couldn't even fund a gym to play basketball. All the money was diverted to be spent in the wrong places. People like Greg Flanken felt no responsibility to educate disadvantaged students. The heads of the school boards and unions were phonies who lied. They believed paying high salaries to teachers and administrators with no accountability was acceptable. Actually teaching children academic fundamentals was a visible afterthought. So the top one percent of local government received the first fruits of collected tax dollars for chauffeured limos, lavish offices, and lavish dinners. And the ignorant ninety-nine percent didn't complain when a child couldn't read or write.

"When funds ran low, the school administration would find a journalist trying to uncover the next Watergate scandal. He'd be led to a school to observe children who'd been deprived because of lack of funding. The next stop would be to a school supply warehouse, to observe clandestinely as school supplies were sold on the black market to other districts or businesses. The reporter finds out the proceeds were deposited in personal bank accounts. The reporter is in shock and demands an investigation that results in higher levels of funding for schools. The cycle is complete."

"I agree. So how do you reverse Detroit's fortunes?"

"I'm the only guy who can fix the problem. That's what interested me in becoming the budget director when Hatcher asked me to join his crew. The high livers like Odetta and her husband will find slim pickings. The teachers union will call for my hide. I have a soft spot for doing things right. I have a conscience. But there is a caveat. If things don't improve, woe to the schools of Michigan. I'm going to join in stealing money when the new cycle of thievery starts."

"You aren't serious?"

"Oh yes, I am. The difference is I know where to hide money where nobody will find it. I'd like my motto to read 'Fix the Roads.'" Alexander said this in a loud, firm voice. "But I have another motto, if necessary." And this he whispered, *"Steal the money.* When you speak about the government, it's always 'Steal the Money.' Everyone's in the pool. Logic, honesty, reason, or responsibility are just words in a dictionary. Where's their rectitude? Sincerity?"

Margarita looked in disbelief at Alexander. "I never saw you openly display this kind of dark side."

"So, will you join the act and be my *shill*? Be a hostess and—if necessary—back me up while I steal the money?"

Margarita was silent.

After waiting a moment, Alexander said, "Let's go back to our fans. They're awaiting anxiously to find out if I've composed any new material. What do you say?"

"Taking part in my husband's scheme to steal money? My father would never have allowed me to marry you."

"I see you're in for fifty percent."

"What about your motto, 'Fix the Roads'?"

"Fixing roads or anything else is based on the squawk-o-meter. Washington and Lansing don't worry about the size of potholes or erosion. They pay attention when the repair becomes a concern, when the public squawk-o-meter becomes loud and irritating. Then the state transportation department rolls out the Florida orange juice-colored barrels to advertise the repair activity. Within hours, people and newspapers bitch about the construction. But in the end, all complaints are forgiven when the barrels are removed to reveal a dazzling road free of pockmarks. And unseen pockets fatten with over-payments and bribes."

Margarita and Alexander started back toward the pool. "I'd hoped this cruise would calm you down. Back home, you've insulted everyone. I have no first-hand knowledge, but I'll wager many organizations are upset with you. Here, you've insulted fellow passengers, but they gave you a break. They laughed at your jokes. They don't know how obnoxious you are. I have an idea. I'll announce over the loud speaker that everyone should forget the name Alexander Haralson, comedian, when they disembark. I'll shout that doing so is in your best interest, to keep your mental state in perfect balance and health."

Margarita and Alexander reached the lounge chairs and lay back down. Alexander commented, "We're alone. We have to re-learn how to be a family—us and the state."

"I sense once you're an elected official, you'll be planning a war."

"Our country has been good to the needy. What we expected back was a simple 'thank you.' But what did we get in return? Whining, incivility. The politicians engineered a way for the poor to become needier, a path that led to higher benefits for others who lined their pants pockets with wads of money.

"I don't care if they're poor. I plan to rip them a new asshole, to wake them up to a reality. The politicians they've supported come at

a price. I plan to build first-class roads for workers and wage earners. The roads will be sturdy, so tanks can travel on them. I'll tear
up the others. If you don't work, you don't need paved roads—you
need gravel roads. Remember August 6, 1945? That was the day
Japan woke up and reversed a flawed political and military-based
economic mess. Detroit awakened and went into reverse."

"What color will your uniform shirts be? Brown?"

Alexander ignored her remark. "I'm going back to Michigan
to join a card-carrying political machine that will turn plowshares
into swords. The sword will be mightier than the pen. I plan to bring
change to a world where the devil becomes the earthly deity. The
Ten Commandments will be known as the 'I Don't Need To Obey
These Stinking Laws.'

"And no, dear, the shirts will not be brown. My campaign shirts
will be Stalin's favorite color—crimson red. I tried to find kulak red,
named after the Russian *kulak* 'class enemies' who opposed Stalin.
I liked the idea of land-owning peasants standing up to the big guy.
But according to Bolshevik lore, the dye needed is gathered from
real blood."

"Oh, I hear you now. To enlist, I see I'll need to switch from
vino to vodka. I'm ready, captain. I'll follow you into your cabin
anytime."

"Let's go now. I need to rant, tell more jokes."

Chapter Nine

ALEXANDER RETURNS TO STARBUCKS

The Haralsons returned home from the cruise more upbeat about life than rested. With success on the cruise, Alexander decided to return to Starbucks for one last fling. The coffee shop was located on Woodward Avenue on the main thoroughfare through Birmingham, Alexander's favorite street. When you looked at him, you could swear Woodward Avenue's public lighting beamed from Alexander's inner electricity. Other coffee shops—Einstein's, Panera Bread, and Bigbys—fronted on Woodward. Alexander patronized them because friends congregated there in the morning.

At the Starbucks located in downtown Birmingham—acting as if he were a high-profile personality—Alexander pulled the door open to the limits of its hinges. It was a marriage made in heaven.

The old timers' breakfast group turned their heads, quieted down, and stared as they saw Alexander swagger through the entrance. They looked at one another wonderingly as they observed the outrageous costume of their friend's latest persona. Alexander was chomping on an unlit cigar, under a wide-brimmed straw "gambler" hat. That was the name the salesman had given the hat when Alexander purchased it. Alexander had replied, "Screw the name. Will the style make my audience take notice?"

Alexander's original plan as a comedian hadn't been working out. So he'd decided to experiment with a change. He'd perused

Henry the Hatters for the perfect flair that would fit his act's new persona. He thought the purchase might spruce up his appearance. He threw money at buying clothes. Maybe he would get recognition for dressing clownishly, and the laughs at his jokes would follow. A dull comedian can't get laughs dressed in a T-shirt and jeans. The hoots and boos get to him. Good jokes were important, but so were the body movements, and so was the garb. Up until now, grabbing the microphone was a crutch, a phallic security blanket. No, no, never again would he do anything halfway or overlook any minor detail. He was excited to show off his new comedy routine to his friends at morning breakfast. He couldn't wait.

They'd heard every old Jewish joke that was ever told one hundred times over. Anyone who repeated it got howls of laughter, except Alexander. His delivery had carried lead weights. He knew the material. But the moment he opened his mouth all traces of funny disappeared. He'd tried a contorted face, a falsetto, and obscene gestures. Every effort had failed.

Once inside Starbucks, Alexander changed his gait, jiving into toe walking, with knees together swishing side-to-side. His wardrobe complemented his jeans—a polka-dot silk shirt, soft leather loafers, and skin socks. Without any hesitation, he walked straight up to Itzy, wiggling his cigar effeminately to get his attention.

Itzy looked up in disbelief from his conversation with Hymie Schwartz. "What am I seeing? It ain't Purim, and it ain't Halloween. Are you trying to prove something? Do you think your clothes will make you look or feel younger?"

"As a matter of fact, yes. They're tailor-made so no one will notice any urine stains or bulges from wearing Depends."

"We've been waiting for you to finally turn up again, Mr. Know-Everything. Let me tell you something. I went home and told Rose about the redness around my left eye. I told her you had an old grudge and hit me, but told her not to call Margarita. Leave it alone, I said."

"Itsy, you haven't changed. You're still a snitch."

"Rose called the police. They told her to take me to Beaumont Hospital."

"You're a lucky man who has a caring wife. It should happen to me. So you went to the hospital and told the triage nurse your sore eye story. I'm glad you didn't tell her you had an erection that lasted more than four hours."

"Get lost, you *schmuck*. What are you doing here anyway? Come to aggravate me? Don't make me have Rose call Margarita."

"Itsy, I didn't come here to fight. I'm sorry I slugged you. I was out-of-bounds. I forgive you. The incident happened sixty years ago. I'm willing to let bygones be bygones."

Alexander waited for Itzy to reply. Itzy started to say something, but the sounds Alexander heard resembled grunts suggesting evidence of Itsy relieving himself of gas. "Come on Itsy, can't you say, 'I forgive you, Alexander?' Christ, you proposed to your wife faster."

"That joke's older than Adam and Eve. When will you learn, Alexander, you're just not funny?"

Alexander, inwardly upset, threw the cigar in a domed trash container and walked to the counter to order a Frappuccino. From behind, he heard Itzy talking with Ben saying, "Forgive him? Hah. I'll forgive a dog infected with rabies for biting me. Who is he supposed to be, anyway?"

Alexander turned around and replied, "My, my, Itzy. You've completed two sentences without asking a question."

Hymie interjected, "Enough! Both of you." The morning crowd of gray heads and lined faces looked at Hymie and then at Alexander.

Conversation resumed as Alexander bellied up to the order station. At the pick-up station he struck a pose as he looked at Itzy's table, slouching against the counter with one elbow resting atop. It was not what you'd expect to see a typical accountant do. It measured closer to a gunslinger in a western movie, drinking libations from a shot glass instead of the Frappuccino.

"What do I see? A bunch of miserable married men," Alexander announced. Conversation quieted again. "Gentlemen, I can save you. My idea will throw off the shackles of an unhappy life and allow you the opportunity to transform your lives for the better. The key is to unburden yourselves of your wives. Don't give me any shit how wonderful they are, or how much you love them, or how happily you are married to them. Today, you're in good company because I can give you a gift that is the envy of every henpecked husband in the world—a dead wife. Think O.J. Simpson. I've changed professions from accountant to hit man. No more worry whether your wife will leave you and have her divorce attorney hang you out to dry, penniless. And don't forget, in case you haven't noticed, another bloodsucking group that has you in their sights—*Them*! Your overindulged children. I can help. Watch me unleash the moorings. You agree? When you're breathing your last gasps of life, you may think they're praying to God, asking Him to restore you to health. No such luck, chumps. Their supplications rest with the hope you check out ASAP. Count De Money isn't some aristocrat in a Mel Brooks movie. They want your money to spend on a lavish lifestyle. They'll sit in a hospital waiting room only under one condition—a copy of your will is in the magazine rack."

Heads turned away. Hands covered faces. Dead silence filled the coffee house. The employees stopped working to listen. "Oh my. Did I cause you embarrassment? Are you worried your heirs might learn how much they overestimated the money they'd receive, like fifty million, when the payoff will be only two million? As your star accountant, let me inform you that the shortfall amounts to forty-eight million. They'll hate your guts when they realize the inheritance gap rivals the Grand Canyon chasm. Listen to me. Reading your will comes before the burial. And when they read the fine print and find out you bullshitted them on how much you were worth, forget a mahogany casket. They'll drop you into the ground wrapped in a horse blanket.

"Listen to me!" Alexander's voice was raised in almost manic supplication. "Don't die unhappy. Don't wait to see your family stand over you while you lie on your deathbed. They may encourage you to get better with a smile, or pose a solemn look of concern. But know this—inside, they loathe you. Arrange through me a plan to kill your wife and kick your children out the door. You'll be free. No more dependency. My fees are reasonable. Twenty-five thousand, with half down before the hit man gets started, and then watch your wife's credit card charges plummet to zero. That's when you owe the other fifty percent.

"Included in your package is disposal of the body. First, I'll arrange for a wood chipper to grind her to pieces and then have her buried under a super highway. No one will ever find her."

Alexander heard Morty ask quietly, "You can actually do this?"

"You're my first customer. See me later. Have cash ready."

Alexander raised his voice further, as if reaching an epiphany. "What are you waiting for? When she's dead, you can spend or do anything you want with your money. Work out with a personal trainer instead of dreaming over a cup of coffee what your body is capable of doing. Get in shape. I can tell you, on good authority, that when a physical therapist asks if you're able to do social activity, she isn't talking about dancing. Get a hooker. Get yourself laid. Make sure you use a credit card so you can earn airline miles."

Someone asked, "Did you switch professions? Are you a mortician?"

Hymie broke in. "Alexander, may I ask if you are planning to kill Margarita?"

"Ah, my benevolent dictator. She reduced my sentence from twenty lashes to ten. I'm sure you've heard about an arms-length transaction in business. Margarita and I have an arms-length marriage. At times, that's too close. My latest love and I are separated by a two-inch piece of glass. She's in prison."

Hooting and shouting began. "Alexander, you're crazy," and "Alexander, call a therapist." The sounds of good will conversation among the morning coffee drinkers, which had before filled Starbucks, were now drowned out by clamoring calls for quiet. That included Alexander's big mouth. Conversations were in an uproar. Calm was suspended.

Alexander spoke even more loudly, trying to transcend the clamor so all could hear.

"Gentlemen, gentlemen. Beware. I know this will be hard to believe, but my new love is a woman who got fed up with her old man and decided to end the misery. They kept a gun in the house. She went to the living room with the weapon to ambush him while he had his bare feet propped on a plywood coffee table, watching TV, sucking back a beer. When he saw her, he dove through the front window."

Hersh Finestein neared Alexander. "What the hell is going on with you? Do you hate everyone?"

"Hersh, when they call my name at a meeting, it means I'm alive, literally. My reply isn't about whether or not I showed up. It's about me. I'm living. I want that wakeup call that says, 'Get your ass out of bed and stop being miserable.' I want a pin stuck in my ass that says *Alexander, you're alive. Do something with your life*. I won't be remembered as the guy who late in life went on an excursion to Jurassic Park and only lounged by a pile of dinosaur shit. When I'm in shape, a day jogging at the beach looks and smells a hell of a lot better. My mind is sharp. I can't wait to do the next sneaky or dirty trick. I've been a gentleman all my life—a caring husband, a supportive father, and a finance professional thinking through client problems before advising the best course of action. All that shit's over."

"I don't know what to say. Does Margarita know about you, this... whatever you call it?"

"Metamorphosis. I'm Kafka, having changed into a verminous bug. Call me Boris the Bad or Alexander the Despicable. Take your pick. I've changed because of a conscious effort to make the world a more miserable place to live in. As for Margarita, do you mean my housekeeper?"

"Jeez."

"Look, Hersh. I may sound like an extremist, but I'm a centrist. Lenny Bruce was an extremist. He wanted everyone to walk off a cliff because he felt his political and moral positions on life were pure—the equality of mankind."

"So?"

"So, there's no life, no verve, when you listen to Lenny's rants. He was a government agent. He felt you should allow the government to enslave you. Lenny wanted you to wise up and be a schnook. Do what they want. They're smarter than you. And no dissent. You're a dummy. You're brain dead. I, on the other hand, want you alive—miserable, but alive versus brain dead. I want you to enjoy inhaling polluted air. I'm your friend. I'm trying to have you become miserable because I'm your friend. Are you with me, Hersh?"

Hersh backed away from Alexander, turned, and returned to his seat with trepidation.

Alexander picked up on Hersh's silent walkoff. "See, Hersh, you're a centrist. You're miserable and thankful the liberals haven't arrived to squeeze your nuts for more taxes. Keep telling yourself, 'I'm not brain dead.'"

Alexander was relieved that quiet had finally been restored inside Starbucks. What he didn't understand was that this quiet stemmed not from acquiescence, but from growing horror. All eyes looked straight at him as he *kvelled* from the attention. He was sure the jokes in his next routine would bring the laughter he sought.

He boomed, "I misspoke earlier. The hitman routine is not what I meant. The norms are between brain dead and miserable. I want to spread misery. Killing your wife will make you happy. And happiness is a variation of brain dead. You can go through life brain dead or miserable, but never happy." Alexander paused. "Raise your hand if anyone here thinks I'm nuts?"

All hands raised with outcries, one that hit the mark. "Alexander, the seventh floor at Beaumont Hospital awaits you."

Alexander broke out into a hysterical laugh. "I love you guys."

Christina, the store manager, edged up to Alexander and flashed a growling face. She flexed her muscular shoulders. "I need you to leave—right now."

"I came in to use your men's room facilities. Burger King's are overrated. Yours are well designed and, mechanically, the best. Your urinals are in vogue, especially the wall-hung ceramic model with a deep bowl. I love how it allows you, having drunk all that coffee, to fill it to the brim. Although I must say I prefer the trough design. The flow to the drain is scenic."

"Get out."

A supporting consensus among the morning group encouraged him to leave, with "Enough already. Leave Alexander."

"Leave before I expect to be served my exorbitantly priced Frappuccino? Where is it? I dare say your physical frame can man-handle me through the front door. But hear me out. Starbucks is not a charity." Alexander looked at the manager's name tag and said, "Wanda. Be a dear and check on my order. Make sure the barista prepped the whipped cream topping in a swirl designed like a breast with a nipple atop."

"Get out. And my name is Christina."

"And have your customers miss out on the best theater this place has seen?"

The front door opened. Judy Clovener, an old acquaintance, came in. Alexander relished the fun that would continue.

"Judy, dearest. What a performance. What an entrance. Your ass was dragging on the runway from the front door to the order register. You would be a fabulous contestant in a Miss Coffee Grinds Ugliness Pageant."

Christina stood with her hands on her hips.

Alexander's remark did not seem to provoke any anger in Judy's expression. She was probably drunk, he thought. He put his arm around her, turning her to face the morning coffee group. "Gentlemen, this is an example of brain dead. She hasn't changed in twenty-five years." Alexander turned his head back to Judy. "You look like hell."

Christina, with spittle flying, shouted, "Don't mess with me. Get out."

Ignoring her, and looking at Judy with penetrating intensity, Alexander said, "But first, you must save me. I'm being asked to leave by this *froy*, Wanda the Beast. I'll have you know, she's a famous person. Yes indeed, an east side *shiksa* whose picture with her husband appeared in the society pages at the latest McDonald's grand opening. They took a picture with the renowned celebrity, Ronald McDonald, who posed with his tongue sticking out between the soon-to-be miserable couple."

"I'm ready to call the police, fuckwad."

"Christina, I noticed your engagement ring, and oh, how I love it—a pebble set in aluminum foil."

Christina walked behind the counter and pulled out a cell phone. The employees stood still, frozen, as she called 911.

Alexander burst out. "Where's my Frappuccino! The police should be here at any moment. Who is going to defend my behavior?" he cried. No hands were raised in support of his plea. He turned to Judy. "Where's Herman when you need him? Where's that kind and gentle man? He would support me. By the way, you look the type who got up early to hunt for your next husband. Look out with this group. Did you think Mr. Right would be here today? If Herman were alive, and he learned about my new profession, he would have been my first client. I can see him now. He would die a second time if he saw you and realized you would be occupying the grave next to his. No holding hands."

A foggy-minded Judy slurred, "Enough, Alexander."

"All right. All right, Judy. I don't want to lay it on too thick. Find your broom and fly off."

The door opened and two Birmingham police officers entered and approached the counter. Alexander remained in his gunslinger stance. Christina took the officers aside. Customers tried to resume normal conversations while Christina enlightened the officers.

The officers walked over to Alexander. One officer spoke directly to him. "It would be easier if you'd walk out by yourself."

Alexander leaned in to see the officer's badge. "I see you're Officer Varnishka."

"Peterson," came a sharp reply.

"What a wonderful Judeo-Christian name. Did you come to arrest the manager, Wanda the Wicked? I paid for my drink, and I'm still waiting. I think you should do your duty and lead her away."

"Would you like us to call your wife and have her pick you up?"

"Is there another option?"

The officers looked determined. The second officer used his smart phone and punched some keys. Officer Peterson waited.

The second officer said, "Mr. Haralson, have you ever been arrested or involved in a police matter?"

"Some silly little matter in Melvandale. Richard Hatcher, my road repair advisor, straightened matters out with the police chief."

The officers hooked their arms under Alexander's, and in this fashion they walked him toward the front of the store, dragging Alexander backwards.

"Unhand me!"

As he passed his breakfast club group, Alexander looked toward his friends and said, "God will punish you. After you finish drinking, eating, and pissing, you'll be going home to your miserable wives and kids. You forgot I'm your friend who tried to help you."

After being dragged another ten feet, with no response from his breakfast group, Alexander bellowed, "You are all disinvited from my funeral!" Alexander broke into a hysterical laugh.

Alexander was released at the police station, with a warning not return to Starbucks. Officer Patterson advised him, "The next time will be jail time."

Alexander left the station in a calm and satisfied mood. His Starbucks gig, he felt, had been successful. His next stop was home. The comfort of his office would be his time to sit back and plot.

Chapter Ten

FLOSSY IS ON A ROLL

Once released from her stint in prison, Flossy Lovesong's comedy career skyrocketed under the watchful eye of her mentor, Alexander Haralson. For the first time in her life, she earned enough money to make ends meet. And at home in his man cave, Alexander squawked and gloated to himself all day. When he was with Flossy, he complimented her on being at the top of her game. His best advice was financial: "Spend some of your money now, on yourself. And save some for the future." She followed Alexander's advice. Flossy rented a luxury apartment in Lansing, which afforded her a scenic view of the capital, and which she furnished with designer furniture featuring the latest in luxurious bedroom furniture and deep red leather couches in the living room that invited intimate activity.

At Alexander's suggestion, Flossy also purchased a BMW. "You can't be getting noticed driving around town in a thousand dollar clunker with no hubcaps, which you bought in Detroit." Flossy was worried about damage to her car parked in a comedy club lot. Alexander told her to tell the comedy club owner she wanted a special parking place at the club and a guard to watch it while she performed. Not only did she get a security guard to watch her car, she also got a guard inside the club who made sure no customer got a chance to rough her up.

One point concerned her. Flossy knew she must still be on her guard. Security guards worked for the owner, and their egos thought an occasional roll in the sack was included as part of her job description as the 'talent.' Flossy drew the owner's attention to this point, insisting her rules prevailed. "Rule number one—I'm the star, and the security guards had better make sure no one approaches me with any ideas of getting laid. That includes you. If they make it past the security guard, know that I own a gun." Her old boss, who owned The Pubic Hair Lounge, had learned the consequences first-hand when he paid her a visit and tried to get 'into the act.' He went home in an ambulance. According to Flossy, being a successful comedian granted her the right to love any man she wanted. That choice was narrowed to one man—Alexander Haralson.

Alexander had planned to make arrangements for an apartment for himself and Margarita that he could use as an alternative home base. But traveling to Lansing involved a commuter run, so instead he opted for a hotel suite. His state office was located near the capital. Margarita wouldn't be coming to Lansing all that often, and Alexander thought the expense of keeping up an apartment didn't make sense. Even Margarita seconded his idea. She wouldn't have to do extra cleaning and cooking. Meals would be eaten at restaurants with domestic service provided by the hotel.

Flossy was busy with her career, but she chose Lansing as her home base, where she could be near Alexander. They agreed to distance themselves far enough that they wouldn't run into each other in public or get caught nuzzling at a restaurant, which might cause a scene. The paparazzi were always roaming Lansing, looking for scandals that could be sold to a newspaper or used to blackmail the perp.

* * *

Flossy and Alexander were eating carryout orders from a Chinese restaurant at her apartment. Flossy had just finished a gig in Grand Rapids and hurried home, anxious to show Alexander the DVD. The food sat on a coffee table while they lay on the floor in an embrace.

Alexander said, "What could be better than some foreplay before eating?"

She was kissing his stomach when she said, "I'm so excited to show you the GR gig." She pushed the DVD in the player, and it began. She nibbled his ear and said, "You hit me with some great lines."

* * *

They watched together as the on-screen Flossy began. "I'm in a happy mood. Been doin' gigs for months, and everyone loves me and loves what I'm sayin'. I stand on the stage and rip on everyone and everything, especially the government spending money from accounts with negative balances." The audience cheered. "If you're going to spend money, spend it coming to my show. Come on, look at the view in front of you, and compare the view you see every day inside the state offices. I mean, are you guys blind? Those hags sitting behind the desks aren't beauty queens. They don't instill confidence that they know what they're doing." Laughter, howls, and applause erupted. "I'll assume those not laughing are liberals. Forget about you. Why don't you other guys protest in front of the capitol building and let the governor know you're unhappy with ugly chicks? Tell him to hire personnel that don't give you a 'What's the use?' kind of look. The dresses those broads wear look as if they were fashioned and sewed together from rice sacks shipped from China." Laughter started to carry the show. "And the makeup. The lipstick those women wear is raspberry lip balm.

"Everyone has been so nice and civil. Let me narrow the definition of civil in my role as comedian, because I'm a dictionary kind of girl. No one throws beer bottles or cans at me, thinking I'm a target at an amusement park. And no cat calling. Tiny Tim, my watch dog, makes sure no one gets out of line. Meet Tim." Flossy waves, while saying, "Tim, come on out." A large male struts out on stage. "Tim stands about six five, weighs about two fifty, and sports athletic abs. He's known as a security guard and doesn't hurt anyone while the show's running. Management doesn't want the show to slow down. Neither do I. I want down time to be with my man between sets.

"But don't be misled. The parking lot has security cameras, where you've been matched up with the car you arrived in. I suggest rowdies better walk back to work. That will be your best option. You see, management moves cars belonging to any troublemakers to a safety zone inside ghetto-land Detroit. The club'll shuttle you by van and drop you off near your car on a vacant lot near Mack and McLennon. Call it a city bus tour. The scenery is fabulous. We aim to please.

"Very soon, you'll realize you're going to have a tough time recognizing your car, with prime body parts stripped off. By the time you arrive, Mack's Chop Shop, known for its fast and dependable service, will have sniffed out and pounced on your car. It's the same as those African wildlife adventures where mama lion creeps low in tall grass until the gazelle zooms by. Then, the chase is on until the gazelle runs out of gas. Mama lion makes the kill and along with the kids digs in for Sunday dinner. Then her bum of a husband shows up. He growls and everyone scatters. Hell, that sounds like my husband. The papa lion invites some friends over for dinner, and they all dig in for the feast. When the old man and his friends are finished eating, they leave, and papa lion finds a comfy spot to sleep. Then it's mama lion's and the kids' turn. They return to the gazelle's carcass and find out what's left is an ass sniff.

"It's the same thing with your car. Your car's condition when you arrive at the vacant lot is down to looking at scraps. Looking around, what could be better to record for posterity? Notably for your insurance company, a picture, a selfie of you and your car. My, my. There's no shame in taking a crummy picture with your phone. Your hand's shaking. You're not expected to be a camera buff or Japanese. Where else in the world could you capture a picture with your stripped car in the foreground, burned-out buildings in the mid-ground, and the Renaissance Towers in the background? You'll have plenty of time to call 911 for a pickup. For the mama lion and the kiddies, it's stage two. Eat and lick what you can, reach the bone, and scrape your teeth to clean them, leaving the rest for the vultures. But in Detroit, be careful of what lurks in the underbrush. Good night, folks."

* * *

Alexander and Flossy rolled on the floor, howling. Flossy rolled on top of Alexander. "Wow. Have your routines always been this funny? I mean, as a kid, were you as funny?" she asked.

"I don't remember. But as children, Roman and Caroline thought I was hilarious. I guess the answer's yes. But outside friends and family, I can't get any laughs."

"Poor baby. All that matters is that the routines float into your head and get written down. I'll take over from there. Let's eat and do some screwing."

"That's a plan."

They dished food onto plates and began to eat. Alexander chewed his food and looked at the ceiling. Suddenly, he stopped eating and said, "That part about the bodyguard protecting you is serious. Did you see VP Joe Biden's picture in the newspapers?"

"Alex, baby, I can barely read. And I wouldn't recognize a picture of the *president*."

"I'll bring it over. That man is worse than your boss at The Pubic Hair. A new secretary of a department is being sworn in, and Joe is snuggled up to his wife. His arms are gripped onto her shoulders, and his lips are pushing her hair aside to insert his tongue inside her ear. I know you'd give a serious look and request that kind of person back away. But it's a lose-lose problem. If you lose the intimacy of the crowd, the public will brand you a slut, and it might jeopardize your career. If you swing a fist or elbow, kick, or ask Tim to help, the public will view you with suspicion. In public, they want you to be funny and sweet, no matter how creepy the guy trying to take hold of you."

Flossy gave Alexander a caress. "Don't worry. Your hands are the only ones that'll ever touch me."

* * *

Alexander stayed overnight at Flossy's apartment. He fell into a deep sleep, with plans to awake in time for lunch. It was his cell phone that rang, interrupting his sleep. His first thought was to ask Hatcher to hang the inventor of cell phones. The device had become possessive, an amulet that demanded attention. In Alexander's mind, it summoned the biblical verse of Ruth saying to Naomi, "Wherever you go, I shall follow."

He looked over at Flossy, who was fast asleep.

The phone caller ID read, "Alexander Haralson." He answered, "Hello, Margarita, my dear. How are you feeling?"

"Grumpy."

"Is that an Italian word?"

"Don't be funny. How are the living arrangements? I'd like you to take me to Lansing next week. I want to check on the hotel suites."

"An excellent idea. I'll arrange plans for your visit and introduce you to all the political big shots. And by the way, Hatcher's inauguration is next month. Did you want to wait and come to Lansing then?"

"That's a thought. Where are you now?"

"I'm getting dressed for work and sipping coffee."

"Are you doing any comedy work? When I'm in town, I think I'd like to go to a comedy club."

Alexander took a quick intake of breath as Margarita continued.

"Vivian heard there was a good local comedian. I can't remember her name. Sounded something like 'singing bird.'"

Alexander became warm, his face moist. "M, was her name Lovesong?"

"That's it. Do you know her?"

"I've heard staff members mention her name. Apparently, she's very funny."

"I'll look forward to seeing her perform. By the way, have you run into that lady you saw on our cruise?"

"Not yet. Her name is Odetta. I'm sure she'll be here for the big gala."

"Alex dear, do you think I could drive to Lansing by myself?"

"I'm sure you could, but you'd have to check with me first. The roads are in deplorable shape. If I have to, I'll see that a car picks you up and brings you."

"Alex, you've been a wonderful husband since you got out of the hospital. I'm so happy. I love you, dear."

"I love you too."

Alexander clicked the phone off.

"Flossy, wake up."

In a calm voice, she said, "Relax, Alex. I heard you."

"Are you dressed?"

Flossy pulled the covers off. She lay naked as a sheared lamb. She reached up, grabbed Alexander's neck and pulled him closer. "Relax, will you. I'm not done with you. There's still time for more fun."

Alexander looked outside over the window sill.

"Alex, you're on the fifth floor, in case you want to jump. My balcony is a great leap-off point."

"She wants to come to Lansing to see your show. Your show was recommended by her friend, Vivian."

"If she shows up at the club, I'll do an Italian routine." Flossy got out of bed and went to the bathroom. She came back with a towel and started to wipe Alexander's face.

"Alex, when you hear this, promise me you won't have a heart attack. I'll be performing at the governor's inaugural party. The entire staff has been to a show I've done and requested that the governor invite me."

Alex was nonplussed. "Obviously Hatcher didn't tell you he called me to set up a gig. All that aside, I need a routine from you ASAP."

But Flossy pulled back, looking at Alexander with quiet concern. "Wait, baby. Don't move. I'll get you a glass of water."

"Is there any other news?" Alexander asked.

"Yes, there is. I understand your friend Odetta is running against the governor. They've already started to lay the groundwork to take over the governorship in four years. Her husband senses good times ahead, thinking he can line up choice women for himself and his friends. The rewards for large donors will be the pick of the litter."

"How did you find out?"

"From Hatcher."

Alexander looked at Flossy in disbelief. She continued. "Hatcher's idea is to ruin the plan by catching Greg in the saddle, riding a slut in the home stretch, headed to the finish line."

Alex flung himself on his back. Flossy crawled on top of him. "I impressed him, Alex. He knew about the trouble I had firing a gun at Almont. He said that I might come in handy. He likes my toughness in the face of adversity. Big words for me, eh? He wants me to set up her husband in a sex scandal. Alex, don't feel he's cutting in on the action. He's scared about running against her. The plan is to destroy her campaign. He'll never match her issue by issue. And Alex, don't play 'possum."

"Help," responded Alexander, giving into the inevitable as Flossy's tongue started to work on him.

* * *

"Have you heard what the new state budget director plans to do about state finances?" asked Flossy, as she started her routine in front of an enthusiastic crowd. "He'll be cutting expenses right to the bone. He's issued a directive that says, 'Using the word *new* on any state purchases will not be permitted. *Used*, as with used cars or smaller, will be allowed.'" Flossy shaded her eyes. "Come on guys, it can't be that bad. The director's trying his best to get state finances back into shape. The less the state spends, the less those politicians can steal.

"Another banned word will be *larger* or *bigger*. I wouldn't plan on going into his office and saying, 'Mr. Director, I need an increase in my budget.' I can imagine the security department escorting you out of the office and throwing you in the heap with the other beggars. He has ice in his veins. The coffee pots in your offices that used to be free will have a collection box. He's thinking of a number he expects to be collected each month. He's a pimp, so what do you expect? If you're not happy, charge your lattes to your personal credit card.

"His other directive concerns holiday victuals. Turkey giving by state, done in the past, will stop. Instead, you'll be saying your Thanksgiving prayers over pizza slices. Your new cranberry sauce will transform into marinara sauce. The cutoff for meals will be clerks paid the minimum wage. If you're in the lower echelon, I'd think about relocating to another state where they still distribute turkeys. If I know the governor, robots will replace you. And don't whine. The governor will hear you and immediately cut other departments.

"Now listen, no one has laughed. I didn't expect you to. But hey, austerity's a word in the dictionary that sits around waiting for the desirable time when creditors aren't going to lend any more money for your good times. That's your austerity moment. Call it the menopause of finance. Or am I wrong? Maybe you want the cities with negative cash balances to keep on truckin'? The director isn't stupid. He's going to get his ass chewed out, no matter what he does. If he cuts spending, the voters are mad. If he lets spending continue, he gets slammed by frugal mayors. Some mayors want the spending to go on to help their campaigns, and other mayors want austerity. I'm for starting a relief organization. You know, an exclusive soup kitchen for budget directors. I hope the state is smart enough to make sure he's not shot on sight. He's only the messenger."

Chapter Eleven

THE HARALSON'S NEW HOME IN LANSING

Margarita and Alex called relatives and friends, telling them the good news about Alexander's appointment as state budget director. Reaction ranged from surprise to totally happy for such an honor. Margarita squawked her story a hundred times. At first she was upset about Alexander's appointment —"I'll be by myself"—but later came around to a cheerful acceptance. "I learned that there are many Italians who work for the state. Imagine me attending parties and mingling with my *paesanos*." Margarita thanked Alexander for his transformation into a civilized human being. "Alex, you were such a grouch around the house. Now fresh air will again float through the household. My dear, you and your hot air will have to find its new place in a Lansing office."

In the following days, Robert Hatcher held a news conference. He commented on Michigan's bright future: "A bit *schmaltzy*." But what was the new head of state to say? He was asking the federal government to declare the entire state of Michigan a disaster zone. On TV, Alex could be seen standing in the background, waiting to be introduced. The governor-elect spoke about big decisions, mainly that spending needed a new direction.

"State aid to schools, health care, and other needs comprise much of the budget. Keep in mind, our constitution requires us to balance the budget. I agree with that provision and plan to uphold it.

To help me, I've asked Alexander Haralson of Birmingham to be my budget director. His credentials are impeccable, and I expect him to guide us in our quest.

"I should note, and as you already know, our roads are in deplorable shape. The federal government cannot fund the monies needed to help us with our task. So we're going to have to find the funds ourselves to fix the roads. We need good roads if we want a good economy. I know our budget will be strained. That's why I chose Alexander. He is direct and will work to tighten the spending belt."

* * *

Caroline saw the news conference on TV in the social services department office with her colleagues, with open mouths and disbelieving eyes. She wondered if a 911 call for heart resuscitation for her father was a real possibility. The Detroit director, Sheila Barnes, knew Alexander was Caroline's father and gave a significant stare in her direction. Caroline took a deep breath, anticipating a verbal onslaught.

Sheila said, "I sense we're going to be short of money to help our clients."

Caroline replied, "We've got an uphill battle. My father's mindset thinks any spending increase for the agency will be used for higher salaries. And ingrained in his head are government agencies that he refers to as professional mooches. But he's a well-intentioned tightwad." Caroline looked over at the coffee canteen area. Tears welled in her eyes. She sighed and plopped onto a chair. Softening her attitude in recognition that they shared the same goals, Sheila tried to comfort Caroline. "We'll fight. I'll call Kwame to arrange a sit-down session with your father."

"I can't believe my tightwad father's declared war against indigent people."

* * *

Caroline Haralson had moved back to Michigan, prompted by a job opening at the Detroit social services department to help with the city's permeating decay. The work, the environment, and the job location had proved a leap into a fiery furnace.

Alexander thought his daughter was a noble being, but wondered if there wasn't another suitable job elsewhere, just as noble. He worried about her entering the social services building each day. He imagined it as a giant leap into a fire pit.

As if Kwame wasn't doing enough damage, his keen mind kept his priorities straight. His latest job description was to look for any means possible to make withdrawals from bank accounts that were clearly not his. Ex-Mayor Kwame Kilpatrick, convicted for perjury, would soon be arrested and transferred to a federal country club prison. Every day he was a free man another piece of concrete fell from the city's foundation walls. The school system, once the envy of America, had turned into a basket case after fifty years. Kwame kept the good times rolling. He morphed schools into babysitting centers. Teachers were fired on his say-so and replaced with recent college graduates and inexperienced teachers. Kwame fiddled while Detroit burned, spending money on wild parties at the Manoogian Mansion, the mayor's residence, and taking trips to vacation spots with an entourage of a dozen friends or more.

Caroline dedicated herself to changing the landscape by reviving the family structure and working on improved schools for students, hoping to change attitudes for the better. She wanted to educate people who might have abilities to return Detroit to its old glory as the automobile capital of the world and hurl its broken image into a trash can. Deep down, father and daughter had the same civic concerns and the same determination to do something proactive.

Although Alexander and Caroline continued an ongoing political war that strained their relationship, she told him one night at dinner that she would attend his installation as budget director. This made Alexander and Margarita happy parents. Alexander was proud of his daughter and wished their relationship was less strained. Above all, Alexander needed to keep his mouth shut to avoid stress by not talking to Caroline until the installation. He wanted to blast her hypocritical stance on every issue—left turn, left turn, left turn.

Oh, Alexander had ammunition. He wanted to throw up to her that her liberal stance, no matter how noble, was a greater evil with Kwame as her mayor. "You and Kwame believe the same philosophy, yet he has no conscience about stealing money from the school system. And have you met the president of the teacher's union, Odetta Flanken? She lets Kwame get away with thievery," Alexander complained. "I saw him write a check for a hundred grand from the city bank account and deposit it in *his* checking account. Isn't that considered stealing? Odetta's all show on TV, shaking her fist with a mean face at all those evil conservatives, but what has she actually done to stop them?" In Alexander's mind, this dysfunctional act was a comedy routine for Flossy to handle.

Alexander's son and daughter-in-law, Roman and Shirley, maintained an independent stance through all this. Conversation at family dinners was lively, but no one stood up, threw down their napkin, called a family member Byzantine, and left in a huff. The fireworks would last until midnight, when *detente* turned Cinderella's royal coach back into a pumpkin. In Alexander's opinion, Roman and Shirley fired on all twelve cylinders, Caroline on half a cylinder, and Margarita on a cap gun. But somehow the Haralson family always worked things out and held together, just like in his father's time.

* * *

Alexander stood with Margarita at the foot of the stairs leading up to the bedrooms. They stepped up to the second riser, where Alexander would address the approximate one hundred fifty well-wishers. They waved and were showered with hardy *mazel tovs*. When the crowd quieted, Alexander spoke. "It's a Thanksgiving tradition in this house that I carve the first slice from the turkey. Since Margarita planned this brunch, the manager at the deli beat me to making the first cut. There are delicious turkey slices on the tray. Be careful, though, with serving knives and forks. We don't want to see anyone get stabbed, especially in the back." Howls of laughter and applause erupted. "But we're joined together here, once again, this time to celebrate the inauguration of Governor Robert Hatcher, and his asking me to serve as the state's budget director. I have accepted the governor's appointment. Margarita and I are traveling to Lansing next week to be installed." Applause broke out. "Margarita has done it again," Alexander continued. "This brunch was put together beautifully and with love. I'm looking forward to being a part of Governor Hatcher's administration. I never thought I could sort out my life after retirement and continue be a part of an organization. This time, it's the state of Michigan. I plan to save the state from itself. My instrument of choice will be well-sharpened scissors.

"Our plans are to stay in Birmingham. Margarita can be with her friends and family without disruption. I, on the other hand, will commute. I've secured a suite at the Oldsmobile Hotel if I need to stay overnight. We decided this was best. I sure as hell wasn't planning to do cleaning. And Margarita wasn't going to do cleaning or cooking when she stays overnight.

"In case any of you are wondering, my health is good. I sometimes suffer from fatigue, but will keep working out in a state gym— at taxpayers' expense! Thank you, taxpayers. Eat up, everyone. Margarita and I will circulate, and if there are any questions, don't hesitate to ask."

"How much money do you and Hatcher plan to steal?" It was Alexander's cousin, Ashford Haralson.

"Ah, Ashford. Who invited *you*? Yet again, you're embarrassing me in front of my friends and associates. I'll recommend to the governor that you be put in charge of organic foods. In case anyone needs to know, *organic* is the Latin word for 'pig shit.'" Howls of laughter erupted. One guest shouted, "Alex, you haven't lost your timing!"

Alexander walked over to Ashburn. Lowering his voice, he looked his cousin directly in the eye, warningly. "You ungrateful welfare-check jerks think you can spout objections to people who support you. What you haven't thought out are the objections you'll spout when I raise housing rents for your subsidized units. The state will feel less offended knowing they're getting paid to hear your big mouths. Get a plate and feed your fat face."

The brunch consisted of a small offering of pizza slices and a white bean bruschetta on garlic toast. The centerpiece was the deli tray. Smoked fish, lox, and herring were the main dishes. Liquor and soft drinks were the liquid refreshments. Corned beef, salami, chopped liver, and tongue were the deli meats on display. The bread of choice was rye. Coleslaw, potato salad, a noodle pudding, and fresh vegetables rounded out the fare. There was a mad rush to get to the deli tray.

Alexander turned to Caroline and said, "So my dear, what false god do you plan to worship, now that you've returned to Detroit? Tinkerbell?" On any other day, a first for Caroline would have been a march straight to a communication armory for slogans to shout at a budget department demonstration. This being a special day, she merely laughed off her father's challenge and answered that the devil planned to take a day off.

"The devil and you ought to get along," she added. "You're both capitalists. Many people sell their souls to him."

"The devil, I'm sure, hates your guts. You are too opinionated," responded her father. "You'll love your new slave master, Kwame."

The Starbucks crowd showed up next: Hymie, Saul, Itzy, and Louie. The hatchet had been buried, and the enduring strength of long-held friendships reigned once again. "Are you planning to came back to us in the morning?"

"If they let me walk in the front door, I'll be there," quipped Alexander with a self-deprecating laugh.

"Alexander, you are one obnoxious person, but the place would be a bore if you never showed up again."

"Guys, I'll take that remark as a vote of confidence and friendship."

"Do you need someone to give your cousin a lift home?"

"No, no. He owns a Cadillac, the capitalist pig. I plan to move him into new quarters when he can't pay his rent. It's called the Detroit River. I wish I could take him atop the Ambassador Bridge and throw him in. He'd make a big splash."

"Alexander, you haven't changed."

Alexander looked at Margarita and asked, "Did you invite Odetta and her husband here today?"

"No, my dear. You'll have to see her off-the-record."

"My dear, let's mingle."

* * *

Caroline talked with her father before she left. "Knowing you, being the world's biggest skinflint, should I expect a cut in our department's budget for next year?"

Alex replied, "Not necessarily. We'll still give help to your flock. One difference will be goals matched to results. It'll be fun in your office, weaning the professional sponges. I know you can handle it."

"Next you'll be charging office staff for coffee!"

"An excellent idea. We'll charge fifty cents a cup and hire a service. That'll buffer the $2.50 Starbucks lattes charged to expense reports."

"Our coffee is free."

"Was."

Roman neared them, and Caroline appealed to him. "Roman, how can you side with Dad?"

"Easy, Caroline. He's not questioning your work or its importance. Show him results, and he'll see that you're properly funded. By the way, you won't be the only one reaching into the state's pocket. Medicare is a problem for the hospital. I expect Dad and I will have words too."

Alexander interjected, "May we get back to the business of eating a delicious meal?"

So they'd heard it from the horse's mouth—the new budget director would not be an easy target for money.

* * *

Standing in front of the comedy club crowd, Flossy pitched the budget director's warning in more colorful terms—"Hi folks. It's me

Flossy, your favorite gossip columnist. Whoo, whee. Have I got an inside scoop. The state budget will be cut. The governor thinks the overspending was initiated by the city big wigs. I'm a little dense how such an operation happens. I do know when the hospital does an operation, they give you anesthetic. My instinct tells me that's not how they cut a budget. Anesthetic is another of the big words I've learned recently. Apparently, it stays in the dictionary when it comes to budget cuts. I'm not sure if the operation includes extras like cutting off arms or legs, or private parts. For sure, the budget surgeon won't be lathering y'all up for a shave.

"My opinion is simple. When they spent money for votes, none landed in my pocket. I still had to work. I went to the welfare office and yelled, 'Hey, what about me!' And the response from the welfare bank was, 'What about you?' I could sense doing a nude dance for the cashiers wasn't going to pull any strings, but I stood my ground. 'You've heard about the battle of the sexes? Well, the war of words is officially on.'

"I said, 'Listen up, bitch. My day ain't about sitting home all day watching TV or eating until the next check arrives. I work, and the money arrives. You've got a good business going. I've heard fancy names of businesses like The Dexter Group or The Woodward Group. Is your name The Welfare Group?'

"Would you be surprised to hear the security guards grabbed me and took me away? To mitigate the disturbance, all the social worker had to say was, 'Ms. Lovesong, we're adding your name to the rolls. What's your address?'

"For disrespect toward me and the rest of y'all, I say to Governor Hatcher—slice up those welfare cartels!"

Chapter Twelve

THE INAUGURATION

The Haralsons drove the I-96 corridor toward Lansing for the swearing-in ceremony of Robert Hatcher as governor of Michigan and the installation of Alexander Haralson as budget director. The inaugural host committee planned the festivities to stretch over a five-day hoopla. The unspoken theme was if you go home sober, you didn't attend the inauguration. Margarita said she was euphoric. "I don't know what to do first—eat something from every dish passed at a cocktail party, dance drunk with a stranger and fall on the floor, or tell overdone stories hoping everyone will think I'm crazy."

"Why not do all three? Your words match your projected activities as dissolute, decadent, and dumbed down, respectively."

Margarita leaned over to Alex and put her head on his arm. In a giggly voice she said, "I love it when you talk dirty."

With his mind on other things, Alexander was not amused. "Could you do me a favor? They'll be passing out name tags. Please don't wear yours."

"Nothing gets past you, honey bunch."

Alexander thought about the bills for the inaugural affair. Had anyone put pencil to paper and cost out this five-day adventure? He dreaded the thought of calling Kwame Black to learn how to cook the numbers so no auditor would find state funds not spent in the best interests of its citizens. Oh, yeah, I remember. What about

Robert Hatcher's obese budget? He tells me to cut the total budget by ten percent, and on the cruise I see his preliminary budget figures up seven percent. We're going to need a man-to-man talk with guns on the table. I want to make sure when he announces his planned budget that it doesn't include humiliating me.

Alexander gazed at the scene surrounding him. *I need Flossy*, he thought. She's an expert at handling the hardware and bullets. There's going to be a showdown.

Several days earlier, Alexander had advised Hatcher that the event's budget estimates were way overboard. Hatcher told him not to worry. "Major contributors will pick up the tab. They'll be participating in the festivities. I'm counting on them to get stinking drunk and not care where or how their money got spent. I'll see that the treasurer mails them the bills."

Now, in the car on their way home from the swearing-in ceremony, Margarita vented, "Alexander, why is the road so rough? I can't concentrate on what I'm going to wear to tonight's dinner. It feels like a dirt road."

"It is, about fifty percent."

"They must fix it. You'll be traveling on this road often going to work. I worry for you."

"It'll be one of the many worries I'll face."

Alexander thought, *I haven't gone fifty miles, and two spending bombshells have hit. Oy.*

* * *

The inauguration of Robert Hatcher convened at eleven thirty a.m., on the east steps of the capitol building. The temperature was cold, and sunshine beamed over the front lawn. Robert Hatcher and his wife Harriet stood in a group that included the lieutenant governor, secretary of state, attorney general, and justices of the supreme court. The chief justice would administer the oath of office at noon.

Alexander and Margarita waited on the front lawn, along with all the other members of Hatcher's cabinet. A notable man of importance to Alexander was the state treasurer, Jullian Comps. Alexander and Jullian had spoken several times by phone and met during the election interim period, planning to keep in close contact about what was needed to shore up the condition of state finances. Borrowing plans as the deficit receded and spending numbers used to compare with the budget were the main topics. Alexander and Jullian agreed that road repair numbers might upset the budget. With Jullian sporting a bandage on his eyebrow, suffered when his car hit a pothole and his face hit the steering wheel, he was definitely on board for increasing the budget to repair the roads.

The lawn group swayed from hangovers and bloated bellies. Valerie Prima, the lottery commissioner's nitwit wife, held her arms against a prized burr oak tree, doubled over and retching sporadically with loud gags. The culprit was too many bloody marys and screwdrivers with too much vodka for breakfast. Everyone had hangovers. Oh well. Alexander thought about whom to connect Margarita with to go shopping for clothes or comparing recipes, thereby allowing him time alone. Alexander walked to the stairs and suggested to a security guard that the band play an interlude to drown out Valerie. He further suggested an escort to whisk her to a lady's room. The inaugural committee had planned enough gaiety, without any extra improvisations. Her pile of barf would cause a stir if someone stepped into it by mistake.

As Alexander walked back to Margarita, the brass band started up and played some moderate tempo incidental pieces. Like others, Margarita also drank her breakfast. Her performance was highlighted by standing still with a stupid grin. Alexander noticed she wore her name badge. Although he hadn't thought it a good idea at first, he now thought it best after all. If she fell down or got lost, identification would be facilitated.

* * *

The appointed hour arrived. With his wife standing next to him, Robert Hatcher placed his hand on a Bible and took the oath of office. At the conclusion, a delighted crowd cheered. Pleadings of "Hallelujahs" and "Praise the Lord" pierced the sky. Jennifer Granholm, the soon-to-be ex-governor, watched with a grim look. Odetta and Greg Flanken stood by her side. Alexander thought ex-Governor Granholm was mentally comparing the crowd cheering for Hatcher with her own reception after taking the oath of office. She looked lost. Alexander commented to Margarita, in a low voice, that the clothes Granholm wore suggested her new profession had changed from governor to home cleaning services. "Get her phone number. I don't like the way our maid cleans the toilets."

Alexander caught Odetta looking in his direction. He smiled, with a short bow. She replied with her fists knocking together and a smile in return. Greg looked at Odetta, and Margarita looked at Alexander, who commented, "Hey, we're buddies." Alexander thought that Odetta's appearance at Hatcher's inauguration was a dress rehearsal for her own in four years.

On the cruise, Alexander had ripped her husband. He obviously remembered. Where Odetta showed distant friendship, her husband displayed outright hatred. Having watched their exchange, Greg was evidently chewing out her ass. Alexander felt bad and thought Greg needed to back down. He hoped Margarita would continue to act respectfully toward him. Wild thoughts ran around in his head. Was Odetta trying to say something beyond friendship? Was she aware of his relationship with Flossy? Was she aware his marriage vows were wearing thin? Was she planning a blackmail scheme against Alexander? Margarita leaned toward Alex and said, "If you and that plump *knish* start going around together, I suggest your best way out of difficulty is my arranging a firing squad."

"You won't have to waste any money on bullets. I sense something brewing from her side."

Before giving the inaugural address, the new governor strolled to a spot on the front lawn, where nineteen heavy cannons stood. The guns were manned by military personnel awaiting a command to begin the cannonade. Alexander commented to himself that the next five minutes would be a doozy. As Hatcher neared the cannons, four A-10 Thunderbolt Warthog jets flew overhead, their roar ripping the sky. People animatedly cheered. As the jets passed, yelling and more cheers became audible. When clarity of sound returned, Alexander heard, "Bomb them Arabs." He looked toward another section attending the inauguration. A grim group of middle eastern people stood with sour faces. Alexander looked about in the crowd to see who might have made that comment. After failing to see a guilty face stand out, he thought about all the fun Lansing had to offer—drunken barroom brawls, cheating on spouses, and legislators screaming at one another. It was no skin off his back. Hell, he was the budget director in a lose-lose position.

Everyone's attention was directed at the cannons. An officer ordered, "Fire one." Alexander spotted some attendees drop to the ground, probably fearing a projectile might hit them. Margarita chimed, "Wow, somebody popped a bottle of champagne." Alexander shook his head and muttered, "Only eighteen more to go." The officer in charge ordered the remainder of the cannons fired. Smoke billowed across the lawn. When he took the oath of office, Robert Hatcher had worn a black suit. He walked back to the podium to give the inaugural speech in a gray suit. Alexander cringed, thinking how Hatcher's tenure as governor might proceed—bright in the beginning, turning murky as time passed.

* * *

The inaugural dinner was an extravaganza. Although a tight belt was Hatcher's administration theme, the expense of the dinner event went over the top. Every item in the ballroom reeked money—dining chairs covered with linen, sterling silver utensils, crystal water glasses, wine glasses and champagne flutes, napkins folded in the shape of a bird, condiments, caviar, filets for the entree, a centerpiece four-feet tall holding a red floral arrangement, waiters wearing white gloves, and a twenty piece orchestra, to name a few. There was no silver clip holding a number to identify the table. Entering the room, an escort showed you to your table.

Alexander was impressed. "Well, Margarita, is everything to your liking? I don't see any cheap Italian salamis on the table. No minestrone soup or sides of spaghetti. I'm emphasizing we are not dining tonight at some local pizza and beer joint. Try not to embarrass me with your mouth running off that your Italian roots are superior, or talking your Italian jive."

"When will you shut up?"

"Never."

They looked up when they heard someone say, "May we join you?"

Alexander saw Reginald Harrison, the state's social services director, along with his wife, Lida. Alexander helped Margarita stand and said, "Please join us."

They acknowledged the Haralsons and stood by their seats across the table. Alexander and Margarita walked around to greet them and shake hands.

When everyone was seated, the state road commissioner came and joined them.

Alexander was most interested in chatting with Reginald about Caroline. He was aware that Reginald wanted to avoid small talk about Alexander's anticipated departmental budget cuts, wanting instead to provoke him into joining in an expanded conversation. Alexander was on standby, ready to ignite the howitzer fuses.

"Alexander, I understand the formal ceremonies to install commissioners of various departments will take place tomorrow?"

"Yes, that's correct. It's before lunch and before the governor's opening speech, which I imagine will be a pep talk."

"Your daughter works in my department. How do you feel about her serving with me?"

"Reginald. May I call you Reggie?" He nodded. "Margarita and I are glad. My daughter conducts herself as an adult and takes her work seriously. She came to Detroit because she felt her efforts here would have the greatest impact for good. I know she'll do exemplary work."

"She indicated there was some political friction with her parents."

"Our differences are that she believes continuing to support social programs with bigger budgets will change the landscape. I don't agree with that viewpoint."

"People need food and a place to live."

"I agree." The wives looked at their husbands as they spoke. "I want to see state money serve the communities, especially education," said Alexander. "I believe it can be done."

Reginald nodded.

"Take a look around the city," Alexander continued. "Detroit has transformed from being a third world into a fourth world country. In the past, government funded a strategy built on poor planning. In contrast, look at the western parts of the state. They came together and worked on programs that have proved successful.

"Burned-out buildings, vacant lots, and skeletal buildings serving as easels for graffiti artists are everywhere in Detroit. Nowhere in the world does another city exist in this condition. Hamilton, a major thoroughfare in Highland Park, has no cars driving on it. There aren't many people who would dare live along its corridor. Jobs are all funded by government assistance. And what did the city get in return for its generosity? Nothing. Think about how you'd answer this question. How close do you feel the city is to repairing all the damage and restoring Detroit to its former splendor? In my opinion, it hasn't budged an inch. Then research how much money has gone over the cliff into private pockets."

Everyone was silent.

Alexander continued. "My view holds that the landscape must be improved and maintained. I hate any person who has contributed to this fiasco. Hatcher has plenty of enemies, but he didn't contribute to Detroit's downfall. Believe it or not, I know he wants to see the state succeed. And for that I respect him.

"Reggie, you and your friends will have me to contend with if you plan to push him up against the wall with the same old, tired programs.

"I originally planned to ask how my daughter was doing as an employee. Why I had to ask, I don't know. Without your saying anything, I know she's doing excellent work. I'm a work performance guy and would believe she is receiving high marks for her efforts. My wife and I didn't encourage her to relocate and work for the city.

But we're glad she decided to come back. She'll be closer to home, to us. We can have more family visits.

"We may be on opposite sides of the political fence, and she thinks her parents a bore. But we love and respect her. It's too bad your clients don't appreciate her and want to learn from her."

"I knew your daughter would be an asset," Reginald answered. "And I'd like to work with the state to fix things."

"Best news I've heard all night. And, lucky me, Kwame has called to set up a budget meeting. Whoopee."

* * *

During the dinner, Robert Hatcher rose to speak. He thanked everyone who'd worked to make it possible for him to be elected governor. He also thanked the host committee for the grand event. But it was his announcement about the entertainment headliner that brought the loudest cheers. "Flossy Lovesong, Lansing's new-found comedian, will perform in the adjoining ballroom at ten p.m. Afterward, come back here for drinks and dessert."

Alexander leaned toward Margarita. "You'll love her."

Margarita recoiled, showing some trepidation. "What is she going to say?"

* * *

After her introduction, Flossy strolled out on stage wearing a long black gown and satin shoes and bedecked in a diamond necklace and matching diamond earrings. Before she reached the microphone, the applause was thunderous.

"Hello everybody. Welcome to the inauguration of Robert Hatcher as governor of the state of michigan. Wow. When Governor Hatcher called and invited me to be the entertainment, I told him he called the wrong number. I couldn't believe it was me he called. I said, 'Have you got the right person?' He said, 'Yes.' I hung up the phone and went directly to an audiologist to have my hearing checked. I called back and said I would be glad to appear, and asked if my Dale Evans, silver-studded jeans outfit was okay to wear." The audience roared. "Don't stop laughing, folks. My jewelry was rented from a local pawn shop and is due back at midnight with interest. That's when I turn back into a country pumpkin.

"I've never met a governor before. I live in Ferndale. It's a city that's between an upscale and downscale part of Michigan. Birmingham's to the north and Detroit is to the south. Ferndale's okay if you can stomach our porn movie theaters, machine shops, and cemeteries. In Ferndale, urban renewal is a paint job on your shack.

"I expect improvement from our new governor to build new roads. Road building in Ferndale means filling potholes manually. Every day there's some guy on the road with a shovel, waiting for an asphalt truck to show up. It's a coordinated effort. The guy with the shovel, the *shoveler*, lifts a load out of the back of the truck and then drops it in the pothole. To make the road even, the street guy bangs the asphalt. I ask, where's the steamroller? The guy driving the truck sits in a warm cabin, listening to music, while Mr. Outside does his best and in the process freezes. What's wrong with this picture? Am I to understand the reason why the old roads aren't being completely dug up is they're afraid they might unearth Jimmy Hoffa? Come on, they've tried enough times. Did you guys check the cemeteries?

"It became clear that the governor wanted me to be part of the administrative team. So he calls me, all upset. He says his wife wants to remodel his office in the capital. She wants me to take down his gun rack and the swimsuit Betty Grable calendar. I said I'd be honored, but what was wrong with his wife's suggestion? He could substitute Betty's picture with mine, but somehow I didn't think she'd consider the problem solved. Governor Hatcher, you and your wife seem a happily married couple. Let's not start any trouble. Follow someone else's orders this one time. For my sake, please.

"Lastly, every state department will have its hand out. This country girl has an idea. Cuff your hands behind your back and start looking first at what good the state's money can accomplish, and then build it. Usually, when politicians see a swimming pool full of money, they seem to think they were elected to hand it out. Then

they find out the state has already spent the money to build an immediate teardown. 'Oh my, the money went over budget to buy a box
of Cracker Jacks,' they complain. I mean, I don't mind paying taxes,
but taking the money and finding a project to make the money dis-
appear... Please!" A general cheer went up in response to this quip.

"Whoa, I'll take that as a motion to run for governor in four
years. Thank you, and goodnight."

* * *

Alexander and Margarita walked back to the dining room. "Well, M,
what did you think of her? Would you vote for her?"

"She shocked me. A conditional yes."

"Yeah, it'd be quite a contest. Flossy against Odetta. But it
might not be Odetta against Flossy. Her husband, Greg, is in for a
surprise. She plans to use his money for the campaign, and when
the election's over, she plans to divorce him in the home stretch.
Hatcher found out Odetta knows about Greg's extra-marital affairs.
And on the reverse, Hatcher knows more about Odetta's affairs than
Greg does. Odetta's toast."

"Were you sitting in Odetta's bedroom with a camera, or were
you two engaged?"

"Without giving the plot away, I'm not her lover."

"Let's get some cake and coffee and call it a night."

"I'm glad Caroline will be coming to my installation."

Chapter Thirteen

ALEXANDER WORKS THE ROOM

Governor Robert Hatcher convened an administrative meeting a couple of days after taking office. The first meeting to initiate his new term would have all state administrate staff in attendance, with the luncheon meeting being held at the Kellogg Center in East Lansing. About 250 people were invited: members of his staff, congresspersons, state senators, and state department heads.

Earlier in the morning, Margarita was in attendance with Caroline and Roman for Alexander's installation. Everyone was proud of him. The plan afterward kept Alexander in Lansing and sent Caroline and Roman home with their mother.

When Hatcher entered the room and strode to the podium, everyone rose and applauded. Beaming a smile to the audience, he waved to the enthusiastic crowd. The lieutenant governor and secretary of state stood on one side of the governor, while the treasurer of the state and attorney general stood on the other side. When the room quieted, all attendees took their seats. Governor Hatcher stood at the podium. "I think two to three days was enough time to dry out from all the booze." His opening remark was well received with applause and some laughter.

"Thanks for the great welcome. Every day should start the same way—with enthusiasm." Again, the attendees applauded.

Governor Hatcher nattered newspaper talk for about ten minutes. Alexander later recalled that applause seemed to have broken out at the end of every sentence. Hatcher introduced his ten-member cabinet individually. He spelled out a brief overview of their responsibilities and what each member's priorities would be. Specific goals were not yet stated by him, but everyone had heard about the high standards that Governor Hatcher had set for each department in private meetings.

A noteworthy member singled out by the governor was Heather DeLastrata, director of public education. He commented on the importance of education and the difficulty she faced in light of US secretary of education Arne Duncan's published remarks, calling the Detroit public schools "...arguably the worst urban school district in the country."

Alexander listened intently. He thought about Caroline, who worked in Detroit. She sat in the soup, trying to help families whose children attended Detroit schools. Alexander's first thoughts about helping couldn't sidestep the issue of additional money. It had turned him into a flaming liberal for the moment.

Christ, he thought. *Every time money was sent from the state to Detroit, it found its way into the wrong pockets.* In Alexander's mind, money wasn't the issue. Money only fed a system that was already corrupt. For years, the Detroit school board had felt spending money was the only solution. Setting goals was a tease, a set-up to extract more money from the state. Words, clothed in sappiness, promised that with more money everything would improve. In the end, the money just disappeared. No one dared to question where it was spent. In Alexander's mind, that would change. He anticipated Caroline would say, "Dad, give them the money." In contrast, he knew his method of not only denying increased allocations, but decreasing existing spending levels would wake up school boards. Alexander's theory of government spending fit the mold of a diet— lose weight, and you'll feel more energized. DeLastrata had heard Alexander's comments and was in full agreement with him.

Alexander sat back as Governor Hatcher lashed out at the previous governor. "She thinks she's great. Washington thinks she's great. I'll see that funds are budgeted for a one-way ticket out of Lansing." The audience roared. "Look what I have to face. A budget mess. Every department's administrative staff was run as a Keystone Cops routine. Past governors tried to be respectable. The drill was spend, spend, spend. With her it was overspend, overspend, overspend. But I'll show up to work each day with enthusiasm and good thoughts."

Governor Hatcher eventually worked his way to Alexander. "Let me introduce Alexander Haralson, our new budget director." Alexander rose, and applause formed. The metered response failed to hit a fully enthusiastic reading. Alexander smelled their fear. Besides, these people had applauded on and off for the last hour. No doubt they were tuckered out. Governor Hatcher commented that Alexander would put together yearly budgets intended to cut out the bullshit. "Oops, I mean lower the deficit." Hatcher counted on eliminating the deficit by the end of his first term in office. Again applause greeted the governor's words. "Fix the roads. That's the motto. If you fix the roads, the economy's got to improve. Every day I hear about citizens' cars being wrecked after hitting a pothole." He glanced toward Jullian Comps, who smiled. "I've seen some of the pictures of destruction. The roads look like craters, like bombs dropped on them. Alexander will increase the transportation budget. It's an investment. Hell, I'm sounding like Bill Clinton." Laughter and applause erupted.

In his mind, a confident Alexander agreed he would successfully defend the state's budget against hostile political groups. He would have Flossy in his corner. She'd told Alexander to get ready to fight by putting on his helmet. "I'm your spokesman for putting those big spenders back in their corner." Robert Hatcher would handle the voting public, and Alexander would handle his family. What lurked in the unknown? Had anything been overlooked?

"If Clinton can overspend and call it an investment, I can cut spending and call it greed with a straight face," Hatcher continued. Laughter and applause again filled the room. Everyone stood. Alexander looked around to see where news cameras recording the meeting had been placed. Security cameras in the ceiling were visible. He spotted one news camera at the back of the room. *Smile pretty*, he thought. What took place and was filmed would be archived for eternity. Censoring four-letter words out of the broadcast appeared doubtful. A conglomeration of swear words to be avoided warmed up in Alexander's mind. He realized his daughter would watch his every step, today being no exception. Lower budgets for social services and increased budgets for roads, Alexander knew, would evoke a higher level of hostility across the state.

Alexander anticipated arriving at work each day and quietly working in the background. He would employ a staff to help construct a proposed budget, accumulate revenues and expenses for periodic reports, then connect with other government agencies such as transportation, health, and education to secure federal funding, among other things. His department would be an inner sanctum. Who would visit him? The inside of an accounting office depicted the most boring and despairing place in the world. The most boring conversations held in the world consisted of two accountants talking business. Even lawyers finished in second place by comparison.

At the conclusion of Governor Hatcher's speech, the crowd gathered in the reception area before lunch and lined up at a full bar with hors d'oeuvres. As if there hadn't been enough drinks and shrimp cocktails served during the inauguration. A reporter approached Alexander with a camera crew and asked, "Are you in agreement with Governor Hatcher's budget proposals?"

Alexander nodded. "Michigan roads are in a deplorable condition. Many sections of major thoroughfares, Telegraph Road being one, are badly deteriorated. I've seen several stretches I judge passable only by oxen pulling covered wagons."

Another reporter asked about complaints once road construction was started.

Alexander replied, "I'm sure the media will stir the pot. If we don't fix the roads, you'll complain, and now you suggest when we do fix them, complaints await us!"

Another reporter asked how the governor would get the public behind the projects when the state faced high deficits.

Alexander handled the matter magnificently. "There is only one thing the entire world agrees on—roads need to be fixed, and I'll work with the treasury to find the money. Sure, complaints about the detours causing delays will be numerous. Let me ask you. After repairs are completed, is there anything greater or sweeter than driving your car over a newly paved surface? No more orange barrels to obstruct a smooth ride. It's so great. Even on a dreary day, you'll put on sunglasses and say, 'Ah.'"

One reporter smiled and asked, "Better than sex?"

"It's possible."

The reporters laughed, and Alexander moved away, signaling that, for the time being, interviews were over.

* * *

The dining room doors opened, and the guests entered. Camaraderie animated the mood. Alexander found Governor Hatcher and congratulated him. "Great speech, governor. Robert, we need to meet one-on-one soon, very soon. I found some ugly spots in the numbers. Just for today, let's call them discrepancies."

Governor Hatcher thanked Alexander and turned without pausing to a wall of well-wishers that swarmed him. His speech set the mood, and everyone wanted to shake his hand. Alexander pushed his way out from the crowd. Chatter and laughter reverberated. While chatting with aides, drink in hand, Alexander spotted the state education director, Heather DeLastrata, talking and laughing as she mingled inside a group. The event was intended for her to meet other directors, legislators, and state personnel. Alexander was anxious to introduce himself. An opportunity to discuss educational budget business would present itself later. He'd heard through the grapevine about Heather's career, beginning as a teacher, eventually rising politically through the ranks to become a Hatcher appointee. He watched her charm the crowd surrounding her.

Alexander shuffled his way through the crowd to Heather's group of supporters.

Upon seeing him, Heather blurted, "Ah. The famous skinflint I've heard so much about dares to show his face."

"I'm not offended. But with all deliberate speed, may your budgets shrink by twenty-five percent."

Laughter followed.

Heather appeared to be in her mid-fifties. Respectable looking, but definitely not glamorous. Her blonde hair had been colored for the occasion, and she was dressed in a medium-priced, one-piece outfit. Her home city was Grand Rapids. She was a mirror image of a Robert Hatcher conservative and within a short time had become a Robert Hatcher appointee. Her husband, Vito, came from an Italian family background. Heather's was Dutch. That European culture pervaded western Michigan—tight, just like Alexander. Heather's husband, an engineer, worked in the automotive industry. As to family, they were empty-nesters. Three children had completed college and started entry-level jobs. More progressive careers were on hold as they waited for an improved economy.

As Alexander hoped, Heather and he ended up sitting together for lunch. This had worked out well, because no designated place settings had been assigned. Mingle was the word. Alexander looked over at Robert Hatcher. He sat with Reginald Harrison, the state's social services director. Alexander considered him a person of importance. Near the bottom of his organization chart, Caroline Haralson's name appeared. Alexander had met Reginald at the inauguration dinner, but knew his department was weak. Alexander felt he needed to reacquaint Reginald with his department's most important staff worker.

Heather looked at Alexander and said, "You planned to talk with me, didn't you?"

"I did. But a compulsion to work the room can't be ignored. I'll be meeting with everyone in the room, eventually. I met Harrison earlier. It appears, from studying his figures, that we'll be meeting regularly. McNulty, the transportation director, will be another priority."

"Or victim."

"Oh my. Do I detect that you think I'm part of a Viking horde attacking Lansing?"

"You are funny. Your reputation precedes you. I'm not accusing you of being a barbarian. Hatcher thinks highly of you and said how important you will be to the success of his term in office."

"Phew, that's a load off my mind. Now to the crux. I don't plan to do any horse trading on budgets. They will be followed as written. That's why Hatcher hired me. As to other department heads, my social worker daughter works under Reginald."

"Now I see why he's so important."

Alexander smiled.

"Try and keep my next year's budget intact," Heather said. "Let's wait until the following year before considering lower funding."

"You've got a deal. Have your staff submit a two-year and a four-year projection. Even after hearing about level spending now, the dogs will growl. Keep quiet, and I'll take the heat."

"You're taking this job personally."

"I'm the bad boy. A take-no-prisoners mentality is welded into my cranium. You're on notice. Be careful before sweet talking me. I may have to order you locked up in the tower overlooking the Red Cedar River. I hear it's a streaming open sewer. And the Red Cedar's odor shall remain so. I plan to cut the clean waters budget."

"I can't wait to hear your preliminary thoughts on the school budget."

"Are you asking?"

"Not really. Could we just concentrate on celebrating today?"

"Of course."

"I'm a golfer. Do you and your husband play?"

"I do. He's into tennis."

"I'll put you on my list of golfers. Maybe we can take an afternoon off and play. You should be able to beat me. My game has fallen down. Too many worries, too much work."

"I'm game. By the way, they're about to serve the Caesar salad. And a menu option—General Tso's Chicken. With that for an entree, the meal appears to be a military leader's delight. Whose idea was that?"

"Call me Commander Haralson. Someday, someone will concoct a jaw-breaking pastry and name it in my honor."

"Nothing mushy about you."

"I reviewed your department's current year financials. The numbers appear sound."

"The administrative assistants I hired will officially be on the job after the first of the year. Personnel changes will result. Not all happy."

"Ah, I feel blame coming my way. That's okay. I need my ass kicked every so often."

Alexander stated he was upset with the way education money was spent. He explained to Heather that, in his view, it was simple. Money spent had invoices or other evidence leading back to where money had been disbursed. Missing invoices for millions of dollars, payrolls with unaccounted employees, and political payoffs in the form of over-the-top salaries were all equally unacceptable.

"I expect money spent to achieve its intended purpose."

Heather nodded.

Alexander continued, "By the way, do you know Odetta Flanken, the president of the Detroit Teachers Union?"

"She's very sweet on the outside. On the inside, watch out."

Alexander nodded. "Yep." He stopped himself from saying anything further. "Let's talk later, privately."

"Weren't we supposed to have a relaxing day?"

"Yes, we were. Let's get down to business."

* * *

The next day, Alexander went to Flossy's apartment for brunch. She opened the door and let him in. Their eyes met in silence. He took a seat on the couch. Flossy sat beside him, and they began kissing. Suddenly, she pulled back and looked at Alexander. "Were you kidding me about running for governor?" she asked.

"Hatcher's a crook, Kwame's a crook, Odetta and her husband are crooks. Flossy, you're an honest and concerned person. You're without a formal education, yet have the smarts to hire the right personnel and lead the state. You'd do an outstanding job," responded Alexander.

"What about Margarita?"

"Stealing money is an art that takes years of training. There's a big difference between being a smart shopper and being a thief. She doesn't have the tools. You, however, have special skills. Infiltrating the Flanken umbrella proved worthwhile, uncovering evidence to be used for blackmail. Sweet. It's so much the way of the world. Hatcher secretly funded me to find out who Greg's banging and at whose house Odetta sleeps when she's not home. She has no notion that evidence exists to ruin her career. She tried to play me. That was a mistake. In the end, Hatcher disappointed me."

"Will he be recalled?"

"No. Leave him alone. He'll be an old man when his term ends."

"Want some breakfast?"

"I do."

Flossy stood and walked to the kitchen to prepare some food for him.

"By the way, last night your gown looked a tad tight," quipped Alexander, looking admiringly at her curvy buttocks and the slight swell of her hips and belly.

Flossy put the ingredients and utensils on the counter. She came back and sat next to Alexander. She rested her head on his shoulder and began kissing him with passion.

"Something wonderful's happened." She licked his ear. "I'm pregnant."

"You are? Who's the father?"

"Silly! You are. Right now, I'm delirious."

Flossy stood and lowered her slacks to expose her belly. She took Alexander's hand and placed his hand on the slightly swollen mound. "Three months."

Alexander's response was immediate. "I wish I could dance, jump up and down without having a coronary. I love you, baby. And the baby."

"If it's a boy, I'll name him Stalin, in honor of your stage name."

"And?"

"And if it's a girl, I'll name her Czarina."

Alexander laughed and began to cough.

"Take it easy, *Daddy*."

"I will. I've got new responsibilities."

"Alex, with a baby on the way, my life will require me to make a huge change. I've had time to think, and I've decided to quit comedy."

"What? Why?"

"I've noticed audiences are hearing about fifty percent fewer four-letter words from me. Jesus, listen to me. I sound like a statistician. The laughs coming from my jokes sound tame, no zip. I'm replacing a lot of words with real vocabulary. I'll have to throw the dictionary away to get my old voice back. Alex, you changed my life for the better. Whatever happens, I'll always love you. And don't you dare suggest I try to make it being a Jewish comedian. Alex, I'm quitting on top. I don't want to see my career crash and burn. Know that I'm not sad about quitting. I'm walking away from comedy to have a child. Wow, eh?"

"Yeah."

* * *

Alexander kept busy and met Kwame Black, Detroit's mayor, inside the old GM building donated to the state. The governor arranged limousine service for Alexander. He would stay overnight at home and be driven back to Lansing after a couple of days rest. The mayor's office was located on the penthouse floor and had a picture window with a view of downtown Detroit and across the river into Canada. After waiting an hour for His Honor to finish his chit-chat, Alexander was escorted inside. He was met by the mayor and his six-man entourage. Handshakes were converted into fist bumps, and "How y'all doin'?" Alexander felt as if the scene were a time-out diorama where he was the basketball coach surrounded by his players. An internal "Oh, shit" was his response to discovering that Kwame's two eyes looked in two directions. He'd heard rumors about the mayor's eye defect. Up close, it was hard to tell if the right or the left eye was looking at him.

"How d'you like our view, Alex baby?"

Alexander didn't want to pick a fight. The mayor was twice his size, about six-five, and two hundred and fifty pounds. On the other hand, once the meeting got going and Alexander told Kwame his budget was going to be cut, it didn't matter whether he insulted the mayor or not. An altercation was going to happen. "It depends what view you're referencing."

Kwame looked at Alexander, frowning suddenly.

"D'ya like the view into Canada? Me and Governor Granholm pulled the rug out from those crooked GM managers. Now I got the only view in this room." His friends were all smiles and giggles. "I can look down and keep an eye on my property."

Which eye, Alexander continued to wonder? The internal comic took over as he internalized a silent response. "Let me say this with sensitivity, as best I can. The view I'm talking about is your eye defect. It will be hard to look at you and concentrate." In Alexander's internal reverie, the mayor's homeys stood up, ready to pounce and shred him into pulp. "When your group is beating me up, tell them to be sensitive," his inner self pleaded. "I have a heart condition."

"You pretty cool. Speak in a low tone of voice," the mayor said, as he turned to his hoods. "He got backup."

Alexander kept the bluff alive, and nodded.

"The governor think he hot shit. Keep that bluff going about diggin' up the streets to find Hoffa. All he doin' is putting money in his pocket."

"Or digging up the streets for new burials."

Kwame stopped and smiled. "Okay, Alex. Let's talk. I want a fifteen percent across the board increase in the city's budget. And don't give me no shit answer."

Alexander felt caught off-balance, trying to concentrate on maintaining a non-confrontational manner while trying not to be distracted by wondering which of Kwame's eyes was dominant.

"You're dreaming," he responded. "You're about to be relocated inside a building they call Leavenworth. That means your power has deflated to about zero. The governor wants to leverage the city budget to ensure you're on the bus to Kansas. He's cutting the budget by twenty percent and will grant your wish when he's waved goodbye to you. The new mayor will take over, and will get the credit for the increased budget." Quietly, but firmly, Alexander stood up, signaling that the meeting was over.

Chapter Fourteen

THE POKER RUN

Robert Hatcher arranged what he dubbed a 'brainstorming' meeting with Alexander at his personal retreat located near Clare, Michigan. Alexander hoped this time away from the Lansing hubbub would help ease the bubbling hostilities standing in the way of their working relationship. Recent matters had turned testy. Lately, trivial issues that might once have been easily resolved on both sides surfaced as mountains.

Alexander arrived late for business meetings, reasoning time spent with Flossy was better utilized. Hatcher scolded him. "I can see you hold your girlfriend in higher esteem than your work." Alexander's response was a smile.

At meetings, Alexander became equally offended when Hatcher slouched or doodled. "Getting comfy for a siesta or drawing chicken scratches is more important than what I have to report to you?"

At one important budget meeting, Hatcher proposed increasing the size of a road project. Alexander said the original cost had risen for some unexplained reason and he wanted to investigate why. Hatcher was offended. Alexander accused him of illegally pocketing money from the job. The two men needed to be pried apart when aides found them clutched in a fight, holding onto each other's suit coats. An early morning ride one hour north of Lansing would bring them to a paradise, hopefully providing them with privacy and time to try to settle their differences.

With growing reservations, Alexander watched Robert Hatcher pattern himself increasingly after Vladimir Putin—publicly riding a motorcycle, openly living his extravagant life, letting Michigan citizens see that they'd elected someone who didn't hide behind closed doors. Meanwhile, travelling in a chauffeured limo allowed Hatcher time to drink liquor or get laid in the passenger section. Robert evidently loved the excitement of it all, especially the action passing the capitol building on the way to a meeting.

Two parked Harley motorcycles at the front steps of the capitol building awaited their riders as they started their retreat. Alexander and Robert, dressed in leathers and sporting custom-designed helmets, straddled their bikes, started their engines, and rode off, raising the decibels to a window-shattering level. A security detail followed them out of town.

Alexander had ridden a motorcycle in his younger and wilder days. He was a little rusty but managed to keep pace with Hatcher. On off-times he practiced his riding skills, sometimes picking Flossy up from work. She once cooed in his ear, while holding him tight. "Alex, baby, I'm your bitch for life." From then on, Alexander always found extra time away from the office to meet and ride with her. He was having the time of his life. Flossy helped him live it to the fullest.

Mid-Michigan was eclectic. They passed through a vast farming area north of St. Johns, passed the Flying Eagle Casino in Mt. Pleasant, passed several Amish families traveling by horse and buggy, and passed Jay's Sporting Goods store with an inventory of about ten thousand armaments for sale. They then passed through a gate with a header that read, "Robert's Soft Landing." The road inside the grounds to the lodge was about a half-mile long. The governor's security spread out to cover all areas of the complex.

"Be back here in an hour, ready to defend yourself," was Hatcher's curt directive. Alexander knew a tough day was about to commence. After settling in his room, he returned to the outdoor barbecue patio, wearing khakis and a polo shirt. Hatcher was waiting for him in his green and yellow golfing outfit. As gentlemen, they had overdressed to attest their rank. Should an unexpected visitor arrive, they would then be already properly attired. In truth, both preferred Levis and a T-shirt.

Steaks were being cooked, and a bottle of vodka with two shot glasses stood on the table. The two men filled their glasses, toasted each other, and slammed the drinks back in a gulp. Alexander stripped off his shirt and threw the first punch. He missed and fell on the ground, quickly standing and evading Hatcher. Hatcher didn't wait and kicked Alexander in the ribs. Alexander rolled way to avoid another kick. They reengaged in a fighting stance. Alexander gave a kick that caught Hatcher's groin. A follow-up right hand landed Hatcher on the ground. "How're you feeling, you old goat?" spouted an exuberant Alexander. Hatcher threw dirt at Alexander and charged him. His head butted Alexander in the stomach, sending them both back into a mud puddle. Alexander reached for some mud and pummeled some of it into Hatcher's face. "That's for your stinking stupidity."

Guards stood nearby and observed the commotion with a watchful eye. Hatcher freed himself and ran, dripping mud, to the kitchen counter. He pulled a butcher's knife from a drawer and threatened Alexander. "You conceited high and mighty pencil pusher. I'm going to make this a quick fight."

Alexander got up and ran for something resembling a shield. He found a cutting board. Alongside it was a bread knife, which Alexander in a state of exhaustion flung toward Hatcher. His aim was off the mark, flying instead at a security officer, nicknamed Muscles, who ducked away.

Both men were breathing heavily and had to be pushed away from each other by the security detail. Muscles grabbed Alexander. He spoke with his 225-pound, broad-shouldered frame. This was a sensible strategy because both Hatcher and Alexander were exhausted. Muscles escorted Alexander to a nearby gardening shed. Hatcher came under his own power, walking with an officer. They were hosed down with water. When done, they laughed, hugged, and walked to the outdoor dining table. Throwing back another shot of vodka, Hatcher opened the discussion with, "Alexander, out with it. You've got something on your mind."

"Yeah, I do, Robert... Robert, you're a fucking crook. You cooked the books."

Alexander dropped his glass, doubled over, and collapsed on the ground.

Epilogue

FLOSSY SAYS GOODBYE

Flossy exited the elevator on Mid-Michigan Hospital's ICU floor in Clare, Michigan, where Alexander had been hospitalized. Earlier, she'd been visiting her sister in Indiana when her publicity agent got ahold of her by cell phone. The agent said, "A nurse from Beaumont Hospital called me. Do you know a Jennifer Reynolds?"

A fearful Flossy replied, "Yes."

"She said it would be better if I called and told you the news." Flossy learned that Alexander had another heart attack and was hospitalized in critical condition in Mid-Michigan Hospital. "He might not survive the day." Flossy immediately jumped into her car and drove to be near him. Flossy cried the entire six-hour drive, afraid he might expire before she arrived. She parked her car in the emergency lot and dashed through the emergency entrance.

Flossy asked the emergency floor nurse for Alexander Haralson.

"They took him to the ICU, third floor, room 674."

On the ICU floor, she asked the floor nurse the direction to Room 674, Mr. Haralson's room.

"Halfway down the corridor, on the left."

"Is he alone?"

"Yes. His wife was taken home by her son about an hour ago."

Flossy thanked the nurse and walked toward Alexander's room.

The time was around ten p.m. The corridors were quiet.

Flossy saw Alex through the large window that fronted his unit. He wore nasal tubes for oxygen, an IV line attached to the top of his hand carrying medication, a catheter hanging at the side of the bed attached to a bag, a pulse clip was attached to a finger, and a blood pressure cuff wrapped around his bicep.

Flossy entered the room and walked up close to him. She made eye contact and whispered, "Thank God you're awake. Are you in any pain?"

Alexander shook his head and smiled. His breathing was labored, but he spoke with a quiet voice, "I'm okay." He raised his hand, which Flossy grasped and began kissing.

"Alex, I love you so much. The nursing staff knows I'm here. If someone comes in and asks, I'll tell them I'm your daughter. Last time I was your niece. Remember?"

Alexander smiled weakly. "Great line."

"You remembered."

"I'm an expert at deception."

Flossy kissed Alexander. "The best." She started to cry. She stood, walked to the entrance, and closed the door. She sat close to Alex's ear.

"I was visiting my sister in Terre Haute. She knows I'm in the family way. When she saw me, she was ecstatic. We screamed and yelled for an hour. She asked me who the father was. I told her it was a man who cared about me and loved me very much. I told her how much I loved you and how happy I was. I'm going home to Indiana to have the baby. But not back to my home town. Christ, every guy will point the finger at the dumb broad and say, 'There's Flossy. Remember her? She's that slut who screwed every guy in town.'

"My sister's invited me to stay with her until the baby is born. Afterward, she'll find me a place to live near her."

"I want to help you with support."

"I don't want any support. I've made a zillion dollars because of you. You made all your clients rich, or did you forget? You taught me how to balance a checkbook. You said that was the first thing to do—to become financially self-sufficient. I've got tons of money invested with an investment manager and three safe-deposit boxes filled with Benjamins."

Alexander lay quietly.

"My agent called and told me the news about you. I'll be staying around until you improve. Do you remember Jennifer Reynolds, your cardiac nurse? She and I will be staying in my Lansing apartment. When the baby's ready to arrive, I'll be turning into a ghost. Where I'm going, no one will know your name, where you live, what you did for a living, or how rich you are. Your family will never find out anything. They don't know me. They won't suspect you have a love child."

Alexander teared. "I want to see the baby."

Flossy covered Alexander's mouth. "Shh. For a long time, we've faced the possibility of having to say goodbye. Know I'm here with you. Know that I'll think of you always.

"I'll pray that you see our child. It will be raised in a caring, hard-working family. I'll have the child you've always wanted. Roberta needs a firm hand to straighten out her life. I'll make sure the child we have won't be temperamental. I could have been the daughter you wanted. Your daughter Caroline is confused and needs to take a detour. I could have been the wife you wanted. Your wife is crazy. You met a woman who loves you more than she thought she ever could or will again. Now she needs to take a detour back into the reality of a low-keyed life.

"Alexander, you fixed the roads in my life. Meeting you at the comedy school was the happiest day in my life. The next happiest day was seeing you again at Ray's. There are more happy days ahead.

"Your child will know you are its father. I've got pictures and movies of you. Want to hear something funny? Maybe the baby will become a comedian. I've got your Joe Stalin cap. The child will wear it with pride and know his dad—my lover—kicked everyone's ass. You worked to change the schools to be places where kids learn. Your effort was above money."

"You're really going to walk away from your career?"

"I'm done. It was a great run."

"Promise me you won't go back and do nude dancing?"

"I promise."

Alexander and Flossy embraced and sniffled.

Flossy said, "Goodbye," stood, and left the room.

A nurse who'd been standing by the door entered and walked over to Alexander. She saw that his face was wet. "Is everything okay, Mr. Haralson?"

"Just a little homesick."

The nurse checked the medication drips. As she closed the door to leave, she said, "Buzz me if you need anything."

Alexander looked up and saw Flossy through the window. She blew a kiss and left.

* * *

A few day later, Jennifer, Flossy's sister, came home from grocery shopping. She found Flossy serenely sorting out some baby clothes and quietly told her the radio had just announced that Alexander had died about an hour earlier. Quietly, Flossy started to cry.

Jennifer took her sister in her arms, comforting her. "Alex loved you for awakening him to a new life. His whole life in business and family had been rigid. He met you and everything changed. He got the chance to tell everyone what he thought, and do what he wanted. I'm so sorry to have to break the news."

Flossy laid her head on her sister's shoulder, just as she'd done with Alexander in happier moments. "He was so wonderful. I'm glad I'm pregnant and that he's the father."

"He was really happy," Jennifer reminded her. "And I'm really happy for you. You can start a new life. I'd like to help you with the baby."

"How does babysitting sound?"

"Perfect."

"Jenn, thanks for keeping me up to date about Alex. Telling me must have been tough."

Jennifer hugged Flossy, then pulled back to make an announce-ment. "With all the tension, I've been meaning to tell you something personal. I'm getting married."

"You are? I'm happy, Jenn. Congratulations. Who is he?"

"Captain Rodger Suchmore, Marine Corps. I had a friend in physical therapy. I dropped over to visit her, and there he was, learn-ing to walk with a prosthetic leg. Roger and I talked during a break. He's super. Kind and handsome."

"I'm so happy for you."

"I want you to come to my wedding."

Flossy sniffled. "I will. Send me an invitation. I want to see you walk down the aisle. I'm counting on seeing Rodger in his dress uniform."

"You will."

"I want to visit Alex's family. Are they still in town?"

"Yes. Do you want me to accompany you?"

"No. I'll do it alone."

That afternoon, Flossy went to the emergency area to find the room where Alexander had been treated and died.

Roman stood at the room's entrance, while Margarita silently sat beside the bed. When Flossy approached, Roman asked, "Can I help you?"

"I knew your father," Flossy said hesitantly. "I want you to know how much he loved you."

Roman glanced at Flossy, noticing that she was in the family way.

Flossy took a deep breath. "I loved your father." Then, looking down at the slight swelling of her belly, she added, "It's your future brother or sister."

Flossy was about to step away when Roman stopped her, "Don't go. Let me introduce you to my mother."

Roman led Flossy to Margarita. "Mrs. Haralson, I'm sorry about your husband. I'm very sad. We all lost a very special man." Caroline walked toward Flossy and hugged her. "I'm the family lib-eral. I can handle your getting pregnant by my father. We were all aware of my father's unusual activities, and we know that was just part of what made him the man he was. I'm really happy for you, and for us."

"Thanks."

Margarita spoke up. "You were the comedian at the inauguration. I knew it. He set you up with all your jokes."

Flossy nodded and started to exit. Roman walked her to the hallway. "Please keep in touch with us. Call me at the hospital, anytime. We want to know all about our new family member. By the way, where can we reach you?"

"Do you know Jennifer Reynolds? She's a nurse in the cardiovascular surgical department at Beaumont Hospital."

"Oh, sure, I know her. She cared for my dad."

"Yes. And we became good friends."

"Where do you work? I'd like to see a show."

"I'm quitting comedy. Alex taught me to think differently. Jewish jokes, told by an Indiana schichsa, don't sound so funny anymore. I'll still be working. My application for my next job has been accepted—motherhood."

Roman and Caroline hugged Flossy goodbye.

"By the way, did you pick out a name?"

"Stalin. Stalin Haralson."

"Oh, my God. Someday, please explain that name. Imagine, I'm going to be Stalin's uncle."